BURIED LIES

Peter Rennebohm is also the author of:

Be Not Afraid: Ben Peyton's Story (ISBN: 0-87839-205-X) Non-fiction.

French Creek—a thriller. (ISBN: 0-87839-211-4)

Blue Springs—a suspense novel. (ISBN: 0-87839-227-0)

Buried Lies

Peter Rennebohm

NORTH STAR PRESS OF ST. CLOUD, INC.

St. Cloud, Minnesota

Cover art by Mark Evans
www.cloudmover.net

ISBN-10: 0-87839-291-2
ISBN-13: 978-0-87839-291-9

First Edition
September 1, 2008

Printed in Canada
by Friesens

Published by
North Star Press of St. Cloud, Inc.
P.O. Box 451
St. Cloud, Minnesota 56302
<northstarpress.com>
<info@northstarpress.com>

1 2 3 4 5 6 7 8 9 10

Dedicated to:

Julie Kay Webster
10/10/47 – 08/02/06

A good friend who was confused at the end but never really alone

Acknowledgements

As each book becomes reality—an actual bound narrative awaiting readers, my list of "thank you's" grows and expands. The summer of 2008 has been eventful in many ways. Getting another book published is always exciting, but beyond that, I've been forced to lay low due to ill health and thus have had time to consider some of the real important "stuff" in life. I came away with a deep appreciation for my family and friends—all of whom have left a profound impression on my soul. Thank you all for being there at a low point in my life.

My wife, Shari, is very simply, the best person I know. I'm a very lucky man.

Our daughters, Emily and Jenny, remain close in so many ways and have become our trusted friends.

To my first, early readers: Becky Planer, Tom Carlson, Louisa Mayer, Michael O'Rourke, John & Nancy Peyton, Bill Vann, George Webster, and Walt Seibert—many thanks for your words of encouragement.

Special thanks to Holly Watson for providing needed perspective and counseling on the hearing impaired.

Thanks to Robert Walker and Theresa deValence for all their help with Buried Lies.

Heartfelt thanks to Jenny Barnes, my daughter, who managed to survive working with her impatient old man on the dust jacket cover.

And finally, many thanks to the great, highly-respected authors who not only read the manuscript, but offered words of praise: Thomas Perry, William Kent Krueger, Alafair Burke, Shane Gericke, Vince Flynn, and Chris Grabenstein. These are all award-winning authors, and I am most appreciative and humbled that they took the time from very busy schedules to read *Buried Lies*.

Thank you, thank you, one and all.

Prologue

The laughter of the children echoed through the deep green valley. As the sun reached down to touch the top of the tallest mountain, the women came and brought the youngest ones to the lodge of the Ancient One.

The children stood in the dim light, huddled just inside the door.

"Come and sit," the Ancient One commanded. "I will tell you a story."

The children shuffled close to the fire and sat cross-legged in a half-moon on the far side of the Ancient One.

And when it was quiet enough to hear a spider crawl, he began. "This is what I have to say:

The Creator gathered all of Creation and said, 'I want to hide something of great value from the humans until they are ready for it.'

'And what is this thing you speak of?' All of Creation asked.

'It is the realization that they create their own reality.'

The hawk said, 'Give it to me. I will take it to the moon.'

The Creator said, 'No. One day they will go there and find it.'

The salmon said, 'I will hide it on the bottom of the ocean.'

'No. They will swim down and go there, too.'

The buffalo said, 'I will bury it on the Great Plains.'

The Creator said, 'They will cut into the skin of the earth and find it even there.'

Grandmother Mole, who lives in the breast of Mother Earth, and who has no physical eyes but sees with spiritual eyes, said, 'Put it inside of them.'

And the Creator said, 'It is done.'

The Ancient One filled his pipe with tobacco, and when the smoke had warmed his tongue said, "You all have this gift from the Creator. Do not lose it, for with this gift, all things are possible."

He waved his leathered hand over the fire toward the wide-eyed children. "Go now, for that is all I have to say about this."

One

SCISSORS FLASHED JUST BENEATH my nose. A meaty hand pressed hard atop my head. Eyes once closed flipped open to estimate the risk of permanent damage. And then, the scissor-point nicked my cheek. Pitched back in the chair as I was, there was no escape. I pretzeled into an awkward wry-neck pose, lost sight of the scissors, but sensed they hovered dangerously close. Perspiration dampened my shirt. This was cold sweat; fear induced, not desert heat. Trapped, I held my breath and waited for the inevitable skewering.

The crazed old man was distracted, unfocused—like a confused animal—and that was problematic . . . for both of us. With a vacant stare, he carelessly waved the scissors. Unable to predict what his next move might be and struggling to retain my own focus, I felt my spine lock in an even more awkward angle, eyes riveted on the end of those dual blades. The end was near; the old man's trembling hand would surely jab the scissors up a nostril to implant the hardened steel somewhere deep within my brain pan.

"Frank. Frankie." I was pleading now. "Watch what you're doing. I need a haircut—not a frontal lobotomy."

The old guy's eyes cleared a bit. "Huh?" He looked at me as if for the first time. "Gus?" He looked at the scissors as if they were a pair of hedge shears. His arm dropped. "Sorry about that. Must've had a brain fart there."

"Guess so."

He fumbled around and made light of his slip while the tension in my body eased. My aching back found relief. "That's all right. You were telling me about that book." I straightened, but was prepared to slide out of the chair at any moment.

Frank shook his head and continued. "Oh, yeah. Right. The book. Anyway, shortly after I was mustered out, I received a package in the mail . . ."

AT ELEVEN-THIRTY THAT MORNING, feeling restless and slightly depressed, I'd driven into the unremarkable strip mall that housed Frankie's Barber Shop. It was a detached single-story building with cracked, adobe walls faded to a rosy pink. A pair of fissured wooden beams supported a slate canopy over the door. A single window with a yellowed sign indicated Frankie was open for business. I imagined the old barber laboring earlier just to lower a green sunshade in a token effort to shield his shop from the blazing desert sun. No other cars were parked in front. I slid from the mini-van, hitched up my shorts, and strolled into the barbershop. A golf date later with my brother-in-law and other friends would complete another unremarkable day in sunny Chandler, Arizona.

Inside, Frank lay asleep in the only chair, head back, mouth open. For a brief moment, it seemed the old guy might be dead. With some trepidation I called, "Frankie? You okay?"

Having rented a small home in Chandler, I'd been coming to his shop since November, and always enjoyed our monthly chats, but now there was no immediate reaction from the old man. The floor beneath the ancient barber chair was relatively clean; only a few fresh cuttings evidenced the morning's work. Business must've been slow. Stepping closer, I touched his shoulder and shook him a little.

Frank choked back a snore, jumped slightly, and opened both eyes. He blinked twice and uttered a dry, "Hrumpf." He licked his lips and cleared his throat. "Huh? Who? Oh, Gus. Sorry. You wouldn't believe the dream I was having."

I smiled at that. "Really. Should I come back later? Maybe let you finish?"

"Too late. Boy, she was something though: long-legged blonde with breasts you could take shade under." He scraped at the bristle on his chin and yawned. "Oh, well. Story of my life."

"Sorry, old timer. Next time I'll leave you to your dreams." The old man's eyes crinkled, reminding me of an old baseball glove I had as a kid, and wondered if on careful examination between the folds of Frank's skin, Phil Rizzuto's scrawl might not appear. Frank's leathery face provided a perfect canvas for deeply set blue eyes topped by bushy white brows. It was a face that invited scrutiny . . . and trust. His humped back spoke to the thousands of dissimilar heads of hair the old guy had stood over for decades. Old Frank was one of the good guys, and I liked him a lot.

"Sit yerself down, Augustus Ivy."

"Only two people ever called me that, Frank: Miss Carlson, my fifth-grade teacher, and my mother. Always tense up when I hear that. Usually meant I was in deep shit." I stepped into the chair as soon as he cleared it.

"Well, now there's three of us, and far as I know, you're not in any sorta trouble. Something almost presidential about yer name . . . Augustus Ivy. You ever run for office?" Frankie snapped the nylon cape and let it collapse over me—the strong cologne on his fingers telling me he'd had at least one customer before me.

"No, not since Miss Carlson's class. I lost."

"Too bad." He tilted my head back, and fastened a tissue paper collar snugly and mouthed an old bromide he thought quite funny. "Don't worry. You won't feel a thing."

The scent of talcum powder drifted up and mingled with a pungent, ozone-like odor from Frankie's aged electric clippers with their ancient, fabric covered electrical cords. Feet propped on the edge of the footrest, I relaxed and gazed around the shop as Frank busied himself behind me.

Six customer chairs occupied one wall, the red leather of each shiny despite a spider web of irregular cracks. A rusted spring dangled from the end chair nearest the door. The linoleum beneath each was a darker shade of green than the rest of the shop; like a dusty field bordered by a thick, dark forest. The yellowed Burma Shave clock with its foggy face was forever ten minutes slow. A wooden shelf held half a dozen jars of Butch Wax, slender bottles of Brylcreem, and a warped card of black combs still priced at twenty-five cents each.

Stacks of old magazines occupied one full corner but failed to hide crooked fissures in the linoleum. Each pile held ancient copies of *Look*, *Life*, brittle *National Geographics*, *Boy's Life*, and *Sports Illustrated*. A large Norman Rockwell print of a small boy's first haircut set a perfect, timeless mood. Fear and pain colored the boy's face, deftly drawn as the white-haired barber hovered over the lad on a raised seat. The boy's wide eyes focused on a large pair of scissors reflected in the mirror; he looked ready to bolt at any moment.

I wondered how much of Frankie's life had been centered within this small, one-chair shop. About all he'd heard from his customers over the years about their jobs, wives, hobbies, habits, childhoods, hometowns, families? How many secrets, shenanigans, tall tales, angry complaints? Had he taken any of it home to share with his wife?

The old man fingered the hair over my ears. "You don't really need a haircut, Gus. Must be bored outta yer skull. Nothin' better to do than come yammer with me?"

"Maybe. Not sure this life of leisure out here is right for me, Frank."

"How's that?"

"Nothing else to do besides golf. Game gets old fast. Too hot, too much effort." I turned my head and studied myself in the mirror. "Just take a little off around the edges then, Frank."

"Will do." He caught my eye in the mirror. "Memory's gone to hell, Gus. Tell me again what you do?"

"Construction."

"Oh, yeah. That's right. Shoulda remembered from your hands. Not a behind-the-desk kinda guy, are you?"

I studied the backs of my paws. "They are pretty ugly aren't they? No. Always wanted to be outside." He started in with the scissors as my eyes returned to a cardboard box spotted earlier. "What's in the carton, Frankie? You planning on going someplace?"

"Huh? Oh, no." He stopped cutting and looked in the corner. "Had a strange phone call yesterday. Lady asked if I still had a certain book I received as a gift a long time ago. Said I didn't know but would be happy to look. So I dragged that carton out of a closet this morning to see if I still had it."

"Did you? Have the book?"

"Yep." He cranked the long chair handle, spun me a quarter turn, and resumed cutting. The scissors clicked rhythmically at the nape of my neck. *Snip, snip.*

My gaze returned to the box. "Those *all* books, Frank?"

"Yeah. Figured as long as I drug 'em out, I'd take the whole mess to the Goodwill or maybe donate 'em to the library."

"And the book this lady was asking about? She wanted to buy it off you?"

"Don't rightly know. 'Nother call come through. Never could get the hang of that hold feature. Anyhow, she got disconnected and never called back."

"I'm a collector, and my curiosity is aroused, Frank. Mind if I take a look?"

"You? A collector?"

"Yeah, I know. I'm strictly small time, but still know the difference between a true first edition and a book club printing."

I knew that age did not necessarily relate to value, but sometimes if the book had been signed by the author, and had the original dust jacket on a first edition, its worth multiplied significantly. "My favorite authors are all dead—writers of old westerns."

"Ahhh . . . like Zane Gray?"

"Yeah, and others like Max Brand, Robert Horton, and Peter Dawson."

"What's your collection worth?"

"Wouldn't call it a collection and it's not worth much."

"Then what drives ya."

I shrugged, and he almost nicked me. "The hope of discovery's a constant draw, Frank."

"Like a guy with a metal detector and twenty miles of beach, huh?"

I laughed. "Sort of. I've spent quite a bit of time digging through secondhand bookstores over the past few years."

"Well now, you just dig right into that box, Gus. Enjoy yourself." Frankie spent another five minutes working on my hair. As he stopped to clean out his clippers, I rose, stepped toward the dusty box, and pulled back the flaps. Lying atop the pile was an old hardback copy of *The Cavity Lake Gang* by M.B. Bower. I returned to the chair and paged through the book.

The dust jacket was in excellent condition, and the book itself pristine. In fact, I'd have sworn it'd never been read. The title along with the author's name took up a third of the front of the jacket—a striking prairie scene reminiscent of a Frederick Remington painting filled the rest. It depicted a group of riders in the foreground—cowboys or bad guys and presumably an Indian guide—atop their horses at a desert watering hole. In the background ranch buildings and a windmill. The colors were spectacular: muted shades of red, orange, and brown. Frankly, I'd never seen anything quite like it on a dust jacket before. Nowhere inside could I find information about the cover artist, though.

"Whatcha think," asked Frank over my shoulder.

"I know the author well, own all of her books, or so I thought, but I'm unfamiliar with this particular title. M.B. Bower and Zane Gray are among a select group of Western authors with a devout following."

"No kiddin'."

"Together they've created a genre, loosely referred to as 'Sagebrush Westerns.'" I was puzzled about how I could've missed *The Cavity Lake Gang*. "Copyright page usually gives more information about publication history." I opened the book. "No printing date, no copyright number."

"What's that mean?"

"Well, it's very old, but beyond that? Not sure."

"It is old," he added wistfully.

Excited to add to my collection, I blurted, "I'll give you fifty bucks for the lot, Frankie. There might be a few more books here I'm interested in, but I'm really curious about this one." I held out the Bower book and glanced at the Burma Shave clock. I still had an hour before golf. "I'll have to get my checkbook from the van."

"Ah hell, Gus, them books aren't of any use to me anymore—just take 'em."

"No, I want to pay you for them. Is this Bower book the one the lady inquired about?"

The old man took it and slipped on his glasses for a closer look. He stared at the cover. "Yep. Sure is. Must be sixty years old at least. Strangest thing, how I came by this book . . . " He closed the book and ran his rough hands over the smooth, faded, paper cover—side to side, then top to bottom, as if rubbing a magic bottle . . . hoping to rekindle a long forgotten memory.

"Ah, yes," he whispered. He studied his reflection in the mirror, handed back the book, picked up the scissors, and resumed cutting. Let me tell you about Preston Kittridge and his book. . ."

Two

Frank. Frank. You were telling me about the book." I'd had enough of his wayward scissors by this time, and considered myself fortunate to only have the one bloody nick on my cheek.

After a brief, silent remembrance, the old man was back. "Oh, Yeah." He noticed the drip of blood. "Shit. Sorry about that, Gus." He tore off a scrap of tissue to stop the bleeding. "There. Think I'm done."

I knew I was. "Good. Be right back. I want to buy that box of books." I threw off the sheet and headed for the door, happy to be out of Sweeney Todd's torture chair.

"That's fine. Can't think of anyone else I'd rather let have 'em."

I left him in mid-sentence, went outside, unlocked the van, and grabbed my checkbook from the door pocket. Suddenly energized and pumped about my purchase, I hurried back, anxious to know more about the Bower book.

I returned to find a distant, thoughtful look on the old man's face. His brown eyes glistened, and his lower lip drooped just a bit. "Frank? You okay?"

"Yeah." He sniffed and ran fingers over his face in embarrassment. "This book brings back a lot of memories, though." He held it against his chest as if he had changed his mind about selling it.

"Tell me about it," I said, my interest genuinely tweaked now.

He held both arms out, handed me the book, and collapsed into the barber chair. "When I was mustered out of the Army in '46, I had ninety-

7

seven dollars in my pocket, a few souvenirs from the Philippines, and no future. Wasn't much call for a munitions expert after the war. Came back here and went to barber school. Pretty soon, this book showed up in a box with my name on it." He paused and looked through the window.

He was off again. "Frank?"

"Huh?"

"Who's this Kittridge you mentioned earlier?"

"The guy who sent me the book. Inside the box was a letter from old man Kittridge—the father of one of my buddies, Jack, our squad leader. First lieutenant and a real good guy." He shook his head just a little. "Jack was from Montana—forget which town. He and his father were damn close. I gathered the old guy owned some kind of manufacturing company, but for the war effort, he'd converted everything over to making stuff for the War Department."

"What kind of stuff?"

"Hmmm . . . think a minute, Frank," he scolded himself. He put his feet up on the rest and tilted his head back. His head jerked forward. "Aw, I can't remember. Don't recall things too well no more. Like the guy said, 'I meet new old friends every day.'" He smiled at that.

I laughed and asked about the letter.

"Well, first off, you have to know that Jack never came home from the war. Our unit, the Eleventh Airborne Division fought in one of the last battles in the Philippines. We were Charlie Company—attached to the Sixth Army. In June of '45 we were airlifted by glider plane and dropped behind the lines in northern Luzon. Army called the campaign Task Force Liberty Bell."

Frankie's voice dropped to a whisper. I could barely hear him. It was clear this remembrance was painful for the old man, and I could certainly identify with that. "You don't have to tell me anymore if you don't want to."

"No, it's okay, Gus." He cleared his throat. "Probably good for me after all these years. God, I was close to those guys . . . hell, we grew up together." He looked out the window. "We were supposed to seal off the Cagavan Valley so the Japs'd be left with nowhere to run." His eyes blazed and the lines on his face flattened as he told the story. "We destroyed twelve pill boxes, and when it was over the Eleventh had killed over five thousand Japs in less than a week. Jack Kittridge was killed on the last day of the battle—June 17th. Never forget it. Sniper's bullet hit him in the throat." He laid a mitt up beneath his chin as he spoke. "We lost four more guys that morning. Only nine of us came home." Frankie's eyes glistened and his voice trailed off to a whisper.

"Aw, geez, Frankie, I'm truly sorry." I really felt bad for the old guy.

"It's okay, Gus." He took a deep breath and continued. "Jack's daddy apparently had this book published that same year and sent to the survivors of Charlie Company."

"What a strange thing to do," I said. "How many men did you ship out with?"

"Hundred ninety-two."

"And how many came home?"

"Ninety-six, actually, in one kinda shape or another."

"Good Lord. Did you stay in touch with any of them?"

"For a while, but, you know . . . once we all got back home—"

"Sure, you wanted to forget about the war."

"Did get together in Chicago about five years later, though—entire company. Only guy in our squad who didn't show up was an Indian fella attached to our unit. Never said much, but he was from around here some-place—Navajo. Eddie something or other. Two-Feathers. Eddie Two-Feathers. Our radio guy."

I wanted to know a lot more, but time was short. "What was in the letter, and why the book?"

He was lost in the memory again. "Hmmm?"

"The letter. What'd it say?"

Frankie bolted upright, reached for the book, and leafed through it. "Ya know, I might've just . . . yep, here it is. Tucked in back of the book." He slipped out a thin, yellowed piece of paper folded in thirds. His thick fingers flipped it open. "Boy, oh boy. Whaddaya know."

"Can I see it, Frank?"

His eyes misted as he held out the brittle paper. I read aloud:

December 24, 1945.

From Mr. and Mrs. Preston Kittridge.

To: The brave soldiers of Charlie Company, Eleventh Airborne Division. Sixth United States Army.

Gentlemen: You fought for your country during a time of great need, alongside our son Lieutenant Jack Kittridge. Like many of your comrades, Jack did not return home from that last battle, and his mother and I mourn his loss. However, in his letters home, Jack spoke warmly of the brotherhood that developed between you courageous men, and how much he appreciated serving with you. Words cannot express our sincere gratitude for your service to your country.

Enclosed, please find a fine book written by the well-known author, M.B. Bower titled, *The Cavity Lake Gang*. It is a western, and I'd encourage you to read the story first for enjoyment, secondly for direction and content. The discerning reader will be rewarded.

In closing, I urge you all to stay in touch with your friends. Maintain and draw strength from that friendship. There is great wisdom and knowledge to be had from sharing. Open your eyes to all that is possible. Study the words. Catch your dream, and enjoy the fruits of your labor. You are all in our prayers, and we wish you great success.

With gratitude,

Preston and Ellen Kittridge.

"What do you suppose he meant by the last paragraph?" I pointed to the passage.

"Let me slip my glasses back on, Gus." He then straightened the crisp paper and silently read the paragraph, his lip quivering. "Ya know, we all puzzled over that back then. Never did figure it out. Main thing was that Jack's dad wanted to thank all of us for serving with his son. I guess he loved Westerns and hoped that if we all read the book, it'd take our minds off the war. Don't rightly know." He handed back the letter.

The tone of the first part of the letter exuded deep gratitude. Beyond that, it appeared to be nothing more than an old man passing on wisdom of some sort. Still . . . that last paragraph almost sounded like an invitation. To what? Fingering the bottom of the sheet, I asked, "Looks like the bottom was cut off, Frankie. Was there anything else?"

"Huh? Let's see." He took the letter back. "Oh, yeah. Some sorta quote from Shakespeare. My wife was taken by it and cut it off for some damn reason."

He closed his eyes and knuckled both at the same time. "What the hell did it say? Something 'bout a 'fortune and a flood.' Ah hell, Gus, that was so long ago. Never did understand what it meant. Funny old coot."

By this time my curiosity overshadowed the pending golf game. "Did you read the book?"

"Naw. Never much of a reader myself. Might've started it, but never finished."

"And that's it? Just this book and the letter?"

"Oh, no. Best part of the whole deal? The money. Jack's dad must've been rollin' in dough, 'cause he sent each one of us a check for a thousand bucks."

"The entire company?"

"Yep. Opened this shop with that money. Never forget such generosity."

"Guess so. Thousand dollars in 1946? Great deal of money." I checked the time again. "Listen, Frank, I need to get going. I'll haul this box out and be right back, okay?"

"Sure." His voice was barely audible.

I replaced the Bower book with the others, closed the carton flaps and carried the box out. On returning, I watched a guy in blue windbreaker and red ball cap slip in ahead of me. A fresh, unknown scent drifted past my nostrils as I trailed behind. It quickly mingled with the talc and shaving lotion, then vanished. Frankie greeted the newcomer with a curious stare followed by, "With you in a minute, bud. Take your jacket off and climb into the chair."

I didn't recognize the stranger—no surprise there, but it seemed Frankie didn't either. The guy never replied; just stepped to one side and made no effort to remove his jacket—or hat. Instead, he turned away and looked out the window.

I hurriedly wrote Frankie a check for seventy bucks—fifty for the books and twenty for the cut. "Check back with you later, Frankie. I'd like to hear the end of the story."

"Don't wait too long, Gus. Won't be here forever, you know."

"Sure you will. Thanks, old-timer. See you soon." A sideways glance at the stranger revealed nothing more about his identity. I shrugged and left.

Excited to read the Bower book, I also wanted to know more about the book's provenance—where the hell'd it come from, and where'd it been since its origin. For the first time in months, I had something interesting and intriguing to ponder.

I drove out of the Mesquite Mall, decided to forgo the golf game, and headed home to read.

Three

I PULLED INTO THE SINGLE-CAR garage, hopped out, and gave Sam, my ninety-pound golden retriever a quick scratch behind the ears. His tail slapped the tin of the van as he leaned into my leg. Together we squeezed through the kitchen door. I opened the fridge, grabbed a Bud, twisted the top, and tilted the bottle back. Sam, his big head on his paws, stared up at me with a familiar forlorn look. Pissed for not taking him with me to Frankie's—something I would have routinely done back in Minnesota, but Chandler's desert heat was a killer, so unless it was a short trip, he stayed home. "Hey. I'm sorry. Come on. Let's take a walk." After another pull on the longneck, we left the house.

As we walked up the block and around the corner, I thought back to my conversation with Frankie; specifically about the origin and history of *The Cavity Lake Gang*. Something he had said nagged just out of reach. What was it? Need to read the book. Maybe it would come to me.

We arrived at a small park, and once Sam was off the leash, he bounded off across the shallow pebbled surface. He located a suitable spot to do his business, spun a couple of times, and looked away. I half expected him to cough. After a dozen toss and retrieves of a tennis ball, we were ready to return home. On the way back, I spotted someone coming from my house. Whoever it was, the figure glanced our way, hurried to a brown sedan, and clambered in. The man put it in gear and sped away. Meter reader? Salesman?

The front door stood ajar as I'd left it unlocked. Bad habit born of living in the country. A quick look inside gave no clue as to whether the guy'd actually been in the house, had taken anything, or not. Wait a minute. My checkbook. Thought it was on the kitchen counter. Bastard stole my . . . wait. Frankie's. Must've left it there. I picked up the phone. Information supplied the number to his shop, but the line buzzed busy. Ten minutes later, same thing. But Frank should still be there. It's only 2:00 p.m. A call to his home went unanswered as well.

"Come on, Sam." The rattle of the keys was all he needed as he padded to the back door.

The Bower book was still in the back of the van in its cardboard home. I lugged the box inside the house, locked the doors, and we drove to Frank's shop. Ten minutes later, I found the shade down, and the "OPEN" sign flipped over to "CLOSED." No one answered my repeated knocking. I went next door to the beauty parlor and asked, "Anyone know where Frank is?"

"Nope. Haven't seen him since this morning," said the owner. "SALLY" was stitched on her blue frock.

"Would you recognize his car?"

"Drives an old station wagon. Ford I think. Green. Usually parks in back." She put down the dryer, tapped the lady in curlers on the shoulder, and said, "Hang on a minute, dear." After a short walk to the back, she opened the door and stuck her head outside. "Car's still here," she said. Concern painted my features, and Sally noticed. "Frank's been known to lock the place up and take the phone off the hook mid-day."

"I see."

"Gets tired, snoozes in that old barber chair."

She barely satisfied my growing concern. "Okay, but will you check in on him later?" I plucked her card from a jar on the way out. "Think I left my checkbook in Frank's shop and would like to get it back. I'll call you later, all right?"

"Of course. And your name is?"

"Gus. Gus Ivy, and thanks. I'm probably worrying for nothing."

"I'm Sally Evans. Pleased to meet you." We shook hands, and she held mine a bit too long. I left the shop, and Sam and I drove home.

After lunch, I sat down with Bower's book. Sam flopped down at my feet and began gnawing at a chunk of rawhide. After an hour or so, I stopped to consider what I'd read. After just a few paragraphs, I knew there was something different about this book. Bower's writing style was usually pleasant, but this novel didn't flow as smoothly as any of the author's other works. The story itself, typical of the genre, wasn't what bothered me. It was the way the words lacked her usual cohesiveness and appropriate pacing. Puzzled, I laid the book down and tried Frank's number again. Still busy. "Phone's off the hook," Sally'd said. Another call to Sally revealed nothing new.

"Come on, Sam." We left the house, and I drove to Frank's for the third time that day. My throat tightened and pulse pounded as I pulled in front. Something wasn't right. I looked around. Nothing caught my eye. I went into the beauty shop and walked over to the owner. She was in the middle of a color rinse or something as her customer had her head over a wash sink. "Sally?"

"Oh. Hi, Gus. Still haven't seen Frank, I'm afraid. When I went out back for a smoke a while ago, saw his car's still there."

"Do you have a key to Frank's shop?"

"Wish I did. Hey, the owner of the building does. He's in the insurance office other side of Frank's. You don't think Frank's like hurt or something, do you?"

"Dunno. Think I'll get the key, have a look."

After a brief explanation to the insurance agent, Jacob Marley, the wheezy old man rifled through his desk for the key, and locating it, walked me next door. Marley unlocked the door, and I followed him in.

The shop was dark. Quiet. "Frank? You here?" the agent called. He stopped, gasped, and said, "Oh, my God!"

My eyes had adjusted and followed his extended finger. Marley pointed to a pair of legs protruding from behind the barber chair. A dark pool of congealing blood had flowed from beneath Frank's head. White tufts of hair—my hair—had been carried on the bloodstream, miniature icebergs in a crimson sea.

A pair of Frank's long-bladed scissors protruded from the back of his neck. The same pair he'd used on me! I recalled that moment he'd gone off on a reverie and almost took out an eye.

I stepped around the quaking Marley, avoided the red pool, and knelt near the old man's head. No pulse. "Better call the police."

"He's dead, isn't he?"

"'Fraid so."

"This isn't right. Who'd want to hurt Frank?"

I wondered the same. Why kill this nice old guy? Bile rose in my throat, the taste bitter and foul. What the hell's going on here? I stood and backed away. A quick look around the shop revealed no checkbook, but I did notice the phone off the hook and the cash drawer open. Whoever'd killed Frank now had something that belonged to me—something with my address on it.

A chilling thought, but again why kill Frankie?

A quick call to the bank would put a stop-hold on any checks written on my account. I guessed the killer-thief could purchase enough for a short while to justify the theft. But was it worth killing for? Have things gotten that bad? The scissors sticking out of his neck seemed particularly brutal in its irony. But wouldn't a murderer have brought his own weapon to the scene of a crime?

Something didn't add up. Only saving grace, as small as it felt right now, was the fact my checks only had my rural address and phone number back in Minnesota blazoned across them. Still, thieves and con men could get pretty creative with the Internet. But why go to all that trouble? My thoughts raced like birds on a strong wind. I'm not a rich man. I don't have anything of value.

A call to my friend Bryce, a brother-in-law ex-cop was in order. His advice would be useful, as I wasn't certain about what to tell the police. Instead of contaminating evidence in the shop, I left with a pasty-faced Marley on my arm, and we went next door to wait for the authorities.

Two hours and a hell of an interrogation later, I returned home. Bryce came over. We were supposed to leave on a trip in the morning. "I don't feel like going to Lake Havasu, Bryce."

"There's nothing you can do here, Gus. You told the cops everything and they know where to get a hold of you."

"Yeah, but I still feel somehow responsible for Frank's death."

"This is not on you, Gus. Probably a couple of punks after drug money . . . that's what the cops think, anyway."

"What about the book?" I asked.

"What about it? You told that detective that you paid Frank fifty-dollars for a box of old books he was going to give away. What am I missing?"

I told him about the call Frank received from the woman the day before, the origin of Bower's book, the letter from Kittridge, and what made a first edition valuable.

"And about the guy who went into the shop just after you left."

"Right. And the guy in front of my house I told you about."

He waved his hand as if dismissing class. "Enough already. You're trying to create some sort of sinister plot here, Gus." Bryce frowned, his palms turned up. "Have you read the book?"

"Not entirely."

"And you don't really know if it's worth anything or not, right?"

"No . . . but I know who can shed some light." I picked up the phone, called information, and in one minute dialed the number to a mystery bookstore in Minneapolis called, Once Upon A Crime. The owner was a respected collector of first editions. I had recently done some work for him and he owed me. "Gary? It's Gus Ivy."

"Gus. How are you?"

"I'm fine. Say, I want to ask you a question."

"Go ahead."

"I just picked up a book published in about 1946. It's one of those old Sagebrush Westerns by M.B. Bower."

"Gus, we're a mystery bookstore, remember?"

"I know but give me some guidance, here. What should I look for in a book this old? If it doesn't say 'first edition' or 'first printing,' what am I looking at? Also, there is no copyright number, no date of publication per se, and the publisher is different from all the other Bower books."

"Was it published for a limited readership, then?" Gary asked.

"Apparently. Maybe fewer than two hundred copies printed."

"Well, then no doubt it's a first and only edition. Without a copyright number, it was probably never meant to be sold to the public. Almost sounds like an advanced reader copy."

"Yeah, but it isn't. It has the original dust jacket and otherwise looks like any other hardcover published in mass quantity. Here's something else: I own all twelve of Bower's books, and my research never indicated a thirteenth."

"Well, now you have sort of a baker's dozen. That fact alone could be worth a great deal to another Bower collector. Has it been signed by the author?"

"Yes."

"Good. That doubles its value."

"To what? Rough guess?"

"Hmmm, maybe a couple grand. You need to do some more research, Gus. Good luck. Stop in when you get back."

"I will, Gary. Thanks and say hello to Pat for me."

"You bet. Take care."

I turned to Bryce. "So, if there were only a few copies printed, how many could possibly be left after sixty years? Gary thinks I've got a collector's item on my hands."

"You think this thing's what got Frank killed?"

"Could be a robbery gone bad, of course. My checkbook's still missing, and Frank's till was cleaned out. But something's definitely weird here, Bryce."

His eyebrows rose. "So you think the lady who called Frank wants that book so bad she'd kill for it? That's a stretch, Gus. I still don't see the connection."

"What about the guy who came in the shop as I was leaving . . . blue jacket, red cap? Never said a word. Seemed to be waiting for me to leave?"

"He was a customer. How many times have you struck up a conversation with a stranger in the barber shop?"

He had me there. "But, what about the guy outside my house?"

"Did he have a red hat and blue jacket?"

"No. White, short-sleeved shirt. No hat."

"Okay, then. Two entirely unrelated events. Bet if you call the gas company you'll find they sub-contract their meter reading, and the guy you saw was late making rounds. Had a friend who did that one summer . . . John O'Rourke. Had keys to get inside peoples' homes 'cause the meters were usually in the basement. Made a habit of using the homeowners' bathroom whenever he found no one home. One day he was taking a crap, reading the paper when the lady of the house returned."

"What happened?"

Bryce laughed. "She screamed bloody-murder and ran out the front door. He screamed, pulled up his pants, forgot to flush, and ran like hell out the back. That was the end of John's meter reading career."

Good story, but I wasn't convinced. "And your point is?"

"These guys are always in a hurry. Always behind schedule. The guy you saw outside paid no attention to you or anyone else. He finished the read, jumped in his company car, and left."

"Could be."

"That's all it was. Look, I have to go home and pack. Why don't you relax, read some more of the book, and I'll see you in the morning. You'll feel better after a good night's sleep." He polished off his beer, gave Sam a pat, and left the house.

I thought his explanation made sense and as an ex-cop, he ought to have a pretty good feeling about cases like this. Still, Frank's death weighed heavy. He was a good guy and didn't deserve to die like he did. The trip to Havasu had been planned for quite some time, however, and we'd only be gone a few days, so why not go? I picked up *The Cavity Lake Gang* and continued reading.

At seven o'clock I stopped and carried the book into the kitchen. Sam gave me a familiar, hungry look—impossible to ignore. He pranced while I filled his dish. My own dinner consisted of a bologna sandwich and plate of chips. After wolfing down a chocolate chip cookie, I rose, poured a cup of coffee, and stepped out on the rear patio.

The western sky had taken on a hue and shading that began as reddish-orange at the lower edge, gradually blending with a pale-blue above. Higher up still, a deep indigo highlighted a few brilliant, early stars. I looked at the book in the fading light. It was three hundred and twenty-five pages with fairly large type. Knowing the author's work well, this was not one of her best, and that bothered me. Disjointed. Choppy. Almost as if Bower had written this one in a hurry. Lots of punctuation errors. Homophonic mistakes are rare . . . any good editor would have caught all of 'em. I was puzzled.

Back inside, I went into the bedroom and packed a bag for the trip. Together with Bryce and two other friends, we planned to fish, gamble and play more golf. After the duffle was packed, I settled into a chair and continued reading.

Sometime later, with the book parked on my chest, I woke up drenched in sweat. After a trip to the bathroom and a clean t-shirt, I slipped into bed. Still fuzzy from the nap, my brain struggled to recall what'd been a disturbing dream: fractured images of mustangs, rustlers, and cowboys. Completely out of context, there were stacked boxes of old books—all without dust jackets in a closet as dark as the night sky. Weirder still, was the presence of a large, brown car that kept driving over my legs—backward then forward. After a few minutes, my breathing slowed, the images faded, and a deeper sleep followed.

A DEEP-THROATED, GUTTURAL, engine-like noise woke me just before dawn. Sam was growling. Something had startled him. He rose from the foot of the bed and padded out to the kitchen. Each growl became a short "huff" with every step. In the kitchen, I found him with his nose at the patio door, sniffing and huffing. "What is it, Sam? Coyote? Javelina?" Both critters had come up from the wash bordering the backyard on previous occasions. Either one would make a mess of a golden retriever—even one as big as Sam. "Hush. It's okay. They're gone now. Shhh." He settled a bit, but the hair on his neck stood as he continued a low growl. My heart slowed. I checked to make sure all the doors were locked. Could have been anything . . . or nothing.

With all the lights on, I fixed an early breakfast. *The Cavity Lake Gang* kept me busy until time for our morning walk. I took a quick look outside with Sam to see if what had upset him might still be lurking.

No footprints anywhere. With desert sand and stone for a "lawn," I really didn't expect to see much. A glance at the patio door revealed a slight scratch on the glass just above the lock. Hadn't noticed that before . . . still, I'd never looked that close either. An attempt to break in? Nah. Why? A tally of all the weird events of the past twenty-four hours all led me back to the book.

Who knew I had it other than maybe Frank's killer? A brief shudder trickled down my back and settled at the base of my spine.

I loaded the van and let Sam climb in. The Bower book rested on the passenger seat. My eyes focused on the cover as it cast a strange, eerie reflection from the bright morning sun. It almost looked like the cowboys on horseback were moving. I blinked, turned the key, and backed out. As the van shook and trembled over each speed bump, the riders on the cover shimmied and bounced as if poised—ready to leap from the cover. Pay attention to the road, Gus. Forget the damned book. By the time we reached Bryce and Allison's, my over-active imagination had retreated, and the book no longer radiated its animated activity.

Bryce waited for me as I parked and let Sam out. "Come on, Sam. You're going to keep Allison company." Sam didn't need to be coaxed. My sister habitually spoiled him more than I. "Hey, Allie. Ready for Sam?" I called out.

Allison, unlike her older brother, had a perpetually cheery disposition. She stood with the door open, a lady always parked on the positive side of the street. "Of course, I am. Hi, Sammy. Guess what I have?" Sam promptly planted his rump and gazed up adoringly as he knew what was coming.

She placed the biscuit on his nose. "Bryce told me about your barber, Gus. What a horrible thing. Was he married?" She waved and Sam snapped the treat out of the air.

"Wife died a few years ago, Allie. I think he had a daughter living in California."

"Bryce says there's nothing you could've done, Gus. Everything's going to hell in a hand basket, as Dad used to say."

I smiled at hearing another of my father's favorite sayings. "I guess."

"You guys have fun and don't worry about Sam."

"Okay. See you in a couple of days. Be good, Sam." I gave Allie a quick peck and rubbed the big dog's head. "Have fun with Aunt Allie, boy!"

We loaded Bryce's Suburban and drove off. Our two friends, Dick Gates and Norm Kiff, were waiting as we drove up. Bryce hooked up Norm's boat to the hitch, and took off. The drive to Lake Havasu would take about three hours. I managed to read a little bit more of the Bower book on the way, but spirited conversation from the other three intruded, so I laid it aside.

We pulled into the marina shortly after noon. Bryce backed the boat to the launch. After it was released, Dick blurted, "Can you imagine that some dumb ass actually paid to have that thing torn down and moved here?" He pointed to the London Bridge, which had been moved from the Thames River in 1958 to this new home in the desert. It spanned a portion of the lake from Lake Havasu City to a small island some distance beyond. It was an ugly juxtaposition of a structure built for a different time and place. We were unanimous that it should be torpedoed. It didn't belong in the desert. And privately, I thought neither did Frank's being murdered belong in Chandler.

Still, the lake shimmered like aluminum foil, and despite the hideous bridge, a sterling, fantastic day awaited us. Bryce parked the Suburban, and five minutes later, we were motoring away from the dock.

A flock of perturbed gulls squawked and lifted from the bridge as we passed by. Long, white streams of excrement floated down and landed on various parts of the bridge. Perfect.

Once we cleared the harbor, Norm goosed the throttle, and we sped down the lake. For the balance of the afternoon, we fished, drank beer, and told outrageous stories.

Four

T FIVE THIRTY WE RETURNED to the dock. Norm eased the runabout into a slip, hired a kid to clean our fish, and gave instructions to the dock master to keep the fish frozen for us. The Arizona sun had fried my face and arms despite the SPF-50 screen, and I imagined a sleepless night of pain.

We stowed everything away, put the cover back on the boat, and drove across the highway. Bryce parked in the casino lot. He locked the truck, and we traipsed across the blacktop with our bags. "A quick shower and then meet in the restaurant?" he asked.

Everyone agreed. We checked in and took the elevator to the third floor. My room adjoined Bryce's. I went inside, stepped out of my fishy clothes, and jumped into the shower. The sting of sharp spray on sunburned skin proved unbearable. Adjusting the temperature control to cold helped a bit. A gentle toweling-off left me half-dry. I carefully pulled on a golf shirt and jeans, stuffed a wad of cash in my pocket, took a quick look around the room, and opened the door.

The boys were waiting downstairs, ready to eat and take on the casino. After a quick trip through the buffet line, we chowed down, paid the bill, and marched a short distance to the casino floor. Norman and I made a beeline for the craps tables, stopping at the first to watch the play. I glanced at Norm and tipped my head invitingly. He nodded in compliance and together we edged to the rail. I withdrew five hundred from my pocket and threw the bills down on the felt.

Craps is a game that requires patience, a great deal of luck, a small amount of skill, and knowledge of the odds that any combination of two dice will appear before seven is rolled. It's no more complicated than that, but it requires nerves of steel to step up and play the first time around. I gathered my chips from the dealer and placed a five-dollar chip on the Pass Line. For the next hour, we suffered through a "cold table." The dice worked around the table twice to find my cash and my sense of fun diminished by half.

The stickman retrieved the dice and in monotone said, "Seven out. Line away." And with that we'd lost—again.

"Whataya think, Norm?"

"Dunno. This is brutal. Next guy looks like he may be a player."

Someone called his name. "Come on, Red." He selected two of the six dice offered by the stickman, rattled both in one hand, and pitched them across the table toward our end. Everyone watched with interest as the dice struck the padded wall and settled.

"Eleven. Winner," intoned the stickman as he hooked the dice and slid them back. Red threw the dice four times. All winners. There were seven players at the table, including Norman and me. We all leaned on the padded armrest and stared down at the crimson cubes as they hit the felt.

"Six."

"All right." Norman leaned over and said, "That's more like it. Let's bet the Hard Way Six."

"I'm not so sure." Typically, I avoided the long shot proposition bets.

An older gentleman slipped in on the other side of Norman and must've heard our conversation. He turned to Norman and said, "I think he's right. That fella will crap out on the next throw."

Norman grunted, "Humpf. That's encouraging." We scooted over to allow more room. Red picked up the dice and heaved once more. The red cubes settled, and as everyone had bet the Pass Line, all lost.

"Damn." Norm turned to the older gentleman on his left and extended his hand. "Name's Norman. And you are?"

"Smead. Limas Smead. Pleasure."

I leaned over and said, "I'm Gus Ivy, Limas. How'd you know he was going to roll the seven?"

"Pleased to meet ya, Gus Ivy. Studied this game a long time. Always watch the shooter. The tell is in his eyes—and his hands," Limas replied. He tossed a hundred on the felt. "Craps is not for the timid, boys. Newcomer doesn't understand the game, he'll drift away like a cork on the open sea. Secret is to hang around long enough for that one, great roll." A shift change brought a halt to the action.

Norman asked, "Whataya do when you're not playing craps, Limas?"

I studied the old man as they talked. Slightly built, he had a narrow face, and prominent chin. A Chicago Cubs jacket hung loosely, sleeves much too short, faded ball cap cocked to one side. When he removed it to scratch his head, I noticed a full head of gray hair combed straight back. He had a well-worn face with deep laugh lines etched at the corner of each eye. His hands were long—capable, with large veins—and looked like saddle leather.

"Oh, I move around quite a bit," Limas was saying. "Sometimes I play here, sometimes Vegas. Rest of the time at the track. Once a gambler always a gambler." He shrugged apologetically.

"Sounds like you've spent a fair amount of time at the tables, Limas," I offered.

"That I have. Can't say it's made me rich, though." He smiled at that.

"We all need to learn when to walk away, don't we?" I offered.

The pit boss approached a chubby, crabby guy across from us and said, "Manny? If you don't mind?" He extended a chit for Manny, an obvious regular, to sign. Manny's dour expression indicated he'd been losing steadily.

The shift change completed, the stickman stood ready to pass the dice when Manny asked, "Who's the next shooter? Is it you, Mickey?"

"Looks like it," the shortest guy at the table replied.

With great deliberation, Mickey selected two dice from the cache offered by the stickman. He stacked one atop, lifted the dice with two fingers, and then flipped both. The pair hit the sidewall, bounced twice, and stopped.

"Seven. Winner."

"Sweet. Atta boy. Do it again, you goofy lookin' little runt," Manny muttered, a gold chain swinging from his open-collared shirt just below his double chin.

Mickey stacked the dice again and gently tossed them into the air. Unfortunately, he crapped out, and the dice were passed. It continued this

way for some time. A new shooter would roll a seven or eleven, get everyone's hopes up, then crap out.

A blonde woman in a low-cut blue silk blouse, tight white capris, and
high heels slipped in to the right of Manny.

"Looks like she forgot her underwear," Norm mumbled.

"Appears that way," I replied. "You know her, Limas?"

"Nope. Never seen her before, but I've a hunch our luck's about to
change real soon." Limas bet fifty dollars, while the blonde threw a hundred
on the felt.

The dealer turned to her and asked, "Reds and whites okay?"

"That's fine. How's the action?" she asked.

"Kinda slow," the dealer replied, exchanging her money for chips and
slipping a stack to her as he stole a peek down her blouse.

"Slow?" Manny repeated the dealer's word for the night. "You got a
gift for understatement, Roy." Manny then turned to the blonde and said,
"Hi, doll. Name's Manny."

"Hi, Manny. I'm Doreen."

"Welcome. Hope you're bringing some luck with you." He held out
a meaty hand with buffed fingernails while flashing a mouthful of
bleached teeth.

"I'll do my best, sugar." Ample breasts moved beneath the thin fabric
of her blouse. She arched her back. Tall and lithe, it took a while to observe
all of Doreen.

All at once, a faint scent of lilacs reached my nostrils, but it wasn't
coming from Doreen. I turned and locked eyes with another woman who
stood a few feet behind. Casual dress with taste, I thought. She wore a beige
cashmere sweater, jeans, and cowboy boots. A small black purse with a thin
strap hung next to her hip. The strap crossed her chest in a way that was
quite alluring. She looked to be about forty—give or take—her eyes a
bright, sky-blue, and she carried herself with grace and style. However, she
seemed uncertain of her next move and as soon as we exchanged glances,
she averted her gaze and squeezed in at the rail on Limas's left.

The scenery at the craps table had just improved by a hundred percent.
The cashmere lady had short auburn hair, fair skin, and full pouty lips. She
wasn't exactly beautiful, but striking—unforgettable, really. In fact, I had a

strange sense that I might've seen her someplace before, but I couldn't imagine where. She really didn't look like someone who traveled in my circle.

Cashmere observed the action for a while. After scanning the table, she turned to her right, and we locked eyes for a second time. She smiled, dug a hundred out of her purse, and dropped it on the table. This wasn't the same sort of practiced move as Doreen's, and she seemed uneasy—as if she'd rather be anywhere but here.

Soon, my attention returned to the flashier Doreen, a bottle-blonde who looked to be in her mid to late thirties. It was obvious that she kept herself in shape. Everything about her screamed, "Look at me." With her turn to roll, Doreen milked the moment. She placed a single red chip on the Pass Line and waited for the dice. With elbows on the padded rail, long hair spilling over the edge, Doreen suddenly looked directly at me, as her painted nails rattled her chips.

"Hi, there. Any luck tonight?" she asked.

Norman jumped in before I could reply. "Nope. But maybe it'll change now that you're here."

"I'm Doreen. And you boys are?"

"I'm Norm. The old guy with all the white hair is Gus. Young fella on my left is Limas."

"Pleased to meet all of you." She casually selected a pair of dice offered by the stickman.

Limas studied the blonde. He seemed to be looking for a clue as to who she was or what she was all about. "She's loose as a goose," he stated quietly. His voice rose and he licked his lips. "If she makes two passes, she'll get on a roll. Climb aboard, boys," he said with a wry flicker of one eye. "Looks like she knows what she's about." He doubled his bet.

Doreen tossed both dice with authority across the green. They collapsed against the sidewall. Her follow-through left Norman wide-eyed as he stared down the front of her blouse.

"My-oh-my," Norm muttered.

"Seven. Winner. We have a new shooter, gents, and she's hot," the stickman shouted as he threw a wink Doreen's way.

Doreen squealed with delight, shook her upper torso, and collected her chips. She pressed her bet, as did everyone else. Once again, she picked up the dice and in one swift motion, tossed them the length of the table.

Eleven. Another winner.

Doreen rolled three more sevens, then eleven. She was making money for all of us.

Cashmere Sweater stayed on the Pass Line with an odds bet, but that was as far as she went. Unlike the bolder Doreen, Cashmere never introduced herself, and by this point, we were all so caught up in the action that no one asked her name.

I threw a green chip out on the Hard Eight—the prop bet I usually avoided. Doreen swept up the dice, blew a kiss into both red cubes, and flicked them the length of the table. They tumbled back off the side, struck two separate stacks of chips, and landed—a four exposed on each die.

"Hard Eight. Winner."

The table erupted with loud cheers. Manny reached down, lifted Doreen's hand, and planted a kiss on her knuckles. She giggled and jiggled, having a wonderful time. The bets paid off, Doreen picked up the dice. Once again she blew a kiss and let the cubes fly.

She next threw three straight sevens—all winners. It seemed she couldn't miss. Doreen glanced down at the chips the dealer stacked before her. She stared for a few seconds, and I could see she was counting the stack. Her face darkened. Chameleon-like, her demeanor toward Roy, the dealer, changed. "You're short," she snapped. "I counted the stack. You owe me six red ones."

Amazing, I thought. In the middle of a hot roll, she figured out how many chips the dealer owed her. Might be more to this babe than she's showing.

The pit boss nodded, and six additional chips were added to Doreen's stack. "Thank you." She stood taller, picked up the dice, and rolled three more winners.

"Stay with her, boys." Limas said. "She's hot. She knows it, and so do the dice."

A new player edged into the rail between Limas and the cashmere lady. He dropped a green chip on the Don't Pass line. This anti-play did not go unnoticed by everyone playing the opposite.

Just before Doreen threw the dice, the stickman barked, "Eight's the point! Hands high." Too late. The dice hit someone's hand, lost momentum, and crumpled before hitting the end wall. Like a pair of exhausted lovers, the dice collapsed, their vitality gone. "Seven out. Line away." The stickman shrugged. "Pay the Don't Pass bettor on my right."

"Sonofabitch." Manny muttered.

"Shit." Norm added.

It was over. We all knew what had happened. The new guy broke the spell. As one, we hated him for intruding.

Doreen looked astonished, disbelieving. She now looked at the guy who'd just squeezed in and jinxed it all, and her ire was evident. It was as if the door to a meat locker had opened and a blast of cold air settled over the table.

The object of our combined dislike, the new guy, was about forty-five—tall, mean looking, with coal-black eyes, a radish-shaped nose, and greasy hair worn in a mullet. He had a gaunt, collapsed face that'd scare a skunk.

This guy's bad news . . . someone to avoid, I told myself, and glanced around to see if anyone agreed. Sadly, I realized that the cashmere lady had stalked off. Nuts. Sorry to see her leave, I wondered about her story.

Five

MANNY STUDIED THE SIX DICE. "No problem, folks. Let's ride this horse for a while and see what happens."

"He's right," Limas offered. "Luck's still down here."

Mullethead was bored apparently. He picked up his chips and followed Cashmere. I looked at my watch. We had an 8:30 a.m. tee time. Golf seemed a distant concern, however. Caught in the excitement and frenzy of the craps game, I wasn't ready to pack it in just yet.

"Pick two, doll." Manny had Doreen select a lucky pair, and rotund, gold draped Manny picked them up. Doreen blew a kiss, and he flung the cubes down the table.

"Eleven. Pass Line winner."

Manny threw three more winners, a loser, and four straight sevens. Prior to each throw, Doreen leaned over and affectionately blew in his chubby, sweaty hand. "Come on, Manny. Hit that eight."

Manny made twelve straight passes, making money for all of us. The casino changed dealers in a lame attempt to end Manny's run. I stuffed black chips in my pocket, backed away and said, "Have to take a leak. Be right back." I left the table and entered the men's room.

Coming out head down, I ran smack into Doreen. "Whoops. Sorry, Doreen. Didn't see you coming." My hands rested on her shoulders. Bare skin beneath the thin veneer of blouse fabric was enticing. She didn't move an inch, but smiled coyly.

"But I saw you coming." Her fingers lingered at my waist. She smiled. "It's Gus, right?"

"Yes." Embarrassed, I withdrew my hands.

She stepped closer and ran her fingers up my arms. "You know . . . if you'd like to party later . . ." A scent of Doublemint gum trailed her wetted lips.

Her invitation was obvious but not really tempting. Doreen was lubricious, delicious, and conspicuous as hell, and I was no choirboy, but the image of the cashmere lady intruded. My face flushed, and I felt stupid for letting the byplay continue. "Sorry, kiddo. Think I'd better stay on the Pass Line."

Undeterred, Doreen pressed against me. After a brief moment, she stepped back, arched to expose rigid nipples, and looked down at the front of my jeans. A single, carefully plucked eyebrow arced. "You sure about that, Gus?" A smile played across her moist lips.

I looked down at the bulge in my pocket and chuckled. "I'm flattered, Doreen, but that's not me—just a roll of chips."

Doreen covered her mouth, giggled, and drew back. "You look like a guy in need of a little fun in your life, Gus." She threw a slender leg out and rubbed my knee with hers. "You're a big one, aren't you? I'm very, very good, Gus. Your friend won't even have to know, if that's what you're worried about."

"Look, Doreen, I'm a big boy and don't need anyone's permission. Why don't you take a run at Manny? He looks like a party kinda guy." I separated and tried to step around her.

"Not interested in Manny. Don't see a ring on your finger, Gus. What's the problem?"

"I came here to gamble and play some golf, Doreen. Some other time, okay?"

Her cheeks flushed. Her eyes flashed a warning. "You don't get it, do you, Gus"

"Get it?" I instantly knew I shouldn't've asked.

"That I usually get what I want." Two scintillating fingers brushed my cheek, and next ran down my chest. The tips of her fingers dipped inside my belt. "Change your mind?"

"Sorry. Nothing personal." I removed her hand, slipped past, and returned to the table. Air escaped in a rush. Christ. *What was that all about?*

Doreen returned a few minutes later. She looked different, somehow. Her face was flushed. Our eyes met, and she turned away. Manny continued his momentous roll for another thirty minutes. The table was covered with chips; every color represented, but mostly black. The value of each hundred-dollar chip seemed lost in the frenzy. I didn't dare speak. Whatever magical spell Manny had on the dice was sacred. Sooner or later, however . . .

"Come on, Manny," Doreen shrieked. "Baby needs a new pair of shoes."

He couldn't lose. We couldn't lose. It was unbelievable. I'd never experienced anything close to this, and doubted I ever would again. Giddy with delight, the chips piled in front of me while Manny made thirty straight passes. The noise from the table had reached a crescendo. Manny picked up the dice one more time. I had over four hundred dollars riding on this one roll. We all wanted Manny to roll a six—the hard way, two threes.

Doreen raised her arms and shimmied. Everything shook and wiggled at the same time. Manny laughed, picked up three black chips, and shouted, "Three hundred dollar Hard Six!" The oval table rocked with anticipation—green felt shimmering like a calm sea before a storm. The table resembled a child's game board—stacks of chips covered every conceivable wager offered. The stickman fingered his miniature hockey stick. All bets placed, everyone leaned in, ready. Doreen kissed his cheek as Manny shook the dice. He leaned out and pitched them over the cloth. The dice chugged through a maze of tiny missile silos, bounced to either side of the table, and settled.

"Seven out. Line away," the stickman said. Manny's magical run ended.

"Son-of-a-bitch!" Norman declared, ecstatic. We all were.

The dealers began collecting chips. All the energy and excitement that enveloped the table vanished like a soap bubble on a spiny cactus. Someone clapped and soon all the players joined in. The applause lasted two minutes. Manny bowed and accepted the kudos.

"Time for bed, Gus?" Norm nudged me. "Got golf in the morning."

"Yeah, I'm ready, Norm, but God, that was fun." I left a generous tip for the dealers, and Norm did as well.

The pit boss sent a guard over with plastic trays to collect our chips and escort us to a cashier window. "Well, it's been quite a night, Limas," I said to our newfound friend. "We still have a long day ahead tomorrow." A glance at my watch said eleven thirty. "You gonna hang around?"

"No. Think I'll quit too." He collected his chips.

"I'm too wound up for bed. Can we buy you a beer, Limas?" I asked. "We owe ya at least that."

"Well, thanks, boys. Might have a soda, rest my feet for a spell."

Cashmere Sweater had vanished long before, which was really too bad. I expected Doreen to be draped all over Manny, but she still had other ideas. The slinky blonde came over, leaned close and whispered, "Not too late, Gus. Think of all we could do together."

"Thanks, but I'm beat." Curiosity intruded. "Why me, Doreen?"

Her warm breath lingered on my cheek. "I like a challenge, Gus. That's all." She kissed me and stepped back.

I was too tired to continue bantering. "'Night, Doreen. Thanks for the pleasant dream."

"Sure." Unaccustomed to rejection, she seemed unsure of her next play. Doreen looked deflated, nostrils flared, eyes pinched into narrow slits. "You aren't normal, Gus." She spun around and stomped off.

I briefly wondered about her abrupt change in mood, but anxious to collect my winnings, I joined Limas and Norm. "I'll be damned," I counted six thousand dollars along with my original stake.

Norman collected his stack of bills and said, "Eight thousand. Wow." His face flushed.

Limas riffled the hundreds in his hand and folded them up. The three of us left the casino floor and walked into one of the nearby cocktail lounges, where we ordered two Buds and a soda to toast our amazing luck.

"How much, Limas?" Norm asked.

"Oh, 'bout three thousand, I guess. Not a bad night, all things considered."

The waitress returned with our drinks. "Never been very lucky at craps," I offered. "Usually go home a loser. Not tonight, thanks to you."

"You get here often?" Norman asked.

"Once in a while . . . travel quite a bit." He appeared uncomfortable.

"Where's home?" My turn.

He sipped his soda. "Move from place to place. Been livin' out in L.A. for the past few years—since I retired. Plenty of tracks and Indian casinos to choose from."

"Retired from what?" Me again.

"Security business." He scanned the room.

That could mean most anything. "Why'd you give it up?"

"Contract expired. Wasn't renewed." I caught a touch of bitterness.

Bryce and Dick found us in the bar. I introduced Limas while Norm bragged about our great luck. Tired and in need of a good night's sleep, I tried to stifle a second yawn.

"I'm keeping you boys up." Limas downed the last of his Coke.

Norman paused long enough to say, "Take care, old-timer. Thanks again for everything." He extended his hand.

Limas pumped Norman's hand then turned and grasped mine, his grip warm and firm. "So long, Gus. Keep your eye out for Lady Luck. Never know when she'll pop up."

"I will, Limas. Hope we meet again. Stay healthy, okay?"

"Sure thing." He looked across the darkened room and added, "Spotted an old friend. Think I'll go say 'howdy.' So long, fellas." Limas maneuvered around the tables and disappeared.

Norman was on stage. "Here's what it felt like. Remember when you'd get to second base with a girl in high school? You know, when she didn't push you off just 'cause your hand slipped under her cardigan?" Everyone nodded, not sure of the analogy but familiar with the event.

"And when you finally got those damn hooks open . . . remember how exciting that was? That's what this felt like tonight."

The guy had a way with words. Bawdy but poetic.

"That about right, Gus?" he asked.

"Pretty accurate, Norm." The banter continued awhile longer, then tailed off. It had been a long day. "I'm bushed," I said pushing my chair back. "Anyone else coming?"

We left a tip, and headed for the elevator. When the doors opened on the third floor, Dick and Norm went left, Bryce and I right. "Sleep tight, Bryce. Knock on my door in the morning, okay?" I passed his door and stopped at the next.

"You got it, Gus." He unlocked his door and went inside.

I dug the card key from my back pocket, drew it across the slot, and opened the door.

Six

AFTER SAYING GOOD NIGHT to everyone, I fully expected to get a good night's sleep, but when I stepped into my room and reached for the wall switch, I never made it to the bed. Someone grabbed my arm and spun me against the wall—face first. Pain tore through my skull. Thousands of white spots drifted behind my eyes. I heard, then felt, gristle and tissue grind as my nose struck the wall behind the door. Blood gushed from a certain broken nose.

Stunned, eyes watering and lacking the strength to defend myself, I was a rag doll. The room was a dark cave, but even if I'd managed to flip the switch, I could not possibly focus. All the euphoria and giddiness of the past few hours evaporated like a bead of sweat in the desert sun. Trembling now, breathing came in short gasps. The sudden loss of oxygen sapped all my energy. My legs had gone limp, arms too heavy to resist further harm. My head wobbled like a dashboard doll. Unable to draw a breath, panic ensued.

The intruder leaned against my back. "Don't turn around. Don't speak until I tell you to. Is that clear?"

With my mangled nose and mouth full of blood, talking was problematic. Somehow I had bitten into my tongue, and it hurt like hell. "Ah, y-y-yes." The money from the craps table.

"Good. I have a thirty-eight Smith & Wesson with a silencer. Twitch and I shoot you in the foot. Understood?"

The urge to vomit was powerful. I sucked a mouthful of air past a couple of loose teeth, regained a spark of courage, and managed a weak, "Yeah. Money's in my pocket." My whole head throbbed.

"Where's the book?"

"What? What book?" The barrel of the thirty-eight dug deeper and prodded my kidneys.

"Don't be stupid. You know what I'm talking about. You bought it from the barber. The *Cavity* book."

"Don't have it." And then boldly, "Left it at home."

My ear suddenly exploded and the rainbow of dots re-appeared as he whacked me with the gun barrel. "Nice try. Next time I shoot your ear off. "We looked through your house. The book wasn't there. Where is it?"

Adrenalin pounded through my veins. My system filled with a strange cocktail of fury and terror. *Careful, Gus. Use your head.* Sweat poured from beneath my arms. I flexed my fingers, unsure of what had to be done to save my ass. *Wait. Wait for the right moment. No second chances here. Guy has a gun. He's in control. He knows it, and so do I.*

Another poke in my tortured, sore ribs reminded me not to press my luck. "You're wasting my time. The book, Ivy."

This maniac knew my name and had somehow gotten into my room. He pressed my face against the wall again. "All right," I wheezed. "You've made your point. Need to wipe my nose. Can't breathe. Can I get a handkerchief from my pocket?"

He paused. I heard the rustle of nylon as he glanced around the small room. "Hurry up. No funny business."

After a swipe at my broken nose, I spit into the cloth. A quick check of my front teeth indicated all were still in place. *Buy some time. Give him the book and you're a dead man. Think. Get out of the room. That's the play.*

"Where is it?"

I recalled Frank's bloody corpse like a bad Kodak moment. "It's in the truck. The Suburban." All the air in the room vanished as I waited for his response. If fear had an odor, it worked past my clogged nostrils; either that or I smelled my own blood, metallic, coppery. The barrel prodded an untouched area of my back. "Ow! Jesus Christ, back off. I can get it."

He didn't say anything at first, but I sensed his growing concern. The entire episode had taken too much time. He fired back a question I'd anticipated. "Who has the keys?"

"My friend, Bryce. It's his truck."

"Which room?"

"Next door. Three twenty-one."

He put his free hand on my shoulder and guided me to the bathroom. "Clean up your face." He flicked on the light.

I wet a cloth and wiped off the blood. My nose had begun to swell. I stole a glance in the mirror at the gunman. It was Mr. Ugly, the mullet-haired goon from the craps table. Now I really hated him.

"Let's go, pretty boy." He waved me out of the bathroom toward the main door. "Open it and check the hall. Don't get cute."

I stuck my head out, and scanned the corridor. "It's empty," I whispered and retreated into the room. My assailant had a problem now. He must somehow get the car keys from Bryce without being seen, escort me into the elevator, and downstairs to the parking lot; all without drawing attention.

"Wait." He turned away. The pressure against my back eased. The rustle of nylon indicated he was removing his jacket. "Okay, here's the deal. The gun's tucked under my jacket. Once we get to your friend's room, I'll step to the side. When he opens the door, don't let him into the hall. His life's in your hands, Ivy. If he spots me, he's a dead man. Just ask for the keys and leave. Got it?"

I choked out, "Yes." I feared my legs would buckle. *God, now I've endangered Bryce.*

"Let's go. Remember what I said."

We edged out into the hall and stopped. I took a deep breath, knocked twice, and waited.

The door opened a third of the way until he recognized me. "Gus? What's wrong?" He squinted at the bright hall lights.

I squeezed into the doorway blocking his view. "Nothing. Need your car keys is all. Left something in the car." I covered my nose and mouth with one hand to hide the damage.

"Yeah, sure. No problem. Hang on." Bryce's eyebrows rose as if he wanted to question me further, but he didn't. In five seconds, he was back. "You okay, Gus?" He moved as if to open the door further.

I quickly reached out, patted his shoulder, and replied, "Go back to bed. I'm fine. Stomach's a little upset is all. Left my toilet kit in the car and need some Rolaids." I grabbed the keys. "Must've been the horseradish. I'll return the keys in the morning."

"Okay. 'Night, Gus." He retreated looking puzzled.

I waited for him to close the door and wondered if I'd ever see my friend again.

Alone again in the hallway with Mullethead, I was shoved toward the elevators. "Hurry up. Move!"

Once inside the elevator, he spun me around and slipped behind me again. The doors closed. "Push the Lobby button," he said.

Muzak piped into the small space seemed particularly obscene right then. The lift dropped, along with my courage. Maybe someone'll step in from another floor. And then what? Distract him. I was running out of time. Wait for the right opportunity. Be ready to move. The door slid open much too quickly.

"Try anything stupid—anything at all—and I shoot the first person I see," Mullet muttered.

There it was. If I didn't give him the book, he'd kill me. Probably would anyway. Something inside my chest broke. A stab of pain that wasn't physical. It was my heart counting down to zero; a reminder of the precious few minutes left.

It was past midnight yet the tinkling and jingling of the slots was a mere whisper compared to earlier in the evening. Mullethead nudged me forward, and we shuffled toward the front doors. Within minutes, we were outside—moving faster.

"Where's the truck?"

"Over there." I pointed with a limp wrist.

It took only two minutes to reach a well-lit area of the parking lot away from the casino. My time had expired without a cogent plan. When we stopped next to Bryce's Suburban, I feared myself dead for certain.

The gunman stepped back. "Hold it." Once again I heard the rustle of nylon. He was putting his jacket back on. He stepped in front of me and glanced around, clearly unnerved by the bright light directly overhead. "Now, where's the book?"

All at once it came to me. I knew what had to be done. "In the glove box."

"Open the door and get it—quick."

I didn't feel particularly brave—pissed off was more like it. I wanted more than anything to rewind the last fifteen minutes of my life, but that wasn't going to happen. This was all very real. I'd have only one chance to take control of the situation. I aimed the electronic door opener at the truck and waited for the "click." After it unlocked, I lifted the handle and leaned in to open the glove box. The next move was critical. I fumbled and let the keys drop.

"What's the matter?"

"Ah, damn . . . dropped the keys. Need 'em for the glove box. Here they are." I inserted the key and was just about to pop the glove box when I heard Mullet say, "Hold it."

"Hey, what's going on over there?" A third voice called. It sounded familiar.

"Shit," the gunman muttered. "We got company."

As the glove box popped open, I twisted back and saw that Mullet had turned and was looking toward the rear of the Suburban. A glance through the glass showed it was Manny, from the craps game. On his way home, unaware of what he had stumbled into, he'd provided the diversion I needed. There was no better time to make my play. I reached into the glove box and grabbed Bryce's service revolver—a nine mm Beretta. With the gun secretly jammed between my ribs and the seat, I waited to make my move.

Seven

MANNY HAD APPROACHED the truck from the rear. As he drew closer, he must've noticed Mullet's gun. "What the hell?" Manny's words came tentative and fearful.

The gunman didn't hesitate. *Pop! Pop!*

Manny staggered back and sat down on the striped blacktop. He looked down at two dark spots on his chest, then back toward the truck. He tried to speak, but blood filled his mouth. He was still upright when I jumped from the truck.

Mullet had turned to face me, but hadn't completed the move. I pointed the Beretta at his head. Strangely composed, I knew control had shifted in my favor. I had the advantage, but for how long? "Do me a favor—do something else stupid, asshole." My finger tightened on the trigger. A surge of venom coursed through me. I ached to blow a hole in Mullet's fat head. I resisted the urge and said, "Drop your gun."

He hesitated, calculating my resolve and his chance for escape. He decided to live. He leaned down and laid the Smith & Wesson on the tarmac.

"Step to the side," I called. "Away from the door." He shuffled sideways.

"Turn around and drop to your knees." Again, he complied. I edged past him and backed over to Manny, who was gasping for air. I knelt down, facing Mullet.

Raspberry-hued chest wounds pumped gobs of blood. One of the slugs had entered a lung—bubbles escaping through his chest along with the blood. I eased Manny on to his back, and with my free hand, pressed hard against what appeared the worst of the two wounds. Blood continued to pulse through my fingers. *Where the hell is security?* There was little more I could do. "Manny? It's me. Gus. Hang on, pal. An ambulance will be here real soon."

His eyes pleaded for salvation. I had none to give. He was mortally wounded. Mullet remained on his knees, so I attended to Manny. His lips moved, the words unintelligible. His eyes searched mine, and after one final rattle from his throat, all sentience clouded over.

"Manny? Stay with me, Manny." When I looked up Mullet was gone, his weapon still on the pavement. I stood and caught a glimpse of him as he darted between cars and vanished from view.

Drained and deeply saddened, I collapsed next to Manny's corpse and gently closed each lid. My conscience was now burdened with two deaths. First Frank. Now Manny. The pavement felt as cold as Manny soon would be, and as cold as my heart had already become. "I'm sorry, Manny. Truly sorry." The pool of blood beneath the hefty body jelled, as though frozen. My scream filled the parking lot. "All this because of some damned book!"

Sirens howled in the distance—first one, then many. They joined to form one loud mournful declaration of another senseless death. Never even knew his last name, I thought.

I stood and held my arms out like a cormorant drying his wings and waited for the cops.

THIRTY MINUTE LATER, I was in a small room somewhere deep inside the casino, imagining Robert Deniro and Joe Peschi with a baseball bat, but the security guys that had me were just the opposite of what you'd expect from the movies. "Can we get anything for you, Mr. Ivy?" the guard asked.

I withdrew a towel from my swollen, clogged nose. "Maybe some ice?" I mumbled.

"Certainly." A second guard scampered off soon to return with a small bag of ice. Trailing behind was a cop. He wore khakis, a golf shirt, and dark blue windbreaker—badge clipped to his leather belt. His partner followed close behind. Dressed much the same, this guy looked like a middle linebacker for the Arizona Cardinals. Ratface and Dick the Bruiser. I've always had this annoying habit of tagging people due to some physical attribute. Picked it up in the service in an effort to preserve my sanity.

"We'll take it from here, Cliff," Ratface said to the casino guard. "Would you set up a screening of those security tapes for us?"

"You bet. Won't take but a few minutes," Cliff replied.

From behind the ice pak, I studied the two cops and waited.

"I'm Detective Badger, Mr. Ivy. And this is my partner, Sergeant Carvel. Mohave County Sheriff's Office. We'll be heading up the investigation here." Badger had round white circles around squinty eyes from a pair of absurd Polaroids that dangled from his breast pocket. "You stated that the attacker wanted a book?"

"That's right." I then recounted all that'd happened since my purchase of the Bower book—including Frank's murder. No reason to hold anything back at this point.

"Sergeant, call Chandler PD and get the details." Bruiser hustled out of the room. "Do you believe your attacker acted alone or in consort with others?"

"The guy said, 'We looked through your house and didn't find the book.' So, yes, there's likely others involved." I groped for additional answers. "There was a woman at the craps table that seemed way too persistent. She wanted to 'party.' Wouldn't take no for an answer."

"She a hooker?"

"Thought so at first. Now I'm not so sure. Name was Doreen. Couldn't figure why she didn't go after Manny."

"Why so?"

"He bet large. So did my buddy, Norm, for that matter."

"Larger than you?"

"Absolutely, so anyone casing the table for this kind of action should've hit on Manny, but instead Doreen comes on to me."

"Would you be able to identify her again?"

"Pretty hard to miss. Blonde, mid-thirties, maybe five-foot-six. Dressed to attract attention."

"She'll be on the overhead camera. Anyone else beside the blonde?"

I didn't answer right away. I just couldn't think of anyone else that took a particular interest in me—except for Limas.

"I don't know . . . an old guy wearing a Chicago Cubs jacket. Said his name was Limas Smead. Smart player—knew the game inside and out. Said he was from L.A. Retired from the security business. Gambler. Nice enough. Seemed harmless. Norm and I had a drink with him afterwards."

"Anything he say make you uneasy?"

I considered that, the cold pak getting warmer. "No, not really. He left pretty quickly when he spotted someone in the bar. That was about it."

"Recognize the other guy?"

"Nope."

"Is there any reason to think that this Limas and Doreen were some-how connected?"

"Can't say. Possible, I guess. They never spoke to each other that I recall. She came at me again as we were cashing in. When I turned her down a second time, she looked pretty pissed off."

"But you can't say why, Mr. Ivy?"

"Damned if I know why! Like I said, she coulda had Manny with a wink and a wave, so I couldn't figure it out." I stood up and laid two fin-gers alongside my swollen, mangled proboscis.

"Okay. Let's go take a look at the security tapes. See if we can iden-tify any of these characters."

My chair scraped on the tile floor as I pushed away from the table. The noise fueled my frayed nerves. "Can I get something to drink? Mouth's pretty dry."

"Sure. Come on. There's a vending machine in the hall." Badger led the way when I had a revelation: Mullet and his pals knew more about the value of the Cavity book than I did. I've got some catching up to do. Someone wants that book badly enough to kill for it twice over, and I've gotta determine why? If I wait for the cops to get on the right page here I'll be number three.

Detective Badger escorted me up to the tape room. I plopped down in a chair and took a sip of soda. "Now, we want you to look at some video, Mr. Ivy. This first tape is of you and your assailant entering the elevator, exiting, and then crossing the lobby."

I edged closer to the screen. The hair on my arms stood up as Mullet's face filled the screen. It was a flickering image, but he was as ugly as ever.

"We'll get a print made. See if we come up with a match. He didn't wear gloves, so maybe we can pull some from the room. Wasn't any too careful about being seen either, was he? Sure you've never seen him before?"

"Nope. I'd've remembered."

"Run those tapes from the craps table, will you, Bill?"

Bill punched some keys and an overhead shot of the craps table suddenly appeared. At the time, it seemed Norm and I had spent hours at the table, but the entire tape was no more than an hour in length. "That's Doreen. Next to Manny," I pointed. "By the way, what'd you say Manny's last name was?"

"Siragusa. Owned a Mercedes dealership. Which one is this Limas fellow?"

"Across from Doreen. Old guy with the ball cap."

"When we're done, scan the tape for a good close-up and have it printed for me, will you, Bill?"

"Sure thing. Anyone else?"

"The old guy, and . . . ah hell, get a print of all of 'em."

We watched the entire tape in silence. When it was almost over, Badger asked, "Who's the dark-haired babe next to Smead?"

I leaned forward. Ah, yes. The pretty cashmere lady. "Don't know. She came in late, never said a word, played for a while, and left."

"Did Smead speak to her?"

"Nope. Not that I ever noticed. She didn't speak to anyone, near as I recall."

"Okay. Here's our guy again."

My blood surged at the sight of Mullethead—the Don't Pass bettor. The grainy tape enhanced his ugliness—wedge-shaped head, acne-scarred skin, and ears that stuck out like sails. His maroon-patterned shirt looked like a seat cover from the State Theater. "Should've kicked in his face when I had the chance," I muttered.

"What's that?"

"Nothin'."

"Did he say anything to anyone at the table?"

"Nope. Bet against the crowd and pissed everyone off. Quit after about fifteen minutes."

"Bill, have you got a tape that covers the area outside the men's room?" Badger asked.

"Yes."

"Punch that up."

Soon we watched a steady stream of traffic in and out of the men's room. My white head appeared next to Doreen's. After our encounter, another guy walked up and stopped in front of her. He seemed to be questioning her, and when she shook her head, he stomped off. Doreen lifted her chin, adjusted her blouse, and left the area.

"Ever see that man before, Mr. Ivy?"

"No, but it sure seemed as if they knew each other, didn't it? Could be her pimp."

"Maybe. We'll run both through the computer and see if we get any hits. Don't think she's from around here—we know the locals." Badger turned back to me. "Not much more we need from you, Mr. Ivy. Sounds like that book you bought is pretty valuable, so I'd keep an eye on it. Where is it, by the way?"

"Locked in the safe in my room."

"Smart move. You were extremely lucky to've escaped. I'm confident had you given up the book, we wouldn't be having this conversation." His eyes bore into mine. His message clear. "Your room is part of the crime scene. It's taped off, so Sergeant Carvel will escort you to retrieve your belongings and move you to another room. Please leave a number where you can be reached?"

"Certainly. I hope you catch this guy, Detective."

"We'll do our best." He reached out his hand. "Good-bye."

"Good-bye, Detective." We shook, and I followed Bruiser out the door.

AFTER A COUPLE OF HOURS of fitful sleep, I met the boys in the Mohave Grill. It was Saturday. I slid into the booth next to Norm. "Gentlemen?"

"We heard what happened, Gus. Jesus!" Dick's eyes widened. "Are you okay?"

"Yeah, a little sore, but I'm fine." I gave them an abbreviated version of what happened, and the bandage across my nose told the rest. "Poor Manny was in the wrong place, Norm."

"You're lucky to be alive, Gus." Norm put a hand on my shoulder and patted twice. "And all of this over some old book?" He noticed the *Cavity* book on the vinyl seat. "Let me see that." He reached for the book and studied the cover. "Beautiful painting on the jacket. This one of those old westerns you like to read, Gus?"

"Uh huh. Still haven't finished reading it. It's time to find out what makes it so damned important to someone, Bryce."

Bryce hadn't said a word but considered my question, and finished his coffee. "I'm beginning to. Look, no one's in a festive mood after all this, and you look like death, so I suggest we finish eating and check out."

Everyone concurred. Our little vacation had come to an abrupt and tragic end. We were anxious to go home. We ate sparingly and conversation flagged. We were a subdued, tired group, and I could barely keep my eyes open. "Come on. Let's go." I slid from the booth and dropped a tip next to my plate.

We paid the bill, checked out of the hotel, and climbed into Bryce's Suburban. The pool of blood on the tarmac had been washed away. For a moment, Manny's dull eyes flashed. I shook my head to clear the image. When we reached the lake, Bryce backed up to the boat ramp.

"Son of a bitch!" It was Norm. "Someone's ransacked the boat!"

"Anything missing?" Bryce asked.

"No. Don't think so. Everything seems to be here. Suppose it has anything to do with last night? With your book, Gus?"

"Wouldn't be a bit surprised," Bryce offered.

"Had to be the same bunch. Geez, I'm sorry, Norm."

"That's okay, Gus. No damage done."

We loaded the boat on the trailer and put everything back in place. Once the cover was snapped on, we piled into the Suburban and drove away from the marina. We stopped for gas at a 7-Eleven outside the marina. Once gassed up, I laid my head back, fell asleep, and never moved until we pulled in front of Norm's house four hours later.

I WOKE WITH A STIFF NECK, a sore swollen nose, and still felt tired. The events of the previous evening flashed and settled like a cloud of dust. Depression is a funny thing—appearing without warning to linger like an unwanted memory. My heart felt as cold as the moon, as I couldn't shake the conviction that Manny would still be alive but for me. I stretched and stepped out. Norman collected his stuff and Bryce unhooked the boat.

"Keep me posted, Gus." My craps partner gave me a hug and finished with, "At least you came home a winner." The word winner fell flat and hollow.

We dropped Dick off and drove to Bryce's. "Gus? I've been thinking about all this. You've got yourself a shit-load of trouble." His look of concern was unnerving as he'd put into words precisely what I'd been thinking.

"Listen, Bryce. This is my problem. I don't want to get you involved . . . you've got Allie, a family to worry about. I can take care of myself."

"Really. And if they come to your house tonight? What're you gonna do? Sic Sam on 'em?"

Stubborn as a mud fence, I thought. Bryce's support would be comforting, but how could I drag him into my mess? He wouldn't always be there to bail me out, but on the other hand, I knew he'd rather be in on the action exclaiming, "Damn, that was fun!"

"If anything happened to you, Allie would never forgive me, Bryce. I can't let you get involved."

We slowed and pulled into Bryce's driveway. He turned off the engine. "I'm a big boy, Gus. Allie's used to the risks associated with my job. Besides, if I stood back and didn't help, and you got whacked, what do you think Allie'd do to me?"

Too tired to argue, I said, "Let me finish reading the book and do a little research. And if you want to lend one of your guns?"

His eyebrows shot up. "Fair enough, but keep me posted."

"Agreed. What do we tell Allie?"

"Hmmm. Hard to keep secrets from her. Never was any good at lying to her. She always knows. Here, take the Beretta and an extra clip with you. Go home. I'll tell Allie later when the time's right."

Sammy and Allison greeted us at the door. I stuffed the gun in my bag. "Hi, sweetheart. You and Sam get along okay?" Bryce asked.

"We certainly did. He slept at the foot of our bed." She noticed my mug. "Gus, what happened to you?" Allison stepped close for a look at my battered face.

"I'm okay. Bryce'll fill you in." After a quick buss on the cheek, I said, "Don't look so worried. I'm okay. Just tired. Come on Sam."

As we left the house, a blue car pulled over and stopped a couple of houses down. The driver didn't get out. Nerves raw by now, the hair on my neck bristled. I stared the guy down, daring him to get out. But whoever it was, he shoved the car in reverse, made a three-quarter turn, and sped away.

Jesus, I've got to figure out what the hell is going on here.

Eight

SAM AND I STEPPED inside the house. He bristled and trotted off, nails clicking on the cool tile. The interior was a mess. Papers and books were strewn everywhere. Furniture overturned, drawers left open; the place had been ransacked.

The house wasn't big; two bedrooms with a full bathroom near the master, powder room off the kitchen, and a big family room adjoining the kitchen. Maybe a thousand square feet, but every inch had been searched. Every room left a shambles.

When I finished describing the scene to Bryce, he said, "Lock your doors and keep the gun handy, and listen, I talked to Jacoby with Chandler PD?"

"And?"

"Not good. Frank was tortured before being killed outright."

I sucked air through my teeth and sat down. "Tell me."

"When they didn't find what they were looking for, they tried to force the old man to talk. Broke four fingers, Gus. Stuffed a rag in his mouth. No one heard a thing."

As chill filled the small space. I was quaking with white-hot anger. "Any clues about who it was?"

"No. These are some mean bastards, Gus."

Saliva collected in the back of my mouth. The taste of bile was strong. I found my voice and asked, "So they found me from the check I left at Frankie's, right?"

"More'n likely. How'd they know about your trip to Havasu, though? You leave a note for anyone?"

49

Of course. "Yes, for the cleaning lady." My stomach churned.

"That's it, then. Keep the gun close and doors locked. I'll check in later."

"All right."

It took me two exhausting hours to clean the house. Sam and I ate a late supper, and I rolled into bed with Bower's book. It didn't take long to finish it. Quite unremarkable, I thought. So why all the interest? Because it's rare? I dropped into an easy sleep. Someone knew more about the books' value than I.

I WOKE LATE SUNDAY MORNING, bathed in sweat. This was becoming routine. I rubbed my face to rid my head of a horrible dream. All I could recall were fuzzy images of the desert and cowboys and cops; all disjointed and weird. I changed my T-shirt, brushed my teeth, and snuck a quick peek in the mirror. The swelling of my nose had leveled out. *Probably look like a racoon by tomorrow*, I silently told my reflection.

Doreen's interest in me still lingered. She hadn't hit on me because of my good looks, so why then? Something else was going on, and I was beginning to believe it all related to the *Cavity* book. I ran a brush through my hair, strolled into the kitchen, and turned on the coffee machine. "Come on, Sam. Let's go."

The phone was ringing when Sam and I returned from our walk. "Gus, is Allison over there?" Bryce sounded concerned.

"No, why?" I glanced at the wall clock. It was 9:00 a.m. I had slept for almost twelve hours.

"I dunno. Something doesn't feel right. She's not here. I woke up late, opened the door to the garage, and found her car gone."

"What day is this, Bryce?"

"Huh? Oh, yeah. Sunday. Church. Sure. Nine o'clock mass, just like always." His relief was obvious.

"Why don't I come over? I've finished the book, and we can talk about it."

"Sounds like a plan. See you soon."

After a shower, shave, and another cup of coffee, I felt normal. I grabbed the book, let Sammy through the door, and the two of us piled into the van. I stopped at a 7-Eleven near Bryce's and picked up a box of Krispy Kremes.

"Hey, Bryce. Allison back yet?" I called from just inside the front door.

"Nope." He came from the bedroom. "Not yet." He spotted the donuts. "Here, I'll open those." He grabbed the box, peeled back the cover, and popped half a donut in his mouth. "Come on in."

For the next hour, we stuffed ourselves with donuts, drank coffee, and rehashed all that'd happened the past couple of days. "Tell me what you think about that cursed book, Gus."

"Something about the dust jacket isn't right."

"Why's that?"

"Well, the book itself isn't one of the author's best, but the artwork on the cover is spectacular. . . with no mention of the artist. It's like the dust jacket is superior to what's inside." I held up the book. "None of her other books look like this."

"Who could shed light on that disparity?"

"No one I know. Best bet is to get online and start digging. Think that's what I'll do." I rose to leave.

He looked at his watch. "Think I'll drive down to Chandler PD before Allison gets home. I want to find out if Jacoby's been in contact with the Mohave Sheriff's Department. Maybe they got a match on the video. Love to know who we're dealing with."

We left it at that.

IT WAS ONE O'CLOCK when the phone rang. After a couple of hours poking around the Internet, I'd been napping. My heart pounded, and it took a few seconds to orient myself. I cleared my throat. "Hello?" My voice sounded like broken glass.

A muffled voice said, "Ivy? We have your sister. If you do exactly as we say, she'll be returned unharmed. If not, you can pick up pieces of her in the desert." Blood drained from my face. I couldn't breathe. The air in the kitchen collapsed. This can't be real. Not Allie. My head pounded; spikes were being driven into damaged sinus cavities.

"Am I getting through to you?" the stranger continued.

"Allison? You have Allison?" My voice was distant, detached, as if another me had taken over.

"That's right. You've caused us a great deal of trouble, Ivy. Two people are dead because of you. If you don't cooperate, your sister's number three. Our patience is exhausted. You still have the book?"

"Yes, I have the book."

"The book you bought from the barber?"

His words brought back brutal visions of a mutilated, tortured Frankie. "Yes."

"What's the title?"

"*The Cavity Lake Gang* by M.B Bower."

"Good. We want to make a trade—the broad for the book." He hesitated, allowing this to sink in. "But we have to be certain you and your friend don't do anything stupid. You have any notions of calling the cops?"

"No. I don't care about the damn book. I want Allison back—alive."

"Perfect. That's what we want to hear. But just to be sure, we'll wait and watch for a while. Expect another call later this evening. By the way, a certain gentleman in our group has a passion for inflicting pain. He really gets off on that sort of thing, and he doesn't discriminate along the lines of gender."

My throat was frozen. The room spun crazily. This had to be a nightmare.

"Ivy? Have I made myself clear?"

The fog lifted. "Perfectly."

"Then do exactly as I say. Call your friend Hamilton. Get him over to your house." The line went dead.

"Wait." I wanted to hear Allison's voice. Too late.

Trembling like a dry leaf in a strong breeze, I sat and replayed the conversation in my head. *Get her back, Gus. Forget the damned book.* If anything happens to Allison I'd never forgive myself.

Sam began whining, sensing trouble.

I continued talking to myself: *I swear to God, if they hurt her, I'll .. . What? Kill? Yes.* The Army had taught me how. *Get a grip. She isn't dead. Do what they say. We'll get her back. Can I trust them? No. You can't trust killers. Call Bryce.*

Cold and lifeless, my reserves drained, I picked up the phone and dialed Bryce's number.

It rang ten times. No answer. No answering machine. Keep calling. I didn't dare go over there. The kidnappers might phone again. A wave of guilt filled my soul. The guy was right. I was responsible for two deaths. If I'd just given Mullet the book back at the casino.

Sammy and I waited. I prayed for Allison's safety. Twenty minutes passed—then thirty. Forever, in other words. My chin slumped against my chest. Arms folded, eyes closed, I slipped into a pit that had no bottom. Sammy nudged my thigh. I opened my eyes, stroked his head, and envisioned the worst—Allison tortured, then killed without mercy. My mind was a wall of stone, cold gray.

The phone rang.

I swallowed and cleared my throat. "Hello?"

"Ivy?"

"Yes?"

"I'll only ask this once, and if you're lying, we'll know. Are the police involved?"

Steady, Gus. "No. But I want to talk to Allison." A rush of air filled my lungs.

"Not yet. You call her husband?"

"Yes, but he's not home."

"We'll call again later. You can talk to her then. Be ready to move tonight."

Bravely and foolishly, I blurted, "I need some assurance that she's all right."

"I told you. You can talk to her the next time we call. Remember, no cops or you'll never see Sis alive." *Click.*

I hung up and stared at the phone. This had to be some kind of slow-motion *Twilight Zone* thing—except these were real killers, and they had Allison.

I dialed Bryce again. "Come on. Pick up."

Still no answer. I dropped the phone back onto the receiver, and the thing rang, startling me. "Hello?"

"Gus? Allison still isn't home, and I'm worried."

There was no easy way to say it. "They took Allison, Bryce."

"What? Aw, Gus. No! Why?" His voice shook and trailed away.

I felt like dirt. "Look, they want to trade for the book. We can get her back, but they said no cops." His raspy breath gave no clue as to his demeanor. "Bryce?"

Finally he replied. "Yeah, I'm here. Who called?"

"Same bunch that jumped me out at the casino."

Bryce sounded more in control now. "You didn't call the cops, did you?"

"No."

"That's good, Gus. You did the right thing. Situation like this . . . best to handle it ourselves. I think I found out who these guys are."

"You did?" I wanted names. My hatred demanded a name.

"Gang out of L.A. led by a creep named Micah Knorr—does occasional work for the mob, but the guess is they're freelancing on this one, which might explain the broken fingers."

I shuddered. His words assaulted my fragile psyche.

He continued, "They must've grabbed her when she pulled into the garage. I just got home, saw her car, and assumed she was at the neighbor's. Dammit. I shoulda stayed home."

"Don't blame yourself. If anyone's at fault it's me."

He described a likely scenario. "They probably hid in the garage, threw something over her head, and tossed her into their car. Once she was loaded, they took off. Not likely they allowed her to see their faces."

"They said they'd call again, that we could talk to Allison then. They want to make the switch tonight."

"Okay. That gives us a little time to come up with a plan of some sort. I know how to deal with these people. They only kill when they have to, Gus. They won't be reckless. As long as they get the book and are assured they won't be identified, they'll give up Allison. I'll be right over. I want her back, Gus."

"I know you do. So do I." Maybe I'd wake from this nightmare and everything would blend with the oatmeal in my brain. I shuffled off into the bedroom like a turtle crossing a plowed field. Suddenly I felt every bit my age.

Nine

I DRAGGED MYSELF INTO the bathroom and washed my face. Cold water helped, but a half-dozen ibuprofen were needed to dull the pain in my head. I poured a glass of water and slammed back six red painkillers.

My multicolored face stared back at me from the mirror. Look like a washed out roadmap with coffee rings. *Christ, what a mess. Get a grip . . . Allison's life is at stake. Yeah, well you screwed up before and two friends died, remember? No! This is different. Is it?* An intense melancholy threatened to paralyze me. A boatload of guilt weighed heavily on my soul.

A glance away from the mirror showed the framed needlework that mother had made; a housewarming gift from Allie. It used to hang in the kitchen of our two-story house in Minneapolis. The stitching was meticulous—italicized, in ivory-colored thread against a flowered background. I still knew the words by heart; words that mother lived by:

> Work as if you don't need the money,
> Love as if you've never been hurt,
> Dance as if nobody can see you,
> Sing as if nobody can hear,
> Live as if the earth was heaven.

With a lump in my throat and a new rigidity in my spine, I heated a cup of coffee in the microwave. A cold beer tempted, but a jolt of caffeine made more sense. There was no room for self-pity. *Suck it up, Gus. You're involved . . . period.*

A pounding at the front door shattered the quiet of the small house. Sam barked at the intrusion. "Hush." I unlocked the door and stepped aside for Bryce. We hugged, uncomfortably. "How're you doing?"

Haltingly, he replied, "Managing. Better than you it looks like. Two things have to happen, Gus."

I suspected what he meant, still, I asked, "What's that?"

"Allison comes home unharmed, and we catch these bastards and feed 'em to the buzzards." His fists had clenched, then relaxed. Bryce looked at the *Cavity* book on the kitchen table. "What the hell is so goddamned important about that book?"

I shrugged. "Hell, I don't know. Didn't learn much from the Internet, but there's more to this than just the fact that only a few were published. Once that book is gone, we'll never know, though, will we?" I glanced at the book with growing distaste.

"If they get a whiff that something's not right, this'll go sour in a heartbeat, Gus." His lower lip trembled briefly. Bryce was a take-charge guy. A guy who, in his former life spent chasing down the dregs of society, thrived on confrontation. He cracked his knuckles, moved his head from side to side, and reached behind his back for the Beretta and asked, "Where's the other one?"

"In the bedroom." My pulse raced. "Whoa, Chief. You think I'm going to make the switch?"

"Yup. They've obviously done their homework. They know I was a cop. They won't want me within ten miles when this goes down."

"You really think I should carry a gun?"

"I do. I'm pretty sure these guys will make the trade a clean one, but if something goes wrong, you'll have to react. My guess is they'll set the meet for someplace dark, desolate. Maybe the desert, maybe some parking lot. Wherever it is, you must insist on making the switch all at once. No blind drops, all right?"

"What? Oh, yeah. Right."

"Allison must be secure before you give them the book." Bryce rose from the table, absently washed his hands, and wandered into the living room. I sat and stared at the pistol. The smell of gun oil took me back in time to a place buried long ago—a time best forgotten. An image of four friends flashed briefly. My eyes filled but a blink took the tears away.

"Gus, come here. Quick!" He stood near the front window. "Look. Is that the same car you saw before?"

I edged closer and gazed down the street. A blue sedan approached. It slowed and stopped across from us. The moon was up, creating a blue world with enough light to see the driver's features. "That's him!"

"Him who?"

"The guy from the barber shop."

"You're sure?"

"I'm sure."

"They're watching the house to make sure you don't call the cops. Listen, if we grab this guy, maybe we can . . ."

"What? Maybe we can what?"

"Maybe we can get him to tell us where they've got Allison." His eyes blazed.

I didn't like the sound of it. The risk was too high. "And, if he won't give it up? What if he's supposed to call in at a specified time?"

Bryce was a caged lion—anxious, pacing. This waiting was torture, but did he really want to mess things up now? If we grabbed this guy and it went sour, what then?

"I can make him tell us where she is, Gus." He said this without emotion. "Or force him to reveal when he's supposed to call in. There're ways, you know?" He looked at me for confirmation. "We need an edge, Gus. This may be it."

"But, what if—"

Bryce stared out the window. "It's a risk, but it's mine to take." He started for the door and stopped. "Hold it. What's he doing?"

Across the street, the driver's side door had opened. We watched as the creep, still wearing that windbreaker, approached the walk. Head down, features hidden below the brim of his cap, it was the guy from Frankie's.

The doorbell rang. Sammy barked. I jerked at the sound. "Hush, Sam."

"Answer it." Bryce stood behind the door, pistol in hand.

Without another word, I opened the door. The face beneath the cap looked up. It was a familiar face from another time, another place. But where?

"Mr. Ivy?" the stranger said as he removed his cap.

I staggered a bit. "I . . . I'll be damned." You could have knocked me over with a low whistle.

"I'm Cassidy Bower, Mr. Ivy. May I come in?" Wavelets of hair the color of molasses fell over her ears.

"Of course. Please." I stood aside, pushed open the screen door, and ushered Cashmere Sweater into the bungalow. The smell of lilacs drifted past as she stepped into the hall. That was it. The same scent from the barbershop, from the casino.

Bryce took three steps and parked in front of our guest, his face dark and threatening.

"Oh, dear," Cassidy said.

"Who the hell are you? Why've you been spying on Gus?"

She collected herself, fluffed her hair, and replied, "Because Mr. Ivy and I are searching for the same thing. I believe he beat me to it, however. The others as well."

"What others?" Bryce snapped.

"The people that killed that poor man at the casino. The people that also killed Frank, the barber."

The transformation of this attractive, mysterious woman was like that of a caterpillar to a butterfly. It was incredible. As a man she'd been all but invisible. As a woman she was striking—unforgettable. If Allison's life hadn't been in jeopardy, I might've found this entire mess amusing. But no one was laughing, least of all me.

"How do you know all this, miss?" Bryce continued.

She was a cool one. Nothing in Bryce's intimidating manner seemed to bother her. "Please, call me Cassidy. Frank's death was in the paper. I heard about what happened out at Havasu. And, you must be the ex-cop?"

"That's correct. Name's Bryce, Miss Bower."

She held out her hand. "It's nice to meet you both."

I finally found my voice. "Why don't we go into the kitchen?" and pointed the way.

The three of us traipsed through the living room. Sammy hadn't left our guest's side since she arrived. They seemed like old friends—reunited after a lengthy absence. "Please, have a seat."

She removed her jacket, draped it over the back of the chair and sat down. Every movement was performed with grace and style. Sammy rested his head on her knee and stared up into her pale blue eyes. "Hello there. What's your name?" She stroked his hair and looked up.

If Sam had been a kitten he'd've purred. "It's Sam. You're his new best friend. Normally he's kind of standoffish with strangers."

"I seem to have that affect on animals."

"Can I get you something to drink, Miss, uh . . . Wait a minute!" If an anvil had fallen from the sky and landed on my foot, I couldn't've have been more shocked.

"Are you related to M.B. Bower?" I reached for the book. "The author of this book?"

"Yes, I am. I'm her granddaughter. And, please, call me Cassidy."

Ten

I WAS CAPTIVATED by our guest—attracted to her flame, but cautious nonetheless. I plopped down in a chair opposite her and repeated Bryce's question. "What the hell is going on here?"

Bryce removed the pistol from the table, and sat down next to me. Cassidy Bower never flinched at the sight of the weapon. Here was a good-looking woman who carried herself with elegance and dignity, yet was unafraid of guns. Atop that, Sammy, a great judge of character, adored her. The dog hadn't moved, but rather continued to fawn over her.

"Yes, please, Miss Bower. Tell us more." Bryce asked. "You seem far more informed about all this than we are."

"You're both making me feel like a spinster, and if you don't start calling me Cassidy, I'm going to steal Sammy from you and leave." Her warm smile melted the icy wall that Bryce had thrown up.

We nodded and returned embarrassed smiles. "Sorry, Cassidy," I said.

"Thank you. I do know a great deal about the history of the book, but first we must come to an understanding. If I share what I know, we'll work together. Agreed?"

I immediately said, "Yes, of course. It's clear there's something valuable about this book, but we have no idea what it is."

Cassidy's voice had a deep, resonant quality to it. Not melodic, not rhythmic, but quite different. She spoke deliberately and at a level slightly above a loud whisper. She might pass for a diction coach.

Bryce barged ahead. "Then tell us what you know about Allison's kidnapping."

Her face blanched. She seemed genuinely surprised. "Kidnapped? Who?" Her eyes flitted from Bryce to me, both brows arched.

"Allison. My wife."

"Oh, my God. When?"

I tried to get a read from her face—her body language, but there was nothing. She was stunned, but hell, she could still have some other agenda. "Today. They took her this morning."

"They want the book, right? My grandmother's book, *The Cavity Lake Gang?*"

"Yes. They called and want to make a switch. They said they'd phone again, and that we should be ready to meet tonight."

"Did you call the police?"

"No. We don't want them involved," Bryce answered. "We'll make the exchange only when we know Allison's safe."

"And how will you guarantee her safety?"

"We haven't quite worked that out yet." I confided.

"Before we go any further," began Bryce, "I need to ask you some questions."

"Go ahead." She looked him in the eye.

"Why were you following Gus?"

"Because I knew after visiting Frank Wilson that Gus had the book."

"Why wait so long to make your move?"

"I had to be sure that Gus was an honorable man. When I saw how he rebuffed the blonde at the casino, I—"

"Wait a minute. Slow down," Bryce interrupted. "How'd you know about the dead guy at the casino? Were you out there?" He turned to look at me. "Gus?"

"Cassidy was at our craps table, Bryce."

"No! What the hell? Anything else I should know about?"

I threw up my hands. "Sorry. Besides, Cassidy wasn't much of a player. After she left, I didn't expect to ever see her again."

"Okay. Continue, Miss . . . uh . . . Cassidy."

"I had to get a read on Gus before I approached him. I knew he had the book because Frank told me he'd sold it to him. When Doreen failed to, ah . . . seduce Gus—when he refused her blatant advances—then I was pretty sure he was someone I could trust. I planned to approach him the next morning, but everything fell apart."

Bryce and I exchanged a look, while Cassidy eyed the book and asked, "May I see the book, please?"

"Certainly." I handed it to her.

She reached and drew it close to her chest. She ran long fingers over the cloth cover and sighed heavily. I sensed that the book provided a reconnect with her grandmother. She looked up and asked, "Do you have the dust jacket?" Her eyes lit up. She seemed to be holding her breath.

I'd removed the dust jacket while reading it, a habit of mine.

"Yes. Why?"

"Is it in good condition?"

"Yes. Excellent. Good as new."

"I'll explain it to you later, but right now please keep the jacket someplace safe. It's the key to everything." Her eyes swept from me to Bryce then back again.

I studied her face and noted a pert nose, arched brows with skin like pearl. Her blue eyes were wise. Up close, Cassidy Bower was really something. At the same time, I had no idea what she meant about the jacket being 'the key.' "If we give up the book, then what good is the cover?"

"Because as far as I know, I have the only other copy of the book. Give them your copy, but not the jacket. As long as we have that, we can unlock the secret buried in the book."

Cassidy implied that something else was going on, something beyond the book's intrinsic value. My baker's dozen suddenly seemed irrelevant. But what secret was she talking about? "How can we be sure these guys won't wonder about the dust jacket?"

"Because they still haven't seen an actual copy of the book. As far as they know, the book itself will reveal the clues they need."

"Clues?" Bryce and I stared at Cassidy as if she'd just landed from Venus. My mind sped ahead. All my instincts about the book had been right, but for the wrong reason. A mystery surrounded Bower's book, and the granddaughter seemed to be the only person with answers. First things first. We had to get Allison back. "Do you mean to say that out of almost a hundred copies sent out by Kittridge, only two remain?"

"I think so. My copy, this one, and maybe two more."

"Where'd you get yours?"

"My father had a copy. Laid around the house when I was a child. The dust jacket was long gone, but when the attorney's letter arrived, I dug the book out."

"What attorney?" Bryce leaned on the table. "What letter?"

"An attorney in New York. Look, this is pretty complicated. Let's wait and go through it all later—after you get Allison back. I have much to share with you but this isn't the right time."

She was right. "Okay. So, we have a second book to give them, but how are we going to make the switch? Bryce?" I looked at my friend.

"I have to think about that . . . work out a plan. Be right back." He headed for the bathroom.

"May I have something to drink, Gus?" Cassidy asked.

"Of course. I'm forgetting my manners. What would you like? Beer, Diet Coke, apple juice, a bottle of water?"

"A soda would be wonderful."

"You got it." I stepped behind her, opened the fridge, and pulled out a can. "Glass? Ice?"

She didn't respond. "Cassidy? Would you like a glass with ice?" Still no response. "Cass. . ." And then I understood. Bryce had returned. I set the soda in front of Cassidy, then stepped back. "Bryce. Come here. I want to show you something." I stood behind Cassidy and waved him over. "Watch this."

He gave me a funny look and nodded toward Cassidy.

I opened a drawer beneath the stove, took out a large pan and dropped it on the floor behind her. *Clang!*

Bryce flinched. So did Sammy. Cassidy never moved. She just sat there and sipped her soda.

"What the hell?" Bryce looked at me as if I were nuts.

"She's deaf."

"Huh? No way."

"Yeah? Clap your hands."

He did. Cassidy never budged. "Well, I'll be damned." He scratched his head. "Well, uh, I mean, how's she able to talk?"

"Let's find out." I walked back to the table and sat down. I looked at Cassidy and without actually speaking, mouthed the words, "You are deaf, aren't you?"

She smiled and said, "Yes, I am." Cassidy exhibited little surprise.

"Why didn't you tell us?"

"A bad habit, I'm afraid. Sorry. I learned to read lips as a young girl, and it was always a good exercise to practice when others were unaware of my deafness. I make a game of it to see how long it takes for someone to figure it out. How'd I do?"

"Damn good." I shook my head. "You speak extremely well, Cassidy. How is that possible?"

"Became deaf when I was ten. It's called 'delayed onset deafness.' After a high fever, I lost all hearing."

"Is it, uh . . . hereditary?" I asked.

"Yes, but seems to skip a generation. Grandma Bower was also deaf, but my father wasn't. In her case, it happened when she was seven. Her deafness was syndromic—that is, she had other medical complications related to her deafness."

"Like what?"

"Diabetes. In Grandma's case, she became blind and her kidneys failed."

"I had no idea about any of this . . . feel kind of stupid and insensitive," I apologized.

"Don't feel bad, Gus. Most people are unaware that the deaf have many other health issues. Sammy picked up on my deafness right away. That's why he's being so protective. Animals know when a person or animal is sick. Sam senses my weakness, so he's watching over me."

"You sure read lips well," Bryce volunteered.

"I had plenty of time to practice. My father and mother taught me."

"But why the get-up? The cap and jacket?" I asked.

"I know this is going to sound terribly vain, but I've found that I can move around much easier and draw less attention to myself dressed as a man. People tend to remember and pay more attention to a woman. It's silly, I know, but when you grow up in a world of silence, you tend to become introverted and shy. Isolation is a comfortable place—a safe harbor, for those of us who can't hear. According to my father, Grandmother used to say, 'Silence is safe, for silence never betrays you.'"

"Sounds like good advice for anyone," I said. "You seem to have adapted well." I was fascinated by her story, but Allison kept intruding. Cassidy must have noticed a pained look on my face.

"Look, that's enough about me. Do you fellows have a plan?"

"Well, sort of," I began, pacing now. "As I said before, the kidnappers will probably want us to drop the book someplace."

Bryce added, "They'll expect us to believe that Allison will be released at some other location. But we're not going to let that happen."

"What do you mean?" Cassidy's eyes darted from Bryce to me as she read our lips.

"Here's where it's going to be rough." Bryce struggled with his decision. "We'll insist on a time and place for the exchange—Allison for the book. Period. Not negotiable."

Eleven

RYCE CONTINUED. "They can't have the book until her safety's assured."

"Are you sure that's the best way?" I pressed Bryce. "What if we piss them off?"

"Gus, you remember the Virginia Piper kidnapping?"

"Yes. Back in the mid-seventies?"

"Right. And what did they do with her?"

"Drove her north of the Twin Cities and tied her to a tree in the woods. Mosquitoes feasted on her, but she was found alive. Why?"

"My point is that the Pipers were lucky. Old Harry Piper did everything the kidnappers asked him to do, but he lost control of the situation because the feds were involved. It could've ended tragically."

Cassidy asked, "She was alive?"

"Yes. Virginia Piper never saw any of her captors, so they had no fear of being identified. I doubt Allison has either. All they wanted was the money. I think these guys are of a similar mind. They want the book. That's all."

"God, I hope your right, Bryce. Okay, so what do we do?"

"Like I said, we find a place that's deserted where we can make the switch. Some place they can check out beforehand to make certain we haven't set a trap. Some place with a wide field of vision. We have to convince them that all we care about is getting Allison back."

Cassidy spoke up. "I don't mean to throw cold water on this, Bryce, but what's to stop them from simply shooting Gus and Allison and taking the book? They've already killed two people."

"You're right. I thought about that. We need to create some sort of gimmick so if the switch goes bad, the book will be destroyed—immediately. That's our only ace in the hole." He paced back and forth. "And, if Gus makes the switch, I can cover both him and Allison from a hidden location. That way I can insure their safety."

I didn't like the sound of his voice. "What kind of gimmick?"

"Don't know yet. We need to work something out," he said.

I glanced at my watch and wondered when the next phone call would come. Surely it'd be very soon. "You have a place picked out?"

"The parking lot at Sun Devil Stadium," Bryce declared. "On the ASU campus. Kids're all off campus for the weekend. Parking lot'll be empty and well lit. You can each see what the other's up to. We'll pick a particular area—say under the Panda Bear sign right in the middle of the lot."

"How do you know that?"

"Parked there when I went to a ball game with Norm. It's perfect. We'll booby trap the book somehow, lay it down out of sight at the base of the pole, and insist the switch be made there."

"What kind of a booby trap, Bryce?" Cassidy asked.

"Dunno. Let's kick that one around later. Right now . . ." He checked his watch, "Listen, Gus. You must insist on letting me speak to Allison the next time they call. I'll tell them that I'll pick a spot for the switch. They'll have to call again for details. It's a gamble, but it's all I've got. Somehow we have to gain control of the situation."

"Jesus, Bryce. I don't know." I held my hands to keep them from shaking.

Cassidy reached across and covered my hands with one of hers. Her touch was warm, reassuring. "You can do this, Gus."

Then the phone rang—once, twice, three times. I took a deep breath, stepped to the counter, and picked it up. "Hello?"

My voice sounded distant . . . as if it came from someone else. I listened for a response.

"Ivy?"

"I'm here." Now. Spit it out. "My friend wants to talk to his wife."

Somehow my voice sounded bold—courageous even. Bryce and Cassidy huddled close, even though she couldn't hear. Their presence fortified my resolve. I held my breath. Bryce hit the speakerphone.

"Since when are you making demands?" the voice said.

Bryce stepped close and replied, "Since we have the book you so desperately want, numb-nuts. Let me talk to my wife or I'm callin' in the feds."

The voice on the line hesitated, "Ah, the ex-cop. Hang on."

He covered the mouthpiece, then issued a command we could hear only in its tone. "Ten seconds, Hamilton. Here, lady. Talk."

Allison sobbed. My heart ached at the sound of her voice. "Bryce? I'm scared, honey—"

And that was all we heard. An angry red haze filled my head as I closed my eyes. I had to hiccup and couldn't stop.

"Ivy? Ivy! You there?"

Give me strength, Lord. "I'm here."

"Still no cops?"

"No cops." I inhaled and prepared for what would come next.

"That's good. If you continue to follow instructions, the broad'll be back home in no time. Now, here's how it's going to go down."

Bryce stuck an elbow in my ribs and leaned close. "Hold it, dip-shit. Listen carefully. If anything, anything at all happens to my wife—if I see one scratch on her, I'll hunt you down and rip off your ass and sew it to your face. Understood?"

"Who the hell do you think—"

"Shut your pie hole. If I don't get my wife back in one piece, I'll spend every penny I have to find you. Count on it."

"Brave talk, Hamilton. You're in no position to dictate anything."

"Guess we'll find out. Call back at nine tonight. We'll tell you where the meet'll be and how it'll go down. Know this, though, there'll be no blind drop. Gus'll hand you the book when my wife is safe. This is not negotiable. If you want the book, it's my way or not at all. Call at nine. From now on, you can talk to Gus, just like you asked." *Click.*

He handed me the phone. The world seemed to stop. All the air in the kitchen collapsed. Bryce sagged, took a breath, and nodded. It was done.

Cassidy asked us to repeat the conversation. I did. My heart threatened to bust from my chest. Strength sapped, I flopped down in a chair. "Bryce? You sure about this?"

Bryce stood behind me, put his hands on my shoulders, and gripped me firmly. "Yes. You were great, pal. I'm proud of you. If we'd of let them maintain control, any chance of getting Allison back would be fifty-fifty at best. It has to be this way." His voice broke.

But, if he's wrong about their greed? "Okay." I took a deep breath and continued, "So, what's next?"

He gave me one last squeeze and returned to his chair. "A beer is in order. Then I'll lay it out for you."

Cassidy stood and said, "Let me get it for you."

I watched as she went to the fridge and pulled out a beer. She turned. "Gus?"

I pivoted. "Sure, why not."

"Here's the way it'll work," Bryce began. "I go to the stadium parking lot just before dark and scout out a spot where I can cover you."

"With what?"

"A Ruger Mini-14 semiautomatic rifle. Bought it this winter to shoot coyotes. It has an ATN MK330 night scope and a thirty-shot clip. I'll park on the street, walk in, and find some place high where I can't be seen. If anything goes wrong, I won't be far away. You have to trust me on this."

"What about the book—the booby trap?" I asked.

"Been thinking about that," Bryce said. "If they believe there's something hidden in the text, then we have to rig a device to destroy the book. At the first sign of deception, we convince them that, 'poof,' the book disappears."

"What do you mean, 'poof'?"

"You ruin the book," he said.

"How?"

"Well, that needs some work. Let's talk about that . . ."

Twelve

TWO HOURS LATER an incessant ringing shattered the quiet of the small house. My skull felt like a rotten melon ripening in the sun. I ran from the bathroom and stared at the phone. *It's time.* My heart pounded. I lurched into the doorjamb on the way to the phone. Cassidy was reading her grandmother's book at the kitchen table. She sensed my presence and looked up, eyes wide. I pointed to the phone. She nodded, and I picked it up.

"Ivy?"

"It's me."

"Still no cops?"

"Still no cops."

"Let's hear your plan."

I told him about the parking lot and how the switch was to be made. "We meet at ten thirty. Stop fifty yards away and wait for me to get to the sign. Then I want to see Allison walking toward me—alone." I held my breath.

"Wait a minute. What about the book?"

"As soon as she's thirty yards away, I'll hold the book up and set it on the ground. I have no doubt your man will be armed, so if anything goes wrong you have that advantage."

"I don't like it. Smells funny. You seem to forget you're gambling with the broad's life here."

"I haven't forgotten. It is a gamble, but we're betting you want this book. If so, you'll go along with me on this. There are no cops involved—and won't be. My brother-in-law and I only want Allison back."

There was silence on the other end for a full twenty seconds, and then, "You still there?"

"I'm here." *Please, just say "yes."*

"How do we verify it's the *Cavity* book? We have to have a look at it before the trade."

Damn. He's right. Now what. "Hang on a minute." I covered the mouthpiece and repeated his demand to Cassidy. "Any ideas?" I mouthed.

Cassidy shrugged and threw both arms out—palms up.

"All right. How's this: after Allison is clear, I'll wait with the book and show it to you for verification. If anything's wrong at that point, you've got me instead of Allison."

He covered the receiver. A muffled conversation lasted ten seconds. "We'll do it your way, but if there's a hint of anything cockeyed, your sister's dead. It'll be on your head."

His last words sent a rush of blood to my brain. *Easy Gus.* "There won't be any problems. I'll be there in an hour and a half." I put the phone down.

Cassidy came to my side. "Gus? Everything all right?" She lightly tugged on my arm so I had to face her.

"Yeah. I think so. I've no idea what their reaction will be to Bryce's gimmick."

"What's to stop them from shooting you at that point, Gus?" Cassidy's eyes showed alarm.

"Nothing. Bryce will be watching but other than that, I dunno." There was no way to anticipate how the trade would play out. Suddenly I felt reassured about carrying the Beretta. "I better get going so I can pick up the stuff on Bryce's list."

"Is there a Home Depot on the way?"

"Yes. Open all night. It's at least a forty-five-minute drive to the stadium."

"I wish I were going with you, Gus. For moral support, if nothing else."

"Me too, Cassidy, but this is my deal now." I picked up the pistol from the counter, slammed the magazine home, and checked to be sure the safety was on. I tucked it in the back of my jeans, and left my shirttail hanging out. "They won't get close enough to search me, so this should work. I'm ready. Sammy, take care of Cassidy." I reached down and ruffled his head.

"Good luck, Gus. I'll be praying for all of you."

"Thanks, Cassidy." I picked up the car keys and headed for the garage door. "Look, if things don't work out . . . well, you'll know if we're not back by midnight."

"Don't say that. Everything will happen just the way Bryce said. I'm sure of it." She stepped close and gave me a kiss on the cheek. Her lips were warm and soft.

Lilacs again. The scent lingered longer than the soft, brief touch of her lips. Such a marvelous fragrance. At any other time I might have languished in its goodness. But not now.

Tonight my head was clogged with dreadful premonitions.

THE ORANGE HOME DEPOT sign on Chandler Boulevard stood out like a desert beacon. I pulled into the parking lot near the exit doors. Very few shoppers were around. The cool air was a nice change and on any other night, it would have been worth a pause. I went in and rounded up the supplies, negotiated the Self Help lane, and was back in the van in ten minutes.

Where's the pistol? Panicky at the thought of meeting the kidnappers unarmed, I flipped the light. It was under the seat. I drew it out and put it between my legs. Is this really happening? It all seemed surreal, as if a movie was playing non-stop. A non-smoker for ten years, all at once I craved the calming effects of nicotine.

I pulled out of the lot, entered the ramp for Highway 101, and eased out into traffic. "Take it easy, Gus," I muttered. "If you get pulled over by some eager highway cop . . ." Seventy-five seemed a safe speed; anything slower might draw unwanted attention. A thirty-minute drive brought me to Tempe. The exit sign for Sun Devil Stadium was clearly marked. My heart landed someplace near my pelvis. At that precise moment, I felt more frightened than at any other time in my life. A creeping chill rose from my toes to my skull. It was an icy fear that clogged all five senses. *Suck it up, Gus. Allison needs you.*

Comforted by the knowledge that Bryce was nearby, I quickly scanned the area. He was hidden from view, but knowing he was close helped immensely. At the Panda sign, I stopped, backed up a hundred yards, turned the engine off, and waited. Bright lights directly ahead of me flooded the interior. A vehicle some distance away flashed its brights.

I sucked my teeth, and returned the signal. The car sped toward me—a blue Jeep Cherokee with blackened windows. No way to see inside. It took a pass around me then arced back to the far side of the Panda sign. It was 10:25 p.m.

Here we go. I grabbed the pistol, leaned forward, and jammed it down my back. A light jacket hid the bulge. *Wait. The book. Relax. It's in the back.*

Once out of the van, I opened every door, and finally the rear one, where I picked up the book and walked around to the passenger side, feeling conspicuous and vulnerable. I leaned in, opened the paint can, tied one end of a roll of twine to the wire handle, and stuck the working end of a screwdriver through the cardboard tube. *God, I hope this works.* Leaving the van doors open to demonstrate that I was alone made sense. Besides, this way Allison could jump in unfettered.

With the book in my left hand, the paint and twine in my right, I started toward the Panda sign. My legs were heavy—numb. Each step took forever. My target: a cartoon image of the gentlest creature on the planet. Sweat seeped through my shirt. Each step brought me closer to the pale circle of light beneath the pole. Totally exposed now, my throat felt as if clogged by sawdust.

At an estimated fifty-yard mark, I stopped and waited. Almost immediately, the Jeep's lights came on, and it sped toward me. *Now what?* Of course. These were cautious people. The truck swung wide then eased back toward my van. It stopped alongside the Dodge. A guy dressed in black got out of the Jeep and walked around the minivan with a flashlight. He ducked and looked underneath. Satisfied, he jumped in the truck and sped back.

They wheeled around, stopped at the same spot as earlier. *Turn the damn lights off. I can't see.* With my left hand shading my eyes from the glare, I spotted two silhouettes as they walked toward me. *Please, let that be*

Allison. When the pair was approximately fifty yards from the pole, I shuffled ahead and reminded myself to breathe. Oxygenated blood equals strength. If I panicked, it could ruin everything. *Breathe, Gus. Deep breathing. Bryce is watching.*

When I reached the base of the pole, I set the paint can down in full view, stood with the book in one hand, the twine and screwdriver in the other.

The two darkened shapes stopped. The larger one shouted, "Ivy?"

"It's me." My voice sounded eerily calm. That was a surprise.

"Change of plans, Ivy."

No. Not now. "What do you mean?" I shouted. My voice rose. It felt like a sack of dry cement landed on my head.

"We want the book first. Then we let her go."

Bryce? Was he within earshot? What should I do? Play your trump card, Gus. Take control. "No," I stated calmly. "I explained how it would work. You can inspect the book while Allison gets in my van. We do it my way."

"You're in no position to bargain. She's got a hood over her head and a pistol aimed at her temple. Drop the book on the pavement and walk back to your car now, or I put the first round in her leg."

My knees wobbled. *Goddammit to hell. Don't give in, Gus. Maintain the advantage.* I was weakening, ready to capitulate when suddenly sparks flew in front of and behind Allison and her kidnapper. *Crack! Crack! Crack!* My sister screamed—a blood-chilling yowl that made my hair stand up. The kidnapper wrapped his forearm under Allison's chin and spun her around to face the shots. "You son of a bitch! I warned you—no cops. She's dead, Ivy."

"No. Wait! That's Allison's husband. Those are warning shots. Do this my way, and we all walk away. Think about it. If he wanted to kill you, you'd be dead. With a night scope he can put a round in your ear from five hundred yards." I had no idea if this was true and held my breath. This wasn't going to work. Allison gasped and sagged. "Hang on, Allison," I shouted. "Bryce is close by. It's almost over."

"You got that right, you sonofabitch! Her life's over if he shoots again."

"Allison, can you hear me?"

"Gus? Oh, God, Gus . . . yes. Bryce? Get me out of here."

"Okay, sweetheart. Stay calm."

Please, please, God. Steady, Gus. You've got one shot at this—make it count. "Before we make the switch, there's one last thing."

"What? Whaddaya mean?"

Advantage, me. "You see this can on the ground in front of me?"

"Yeah, I see it."

"It's an open can of red paint. There's a long string tied to the handle. Here's your book." I held it up over my head in the opaque gloom. "Once you've inspected it, I'm going to fan the pages and set it on end right next to the can. I'll back away and unwind the string. If at any time I feel that Allison is threatened, I yank the string. Know what a gallon of red paint will do to your precious book?"

He jabbered into a two-way phone. Brief snatches drifted over. "He's got a can of paint . . . going to pull . . . don't do anything . . . too close to screw up now . . ."

"You ready?" I yelled.

"Yeah, but so help me, Ivy, if you jerk me around any more, you and the broad are toast."

"Let her go safely, the book is yours, and we're out of here." *Enough talk.* "Let her loose. Allison! Take ten paces then remove the hood. Do not turn around but keep walking toward my voice. Okay?"

"Yes." She sounded small and unsure.

I took a deep breath and waited. Nothing happened. More chatter from the two-ways. *Shit! Now what?*

"I'm going to untie her hands. We're both coming over."

Allison stumbled forward as if pushed. She staggered toward me with her arms outstretched, as if playing a deadly game of blind man's bluff. The kidnapper was right behind her, the barrel of his revolver aimed at the back of her head. They closed the distance and once beneath the cone of light, my heart raced as I contemplated what would happen next.

Thirteen

ALLISON AND THE GUNMAN walked toward me. Thirty yards, then twenty. Nothing happened. She was very close. I reached back and grabbed the Beretta. *Steady, Gus. Show the gun.* Ten yards. "That's far enough. Take off her hood," I raised the weapon, and thumbed the safety.

He yanked off the cowling. Allison screamed. "Bryce?"

"Hang on, Allie. Everything's going to be all right. Bryce is close by."

He nudged her ahead. The pistol at her head never wavered. She stopped in front of me. Her eyes glistened. Both hands covered her mouth.

I slowly raised my arm and pointed the pistol at the gunman. Thirty-five years had passed since another man's life was in my hands, and now for the second time in two days, I was prepared to kill again.

He ducked behind Allison at the sight of the Beretta, unsure of what to do next. "The book. Let me see it."

"Let her go first."

"No. The book. Show it to me."

He was too jumpy. "It's right here. Look." I held it out, and twisted it around. "See? It's Bower's book. Now I'm going to open it up and set it next to the paint can."

"Wait! You said I could look at it first."

"Soon as she's safe, you can smell the damn thing, but not until then."

He hesitated. We were at a standoff. He knew it, and so did I. My ace in the hole was a rifle trained on him with a night scope. Take control.

Now! "Allie. Step toward me, sweetheart. That's it. Keep coming." I waited an eternity as she stepped away.

The kidnapper kept his gun pointed at her while I covered him with mine. "Good girl. Okay, walk around me. Be careful you don't kick the paint can." Two or three more steps, and we'll be home free. "Hurry on to my van."

She hesitated, then sprinted away. I focused on the gunman. The sound of Allison's shoes as they slapped the pavement echoed across the lot. The two of us stood toe to toe, his gun pointed at me, mine at him. Two holes in the ski mask were lifeless black seeds. My arm ached from the weight of the pistol. The tremor noticeable, like warm jello. A slight twitch and my finger would propel the slug toward his brain—or not, depending on who fired first.

The air around us was charged with energy—or perhaps fear. We were both locked in a bubble. His arm was rock solid; that was worrisome. Mesmerized by his gloved finger on the trigger, my eyes ached, then watered. I blinked. His finger moved a fraction against the cold steel. In one second my brain matter would be all over the pavement. "Here. Check it out." I fanned the book, knelt, and set it next to the paint. "See this string? One little tug and your precious book is adios."

"Wait a minute. You said I could . . ."

"I lied. Remember the paint . . ." and I backed away from the post. Twine unraveled from the spool. My eyes remained locked on his during my excruciatingly slow retreat. The twine stuck to my damp palms, and I had to shake it loose to free it.

Just as he crouched to grab the book, the unexpected happened. A pair of headlights suddenly appeared from behind me. The vehicle approached at high speed. I stumbled and bit my lip. The taste of my own blood did little to bolster my courage. At any moment the gunman would panic and fire. But, he didn't. That could only mean that they had a back-up plan, and the approaching car was it.

Will Bryce shoot? Should I wait? For what? My heart thumped against my ribs. Bile mingled with blood in the back of my throat. The kidnapper had the book in one hand, his pistol in the other. We stared at each other. He appeared puzzled by this turn of events. This was bad—none of this was part of our plan.

Enough. I turned and ran, expecting a bullet to rip into me at any moment. The twine and screwdriver fell to the pavement. "Allison! Get in the van—hurry!" I caught up to her, grabbed her arm, propelled her toward the open passenger door and shoved her in. I tore around to the driver's side, slid in, and the engine roared to life. "Hang on, Allison. It's almost over." My voice sounded crystalline, ready to fracture with every hard consonant.

Allison, on the verge of hysteria, made a frenetic rasp followed by one jolting gasp after another. "Put your head between your knees," I said. Her eyes widened and her lips quivered, but she failed to react. *What's the Jeep doing? What about the second car?* The SUV darted ahead to pick up the gunman, then spun around and screeched off in the opposite direction. *Get the hell out of here, Gus.*

I turned the wheel and hit the gas at the same time. The minivan seemed to roll up on two wheels, then leapt forward. The exit from the lot was two hundred yards away. We had to pass the second vehicle, which was speeding toward us. I kept my foot on the pedal, prepared for a life-and-death game of chicken. At the last second, we each veered to the right. A raucous shout sounded from the car. The sound of broken glass trailed away, and additional whoops echoed as we passed each other.

Relief washed over me like melted butter. It was only a bunch of kids, college kids out for a good time. I let up on the gas. *What about Bryce? What if he fires at these kids?* I slowed, turned toward the stadium, and held my breath, expecting shots from the Ruger. The kids in the convertible began a series of high-speed turns on the still warm pavement. The sound of squealing rubber filled the night. Oblivious to what had just transpired, the youngsters stopped and turned out their lights. I shuddered at the thought of what might've happened if they'd entered the lot five minutes earlier. *Forget it. It's over.*

"That's it, Allie. We're safe now. Are you okay? Did they hurt you?"

She was sobbing uncontrollably. I reached over and touched her shoulder. "Hang on, sweetheart. You'll be home soon." She was dull-eyed, unresponsive. Tears streamed down her face. I stepped on the gas and headed for the exit. Allison whimpered like a lost kitten. My heart ached for her, realizing the nightmare she had just endured.

"Allison? Listen to me. No one can hurt you now, I promise." We sped off into the night. Allison cowered against the door and didn't say a word.

We arrived home at midnight. We had agreed to meet Bryce back at my house. "Allie, we're home now. You're safe."

She reacted as if in a trance, eyes glazed, dull and gray as lead. I hopped out and ran around to the other side. Once her door was open, I unbuckled her belt and helped her out. She was as limp as a noodle, as if every ounce of energy had been sucked from her body.

We stumbled into the kitchen. Cassidy had been watching for us and came to the door. "Thank God you're both all right."

"Help me get her into the living room, Cassidy." Focused on Allison, she hadn't heard me. "Cassidy?" My fingers covered her hand. She read my lips. We led her to the couch and eased her down.

Allison noticed our guest. "Gus? Who is this?" Her head pivoted from Cassidy to me and back again. The presence of a stranger seemed to dislodge her from whatever precarious perch she'd landed on.

"It's okay, Allie. This is our friend Cassidy."

"Hello, Allison. I'm very happy that you're safe and home again."

Allison stared at Cassidy. Suddenly her eyes widened and she exclaimed, "You're deaf, aren't you?"

Cassidy smiled and nodded. "You're very astute, Allison. You must have worked with the deaf before."

"Yes," she sniffed. "I helped teach a class for the deaf a few years ago." She addressed me next. "Make sure you always face her when speaking, Gus."

"Yes, I will." I smiled, let my breath out and winked at Cassidy.

Just then, Bryce burst through the door, and ran over and took my spot on the couch.

"Oh, Bryce. I was so scared." Allison threw her arms around his neck.

"I know, honey, but it's over now. You're here with me. No one can hurt you. Promise." Bryce pulled her head under his chin and hugged her tightly.

The four of us remained silent for long minutes as Allison struggled to make sense of all that'd happened. "Who were those men? What did they want?"

"They were after Gus's book, sweetheart. It was the same bunch that jumped him at Lake Havasu."

"But why me?"

"Because you're Gus's sister. They knew he'd do whatever they asked."

"Didn't think I'd ever see you again." Allison broke into another round of wracking sobs.

Bryce continued his comforting while Cassidy gently rubbed the back of her hand. Finally, exhausted and spent, Allie stopped crying. She had shed an unwanted skein of fear and her visage brightened. "Bryce? Have you noticed Cassidy's eyes? See how wide open they are? Deaf people adapt all their other senses to a higher degree. You have a wide peripheral field, don't you, Cassidy?"

"Yes." Cassidy smiled, continuing to stroke my sister's arm. "We do learn to see things others don't; to pick up visual keys that broaden our range of awareness. You'll notice I constantly move my head and eyes to see who's speaking. You're remarkably perceptive, Allison."

"Thank you. I've always held great admiration for people who find ways to compensate for loss."

Soon Allison and Cassidy began signing to each other. Their hands fluttered while fingers jabbed at air, speaking invisible words. The pace increased, and before long, I detected a smile on Allison's face. It was pretty amazing, actually. Cassidy's presence, her deafness apparently, was exactly what was needed to jolt Allison from the horror of her recent nightmare. I looked at Bryce and jerked my head toward the kitchen.

He whispered something in Allison's ear and rose from the couch.

"How is she, Bryce?"

"Fine, I think. In some sort of shock, but Cassidy managed to calm her down. We need to have a doctor look at her, though. There's a retired doctor we play golf with. I'll call him."

"Good idea."

He called and waited with the receiver on his shoulder. "What happened out there, Gus? Sounded like everything was about to go south on us. That's why I fired when I did."

"Almost did. Your timing was perfect. He wanted to see the book and wouldn't let Allison go until he did. When we were toe-to-toe, I lost my nerve and backed off, went maybe ten yards until the twine got messed up, then dropped everything and ran like hell."

"You did the right thing. No telling if he'd've shot or not." Bryce's voice dropped. "Almost jerked a round off, Gus. It was touch and go." His face turned the color of bark on a young maple. "And when those damn kids pulled in, I didn't know what to think. Had my finger on the trigger and was about to plug the driver when that beer bottle flashed. Have to admit, I was scared shitless."

"If they'd arrived five minutes earlier everything would've fallen apart. Thanks to you, we pulled it off."

"What do we tell the police?"

He held up a finger and spoke into the phone. When finished, he said, "Doc'll be right over. We tell the cops everything. The main thing is to get the cops after these guys and out of our hair." Bryce then placed a call to the Chandler Police Department and returned to the living room. "Honey? Doc Whitcomb is coming over to take a look at you, okay?" He brushed a stray strand of hair from her face. The mention of the doctor must have triggered a sudden remembrance of her nightmare, as her eyes widened. She reached for Bryce's hand.

Bryce next looked at me and said, "The FBI will be brought in on this."

Cassidy stood and the two of us went into the kitchen. Soon sirens wailed in the distance and multicolored lights flickered through the front windows as the squad cars tore down our quiet street.

Fourteen

OC WHITCOMB ENTERED with a half dozen cops. "Bryce? What in the world?" He went straight for Allison and knelt before her. "Allison, honey? Look at me, Allison."

She raised her head and stared at the retired G.P. It took a few seconds for her to recognize him. "Hi, Doc."

The house filled with cops. Allison was in capable hands, so I left her and went into the kitchen where the police peppered me with questions. I told them everything that'd occurred and only deviated from the truth the slightest bit: Cassidy was introduced as a friend—a visitor from Montana. I never mentioned the second book or the dust jacket.

When the FBI arrived, they took charge. One of the FBI guys asked, "Can we ask your wife a few questions, Mr. Hamilton?"

Doc nodded and said, "Keep it short. She's been through a lot. I'm going to sedate her so she can rest comfortably."

"Certainly." The agent pulled the ottoman close and sat down. "Mrs. Hamilton? My name is Rodriguez. I'm with the FBI. Can you describe the men who abducted you?"

Allison shuddered

"Go ahead, honey." Bryce rubbed her hand. "I'm right here."

She hesitated. "I don't think so. It all happened so fast."

"How did they get in?"

"They were waiting for me in our garage. Bryce wasn't home." She gagged and coughed. "Threw a blanket over my head when I stepped out of my car. Loaded me into some sort of vehicle."

"Was it a car or an SUV?"

"SUV, I guess. Like Bryce's, sort of."

Bryce addressed Rodriguez. "I've got a Suburban, but the vehicle in the stadium lot was a blue Jeep Cherokee. We didn't get the license number."

Rodriguez gave Bryce a studied look and turned back to Allison. "What did they say to you, Mrs. Hamilton?"

"They said they had a gun, pressed it to my head. Then one said that if I made a fuss, he'd shoot me." Her voice shook as she spoke.

Bryce jumped in. "Allison? Listen, honey. I know this is difficult, but if you can give them a description of these guys, there's a good chance they'll be caught. Then we don't have to worry anymore, okay?"

"I'm sorry, but I never saw any of them." Tears spilled. "They tied me up, took me someplace, and locked me in a room. I heard their voices, but that was all."

"How many voices?" Rodriguez again.

"Oh, three, I think."

"All male?"

"Yesss . . . I don't know. I thought I heard a woman's voice one time, but maybe not. Could have been the television."

"Did any of the men have an accent?" The agent asked.

"Certainly not Hispanic. One of them sounded like he was from Eastern Europe. Another could've been from the South. Dunno. I was so scared."

"Do you have any idea where they took you? Could you identify any sounds?"

"Hmmm. Traffic noises. A siren at one point. Once we stopped, they dragged me out. Then we climbed some stairs. I smelled fried food before we went inside. That's about it, I'm afraid."

"Could you estimate how long the drive was?"

"Forty or fifty minutes." She was tired.

"Okay, that's enough," Doc said. "Come on, honey. Let's get you into bed." He helped her to her feet. "She should stay here, Bryce. The more family around her the better."

Bryce nodded. "No need for a hospital?"

"No. Physically she's fine." They led her into the guest bedroom. In a few moments, Doc returned. We shook hands, and I thanked him for coming.

"No problem. She'll sleep most of the night. There's a bottle of sleeping pills on the dresser. She shouldn't need any more. Call me if you need me."

"We will, Doc, and thanks." I stood and walked him to the door. Then, Rodriguez immediately started in on me.

"What were they after, Mr. Ivy?"

"A book. Same guys that jumped me out at Lake Havasu, I imagine." His eyes bore into me. "What happened out there?"

It took a few minutes to tell about Frank, Mullethead, and Manny. Bryce returned and sat next to me.

"Okay. We'll be working with the Mohave County Sheriff, and Chandler PD on this. If it's the same gang, then your wife's very lucky, Mr. Hamilton. So are you, Mr. Ivy. What you did tonight was extremely fool-ish. Kidnappings are always best left to the authorities, sir."

FBI Agent Rodriguez was heavyset with short black hair. Pale gray eyes, the color of alabaster, revealed little of what he was thinking. A no-nonsense, Sergeant Friday kind of guy, but Bryce wasn't easily intimidated.

"Cut the bullshit, Rodriquez. You and I both know that cops can screw up a kidnapping. Perps panic, dump the victim, and vanish. Forty percent of the time the target is found dead. We did what we had to. It was my call." He folded his arms and glared at Rodriguez.

"Something tells me you were once a cop, Mr. Hamilton?"

"Thirty years with the Minneapolis PD."

Rodriguez nodded. He seemed a fractious sort of guy. His cheeks flushed and his thin lips formed a single line. He tried very hard to regain control. "What about this book?"

"One of a boxful I purchased from Frank, the dead barber. That box over there in the corner." I pointed at the carton. Cassidy had glided into the kitchen and now stood next to me. She studied the agent's face and read the conversation with interest.

"Which one of the books was it?"

"An old Western called *The Cavity Lake Gang*."

"Any idea why they'd want this particular book?"

"Nope."

"And the rest of the books? The ones in the box?"

"Never mentioned any others," I said.

Rodriguez studied me with a practiced eye. "Must be a very valuable book, Mr. Ivy."

"Seems that way, but I've no idea why."

He pointed to my face. "Break your nose?"

I touched it reflexively. "Probably. Not the first time . . ."

We parried for another fifteen minutes. I recapped the events leading up to Allison's kidnapping. "Were you armed, Mr. Ivy?"

I was tired and peeved. "Yes. We knew I'd be outnumbered and thought that'd be wise."

Rodriguez shook his head. "Any number of things could've gone wrong."

"It was a calculated risk. They wanted the book—we wanted Allison. It went off without a hitch." Not entirely true, but what the hell. "Look, it's been a long day."

Rodriguez stood constipation rigid. "And what line of work are you in, Mr. Ivy."

"Construction."

A single brow arced. "Care to be more specific?"

"I build things."

"Such as?"

I shrugged. "Lately, nothing. Before nothing, barns and rock walls. Before that, whatever needed building." Funny, how people always looked at my hands when the subject was my occupation. Rodriguez did as well.

He seemed to come to a decision, flipped open his cell, and punched a number. "Jeff. You'll find a can of red paint next to the pole. Dust it for prints." He snapped the phone shut with one hand, turned and focused on Cassidy. "Miss Bower, I'm a bit puzzled over how you just happened to be here during this whole thing. You say that you and Mr. Ivy are friends?"

Cassidy didn't reply. I said, "You'll have to face her directly. She's deaf, but reads lips."

"Oh. Sorry." Rodriguez raised his head and repeated his question, this time louder, which struck me as humorous.

Cassidy nodded, and never hesitated. "Yes. I've known Gus for a number of years. We're working on a project together."

Her quick thinking surprised me as I had no chance to prep her. "Yes, that's right. Cassidy is visiting for a few days."

"I see. That your rental car outside?"

"Yes."

"This is all a bit puzzling," Rodriguez began. "Let me try and sort it all out. Feel free to jump in if I miss something: Mr. Ivy goes to Frank Wilson for a haircut, sees a box of books, hears of another interested party who phoned the night before, purchases the entire box, but leaves his checkbook behind. A few hours later, on a return trip back to find his checkbook, Mr. Ivy and the building owner discover Frank's dead body." He was staring at me now. "Did you say he was tortured, Mr. Ivy?"

"That's what Bryce heard from the Chandler PD."

He clucked his tongue. "Then, after a night of gambling, you're accosted in your room by someone who demands you turn over one of the books purchased the previous day. With a gun in your back, you lead him outside to Mr. Hamilton's Suburban. A player from the craps game, a Mr . . ." He looked at his notes, ". . . Siragusa, wanders by. Somehow in the confusion, you, Mr. Ivy, are able to withdraw a gun belonging to Mr. Hamilton. Mr. Siragusa is killed, you get the drop on the gunman, as it were, but he escapes nonetheless. How am I doing so far?"

The sarcastic tone of his voice left little doubt about his disbelief. "Yeah. Unbelievable, right?"

"I'd say," he continued. "We also have a mysterious customer in the barber shop, another unknown party outside your house, a break-in while you were at Havasu, and now the kidnapping of your sister. All these events are somehow related to a book you gave up to the kidnappers. That about it?"

At this point, it seemed unfair to confuse the guy any further, so I merely said, "That pretty well covers it."

He looked at each of us in turn—for what, I'm not sure. "One last question. Miss Bower?" Again his voice was unnecessarily loud. He leaned over to get her attention. "Miss Bower, is there any chance you called the barber the night prior to his murder?"

Wow. That thought hadn't occurred to me. I studied Cassidy closely. So did Bryce.

"No." She didn't miss a beat. "That wouldn't be possible unless the barber and I spoke through a relay service."

"A what?" Rodriguez asked.

"Oh, I'm sorry. Let me explain. Look at this . . ." She pulled something out of her purse that looked like a pager. "This is a Pocket Speak and Read— similar to a TTY. It attaches to any phone like this." She strapped the device over the mouthpiece. "Now I can call the state relay service and wait for a communication assistant."

"And then?" Rodriguez again.

"The relay service completes my call. My message is relayed to a person with normal hearing, verbally. That person speaks as normal and the assistant types their message into this device where I read their response. It's a bit cumbersome, and privacy goes out the window, but it works."

"And if you're calling another deaf person?"

"They would have a TTY—a teletypewriter, or a device such as this. They would see the call coming in as a flashing light and answer electronically. The entire conversation is transmitted through the same relay service."

Rodriguez persisted. "Word for word?"

"Pretty much. It captures each phrase and sentence, but inflections are lost."

"And if you were out someplace without your pocket gizmo?"

"Airports and other public facilities have special pay phone TTYs. A drawer beneath the phone pops out with a keyboard. Still goes through the relay service."

"Who pays for the service?" the agent asked.

"The phone companies are required to provide it by law."

"So, Frank could have spoken to you through this relay service, correct?"

"But he didn't," I interjected.

Rodriguez spun to face me. "How do you know that, Mr. Ivy."

"'Cause he would have told me about it. Not something that happens every day . . ." I replied.

"Easy enough to check with the relay service, Rodriguez," Bryce added.

"Thank you, Mr. Hamilton. I probably wouldn't have thought of that." Rodriguez's cheeks flushed.

Cassidy jumped back in. "As I said before, I'm visiting my friend Gus." Her face revealed no deceit.

"All right. That'll be all for now." Rodriguez stood to leave, then paused to answer his cell.

Bryce and I stayed put. "She's pretty quick on her feet, Gus," he whispered.

Rodriguez flipped the phone shut. "We found the Jeep abandoned just off the 101 near Gilbert. Stolen in Yuma. These guys are probably from L.A. They're running now, and you should have nothing more to worry about One last question: how would these guys've known about the books?"

"I really couldn't answer that." I lied.

Three distinct lines formed across Rodriguez's forehead. Something still bothered him. "You mentioned being a collector of Bower's other books, Mr. Ivy; twelve others I believe you said. Are they equally as valuable as this latest one?"

"No, not really. Maybe two, three hundred each. Might've been more with the addition of the *Cavity* book, but now?" I shrugged, my palms up.

"Too bad you had to give it up." His eyes flared. "Maybe it'll turn up yet."

"I won't hold my breath," I replied. "We're just happy Allison's safe."

"All right. We'll be leaving now. If they call again, or you think of something else, here's my card." He pulled out a business card and left it on the counter.

"Thanks for everything, Agent Rodriguez." I shook his hand.

Rodriguez said, "Good-bye, Mr. Hamilton. Miss Bower."

Cassidy smiled and waggled a couple of fingers at him to indicate she'd read him. Bryce nodded.

I wondered about Rodriguez's assessment that the kidnappers had fled the state. As soon as they realized the book was useless without the dust jacket—then what? An image of the masked gunman—his maleficent glare down the barrel of that pistol, flickered. A chill filled the room. If we were going to uncover the secret of the *Cavity* book, we'd have to be extremely cautious. My entire body squirmed with doubt. "You were lucky," Rodriguez had said. What if he was right? Then our plan to go forward could be tortuous . . . filled with danger. At this point, however, I wasn't about to crawl away and hide under a rock.

Fifteen

T HOUGHT HE'D NEVER LEAVE." I closed the door; glad to be rid of Rodriguez.

"I imagine it's a challenging case for him," Bryce replied.

"Yeah, guess so."

"I mean how many murders does he see here?" Bryce continued. "The book creates problems for him. How the hell do you trace a book? These FBI guys have an inflated sense of their own importance, by the way. They resent it when ordinary citizens take matters into their own hands."

"Yeah, and how ordinary am I? An almost retired construction worker from Minnesota? I think it cut some ice with him that you were once on the force, Bryce."

"Gus, have you read Grandmother's book?" Cassidy asked.

"Yes. Why?"

"And you've read her other works?"

"I have, yes. Always been a fan. Why?"

"Wondering what you thought of the *Cavity* book."

"To be honest, it's her worst. Almost as if she was ill or not quite herself when she wrote it. The story is pretty typical—rustlers chased by cowboys and an old Indian. The U.S. Marshall is a stereotype, and your grandmother's usual love interest is there, but otherwise I found the writing choppy; lots of mistakes. Seemed to have been written in a hurry. Maybe the editor fell asleep. You've read it?"

"Yes. You're aware that there were only a hundred copies printed?"

"I didn't know the exact number. Frankie told me only ninety-six soldiers from his company returned. Have you found them all?"

"Almost. I contacted the Veterans Administration. They provided a list of the survivors. Took months to track them all down. It's been very difficult. I had eliminated almost all of them when I came across Frank's name."

Bryce jumped in. "And you found Gus through Frank?" She wasn't looking so he repeated himself.

She blinked, looked down, then addressed me directly. "Yes. You beat me to it, Gus. Frank gave me your address when I told him I wanted to purchase it from you. Then I decided to watch you before revealing myself."

"You were pretty well hidden beneath that cap, Cassidy." Still should have recognized her perfume, though. "Let's talk about the book," I offered. "It had a different publisher. All the others were from Grossett and Dunlap. Why the change?"

"I can explain that and probably answer your other questions, but tonight I'm exhausted. How about you?"

"I agree. Been a long day, and we all need some sleep. Would you like to spend the night here? You can have my room. I'll bunk on the couch."

Cassidy considered my offer and patted Sammy's head. "If I'm not putting you out, I think I'd like that. I am tired and would rather not drive back this late. Thank you for the invitation."

"Bryce? Doc thought you and Allison should stay here as well."

"Yeah. Thanks. I don't want to wake her up now."

"I'll just trot out and get my suitcase," Cassidy said. She stood up and stretched.

I touched her arm. "I'll go with you." We walked to the door, and I held it open.

"See you guys in the morning," Bryce began as he made his way to the bedroom. "Thanks for your help, Gus. You came through like a champ."

"'Night, Bryce. Everyone's safe. That's all that matters."

Cassidy retrieved her suitcase and locked the car. The Arizona night hummed with a dead silence. She turned to face me. We didn't speak. Something sparked, though, and I could feel my face redden. She looked away.

"Here, let me take that." Our hands touched briefly, and once again the smell of lilacs intruded. It was an awkward moment. I led the way back to the house. Once inside, I showed her to my bedroom and put her bag on a chair in the corner. "Bathroom's in there, Cassidy." I faced her and pointed out fresh towels and linen.

"Thank you, Gus. You're very kind."

"Not at all. We're in this together now. Actually, there are so many unanswered questions that I can't let you out of my sight until you've explained everything."

"I'll do my best to answer them for you, Gus." Her warm smile filled the room.

"Good night, Cassidy." I turned to leave but stopped and waved to get her attention. "Oh, one quick question. What was the connection between your grandmother and Preston Kittridge?"

She hesitated and grinned. "Mary Beth Bower, my grandmother, was Preston's mistress."

My head leaned against the doorjamb. "What? Then . . . you . . ."

"Preston Kittridge was my grandfather." She said this without shame.

Stunned by her revelation, I was speechless. "Come on, Sam. Let's leave Cassidy alone."

He didn't budge from her side.

"It's okay if he wants to stay."

"He snores." How dumb is that comment?

She laughed. "I'll never notice. Good night."

Red-faced, I managed a weak, "'Night." This mysterious woman with her beguiling family history had my head spinning. Fifty questions flood-ed my brain, but they'd have to wait.

Cassidy Bower had slipped into my life like a warm rush of fresh air. She carried with her an intoxicating scent, the hope of unanswered ques-tions, and was involved in an enigma within an enigma.

At breakfast the following morning, I couldn't take my eyes off Cassidy. She had on a white short-sleeve knit shirt, khakis, and comfortable-looking loafers. Her hair had a coffee-colored sheen to it and sort of bounced when she moved her head. The early light illuminated her face like a portrait. A poem I'd seen recently came to mind, and a particular line seemed appropriate: "Light defined beauty the way longing defined desire."

But all I could say to her was, "Sam bother you last night?"

Cassidy looked at Sam. "No. He's wonderful company. How old is he?"

"Old enough to know better. Nine—going on one."

That's when Allie and Bryce walked into the kitchen, and I asked, "Sleep all right, Allie?"

"Yes. Thanks, Gus. Sleeping pill put me on cloud nine."

"I am so sorry that you and Bryce got sucked into this mess. If I'd've known that book was going to cause so much trouble . . ."

"That's all right, Gus. It wasn't your fault." She looked tired but happy to be with Bryce.

Bryce looked at Cassidy. "That book must be worth a great deal of money."

Cassidy read his lips, sipped her coffee, and didn't say anything.

"Cassidy? Am I right?"

"I'm not avoiding your question, Bryce. I honestly don't know. I'll be more forthcoming in a bit. I do hope we can figure out what secrets are hidden inside, and if you'll indulge me for a moment, I'd like to tell you a story. It's a bit complicated and will sound like pure fiction, but I assure you it is not."

"I love a good mystery," Allison said. "But, I know Gus and Bryce. They're planning something, and that worries me. These are dangerous people. Frankly, I'd like to pack up and go back to Minnesota."

Allison had been through a horrific experience. As my sister, I really hoped she and Bryce would go back home. But, while I regretted what had happened to her, I was like a dog with a fresh bone. The mystery of the *Cavity* book was just too enticing. I had to know more.

"You don't have to be involved, honey. As a matter of fact, I think we should put you on a plane," Bryce offered.

"I think I'd like that, Bryce."

"What about you, Bryce. Maybe you should go too." I knew from his expression that he'd resist.

"Not until we find out what all the mystery is about. Allie can stay with Sarah."

"Okay, we have some decisions to make," I replied while scrambling up an omelet. "If Allison's leaving, then the three of us are in this together, correct?"

Both nodded their assent.

"Good. Then we share everything and try and make sense out of it all."

"I'm going to call Northwest and find out what flights are available," Bryce said.

In a few minutes, he had booked a flight, and we all sat down to coffee and my Tex-Mex egg concoction. "Tuesday at 3:45 p.m., honey." Bryce put an arm around Allie. "We'll stay home today. You can relax. Get your strength back."

This brief return to normalcy was a welcome change. Still, Cassidy's presence was a constant reminder of the vortex we were caught in. Sixty years earlier, Preston Kittridge and his mistress, Mary Beth Bower, had put into motion a plan that now was gaining momentum. They created a puzzle so intriguing it'd cost the lives of two people—and nearly a third.

The price of revelation mounted.

Sixteen

ITH ALLISON RETURNED to the bedroom to make arrangements with Sarah back in Minnesota, and with the book in front of her, Cassidy looked across the table at Bryce and me. "I'm not certain what you have gleaned so far, but think I can provide a fair amount of history. Tell me what you've learned first?" Cassidy rested her chin on her hands and waited.

Bryce jumped in. "No offense, Cassidy, but I'm troubled about something. How do we know you're not here just to get hold of the dust jacket?"

Cassidy didn't flinch.

Bryce caught my glaring look. "We need some assurance that she is who she says she is."

"Do you think that's fair?" I asked.

"Look, Gus, think about it. First of all, she says she visited Frankie prior to his murder. Then she manages to track you to Lake Havasu. And, finally, she stops by your house shortly after Allison's been kidnapped. Interesting timing, no?"

"Yes, but . . ."

"On top of that, she just happens to have a second copy of the book. That's convenient, isn't it? But she doesn't have the dust jacket, which, as she said, 'holds the key to everything.' Pretty clear the book and jacket together are worth a great deal of money. All these coincidences are troubling."

He was right, of course. She could easily be posing as Bower's granddaughter, could have even killed the real Cassidy Bower—if there was a granddaughter at all—and could be part of the murderous gang that kid-napped Allison. "Cassidy? Maybe we do need to clear all this up."

"Perhaps we should see some identification," Bryce suggested.

Cassidy's face reddened, but she said nothing. Instead, she rose from the table, left the kitchen and returned with her purse. She unzipped it, withdrew her wallet, and slid it across to Bryce. "Be my guest."

Bryce withdrew her driver's license, and studied the photo. "Well, this is definitely you." He took a quick look through her credit cards and put everything back. "I have one more concern. When the FBI asked you how you happened to be in Chandler, you came up with a pretty clever answer. But you lied— more than once. Why?"

"First of all, we discussed a partnership. Would you rather that I had told them the truth and forced Gus to hand over the dust jacket?"

"All right, that's enough," Allison said. She stepped close and put a pro-tective arm around Cassidy's shoulders. "If you're finished with your interro-gation, then apologize to Cassidy." She pinched Bryce's earlobe for emphasis.

"That's not necessary, Allison." Cassidy's denim-blue eyes never left me. "I'm sure I'd be equally as suspicious if I were on the other side of the table. No offense, Bryce. Really." Her eyes sparkled with sincerity. She didn't sound at all bitter.

"I'm sorry, Cassidy," I offered. "You were very supportive last night, and that meant a lot to us. You didn't deserve that."

"Cassidy? Old habits die hard, I'm afraid. My apologies," Bryce added.

"All right. Let's get started." For the next ten minutes, they listened to what I knew about the *Cavity* book. "That's about it. Anything you can add Cassidy is welcomed. By the way, had you seen Doreen before?"

"No, I was there to observe you. As I told you, I came here to pro-pose a partnership."

"How did you know we were going to Havasu?" Bryce asked.

"Gus left a message on his answering machine."

I was satisfied. "What else did Frankie tell you, Cassidy?"

"Only that you had the book. He made it sound as if the transaction was quite by happenstance, that you had no knowledge of the book's provenance. I wasn't entirely convinced, however. For all I knew, Gus was hired by Bailey Greyson to acquire the book on his behalf."

"Who?" Bryce asked.

"Bailey Greyson . . . I'll get to him in a bit. When I told Frank who I was, he hugged me and thanked me for coming in. Said he had always hoped to be able to express his gratitude to some member of the Kittridge family. It was quite touching, really. Such a sweet old man . . ." Her eyes turned down and settled on Sammy. Her shoulders drooped, and she sighed.

None of this could be an act. Allison and Sammy vouched for her. I wanted to trust her. "Was Frank the last name on your list?"

Cassidy looked up. She hadn't heard my question. *Have to remember to make sure she's looking at me.* I asked a second time.

"Yes. The others couldn't remember what happened to their copies. Many had no recollection of the book whatsoever."

"Then we can assume the killers did the same thing," Bryce offered.

"Probably. There were two men I couldn't contact. One was Eddie Two-Feathers who lives on a Navajo Reservation in the northeast part of the state. The other lives in Denver and never returned my call."

We moved out to the patio. A bank of violet-and-gray clouds had gathered in the north, but they would break up and scatter before reaching the Phoenix area. The never-ending blue sky was an upside-down swimming pool. It felt refreshing to be outdoors after being cooped up in the house. "Cassidy?" A brief wave caught her eye. "Tell us about your family."

"All right. Most of what I'm going to tell you was passed to me from my father and mother. Grandma Bower died in 1958. Before I was born. She went to her grave with most of the secrets she and Preston shared, intact. However, after her death, certain letters surfaced which father uncovered."

"Where was Preston from, Cassidy?" Allison asked.

"Wolf Point, Montana. Left home at sixteen—in 1920—and signed on as a ranch hand for a large cattle spread near Cut Bank."

"That explains his interest in Sagebrush Westerns," I offered.

"Probably. I'll attempt to encapsulate this, but please excuse me if I sound like a schoolteacher. A bad habit from my days in front of a class."

"You were a teacher?" Allison asked.

Cassidy's eyes darted from right to left as she struggled to keep up with each question. "Yes. I taught at the college level."

I was puzzled. "Cassidy, uh . . . how, if you're deaf?"

"Oh. I graduated from Gallaudet University in Washington, D.C. Are you familiar with Gallaudet?"

Allison said, "Isn't that the college for the deaf?"

"Yes. It's the only all-deaf college in the United States." She spoke with warmth and fondness now. "I taught history and was there until a few months ago when . . . when all this trouble began."

"Why did you leave?" Allison again.

"The letter, the one from Grandfather's attorney. I'll get to that, but want to keep everything in chronological order." She folded her hands. "Grandfather married Ellen Simpson in 1924. They had one child, Jack—born in 1925. Ellen was quite frail, and something must have happened between her and Preston after Jack's birth. I don't know exactly what. Maybe her health deteriorated. I just don't know.

"Preston helped build the Fort Peck Dam in northeast Montana. Took seven years and spanned four-and-a-half miles across the Missouri River. Grandfather had a contracting company to haul rocks for the spillway. Started with a couple of mules and soon bought his first truck. For the next few years, he saved every penny he could. I think this is where he made his initial stake."

She held up her empty cup when I offered more coffee. Then Cassidy continued.

"With the dam completed, he moved his family to Billings and bought a small metal castings company, called Montana Minerals. Grandfather knew the United States would be drawn into the war, so he went to Washington to learn about defense contracts. As a result, he went home and re-tooled the plant to model it after a company called, Comet Manufacturing."

The three of us were an attentive audience. "When did Preston and Mary Beth meet, Cassidy?"

"Sometime before he bought the casting plant, because my father, Ramsey, was born in 1940. Father was never very clear on the circumstances of how they met. Remember, Mary Beth was deaf, so for a shy, introverted young deaf woman to take up with a man like Preston—well, it's hard to fathom. I concluded that grandfather must have met her through her writing. That was grandmother's escape—her writing." She paused and looked at each of us in turn. "If I'm boring you with all this?"

"Not a problem, Cassidy. You have me hooked," I offered. Bryce sat quietly studying our guest.

Cassidy stood, stretched, and paced the small patio. She reminded me of a graceful sloop, the way she glided. Leaning against the brick barbecue, I watched Sam trot over, plant his rump, and gently fall into Cassidy's leg. "I was told grandmother knew of Preston's marriage from the beginning. Because of her deafness, I think she was content to share whatever time Grandfather made available, and was happy living the reclusive life she created for herself."

"When did she become deaf?" Allison asked.

"Earlier than I. Age six or seven. Taught herself to sign from what she learned from the Indians around Billings. She had no formal education. As her writing progressed, Preston helped her find her New York publisher."

"Who was this 'Franklin Press' that did the *Cavity* book?" She wasn't looking and I had to repeat myself.

"A very small publisher Preston subsidized to publish *The Cavity Lake Gang*. Few copies were printed, so he stood the entire cost and never registered the book with the copyright office in Washington."

"That explains quite a bit." I sipped at my last dram of coffee.

"Yes. There's no record of this book ever being published." Cassidy took her copy of the book and opened it to the front page. She laid it down on the table.

"Okay, so what did he convert Montana Minerals to?" I asked.

"Ah. Here's where the real mystery begins," Cassidy replied. "They made toy soldiers." She paused, looked at each of us, and continued. "They were called, 'authenticasts.' Preston copied Comet Manufacturing's molds and turned out hundreds of thousands."

"Authenti-what?" Allison asked.

"Authenticasts. Father had drawers full of blueprints."

"What were they?" Bryce finally demanded.

"Whatever the Defense Department needed in the way of scaled-down replicas: enemy warships, tanks, planes, artillery—even soldiers in various poses. Each model was 1/1000 of the original size—"

"Cast of lead and tin?"

She nodded and added, "Used to train the soldiers by simulating battle scenes."

"Like little boys playing with tin soldiers, eh?" asked Bryce.

"Today they play video games." I offered. "And Kittridge made money manufacturing these toys of war?"

"It added to his fortune, certainly. However, Grandfather resented President Roosevelt's declaration that defense contractors voluntarily cap their profits. Of course that didn't work, and 'Wartime profiteering,' became a game of hide and seek," Cassidy concluded, dropping her gaze.

I tapped her on the shoulder to get her attention. "So, Preston's response was what? Cassidy?"

She brushed a loose strand from her eyes. "He knew what was coming, so early in 1942, he began siphoning off money from the company."

"What'd he do with it?" Bryce's cop instincts bristled.

"I don't know. Father didn't either. I hoped the book would provide a clue."

And there it was, the first solid bit of evidence that this wasn't just a murky dream or figment of collective, over-active imaginations. There might just be something significant beneath Preston's rainbow. This was all very exciting, but so far, it was conjecture. I had to try to remain objective. How much truth is buried in Cassidy's narrative? Is she really who she claims to be? If not, who is she? What's she after? What if this was the make-believe fantasizing of a lonely, deaf woman's sanguine imagination? Preston Kittridge didn't strike me as a man given to whimsy, however. If he was distraught over his son's death, maybe what he did was logical.

"He didn't want Roosevelt to get his money," I said. "So he hid it." I paused for their reaction. "It makes sense. Why not give it to the soldiers who served with his son? Preston and his mistress dreamed up an elaborate treasure hunt. They created the *Cavity* book and buried clues within its pages. They built a map of words to lead some lucky soul to something of value."

"You did say the writing was stilted," Allison remarked.

"Not at all up to the author's usual standards?" added Bryce.

We all stared from one to the other. I stated the obvious: "Then it is a code, a code leading to a hidden treasure."

Seventeen

I LOOKED AROUND AND REALIZED how foolish I sounded. "Sorry, Cassidy. I couldn't resist. Please continue."

"That's all right, Gus. I hope you're right. We have a ways to go before we can claim his prize, however. During this period, Preston bought a ranch someplace away from Billings. No one knew where it was except Preston and my grandmother. They would slip off to the ranch when he was supposed to be away on business." Her words created quite a romantic twist. "The Circle MB ranch provided the privacy they sought, and that was where Mary Beth did most of her writing."

"How'd you know about the ranch?" Bryce asked.

"Father. To this day I don't know what happened to it. Father always thought Preston deeded it to Mary Beth before he died. If so, she must have sold it right away. There's no record of it anywhere."

I jotted down everything that seemed important. "When did Preston die?" Tap, tap. "Cassidy?" and repeated the question.

"1948."

"Are you getting tired, Cassidy?" Allison asked.

"No, I'm fine. At some point, though, we're going to have to dig into the real essence of this book. Here's what I believe: Grandfather had a hundred copies printed, enlisted grandmother's help to both write the book, and insert a coded message within the text. Furthermore, the letter to the survivors was an invitation to gather together and unlock the puzzle."

Bryce leaned over to get her attention. "How do you figure?"

"The last paragraph in the letter. Did Frank give the letter to you, Gus?"

"No, he wanted to keep that. Seems I should've taken it with."

"No matter. I have a copy." Cassidy withdrew the letter and unfolded it. "There are a couple of parts here that strike me as an invitation. First: 'I'd encourage you to read the story first for enjoyment, secondly for direction and content. The discerning reader will be rewarded.'"

"I agree. The last paragraph reiterates that claim. Can I see that?" She handed the letter to me. "Here it is: 'I urge you all to stay in touch with your friends. Maintain and draw strength from that friendship. There is great wisdom and knowledge to be had from sharing. Open your eyes to all that is possible. Study the words. Catch your dream, and enjoy the fruits of your labor.'"

"Yes. Exactly," Cassidy said.

The Shakespeare quote Frank mentioned was typed at the bottom of Cassidy's copy. "What did you make of this quotation, Cassidy? 'There is a tide in the affairs of men, which taken at the flood, leads on to fortune.'"

"That is curious. Grandfather's last little tease, perhaps?"

"You were an English major, Gus. How well do you remember your Shakespeare?" Allison asked.

"Not at all. I only took lit courses 'cause I liked to read. Might be more here we should know about."

"Were you a teacher, Gus?" Cassidy asked with a lilt in her voice.

"No. My post-grad study was of a different sort." I hadn't thought about boot camp or AIT for a good long while. I shook my head to clear the memory and said nothing further.

Cassidy looked around as if she missed someone's comment. It was an uncomfortable moment and up to me to ease. "Who wants to look up the quote?" My question was directed at Cassidy.

"I have a laptop." Cassidy volunteered. "Can I plug it in to your phone line?"

"You bet."

Bryce cleared his throat. "Sure as hell sounds like he was dangling a carrot out there, doesn't it? When was his son killed?"

Cassidy was busy opening her computer. "I'm sorry. I missed the question." Cassidy looked at me.

"Jack was killed in '45? In Luzon?"

"Yes. Their mission was called Task Force Liberty Bell," Cassidy said.

"The book was published in 1946, so he must've commissioned Mary Beth to write it after Jack's death, correct?" I asked.

Cassidy arched a single, gentle brow. "Yesss. So?"

"Why go to all the trouble to bury some secret in a book? He's already decided to give away almost a hundred thousand dollars, so why not just give the rest away? He'd provided for both families in his will, right?"

"Yes. Grandmother's estate was substantial—so was Father's. I assume he left plenty for Ellen as well."

"Then, why the book?"

"We'll never know the answer to that, Gus. Maybe grandfather hid his money from the government long before Jack's death. And after? Maybe he just didn't care anymore and wanted a group of the soldiers to band together and find the treasure. Perhaps he wanted to challenge them—make them work for it. So along with Grandmother, they came up with the idea for the puzzle book." Cassidy continued. "It would've taken some time to get a book written and published back then. He had plenty of time to think about what he was doing. Based on what I've learned, I don't think he was being playful or coy."

"What caused you to go in search of the book in the first place, Cassidy?" Bryce asked.

"The letter from Grandfather's attorney I mentioned. I received it in January."

I asked, "What was in it?"

"I'll show you." She pulled out a typewritten letter with a sheaf of pages stapled beneath. "I won't read the entire document. It's six pages of legal, mumbo-jumbo. I'll try and paraphrase." She found a highlighted section. "Dated January 1 of this year. The letterhead is from Maxson, Moore, and Eldridge, attorneys at law. Addressed to the heirs of Mary Beth Bower and Ellen Simpson Kittridge. The date of the letter is important, by the way.

> Dear Sir or Madam: As the duly appointed trustees for the estate of Preston Leonard Kittridge, and the legal executors of said estate, etc, etc, we are authorized to inform you of the contents of a certain codicil, originally dated and notarized on, January 1, 1945.'"

Cassidy had our attention.

"Here's the essence of the document: 'On this date, ninety-six copies of a book titled *The Cavity Lake Gang* by M.B. Bower, were delivered to the surviving members of Charlie Company, Eleventh Airborne Division, Sixth United States Army, along with a letter from Mr. Kittridge and a check for one thousand dollars.'

"It goes on to state that Grandfather had a number of clues buried in the book that would 'lead a discerning reader, or readers, to the discovery of a certain container.'" She continued, "Whoever found this container would also find 'a notarized Certificate of Ownership providing proof extant regarding legal title to the contents of said 'container' and vicinage.'"

She paused to catch her breath. "Everyone with me so far?"

"Vicinage?" Bryce asked and turned both hands palms up.

I shrugged. A red herring? "Damned if I know. Keep going, Cassidy."

"Here's the problem," Cassidy said. "'If the container remains undiscovered by the anniversary date, July 1, this year, Citadel Bank and Trust is authorized to open a safe deposit box reserved by Grandfather. A map will reveal the location of the container.'"

"Uh, oh. And what happens to the container?" Bryce asked.

"Legally, it becomes the property of the bank." She said. The room was silent as her words registered. "Quote, 'if neither family representative uncovers this container by July 1—six months from the date of this letter—all rights to ownership by either party's interest (Kittridge or Bower) are voided.'"

Cassidy finished with, "Signed by Gerald Moore III, attorney at law." She laid the document down on the table and looked up.

I was right. The old bastard hid his fortune and created a puzzle buried in the pages of *The Cavity Lake Gang*. "I'll be damned." I muttered and nibbled the end of my pencil. "Do you know this law firm, Cassidy?"

"Yes. They're the trustees of Father's estate. I speak with a representative from time to time."

"Why didn't this codicil surface before?" Bryce asked.

"Mr. Moore said that it was Grandfather's express wish that sixty years pass before it became public."

"Was there anything else, Cassidy?" Allison asked. She fingered Cassidy's arm to get her attention.

"The letter was addressed to me as the sole heir on the Bower side and to a man named Bailey Greyson on the Kittridge side. Apparently Greyson is the only remaining heir of Preston and Ellen. Probably a third or fourth cousin. Lives in Denver. I made a few inquiries and discovered he's an accountant with something of a checkered history."

"Well, that explains quite a bit." Bryce offered. "I'd guess it's this Greyson character who hired the bunch that killed Frankie, roughed up Gus, killed the guy at the casino, and had Allison kidnapped."

"Makes sense. He's the only other person with knowledge of this affair," I added.

"And the container's where?" Allison asked. "Someplace in the United States?"

"Who knows? Stands to reason he wouldn't leave the contiguous U.S., right?" Bryce offered.

Cassidy followed his lips, raised both arms and shrugged without responding.

I touched Cassidy's bare arm. Her skin was warm, soft as a dove's breast. "When you spoke to the attorney, did they have any idea what might be in the container?"

"No. Any guess would be pure speculation. When I asked what the bank might do with the contents, they said it'd simply be acquired and disposed of as they saw fit."

My fingers were numb from scribbling. This had become quite complicated. A second and third look at both letters revealed nothing more than we already knew. "Okay, it seems to me we follow the trail of clues and uncover everything we can from the book. I've made a list of significant details. Take a look. If I've missed anything, jot it down."

I dropped the notebook on the table, stood and stretched. "I'm hungry. Anyone else?" My head ached. Somewhere in my cluster of notes was the key, but now my mind was numb.

"I am," Bryce said.

"I'll fix some sandwiches." Allison headed for the refrigerator.

I stood over the table and stared at the items circled on the top page of the notebook. Kittridge and Bower had certainly created a clever labyrinth. Which of the clues are the most important, or do they all tie together? I laid a hand on Cassidy's shoulder.

She looked up.

"After lunch, let's hear why you think the dust jacket is so important."

Eighteen

W E FINISHED EATING and decided to take a break. Allison wanted to go home, and I needed a chance to digest everything we'd heard from Cassidy. An afternoon poking around the Internet could prove informative. Cassidy wanted to return to her motel for a shower and a nap. She looked tired and not terribly healthy.

Allison must have seen something in my face. "What's the matter, Gus?"

"I don't know. You think Cassidy looks unwell?"

Allison smiled and nodded to Cassidy. "Did you read that?"

"Yes. I'm touched, Gus. But really, I'm okay. Tired is all. This has been very trying. Not used to being out in public, I'm afraid. You're very sweet to ask." She reached out and laid a hand on my cheek. Her touch was light and tender, but it was clear she didn't want to discuss this anymore.

My face heated up. Feeling awkward and unsure of how to proceed, I said, "Look, if you're that tired, maybe I should drive you back to your motel. I could pick you up later."

"Oh, no. I don't want you to go out of your way. Besides, I . . . I have a couple of errands to run." Her voice caught slightly. "Would you mind if I took the jacket with me?" Her blue eyes bore into mine.

"Not at all. I'll go get it." When I returned she accepted it as if it would fall apart in her fingers. "Before you go, can you tell us why that's so important?" Her head was down, staring at the jacket. I reached out and touched her hand. She jumped and looked startled. "Why is the jacket so important, Cassidy?"

"Oh. Sorry." She wet her lips and laid the jacket down. "Here, I'll show you." She picked up the book and turned to the very last page. "Read this." She pointed to a page titled, "There's More to Follow!"

I took the book and glanced at the page in question. "I see what you mean." Bryce and Allison looked confused. "Years ago, publishers used the last page to tout the work of other authors in their stable. Might've been something here about Zane Grey's books, for instance. Instead, this reads like a personal note to the reader of the *Cavity* book. This is interesting. Listen:"

> There's More to Follow!
> More stories of the sort you enjoy by the author, M.B. Bower, are listed in chronological order on the reverse side of the wrapper. Look the list over before you lay it aside; there are books here you will surely want—some possibly that you have always wanted!
> It is a selected list; every book in it has achieved a certain measure of success.
> This list is the greatest index you will ever find of valuable and important fiction of the Old West. It represents a generally accepted standard of great value. Every letter, every word, every paragraph, every page has been carefully constructed by the author to present for you a truly memorable and worthwhile journey into the world of fiction and dreams.
> It will pay you to consider the list!
> In case the wrapper is lost, contact the publisher:
> Franklin Press
> 1611 Liberty Bell, Franklin, Pennsylvania
> Good luck and good fortune.

Bryce and Allison studied the last page. "Okay. Now what's a wrapper again?" Bryce asked.

"It's what they used to call the dust jacket," I offered.

Cassidy unfolded the jacket, and we gathered to scan the back flap. Listed were fifteen M.B. Bower titles. Something was wrong with the list though. It didn't look right. The heading on the back of the jacket read, Other Books by M.B. Bower. "Cassidy, are you familiar with all the books your grandmother wrote?"

"I think so. Why?"

"Take a close look at this list. I have copies of all twelve of her books but this lists fifteen. Some of these can't be right. The first one, *Message to the Angels*. Never heard of that. Have you?"

Cassidy leaned close and studied the list of titles. "No. That's not familiar. Neither is the sixth one, *The Long Road Home*. This is very strange." She sounded sincerely puzzled.

"Look at number eleven, *Crossing on the Prairie*. That one certainly isn't one I know either."

"That's three," Bryce said. "Any others?"

"Nope. Just those three."

On the bottom of the flap was the Franklin Press address—again, 1611 Liberty Bell. *Something about that . . . Dunno.* Three bogus titles had been included with her other twelve books. Why? A mistake? Uh-uh. Don't think so.

"Cassidy?" I tapped her shoulder. "You notice anything else peculiar?"

She looked back at the flap. "No. Why?"

"Don't really know." I stared at the address. "Something else we're missing here. Maybe it'll come to me later. For now, let's concentrate on the three bogus titles. Bryce, why don't you see what you can find out about Frankie's unit, the Eleventh Airborne?"

"Sure. I just had a thought, though. What if someone already found the container, and didn't report it? Like to the IRS? He certainly wouldn't have notified the bank, would he?"

"Ouch. Good point. Look, there's no guarantee this won't be a wild goose chase anyway. This Greyson character might've already found it." Cassidy looked distant, preoccupied. She had read my lips but wasn't focusing. "You sure you feel okay, Cassidy?"

A slight smile creased her lips. "I'm tired, Gus."

"Why don't we all go out to dinner tonight?" Allison offered. "It's my last night. How about Boca Chica, say at six? That all right with you, Cassidy?"

She swung her head to catch up. "What? Yes, I'd like that. A short nap'll do me a world of good." She placed the dust jacket in the folder, and tucked it in her purse.

"Good idea, Allie. We can compare notes," I said, thinking that something in Cassidy's voice didn't sound right.

"Do you know where the restaurant is, Cassidy?" Allison asked.

"If you give me directions, I'm sure I can find it. Thank you for your hospitality, Gus. You've managed to make me feel most welcome." She took two steps and kissed me on the cheek. She turned to Allison. "I hope none of what has happened lingers too long, Allison. That was a very traumatic experience."

"Thank you, Cassidy. It's over now. Maybe something positive will come out of all this. We'll see you later tonight." They hugged.

Cassidy approached Bryce and extended her hand. "Take care of Allison, Bryce. She's a brave lady."

"I will. 'Bye, Cassidy."

The four of us walked out together. I opened the car door for Cassidy, waited until she belted in, and gave her directions. She started the car and slowly closed the door. Before she pulled away, she turned one last time, as if to be certain I hadn't called out to her. She wiggled her fingers, smiled and pulled away.

"That woman has lived two lifetimes," Allison said as she approached.

"Huh? Oh, yeah. Because of her deafness." I was already off in another place. "See you guys tonight."

The phone rang at four thirty that afternoon. "Mr. Ivy?"

"Yes?"

"Agent Rodriguez. How's your sister doing?"

Sergeant Friday. "All right, I guess. Last night was pretty rough on her."

"I'm sure it was. Listen, we pulled a print from the Jeep. Matches the gunman from the casino. Name's Edwin 'Hardboiled' Prittie. Got a rap sheet as long as my arm," said Rodriguez. "Hangs out in L.A. Been arrested numerous times. Spent seven years in Folsom for manslaughter. Not a very nice character."

He waited for me to respond. "What about the others?"

"I've a list of people he's known to work with. One named Boris Lesard, another career criminal. They're part of a gang led by one, Micah

Knorr. We've never been able to pin anything on Knorr. Now maybe we can."

Bryce was right. Knorr was the ringleader.

"We think Knorr is taking orders from someone else, but we've no lead on who it might be. This is a bad bunch, Mr. Ivy. They won't hesitate to kill again to get what they want. If you're contacted, call me immediately. Don't mess with them. They're outright killers."

"Duly noted. Anything else?" Tired of dealing with cops, I'm sure I sounded crabby.

"You'll be sticking around town?"

"Far as I know." Not exactly a lie as I wasn't sure where our search might lead over the next few days.

"One more thing. We checked out Miss Bower, and she appears to be everything she claims, but . . ." He let this dangle for a bit. "Do you have any reason to believe she's involved in this?"

The question caught me off-guard. "No, I don't think so. Why?"

"No reason. Just doing my job."

Rodriguez was holding something back. "I'm sure you are. Call me if you learn anything more."

"Oh, you can count on that, Mr. Ivy."

I stared at my notes. It's all here. The puzzle is unraveling. I'm close. Real close. Sam came over and laid a heavy paw on my thigh. "You couldn't care less, could you, boy?"

Depending on what Bryce discovered, a trip up north might be in order. My pulse surged. A spidery tingle worked its way down my spine. I had a strong hunch about what Preston had done. But, were we too late? How much had Knorr and Greyson discovered? What could they do without the dust jacket? More importantly, if we had the only one known to exist, then what?

Nineteen

BRYCE AND ALLISON JOINED me at Boca Chica at a couple of minutes after six. We ordered a bottle of wine ahead of Cassidy. "Cheers, you two." I held out my glass.

We clinked glasses and Bryce said, "I'll feel a lot better once Allison's back in Minnesota."

"Me too." Allison leaned on the table with her elbows. She looked at us. "I want you guys to promise me something."

"What's that?" A large smile plastered Bryce's face.

"That you and Gus won't do anything too stupid."

"Define stupid."

"Don't do that, Bryce. I'm serious."

"I know. Look, we've managed to work our way out of a number of scrapes over the years, but we're both too old to look for trouble."

"We'll be careful, Allie," I assured my sister.

She wasn't finished. "You two guys are like kids playing hooky from reality. One of you gets a harebrained idea, the other naturally goes along. Between the both of you, I don't think you know what caution means."

"Aw, Allie, that's not fair," Bryce complained.

"Really? What about the time in Canada you guys went out fishing against the advice of the lodge owner? As I heard it, all the other boats stayed in that day. Too windy. But not you two boobs. And what happened?"

"Ahh. So we had to spend the night on a muskrat house. Big deal. They came and got us the next morning. Right, Gus?" He winked, as I guessed he never had told her the entire truth about that day.

"Never in any danger, Allie. A little cold, maybe." I looked at my watch. Almost seven. "Cassidy's late. Wonder if she got lost."

"Give her ten minutes, then call her motel," Bryce suggested.

Cassidy didn't strike me as someone who was late for anything. A glance toward the front door didn't relieve my concern. Back to the book. "What did you find out about the Eleventh Airborne?"

"They got creamed on Luzon," Bryce started. "Lost a bunch of men, killed a lot of Japanese. They were flown in by glider."

"Really?" I'd heard about that strategy during Airborne training. Suicide flights.

"Yep. A silent drop. They were the Angels. Trained at Camp Mackall, North Carolina. Left for the Philippines in November 1944."

"Jesus, green recruits with very little training. Sounds familiar," I offered.

"Exactly. Their mission was dubbed Task Force Liberty Bell. You knew that, right?"

"Yes. Anything else jump out about them?"

"You know anything about the code talkers?"

"Navajo Indians recruited to create some kind of secret code. There was a movie a few years ago. *Wind Talkers?*"

"You got it. Apparently the Navajo had a unique language all their own. Only a handful of people outside their tribe could communicate with them. Created from sign language, it didn't have an alphabet, per se, so it was impossible to record as a written language. Unwritten to this day, near as I could tell. Some guy named Johnston encouraged the Marines to use the Navajo language to create secret coded messages."

"Now it's coming back. When were they first used?" I asked.

"In 1943. By the end of the war, over 500 Navajos were involved."

"And the Japanese never did break their code, did they?"

"Nope. A few of the Navajos were loaned out to the Army during the campaign in the Philippines at the end of the war."

"Let me guess," Allison volunteered. "Eddie Two-Feathers was one of these code talkers."

"That's a pretty safe bet," Bryce said.

"You think Preston Kittridge got Eddie Two-Feathers to create a code?" I asked.

"Maybe. The military code was declassified in 1945," Bryce said.

"Kittridge would've had access to that information through his connections in the Defense Department."

"Yep. Something else of interest: each code talker was assigned a buddy whose only job was to keep the talker safe. If he fell into enemy hands, you see, it meant sure torture and torture has a way of . . ."

I finished the sentence. "A way of loosening a man's tongue. So it was the soldier's job to assassinate the talker in the event of capture."

Allison choked on a sip of wine. "What? That's barbaric."

"Maybe, but if the Japanese had managed to break the code, we might've lost the war in the Philippines," Bryce concluded.

Time to move on. "There were a number of Indian words Bower used in the book. I wondered what they meant at the time; now I'm thinking they were Navajo." After a glance at my watch, I rose. "I'm going to call her motel."

In three minutes I was back. "She checked out."

"What?"

"Clerk said she checked out at four."

"Was she alone?"

"Didn't ask. Something's wrong."

"Would seem so. You thinking what I am?"

I shrugged and finished my wine.

"What?" Allison asked.

"She may well've played us for the biggest suckers in the world. Everything she told us—bullshit!" Bryce said.

"Why?" Allison asked.

"To throw us off the track," I put in. "She has the dust jacket now. She doesn't need us anymore."

"I refuse to believe that," Allison said. "There must be another explanation."

Bryce wasn't done. "Like what? Hell, she might have an accomplice we know nothing about."

"Wait a minute, Bryce. We have the only other book," I offered.

Bryce persisted. "Really? What if she's got a third copy? Maybe Kittridge had more copies printed and threw away the wrappers."

"You don't know that," Allison said.

A waiter approached our table. "You folks like to order?"

"Yeah. Let's eat. I'm starved," Bryce said.

I hoped Cassidy would still show, but somehow I knew she wouldn't. More wine was ordered. I nibbled on a sesame roll and poked at a nondescript salad. My appetite had vanished along with Cassidy and the dust jacket. Why didn't she at least call? Bryce was pissed, Allison hopeful. I struggled to remain positive about her veracity, but it was a losing battle.

Just before we left, Bryce said, "Question."

"What?"

"If she has the only dust jacket, where do we start our search?"

"My notes." My reply was weak. "I copied down everything that looked important."

"Even so, how do we know that there wasn't something else? Something she knew about and we missed? Maybe it was on the front of the jacket—the illustration itself. She asked to take it with her."

"I know."

"She didn't strike me as being that devious, honey," Allie said.

"Maybe she'll call in the morning . . ." I offered, not believing it myself.

"Look, Gus, I know you've developed something of an attraction for her, but you aren't thinking clearly here."

My face reddened. "Maybe so. If you're right, then we move on without her. Come on, let's go." We agreed that I would pick Allison up the next morning while Bryce checked in with Chandler PD.

If Bryce and my baser suspicions were right, Cassidy had a big advantage over us and could already be zeroing in on a solution. *Should have kept the jacket, Gus. You weren't paying attention. No fool like an old fool.*

Sammy licked my face as I sat behind the wheel.

"Here ya go, pal." I fingered a chunk of steak from the take-home box. "What do you say?" A hoarse, garbled "ghrrrgh" was all he could muster. The meat disappeared in an instant. With his treat devoured, Sam looked as depressed as I felt. His new friend had disappeared, and now all he had was me, and that was sad.

THE NEXT MORNING BRYCE called at seven thirty. "Any word?"

"No. Nothing."

"Nuts. Now what?"

"We keep on keeping on, that's what. If she played us on this deal, then she has a head start. We have to figure out what our next move is."

"And how do we do that?"

"Will your friend in the Chandler PD help you locate someone?"

"Maybe. But if he won't or can't, I've got someone back in Minneapolis who will. Who are we looking for?"

"Eddie Two-Feathers. I've a hunch he might be important."

"Okay. You want to know where he lives?"

"Yes. Supposedly he's out here someplace. Once you find out where, we should track him down and pay a visit. Maybe he can tell us what the Indian words in the book mean. Gotta start someplace."

"Okay. And what are you going to be doing?" Bryce asked.

"I'm going to play with those three bogus titles. See if I can spot a marker or sequence that leads to something else. I want to research Franklin Press, too. Something's funny about that address."

"Anything else?"

"See what you can learn about those 'authenticasts.' I want to know if what Cassidy told us is true."

"Sure hope I'm wrong about her, Gus."

"I do too, but until we have another explanation, what else can we think? I misread her . . . had my head up my ass. She seemed so . . . genuine though. Ya know?"

"Well, if she was pulling our chain, she did a damn good job. Hang on. Allison has something she wants to say." He handed the phone off.

"Gus?"

"Hi, Allie. You doing okay?"

"I am, but I'm anxious to get back to Minnesota. I've been thinking about Cassidy and want you to consider another explanation for her disappearance."

"Like what?"

"Remember when she was talking about her deafness? Her grandmother's?"

"Yes. Why?"

"She said Mary Beth had other health issues. 'Syndromic' was the word she used; that her grandmother went blind and her kidneys failed."

You're reaching, Allie. "Cassidy didn't say she had any health issues."

"She did look ill yesterday, Gus. You said so yourself." Real concern filled her voice.

"Possible, I guess. Why the secrecy? Why not just tell us she's sick? Why not a phone call?"

"I don't know. Obviously a very private person. What if she had to go home for some sort of treatment?"

I wasn't convinced. "Yeah, well, whatever. The quotation is from Shakespeare's *Julius Caesar*, Allie. There's a message of some sort there: Tide, affairs, flood, fortune. Kittridge wasn't a whimsical guy."

"You're right. The quote was included for a reason. All you have to do now is figure out why. I'd better finish packing, Gus."

"Okay. I'll see you about eleven-thirty." My pulse rose as I repeated the words: tide, affairs, flood, fortune. I'm close. I can feel it. But where to start without the jacket?

Twenty

WHEN I ARRIVED AT BRYCE and Allie's, both were waiting outside. "Where's Sam?" Bryce called.

"Left him at home. Wasn't sure how hot it was going to be." Bryce looked defeated. His mouth turned down, and he wouldn't look me in the eye.

"What's the matter?"

"Change of plans. Allie wants me to go home with her. And I agreed."

I held both arms out—palms up. "What?"

Allie spoke first. "I'm sorry, Gus. I'm worried about this whole affair, and if Bryce is with me, that's one less . . . worry. I can't call you off, but I still have some control over Bryce."

"Hold it, Allie. No need to apologize. I understand." I stepped close and gave her a hug.

"Without Cassidy or the dust jacket, we couldn't do much anyway, Gus. I have to go with Allie.

"Don't blame you a bit." How could I? They had each other and I had . . . Sam. "Come on, let's get your bags in the van."

As we loaded up, Bryce pulled me aside and handed me a small notebook. "Here's my notes. You have a house key. If you leave town, take the Suburban. Remember what's tucked under the back floor panel. There's still the Beretta in the glove box. Don't screw with these guys, Gus. If you face 'em again, shoot first." He grabbed the back of my head and tugged. "I mean it. Call me in a day or so and let me know what's happening, okay?" His dark eyes bore into mine, waiting for me to respond.

"I will. Don't worry. I'll be fine." I helped them finish loading, and we drove off.

Drivers in Phoenix were crazy. They all drove like they were late for something, and ninety miles an hour was routine. We carefully negotiated the notorious Highway 101. It took an hour and forty minutes to reach the airport. I parked in the short-term lot and walked into the terminal with Bryce and Allie. Once they were checked through, we walked to the security checkpoint.

"Have a good trip, you two. Give the kids a kiss and a hug. And don't worry, Allie."

"Please be careful, Gus. I have this weird feeling . . ." Her hug lasted longer than necessary. "Remember who you're dealing with."

"Yes, Allie. Get going before you miss your flight."

"I certainly hope Cassidy's all right," she said over her shoulder.

"Keep your eyes open, Gus." Bryce slapped my arm and followed Allie. They disappeared down the corridor, and I headed for the exit.

The sun was blinding outside. I waited for my eyes to adjust and noticed a tall blonde at the taxi stand. Her back was to me, yet something about her seemed familiar. I'd seen her before, but where? In a hurry to get home, I had to stop at the curb for a break in the traffic. A sideways glance confirmed my hunch—it was Doreen. I had two choices: turn and move on down the walkway, or keep going across the street and look the other way. The latter seemed less obvious, so I stepped off the curb.

After two steps she called, "Gus? From Lake Havasu?"

I turned, shaded my eyes and went for a feigned look of surprise. Unsure if it was successful, I returned to the curb with a broad smile.

Doreen looked predictably sumptuous. She had on faded designer jeans with the cuffs rolled a stylish eight inches and a short tan jacket over a white tank top with "Train Him To Obey!" printed in pink. Toeless two-inch sandals gave her legs the proper attitude. Doreen was hard to miss any time of day. She looked every bit as good as when I last saw her—a little tired, perhaps, but for a working girl, very nice.

"Doreen. What a coincidence." I leaned close for a friendly kiss aimed at my cheek. Her lips lingered and she laid her hand on my bare arm. "Seems as if I just left you at the craps table."

She flashed fabulously white teeth and giggled. "You did, silly. Small world. Where're you headed?"

"Oh, just dropping off my sister and husband. Headed home. How about you?" She was carrying a small overnight case. A white purse hung from one shoulder. "Where've you been?"

"Vegas. Flew up yesterday for the night."

"Any luck? With gambling, I mean." This entire encounter made me uncomfortable.

She arched her back, smiled slightly, and replied, "Oh, a little, I guess. Came home with more money than I left with, so that's all good." She glanced down the one-way street and finished with, "Damn cabs. Never stop up at this end. Say, where're you headed, Gus?" She leaned out over the curb.

Too late, I replied, "Chandler." My eyes focused on her ass. How in the hell did she manage to climb into those jeans? And what was between her and the denim? *Careful, Gus.*

"Oh, would you mind terribly giving me a ride? Tempe is on the way . . ." She batted her long lashes knowing I couldn't refuse.

"Sure, come on." What the hell.

"That's wonderful. Really appreciate it. Saves me thirty bucks." She started off at a languid pace. If she were in a narrow hallway, her hips would bump each wall.

"No problem, Doreen. Car's in the ramp." We jogged across the street. More than one male driver slowed to catch a glimpse of Doreen as her jacket flopped open. Her chest heaved with each step. She removed her jacket as we crossed the hot concrete. She truly was something to look at. From the rear, it looked as if her legs went all the way to her armpits. I shook my head and smiled.

Once inside the elevator, she edged close and pressed against my bare forearm. This wasn't unintentional. Doreen reached out and punched the stop button. She turned, dropped her jacket and wrapped both arms around my neck. Her breasts now pressed against my chest.

"Gus? Seems to me we have some unfinished business . . ." She tilted her head, licked her lips, and in a flash her tongue was in my mouth, exploring and jabbing. The pressure in my shorts was sudden, not entirely unexpected. It had been quite a while since anyone as exotic as Doreen had lit me up. Cassidy came to mind. But this wasn't Cassidy thrusting her pelvis against me.

She pulled away. "Do you ever watch Seinfeld?" A smile played on her mouth.

I couldn't speak . . . just nodded dumbly. I'm sure my tongue hung out to one side.

"Well, these are real." She cupped her breasts proudly, as if displaying homemade muffins.

She took my hand and laid it across her breast. I had to agree with her, and remembering the gorgeous babe played by Teri Hatcher that Jerry Seinfeld lost, answered, "Yes, they are spectacular, Doreen."

She giggled at that, and before I could muster a defense, *zipp*—my shorts dropped around my ankles and collapsed in a heap on top of my Bass Weejuns. I groaned as her fingers found life down below.

"Whoa, Gus. Now that's not a roll of chips, is it? Guess you have a pulse after all."

It had been so long since I'd felt anything close to the heat I now experienced, that I gave in to the pleasure of the moment. Her fingers toyed with me. Horny as a two-peckered billy goat, I wanted her to continue, wanted to throw her against the wall and consummate the deal. But it wasn't to be. Something intruded. Maybe it was the muzak in the elevator. I broke her grip, shuffled aside, and pulled up my shorts.

She stared at me with her mouth open. "Gus? What?"

"Look Doreen. You're incredibly sexy, and I'm truly flattered, but I just can't do this." Truth was, sex was pretty important to me, but not like this—not with a woman as well-traveled as Doreen. Regrettably, I punched the start button, and the elevator lurched to the fourth floor. "Maybe in another life . . ."

"Whatever." She fluffed her hair and straightened her t-shirt. "Don't worry about it. You're a nice guy, that's all." She picked up her jacket, and faced the door.

When we reached the fourth floor, I gestured for Doreen to step out. The entire episode in the elevator couldn't have taken five minutes. "My van's over there—nothing very fancy, I'm afraid."

"This is really sweet of you, Gus." She looked at her watch, then glanced around the ramp.

"Here we go." The unlock button on the key chain snapped the doors open. We both climbed in. "Better crank up the air conditioning. Never get used to this incessant heat."

"Oh, you don't live in the Phoenix area?"

"Nope. Only came down for the winter."

I faced her and asked, "You heard about what happened to Manny, right?"

"Yes. I feel just awful. Such a sweet guy." She pushed back her hair with one hand. It appeared she didn't want to talk about it anymore.

"Sure seemed like you two were friends." I volunteered.

"No, not really." She flicked an invisible piece of dirt from her jeans.

"Sorry. None of my business."

"That's all right." She turned and looked out the back window.

"You know, the police had me look at some security tapes. One showed you in an argument with some guy outside the men's room. You remember that?"

Her brows arced, and she snapped, "That's none of your business." And then, "He's my manager."

"Fair enough. I'm still curious about why you singled me out? Why not Norm?"

She paused. "I, uh, told you. 'Cause you're cute, and you looked like fun. Guess I was wrong about that. It wasn't about money, honest." Her gray-green eyes flashed a new look, one that said, "Leave it alone!"

I didn't think she'd reveal more. I put the van in gear. "Okay. Where to?"

Satisfied that she had put me off, she settled and pulled down the seat belt. "Get off the 101 going south, I'll direct you from there." She tossed another glance behind. Her sweetness returned.

We drove across the lot and started down the ramp. The windows were closed, but the loud squeal of tires sounded through a crack in my window. Within seconds, a black SUV flashed by and climbed up the opposite ramp.

At ground level, we eased out into traffic. From Sky Harbor Airport it was only a couple of miles before we turned on to Highway 202. I eased over to the right lane and kept my speed at sixty-five. Doreen flipped on the radio. Soon she was swaying and bobbing to a Bob Sager tune. Music filled the van.

Before long one of many impatient desert road hogs decided to plant on my tail. I glanced in the rearview and noticed it was a black SUV.

He pulled close, flashed his lights on and off. I slowed—just to piss him off. These guys drove me nuts, so I do whatever I can to make life difficult for them. With a rider in the passenger seat, it was more prudent to avoid a confrontation, however, so I stuck my arm out, and waved him past. "Get your ass over, you moron," I muttered. He had two additional lanes available, so why was he giving me a hard time? My blood pressure rose steadily.

We continued on for a couple of miles. He pulled close a few times, then dropped back. I slowed, and then sped up. Tapping the brakes made little impact. He obviously wasn't about to let me go without further harassment.

Doreen eventually turned and looked at the SUV. "It's a Cadillac Escalade. What's he doing, Gus?"

"He's a jackass looking for a laugh. Enough of this shit." I slowed and pulled on to the shoulder. The Escalade passed by. I noticed the windows were blackened. *Is that the same SUV from the parking ramp?* My heart raced at the implication. The Cadillac stopped fifty yards ahead of us. Now what? This might be something more than some kook with a chip on his shoulder. "Any idea who that might be, Doreen?"

She lowered the volume on the radio. "No. I have no clue."

"Who'd be after you? Jealous boyfriend, maybe?"

"Not likely."

Not likely, huh? I'd had enough. Just ahead was a turnoff to Highway 101. Time to dump this guy. I put the van in gear and pulled out into traffic. After we passed by, the Escalade accelerated to catch up. When he was close, I flicked my turn signal before the exit ramp. Once he was committed to the same exit, I spun the wheel to the left. We bounced over the curb, crossed a patch of gravel, and jumped back out onto Highway 202.

The Escalade braked and tried to turn around, but another car had entered the ramp and blocked the Cadillac. Once on the cloverleaf, we headed north on 101. I took a deep breath to relax, but it felt like every nerve in my body had been jump-started by a pair of twelve-volt battery cables. Doreen was very quiet. The episode with the SUV hadn't seemed to alarm her at all.

She merely turned up the volume on the radio again. REMs new hit filled the cab. Doreen tapped her nails against the window.

Twenty-One

WHEN WE HIT THE END of the cloverleaf, I floored the accelerator and the little van shot out onto 101. Before long, we were cruising at the same high speed as the rest of the idiots that afternoon. "Doreen." She nibbled on a fingernail.

"Doreen." I turned down the radio.

She turned toward me. Her eyes bulged. "What?"

"Talk to me. You're involved. How?"

She didn't look quite so pretty anymore. Nerves frayed, she repeatedly licked her lips. Our brief dalliance in the elevator seemed eons removed. She spoke through clenched teeth. "Money, Gus. It's always about money, isn't it?" Her voice had taken on a steely edge.

Finally. The truth. "How much?"

"Ten thousand if I got the book. Thing is, you didn't cooperate. If you'd just gone with me to your room, none of this would've happened, and poor Manny'd still be alive."

I should have been shocked but wasn't. If these were the same guys that had killed Frank and snatched Allison, they'd chase me until they had what they wanted. "But they have the book, Goddammit! They kidnapped my sister, and I gave it to 'em." I knew the truth: they must've figured out about the dust jacket. I spotted a black spec in the rearview. "What were you supposed to do today?"

"Slow you down. Keep you at the ramp. I dunno . . ." She was jumpy. "They want the damn cover. Said the book was no good without it. That's all I know. Give it to 'em and they'll leave you alone. They only gave me five thousand, and I won't get the rest 'til they get the jacket. That's a lotta money, Gus. Just give 'em the damn jacket, and they'll go away."

"No they won't. Besides, I don't have it—not anymore."

Her eyes looked like giant marbles. "What do you mean? You have to . . . they said you would."

"Yeah, well, it's gone. Someone else took it."

"Who?" She glared at me in real alarm.

"Doesn't matter. The jacket's gone. Use your head, Doreen. These guys killed two people and kidnapped a third. You can identify them. You think they're actually going to let you walk away?"

She blinked. Tears seeped from her heavy lashes. "They promised. I told them I wouldn't talk."

"Grow up. This isn't a game!" I shouted. "You aren't dealing with normal people. These are ruthless killers." The Cadillac had vanished. Air escaped from my cheeks. "Think they're gone."

Doreen spun around, then turned back. Impossible to tell what she was thinking.

We passed a sign for Beeline Highway 2. "Two Miles ahead," I muttered. Jackrabbit Road loomed before 2. It led into the Salt River Pima-Maricopa Indian Community. A billboard advertised, "A 53,000-Acre Agricultural Preserve Owned and Managed by the Pima Indians." A number of irrigation canals were visible in the broad valley cutting through hundreds of acres of cropland. The billboard showed that the Salt River paralleled the Reservation.

"Do you know what's in there, Doreen? Is there another way out?"

"Uh, I dunno. They grow stuff. Broccoli and corn I think."

I slowed and eased onto the loose gravel of Jackrabbit Road. It appeared to run the length of the reservation. Maybe there's a way out at the other end. We had no chance on the highway. Only hope seems to be in the reservation land. We sped down the dusty road. After a couple of miles, tall fields of Indian corn flanked both sides of the road. "Damn sure looks like Iowa here," I joked to ease the tension.

Doreen chewed on a fresh fingernail. "Wonder if we made a wrong turn," she offered and spun around to look out the rear. "Better pull over, Gus. We'll have to turn around."

A U-turn appeared my only option, but I hated to take a chance on meeting up with the Escalade again. I snuck a quick peek in the rearview and noticed a cloud of dust some distance behind us. I edged to the side and waited for the vehicle to pass. As the image in the mirror grew, I realized my mistake. The Escalade drew close, slowed, and stopped behind us. My heart pounded as we waited. Every nerve ending tensed. *Get your ass out of here, Gus.* I cranked the wheel and hit the gas to complete the U-turn. Too late. The SUV made the identical move and blocked the road.

"Shit." My fingers strangled the steering wheel as I slammed the brake pedal. *How the hell do I get out of here?* After a last glance at the SUV, I straightened the wheel, stomped on the gas, and sped off. With eight cylinders, the Escalade stayed close.

Doreen shouted, "They'll run us off the road, Gus!"

"Or we run out of road. Damn, it is a dead end." I was out of options but not determination. "Hang on, Doreen." I cranked the wheel to the right—toward the river, and tore off through the cornfield. Corn stalks slapped and banged against the fender and grill. The *rat-a-tat-tat* jangled my splintered nerves. Adrenalin surged. *One move ahead, Gus.* Sooner or later, though, the soft ground would bury the van, or the bundle of corn stalks snagged beneath the low-slung Caravan would slow us down. I kept my foot on the gas and prayed to get through the field.

"Gus. What're you doing?" Her eyes darted from side to side.

"It's our only chance. Better hope they don't catch us." We rocked from side to side as the van charged through the tall corn. My fingers ached from a claw-like grip on the wheel.

The Escalade plowed over the colorful Indian corn like a combine on a hot August day.

"They're gaining on us!" Doreen pummeled the dash.

The Caravan's engine howled and screamed to stay ahead. The noise blotted out all other sounds. I felt like a turtle rowing through tall grass. The gap closed. And then, one large overturned clod of earth brought us to a jarring halt. I threw the gearshift into park and snapped open my seat belt. "I'm getting out. Make up your mind, Doreen. Stay and die or come with me." My head throbbed. We had only a few seconds left.

She was white-faced, shaking like a feather in a wind. "I-I can't Gus."

Surprised by her choice, I wouldn't argue. "Your call! Maybe you can talk your way out. Good luck, Doreen!"

I hopped out, and ran ahead of the van into the tall corn. Forty yards into the maze, doors slammed behind me. I heard a brief shriek from Doreen. Should have dragged her with me. Too late. The Escalade's engine roared to life. With four-wheel drive, the SUV would have no trouble tracking me down.

I cut to the left for thirty yards and continued down the rows away from my pursuers. Dressed in golf shorts and loafers with no socks, I realized how exposed I was to the sharp edges of the corn stalks that cut into my legs with every step—like being flayed by trolls with whips of piano wire. Every inch of exposed skin burned. It wasn't long before I was covered with a slime of bloody, sweaty dirt. Meanwhile, my eyes were afire, as if doused with acid. Out of breath, I gasped, lungs aching. My heart felt as if it would leave my chest. Panting like a crippled wildebeest, I listened for the Escalade.

After a couple of minutes of heavy breathing, another rush of adrenalin propelled me forward. Sweat poured from every opening. Pissed off, determined not to be caught, I barged ahead. Weaving a broken trail through the corn to confuse my pursuers, I huffed and chuffed and fought for air. *Can't keep this up.* My throat felt like the desert floor in mid-August.

Finally, I stopped to listen. The roar of their engine sounded some distance to my left. Were they stuck? No. Car doors slammed. The SUV was coming closer. The sun was just settling above the horizon on my right. The Salt River should be straight ahead. Unconvinced, I hesitated. One wrong turn at this point and I was toast.

By now, I should've crossed one of the ribbon-like irrigation ditches. *Keep moving.* I parted another clump of stalks and stumbled on. Eyes half-closed to protect them from the sharp fronds, like a blind, drunken sailor, I staggered on. My legs were dead. *Remember your training, Gus. They taught you how to survive.*

And then I broke into the open and fell face down into one of the clouded canals. Ten yards wide, three feet deep, the tepid water was dark, stagnant. It smelled of rotten eggs, like loon shit from a swamp back home.

The water appeared static; I had hoped to see a flow indicating the location of the Salt River. Lost in the maze, I had to keep moving away from my pursuers.

This muddy canal could be my salvation. They'd be unable to cross over to the other side. If they had to skirt the ditch, I could hole up someplace safe. I lay in the water, rinsed my mouth, and waited to catch a breath. The roar in my ears eased as my breathing slowed. My chest hurt. *Don't stop.*

I crawled up the opposite bank, and listened. The Cadillac sounded close. Back in the corn again, I crawled between the rows on bloody knees for fifteen yards before collapsing. The truck slid to a stop at the edge of the canal. Unsure of what their next move might be, I had to get up and run again.

Car doors slammed. Someone yelled, "Can we get across?'

"Too deep. Might get stuck. Follow on foot, Edwin. We'll meet on the other side."

A younger man on foot? Okay. You've done this before. Time for the hunted to become the hunter.

"I'm coming for you, Ivy! Got nowhere to run. Make it easy on yourself. Give it up. All we want is the cover. Even give the girl back. She's no good to us anymore." I recognized the voice. It was Mullethead, Manny's killer.

Find a weapon. Keep yelling, Mullet. Show me your location. I circled around through the stalks to the canal, slid into the murky water, and paddled back until I found his tracks. Within minutes I was behind him; tracking, stalking. *Think, Gus. Don't lose the advantage.*

Mullet lumbered through the corn. I broke off a three-foot stalk with a hard, crusty root ball filled with dirt and rock. *Easy. You've got one shot.* Waiting for my chest to settle, I crept close.

Mullet stopped.

I crawled closer still.

A mere three feet separated us.

He stood with his back to me. His right arm bent at an angle. He held a gun.

Suddenly his back stiffened. He began to turn. I lunged from a deep crouch, and swung the heavy ended stalk at his head. The blow threw him to the left—down to both knees. Without pause, I skipped and drop kicked him in the forehead. Mullet yelped and fell backward, eyes rolling back as he struggled to both elbows. *Finish it, Gus . . . you know how.*

I broke the stalk in half, grasped the short end with both hands, straddled his body, and jabbed the stalk into his open mouth. I sat on his chest as he twisted and bucked, all the while gurgling like a skewered pig. After a second stab deep into his tortured throat, the corn stalk broke in two. Mullet screamed as he flailed, kicked, and grabbed at the stalk. The mangled, bloody stalk remained impaled in his maw.

I picked up his pistol and eased away. A glance behind revealed that each step left a clear imprint in the soft earth. *Damn.* I checked the position of the sun. It was on my left. *Then the irrigation canal is on my right!* Find it again, or another one; they'll lead to the river. I took a couple of deep, painful breaths and walked backward—stepping carefully into my footprints. After twenty feet, I broke off a stalk, jumped aside, and swished the new set. Satisfied, I ran again.

It took only a few minutes to find the shallow canal. I plunged in, lay down, and grabbed a shard of brittle stalk. It settled on the brown surface and slowly the leaf began to move—just the slightest bit. *Yes!* There was definitely a subtle current, flowing south. A slow crab-crawl took me in the opposite direction down the muddy waterway toward the river. My lungs ached, but each breath meant I was that much closer to freedom.

All at once, I heard the sound of someone crashing through the corn on my left. If they followed my tracks, they should get confused and head back the other way. I needed to stay hidden until dark. Down the canal took me away from danger.

Fifteen minutes passed. My heart stopped as a familiar sound reached my ears. I froze in mid-crawl. *Dammit!* The SUV's heading this way. I slapped at the tepid water and crabbed ahead. *Where the hell's the river?*

A horn honked. Someone yelled. *Must've found Mullet.* Doors slammed. The Escalade came to life again. All eight cylinders screamed as the SUV weaved through the corn.

Traversing great swaths of the field as they went, sooner or later they'd find me in the ditch. *Hurry, Gus. Get to the river.* The engine noise grew louder. *They're right behind. Must've reached the ditch.* I'll never make it.

I tried to run, but muck sucked at each foot. Like wading in tar. *The loafers—get rid of 'em.* Each step took gargantuan effort to free myself from the gluey bottom. I left both shoes mired in the ooze. The gun slipped away. A quick search in the muck proved useless. *Keep going. Don't stop.*

The SUV couldn't've been thirty yards behind me when I stumbled against a concrete barrier. My arms reached to cushion the fall. Too late. Both shins still slammed against the top of a water control device used to flood the canal.

I slid over the rim and dropped down the far side. Momentum propelled me head first into the Salt River. Under water too long, I opened my mouth and swallowed brackish river water. *Move your arms. Kick!* With a last burst of energy, I reached the surface, gasped for air, and laid my head back. Floating on my back, face exposed, I treaded water and waited for my lungs to fill.

Now what? Relax. Think they'd expect me to drift downriver, so go the other way—up stream. Setting out across the river was an option, but foolish. *Never make it.* Each arm weighed twenty pounds. *You can do this. It's not far.* I took a deep breath and swam upstream. The current proved strong, my progress slow, but by sticking close to the bank, I could pull myself along. I hoped they wouldn't be able to spot me.

When I could go no farther, I heaved my tired, battered body up on the bank, and crawled into the corn. I was spent. This was it. If they found me here, tough shit. End of the road. Have it out right here. I was exhausted.

Come on, you bastards. Let's get this over with.

Twenty-Two

I ROLLED OVER ON MY BACK and looked up through the dried stalks at a clear blue sky and wished I was up there with the birds. The sun had dropped, and as my breathing eased, I felt chilled. Shivering from both exhaustion and fear, I hugged my chest and closed my eyes. Time slipped by.

I've messed up. Another wrong turn. Underestimated these guys. How many are there? My head's under water. Can't breath! Blood . . . from my mouth, my lungs. Pushing me down. Huge hand on my head . . . down, down. Everything black as coal. Sudden silence. Wait! The scissors! No! Frank? I'm sorry, Frank. Not again . . . please. They're calling now. I have to go. I'm coming! Hands . . . reaching. Who? Head hurts. Ready to burst. Voices . . .

"There he is. Over here."

The motor dropped to an idle. A hand touched my bare foot. *No! Don't!*

A face stared down at me. "Easy, easy. You're safe now." The sudden wash of a bright beam covered my face. A buzz of engines drew close. I could hear the *slap, slap* of corn stalks striking metal. I finally came out of the fog as ATVs manned by deputies from the Maricopa Sheriff's office converged near the riverbank. Multiple lantern beams darted across the darkening sky. Muted shades of pink and purple were visible just above the horizon. My weary eyes focused on Venus—the first star in the western sky. *This isn't a dream, is it?* I edged up on both elbows and looked around, teeth chattering.

"Grab a blanket, Willy. Guy's freezing here."

A wool blanket was draped across my shoulders. My knees oozed puss and blood from blisters and gashes. Both hands were peeled like onion slices. I didn't care. I was safe.

"How'd you find me?" My teeth slammed together and nicked my tongue. Blood mingled with muddy slime.

"Don't know for sure. Seems someone called about vehicles tearing up the Pima's cornfield. Thought it was a bunch of kids 'til we found your van."

"Yeah, but, uh . . . way out here?" I waved my arm.

"Once we shut the engines down, we heard your moaning pretty clear. Spotted a leg—you were jerking and thumping the ground like a wounded bunny."

"What about the guys in the SUV?"

"Long gone. What kind of vehicle?"

"Cadillac Escalade. Black, new, with blackened windows. What about the guy in the cornfield?" I hoped Mullet was dead.

"Someone still out there?" the deputy asked.

"Should be, unless his pals picked him up." I quickly described what'd happened.

"We'll sweep the area. If he's still out here, we'll find 'im. Get a license number?"

"Sorry. What about the girl? Doreen?"

Another deputy stepped close and whispered in his ear. "Come on. Let's get you out of here. Anything broken?" They each grabbed an arm and lifted me to my feet.

"No. Few cut's all." I looked at my limbs; there didn't appear to be a bare spot without a cut or scratch.

"More than a few, I'd say. Happened to your nose?"

"Same guys. Another time, another place."

"Hold the boat steady, Willy. Easy now. One leg at a time."

I sat in the back of the Boston Whaler wrapped in the blanket as dusk settled over the Salt River. I wanted to know about Doreen, but then again feared the news. She was either dead or she'd been forced to go with Knorr. I prayed for her safety. The little good it might do.

The boat slowed and bumped against a long dock. My legs numb and stiff, I stepped out on to the planks like a robot.

"This way, Mr. Ivy."

"What about my van?"

"We'll bring it back later. Don't worry."

Led to a waiting ambulance, a team of EMTs checked me over. Satisfied I'd live, they released me into the care of the deputies. Tired, sore, and very hungry, I wanted nothing more than a hot shower, a warm meal, and deep uninterrupted sleep.

IT WAS PITCH DARK when the patrol car pulled up in front of my house. "Anyone we can call for you, Mr. Ivy?"

"No. Thanks just the same."

I had to let Sam out; he'd been cooped up all day. The door swung open and Sam bounded out. After a quick sniff, he greeted the others and went off to take care of business. I found a pair of sneakers in the garage and grabbed his leash.

"Guess we'll be going then. Your van should be back first thing in the morning. We'll dust it for prints and contact Agent Rodriguez. Anything else we can do?"

"Thanks, Deputy, for all your help. I'm fine now." After a brief moment of getting myself together, Sam and I headed for the park.

Fifteen minutes later, we were back. I was anxious to get into the house. A car had parked in front where the cops had just been, but I paid little attention. As we came through the kitchen door, Sam surged ahead, nails scrabbling over the tile floor. He skidded to a stop, and a voice sounded . . . a familiar, welcome voice.

"Hi, Sammy. Did you miss me?" It was Cassidy. She was back, sitting at the kitchen table. She rose from the table, and exclaimed, "Gus? What in the world?"

"Cassidy, you owe me an explanation." I really wanted to hug her, but needed to hear what she had to say. "Least you could have called. We were worried about you."

"I'm so sorry, Gus. I had to take care of something personal; something private. A phone call would've been awkward." Her eyes pleaded for understanding and forgiveness.

"I thought you stiffed me—that all you wanted was the dust jacket."

"I had every intention of bringing it back, but that is not why I left. Please believe me. I should've called and would've, but now I'm back." Cassidy's eyelids tightened and a flush of crimson colored her cheeks.

"That's it?"

"I'm sorry but—"

"I was almost killed today, and you're not going to tell me more than that?"

"I'm sorry. I can't. Not now. It was important, though and had nothing to do with our agreement. I'm asking you to trust me." The corners of her lips turned down a fraction.

Her face revealed no deceit, and she looked healthier than when I last saw her: Skin less pallid, eyes sparkling again. "That's fine. Sooner or later, Cassidy, you're going to have to tell me what's going on. Will you promise that much?"

"Yes, I will." Sadness appeared in her eyes. Something I hadn't seen before. "I promise."

If I didn't smell like a diseased camel had crapped all over me, I'd have pulled her close just to be sure she was real, that I wasn't dreaming. "It's all okay, Cassidy. It's been a rough day and I'm worn out. Tell me what's going on when you're ready. Right now, I need to stand under a hot shower for about three hours."

"You do smell pretty rank. What happened? What's this about getting killed?"

"Micah Knorr caught up to me at the airport. Used Doreen as bait. They haven't given up. They want the jacket."

She looked frightened, but quickly took charge. "Come on. Let's get you into the shower and clean up those cuts." She took my arm and led me into the bathroom. Before I could resist, she had removed my shirt and shorts. "Don't get modest, Gus. I'm a big girl. I've seen it all before," she assured me.

Too tired to argue, I stepped out of my boxers as she turned on the water. She helped me in and pulled the curtain closed. Remembering her deafness, I stuck my head out and said, "Doreen was in on it from the beginning. She was supposed to slow me down at the airport."

"How?"

"What?"

"How did she slow you down?" I stuck my head out. "Oh. Well, you've seen Doreen's act. Anyway, we got away and wound up in the middle of the Pima Reservation."

Cassidy had her arms crossed. Her mouth was turned down.

What's the problem here? Doreen? "Hang on here. Do I owe you an explanation for something?"

"Certainly not. But please tell me you weren't taken in by Doreen's transparent, tawdry come-on."

I ducked back in the shower. Let her stew a while. She's the one owes me an explanation, for Christ's sake.

After two minutes of silence, Cassidy whipped the curtain aside and said, "Are you going to hide in there all night or come out and talk to me?" A towel draped over one arm, her demeanor was demanding, stern.

After wrapping the towel around my body, I described the day's events. "Doreen admitted her complicity. Paid her ten thousand dollars to get the book from me at Havasu. When she failed, they held back half the money. Finally figured out that the book is no good without the dust jacket and sent Doreen to see if I had it."

"Did you tell her you had it?"

"I did admit to having it at one time."

Cassidy's brows rose. "And?"

"That's all. Never mentioned you had it, or your involvement." It was clear Cassidy wasn't going to move, so I finished drying, dropped the towel in a heap, and put on my bathrobe.

"And Doreen? What happened to her?"

"No idea. I have a hunch they killed her and left her behind. She had no value at that point. Come on. I'm hungry."

I fed Sammy and threw a huge steak on the grill. Two beers later, I began to feel human again. Cassidy wasn't being forthright, but in spite of my misgivings, I was comforted by her presence. I threw the steak on a platter, and we went inside. "You hungry, Cassidy?"

"No thanks. I ate earlier."

I tossed a salad, made toast, and sat down to eat. After five minutes, I managed to ask, "Sure you don't want any?" Dried toast crumbs flew from busy lips.

Cassidy smiled with her chin resting on her palm. "You'll have to repeat that, Gus."

"Oh, sorry." After a swipe with the napkin, I repeated my offer, although there wasn't much left. I took a slug of beer while waiting for her reply.

"I'm fine. You go ahead and finish." She stroked Sam's head and looked into his eyes. "You are so well behaved, Sam-I-Am."

"What was that?"

"A character in Dr. Seuss."

"Hmmm. Never had much to do with kids' books."

"I never asked you, Gus, but what do you do for a living?"

My least favorite question. "Always in the construction business since I got out of the Army."

"That covers a wide spectrum. What did you construct?" She wasn't going to let it go.

I grabbed another beer and popped the cap with my thumb. "Started out as a carpenter's apprentice. Eventually worked into my own crew. Guess I've built just about everything over the years."

"Did you graduate from college?"

She was clearly puzzled by my career choice. "No. Dropped out, and the Army grabbed me."

Cassidy straightened up. "That would have been when? 1968?"

"Sixty-nine."

She must've seen something in my eyes. "Vietnam?"

"Yes. Two tours." The memories came flooding back, but this time it didn't seem quite so bad. Sam came over as if sensing my discomfort, and he leaned against my leg. *What is it about this woman?*

"If this makes you uncomfortable, Gus, you don't have to continue."

I finished my beer and dropped the bottle in the wastebasket. "Normally I don't like to talk about that period of my life, Cassidy. It was an ugly war."

"Is there any other kind?"

I shrugged at her retort. "A war we had no business being in then! A war we couldn't win. Ho Chi Minh knew we'd tire first—and we did. A lot of good boys were lost."

"E-Even the ones who came home?" she asked.

She was quite perceptive—and empathetic. Carelessly, I said, "Only good thing to come of it was my brief time with Abby."

Her eyebrows rose as one. "Abby? Was she someone you met over there?"

"No. My partner. A two-year-old yellow lab. We were part of a five-man tracking team."

"Tracking?"

"CTT. Combat Tracking Team. Military loves acronyms."

"I didn't know dogs were used in Vietnam."

"Toward the end of the war, there were over a thousand in service attached to various units. All trained to track the enemy."

"And you were, what?"

"I was the dog handler."

"Of course." She looked at Sam and nodded.

"Our team had two visual trackers and two cover men. All heavily armed, we were flown in by helicopter."

"To do what?"

"Find the enemy." I looked down at Sam. "Abby could smell Charlie from a hundred yards and run like the wind."

"Charlie?"

"Sorry. Slang for bad guys."

"You must have been very close to Abby. And the men in your team? What were their names?"

Enough. I'm not ready for this. "Maxie, Tyler, Joe, and Ed Tom." *There. I spoke their names outloud.*

"That's six counting you."

"No, Ed Tom was one guy's given name."

"Do you stay in touch with them?"

I stretched. *I can't do this. End it. Now.* "Look, I'm tired and it's getting late. Do you want to spend the night? We can talk about what to do next in the morning."

She looked disappointed. "I'm sorry. It's obviously painful for you to talk about that part of your life, but maybe it'd help, Gus."

"I don't think so. And, coming from you, that all sounds a bit hypo-critical."

Her face reddened. She stood and walked over to the patio door, her back toward me. A very effective retreat. I should try that.

Cassidy turned, composed now and calm. "You must believe me when I say leaving had nothing to do with you . . . or the book. If you can't accept that, then I should leave right now."

I wanted to believe her. Wanted to trust, but instead of saying so, I said, "Look, we're both tired. Stay here and let's see what happens in the morning."

"All right. I'd like that."

"Good. Come on. You can walk with us before bed." Sam headed for the door, and the three of us left the house. It was a clear, cool night. I was just happy to be at home instead of laid out in a parched field of Pima Indian corn. Talking to Cassidy was easy—cathartic, and that was confounding me. My memories of Southeast Asia had been buried a long time, but I had experienced a light sense of relief talking about it. *Careful, Gus. She still owes you.*

We returned to the house, and I helped her carry in her bag. "Need anything else, Cassidy?"

"No. You've been very kind and understanding. Trust me? For a while longer?" She rose up and placed both hands on my cheeks. "Please?"

"I have to, Cassidy."

She smiled and kissed my lips. "Me too." That kiss turned into something more. I watched her eyes as her lips parted briefly. God, she tasted good.

We broke apart. "'Night, Cashmere."

"Why are you calling me that?"

"First time I saw you, you looked so damn good in Cashmere."

"Good-night, Augustus Ivy."

Lilacs. I'll never forget that scent.

Twenty-Three

I WAS UP AT SEVEN Wednesday morning. Nightmares about the bizarre day in the cornfield dogged my slumber. My body ached. Multiple cuts burned like crazy. Happy to be alive, I wandered into the kitchen. Cassidy had started breakfast. "Hi and hello."

"Good morning. Scrambled eggs and toast be okay?"

"Perfect."

"Sam and I already had a walk," she commented.

"You want to move in permanently? Sam'd love it. So would I, actually." She hadn't seen me speak that last line, and I didn't bother repeating it

Time to consider what to do about the *Cavity* mystery. *Tap, tap.* "We need to drive up to the Navajo Nation and track down Eddie Two-Feathers. Maybe he can translate for us. Then, we should continue north to Denver and check out your grandfather's old company. I'd also like to find Bailey Greyson. If he is involved in this, I want to meet him face to face."

Cassidy buttered the toast. "All right, but first we should figure out what the titles on the back of the dust jacket are all about."

Rodriguez called at nine, as I knew he would. "Mr. Ivy?" Rodriguez was all business.

"Agent Rodriguez. How're you today?"

"I'm fine. More to the point, how are you? What is it about you? It's like you have a sign around your neck."

"You heard about last night, I gather. They're persistent, aren't they?"

"I'm not certain you've been entirely forthcoming with us, Mr. Ivy. What were they after this time?"

"Turns out the original dust jacket has a bearing on this affair. The 'book without a cover' deal. Apparently, the book's no good without the jacket. That's all I can tell you, except Doreen, the blonde from Havasu was involved again."

"How's that?"

I told him the entire story.

"And what happened to this Doreen?"

I shrugged. "Once I ditched my van in the cornfield, she stayed behind. Don't know what happened to her."

"Neither do we. We lifted a print from your van, but can't identify it yet. Might belong to Doreen."

"What about the guy in the field? Mullet?"

"Who?"

"Prittie. Knorr's guy."

"No bodies were found. If any of these guys contact you again, call me."

"I'll do just that." Doreen was history, I was certain of that. "You need anything else from me, Rodriguez? Gotta walk my dog before he craps on the rug."

"Nothing for now. Stay out of trouble. I'll be in touch."

I hung up, wondering anew about Doreen's fate.

Cassidy had been on the Internet looking for information on Eddie Two-Feathers. She had read my lips.

I looked at her. "What did you find?"

"I've got a phone number. If you're done, I'll use the phone." She attached the TTY and dialed up the relay service.

Sammy clung to Cassidy's knee, but acted strange; looked as if he was 'worrying a worm,' as my grandfather used to say. He whined and paced under and around the table as she typed into the device.

"Sam? What's the matter? Need to go outside?" I motioned toward the door, but he made no effort to follow.

"What's up with you, anyway?"

Cassidy reached out and drew him to her. He plopped his butt down and licked her hand. Not a couple of slurps but lap after wet lap. I'd seen him do this before when he licked a cut on his paw—or when he was bored.

The vet described it as compulsive boredom behavior, but this wasn't boredom.

"Sam! Leave her alone."

"It's all right, Gus. He just missed me, I think. Lie down now, Sam. I'm okay."

He slid down to his stomach, but never lost sight of Cassidy's face. *Dog's gone bonkers.*

Cassidy finished and disconnected. "Two-Feathers will see us."

"Good. Then that's where we start. I'm convinced the clues Kittridge left in the book involve the Navajo code talkers."

"Why?" Cassidy asked.

"Jack Kittridge was a lieutenant—that means he was the squad leader and would've worked very closely with Eddie. Any message transmitted would've come through Jack."

"That doesn't mean he understood the code."

"I know, but if Jack wrote home about his new friend, a Navajo, Preston may've picked up on that and want to know more. There's very little information on the Internet about the code talkers' dictionary. And what there is, is confusing as hell."

"Why?"

"Here, I'll show you." I opened up my note pad. "Their alphabet doesn't translate literally. They have three different words for the letter A, for instance. The Navajo spelling of a single letter is multi-syllabic."

Cassidy smiled warmly. "Very good, Gus."

"I did learn a few things during my shortened collegiate career." I tilted my head so she could see my lips as I wrote. "Here's an example: one of the words the Navajo's use for A—*cwol-la-chee.* Means 'ant.' *Be-la-sana* is another word for A, but means 'apple.' *Tse-nill*—still another A word— means 'axe.'"

Cassidy looked at me with her mouth open and shook he head in disbelief.

"Stay with me on this, Cashmere. The code talkers created sentences and phrases for verbal communication, but never contemplated any sort of written form of that same language. The Army code talkers were given an English word and when they verbally communicated that word . . ." I flipped through my notes and continued, ". . . Here. If the talker wanted to say the word 'Navy,' he'd say *tsah* (needle) *cwol-la-chee* (ant) *ah-keh-di-glini* (victor) *tsah-ah-dzoh* (yucca)."

"That's unbelievable."

"Right. But here's why the Japanese could never break the code: The talker could also have substituted any of eight other Navajo words, in any combination, to spell that same word, 'Navy.'"

"That sounds impossible, Gus. I mean, how could my grandparents ever have created a message that anyone would decipher? And, remember, back in the forties the average person wouldn't have access to the same information that we do today through the Internet."

"Agreed. Something tells me we still have to talk to this Eddie Two-Feathers, though. We have to drive north to the Navajo Nation, and explore other possibilities at the same time." I stood and stretched. "If you're coming with me, and I hope you are, you should return that rental car."

"Good idea." She rose and Sammy scrambled from beneath the table.

I studied her closely and marveled at her trim figure. "Is there anything else we need to look up before leaving?"

"My laptop has a card that let's me access the Internet through my cell phone provider," she explained. "As long as the batteries hold out, we should be all right."

"Okay. Here. Take my notebook. We can try to work this out as we drive. We'll have plenty of time to sort through these. Bryce left me the keys to his Suburban. I'd feel better driving it this time of year. Never know about spring storms in the high country." There seemed no need to mention the special compartment and Bryce's private arsenal.

Cassidy tensed. Her lips compressed. "Do you expect more trouble from Knorr?"

"Hard to tell, but after everything else that's happened, who knows? Sure you want to be a part of this?"

"Absolutely. Too involved to back out now. Besides, a promise is a promise. I'm in this with you until the bitter end."

That sounded almost prophetic. "Okay, I need to pack. Then you can drive us to get Bryce's truck. We'll go past the airport and drop your car."

"Ready for an adventure, Sammy?" She held his head in her slender fingers and looked into his eyes.

"Be right back. Do you have everything in your car?" Tap, tap. "Cassidy?" I repeated my question.

"Yes."

It was ten thirty when we left. We'd reach the Navajo Nation by late afternoon. My heart skipped a couple of beats as I thought about the trip ahead. One way or another, the next few days would determine a great deal. We left Cassidy's rental car at the airport and headed north out of Phoenix on Highway 17. Cassidy sat sideways with her legs tucked under her to watch me speak. I was strangely ebullient—excited, full of energy.

Sammy sat on the broad backseat. His attention focused on Cassidy.

I thought we had plenty of time. "We're in good shape, Cashmere. Here, I printed this map."

She hadn't seen me speak. "I'm sorry . . . oh, good. A map."

"When we reach Flagstaff, we'll pick up 89 to Tuba City. How'd you find out where Eddie lives?" I was learning to tilt my upper body forward to get her attention.

She twisted and said, "The list I got from the Veterans Administration showed his last known address as the Navajo Nation. I found a Nantan Two-Feathers in Rock Point, Arizona, on the Internet. The search listed his age as eighty-three which seemed about right."

"You speak to him?

"No. His wife. She asked a lot of personal questions about me, which was strange. Anyway, when I explained who I was and why I wanted to see Nantan, she had her grandson give me directions. They live on a ranch on the northeast quarter of the Nation."

"What kind of questions?"

"Uh, she wanted to know my age, if I was married or had any children."

"Anything else?"

She hesitated, licked her lips, and was about to say something more, but didn't. She finished with, "No. That was it."

I had an opening to ask something I needed to know. "Were you ever married, Cassidy?"

She smiled. "No. In a few relationships, but somehow my deafness always interfered." A touch of sadness sounded with that last comment.

"Too bad. You deserved someone in your life." And a couple of lonely souls were we . . .

We were both quiet after that. I kept a watch in the rearview mirror and studied the road behind us. It was empty, but Micah Knorr was never far from my thoughts. Frustrated in their attempt to decode Bower's book without the dust jacket, I was convinced they'd try to find us and finish what they'd begun.

I glanced at Cassidy. Her safety was something I had to consider. The thought of having to use Bryce's weapons was more certain now than ever. I'd left combat and killing behind me so many years before, but I believed I'd killed Mullet just yesterday. If it came to a confrontation, I knew I would respond. But, how would Cassidy react?

Twenty-Four

ASSIDY SPUN AND FACED ME. "Gus, did you jot down that Shakespearian quotation?"

"Second or third page, I think."

She flipped the pages, found it, then opened her ThinkPad. "'There is a tide in the affairs of men, which taken at the flood, leads on to fortune.' I'm using a thesaurus. "Here's a variation of tide. 'Flood tide: a favorable occasion; an opportunity.'" She looked at me expectantly.

"I like that . . . as an invitation."

"I agree. Let's try taken. 'Encountered, catch, discover; appropriate for one's own benefit; a quantity collected at one time, especially for profit.'" She looked at me again.

"Keep going, Cassidy. I think you're onto something."

"'Fortune: extensive amounts of money; wealth; fate; destiny.'"

"Money and wealth sound right," I said.

She watched my lips. "Yes, but destiny might have a bearing as well. How about affairs: 'Transactions; occurrence; personal business.'"

"There's definitely a theme here."

She nodded. "And finally, 'flood: overflowing of water on to land that is normally dry; excess; deluge; surge.'"

"That doesn't fit."

"Well, it does relate to 'tide.' Here's everything, then: 'A favorable occasion; an opportunity; discover; a quantity collected at one time especially for profit; extensive amounts of money; wealth; occurrence; excess; deluge.'"

"Sure sounds like a summons to search for something of value, doesn't it?"

"I think so." She turned away and stared out the window.

I drifted off, imagining all sorts of things beneath Preston's rainbow, but reality intruded. I gently touched her shoulder, and when she looked at me, I said, "Hope is an abusive mistress, Cassidy."

"Where did that come from?"

"Not my words. I get a daily poem from our local public radio station sent as an email. Every now and then a particular line sticks."

"Hmmm. You are definitely more than you appear, Augustus Ivy."

Not really. I studied the surrounding bleak, arid landscape. Like giant brooding animals, saguaro cactus dotted the hardpan for miles in every direction. How could anything sustain itself in this climate? Hell, average rainfall is less than a foot a year. Whatever lives out here must be tough as nails. I checked the rearview again but saw nothing alarming.

Cassidy opened her folder and withdrew a piece of paper.

"What's that?"

"Grandfather's letter to Charlie Company. 'Study the words,' he said." I've read this a hundred times. I'm convinced it's a call to every member of that company to read grandmother's book twice. 'First for enjoyment. Secondly for direction and content.' Direction. Content. Words. It's all right there, I'm sure of it."

My pulse jumped as I considered what she'd said. "Kittridge created a difficult puzzle. He tried to entice the reader. He wanted them to understand it would be worth their time to unscramble his message."

Cassidy's eyes glistened. She threw both arms on the backrest, her chin rested on the top arm. "You know, we could be just hours away from finding Grandfather's fortune." Her voice was sanguine.

"Baby steps, Cashmere. Remember the mistress. We still have a ways to go."

Her face clouded and the corners of her mouth dropped. "I know. Still fun to dream."

"Okay. Just for fun, then. If we find a zillion dollars, what'll you do with your share?" This was the first time we had addressed this subject.

"I've been afraid to think too far ahead. As you know, father left me a sizable estate, so if there's a fortune, it won't mean a great deal to me."

"What then? I mean, why're you doing this?"

"Good question. Father left a portion of his estate to the National Foundation for the Hearing Impaired. I've included a bequest in my will to that same group. There's so many others not as fortunate as me, so it's important I help any way I can."

Cassidy was rapidly restoring my faith in her motives. "So, you'd do what?"

"I'd give any money to Gallaudet College." She turned and gazed out the window.

I tapped her shoulder. My fingers rested there. Something about being close to her—touching her, proved intoxicating. "Your years at Gallaudet must've left a distinct impression on you."

"It did. They did. I gained so much working with those children, Gus." She hesitated, then said, "Your turn."

"Hmmm. I admire your philanthropy, Cassidy, but can't admit to the same selfless purpose. I'm driven by the mystery Kittridge created—the quest itself. My father once said there were two types of people: givers and takers. You are clearly the former. I, on the other hand . . ." *This is serious introspection. Too serious. All meandered speculation anyway.*

"I don't believe that, Augustus."

"Yeah, well so far, all we have is an old book, an attractive and provocative wrapper, a series of hazy references that might be construed as clues, and a unified resolve to unearth a heartbroken old man's dream." In the end, maybe that would prove to be the only story told.

The next hour was spent in silence. I was feeling more pensive than I had for a long time. The more I thought about it, the more I realized that financially I didn't need much. Without a family of my own, what did I need? Besides, if it's unearned wealth, it wouldn't count for much. "Emerson said: The first wealth is health." Cassidy was poking around on her computer.

She looked up and smiled. "Did you say something?"

"Nah. Nothing important." Sammy snuffed in my ear, and I elbowed him back. He sat down with a disgruntled *gruummph.* Tap, tap. "You need to stop, Cassidy?"

"I could use a potty break, yes."

"Sedona's just ahead. I have to get gas and let Sam out."

Cassidy stretched, closed her laptop, and said, "Good. You hungry?"

"I am. What're you up for? Drive-thru or should we go in and sit down?"

"Can we go in and eat? I'd like to stretch my legs."

I nodded and pulled into a Holiday Station. "How about that restaurant next door?"

"Perfect. Think I'll walk with you guys."

"Great. Sammy'd probably follow you right into the restaurant anyway. Never seen him become so attached to another person. It's weird."

"I told you. He senses my disability," Cassidy offered.

"Come on, Sam." I opened the door and stepped out into a totally different climate. "Wow." This was high desert country. "Thirty degrees cooler up here. "Better grab a jacket, Cassidy."

Sam hopped out and waited below Cassidy's door. She stepped out, walked around back, and pulled out a light green nylon jacket. Once she slipped it on, we hiked over to the field.

"By the time we reach Flagstaff, the elevation will be seven thousand feet," Cassidy offered. "This is marvelous. I love the fact we can see Ponderosa pine again."

We waited for Sam to find an appropriate spot to take care of business. "He's kind of a private crapper," I offered apologetically.

"Nothing wrong with a little modesty, even in a dog. A true gentleman." Cassidy smiled. "He's such a nice dog. Do you hunt with him?"

"Used to. Not anymore."

"Why?"

"Figured I'd shot enough birds in my life. Didn't enjoy killing things anymore. 'Though the boys throw stones in sport, the doves do not die in sport, but in earnest.'"

"I'll bite. Who said that?" she asked.

"Plutarch."

"Hmmm. I like that quote, a lot." She was close. Her scent dizzying. She stood on her toes and kissed me. "Good for you."

"Come on, Sam. We're hungry."

Once Sam was back in the truck, we walked over to the restaurant. As we crossed the lot, I felt the hair on my neck stand up, a response acquired in the service that had saved my life more than once. Someone was watching. I looked around. Over there . . . the brown Taurus parked by the Holiday Station. I studied the sedan. I'd seen it on our drive north. The driver remained seated.

"Gus?" Cassidy tracked my gaze across the lot to the sedan. Her brows rose, then she looked at me.

"Thought I'd seen that car before. Probably nothing. Come on. Let's eat." *And if he's still there when we leave?*

We entered, sat down in a booth by the window, and looked at the menu. Cassidy sat across from me. A waitress took our order. "Any more ideas about what we've gleaned so far, Cassidy?"

"Here's what we know for sure—what we think is for sure: Grandfather left a number of hints that the book is more than it appears. Agreed?"

"Yes."

"Okay." She withdrew the notebook. "On the last page of the book is one final attempt to entice the reader: an invitation to study the reverse side of the dust jacket. Listen: 'Books you will surely want—some you have always wanted.' Then, 'it is a selected list, valuable fiction.' A strange choice of words. And then there's this: 'every letter, word, paragraph, and page has been carefully constructed by the author to offer a truly memorable, worthwhile journey—into the world of fiction and dreams.'"

The waitress brought our order, but Cassidy wasn't finished. "There are some key words here: wrapper, surely, always, selected, valuable, journey, dreams. And the sentence about every letter, word, paragraph, and page is critical."

"I'm with you. And, the three titles on the back of the wrapper are bogus." I bit into my burger.

Cassidy turned both palms up, looked out the window as if searching for an answer, and replied, "But what do they mean? Grandfather embedded a coded message, but we still haven't found the key to unlock it." She studied her salad. Poked at it without interest.

"Cassidy? What?" She didn't see me speak. I tipped down and caught her eye. "Cassidy? We'll figure it out. Finish eating. Maybe this Eddie can help." We were deep into a maze without a clear path to the end. If Eddie Two-Feathers couldn't help, then what?

When we left the restaurant, the brown Taurus was gone. "Should have gotten the license plate." I asked if she'd seen it.

"No. Wrong color for an Arizona plate, though. Probably some salesmen taking a break," Cassidy offered. She shivered. "Brrr. Feels like it might snow."

"Could be right. Certainly at a high enough altitude. Hope not, though. No boots." We climbed into the Suburban. Sam reached out with his front feet on the edge of the seat and licked Cassidy's ear.

"Hi, Sammy. Yes, I missed you, too." She reached back and scratched his ear.

"We should stop and buy some winter clothes. Coats, boots, gloves," I said. "We didn't exactly come prepared for a spring snowstorm."

Cassidy didn't hear me. She was busy with her laptop.

I decided to wait until we reached Flagstaff. For the next twenty minutes I studied the scenery. A combination of piney woods, barren tundra, and high studded plateaus, it was the kind of scenery an artist would try to replicate and never succeed unless his name happened to be Russell. A bank of mountains framed everything. A glance in the rearview soon brought me back to now. A flash of brown appeared then vanished. The Taurus.

Cassidy's reaction at the restaurant puzzled me. Seemed a bit too quick to dismiss the sedan. Bryce might have questioned if she had a hidden agenda of some sort. Impossible. *Wait. Think it through.* If someone's tailing us, who else would have tipped them about where we were going? My mood soured.

We approached the outskirts of Flagstaff. I pulled into a Target store and parked. I grabbed a jug of water and poured a small amount for Sam. When he was finished, Cassidy and I went inside. We separated and within fifteen minutes we checked out loaded with heavy coats, gloves, boots, and hats.

As we were leaving the store, Cassidy said, "I'll meet you in the car. I have to make a phone call. Is that all right?"

"Sure. Here, let me take your bag for you."

"Thank you. Won't be a minute." She handed me her bag and headed over to a pay phone.

As she walked away, I wondeered who she'd be calling. Seems like we needed a heart-to-heart. I had to know where she'd disappeared to the other night. Her veracity was still in question.

She returned in a few minutes and offered no explanation about the call. "All set?"

"Anything I should know about your call?" She read my lips.

"Oh, I promised a friend I'd let them know where I was. That's all." She sounded cheery.

My first thought was whether the friend was male or female. *What the hell is that all about? Jesus Christ, I was acting like a jealous high school suitor. This is like high school.*

Once we'd gotten resettled in the car, Cassidy opened her laptop. Silky amber waves molded the left side of her head as she leaned forward to remove her jacket. She fastened her seat belt and settled back. Sooner or later, kiddo, you're going to tell me what's going on. Either that or we go our separate ways.

I again stared in the rearview looking for the Taurus.

Twenty-Five

OUR JOURNEY TOOK US north on Highway 89 to Tuba City, a burg badly in need of reconstruction. It was a depressing small town, just like many similar reservation towns in northern Minnesota. I remembered a line about ghost towns from a Max Brand western: "Where other people decided not to be." We whizzed right through without stopping.

"Look at all the dogs," Cassidy exclaimed.

"I noticed that, too. They're everywhere." Numerous packs roamed the outskirts of town. "Good thing you're in here, Sammy. They'd tear you to pieces and have you for supper."

Sam stared through the cold glass and appeared to have no interest in investigating the scrawny animals. We picked up Highway 160, and by two-thirty that afternoon, passed through Kayenta. We'd been driving through the Navajo Nation for quite some time. Kayenta was twenty-five miles from Utah on the north, and seventy-five miles east of New Mexico. The landscape looked like the South Dakota Badlands, but at a much higher elevation. The sun had burned everything jackrabbit brown, while off in the distance dense green alpine forests and tall, snow-capped mountains reached into the sky. It was the Old West, and reminded me of the cover of the *Cavity* book.

I waved at Cassidy. "Can you check the weather on your computer?"

"Sure. Just a minute." She tapped a few keys. "Good thing we stopped. Sixty percent chance of snow tonight, forty tomorrow."

"Ouch. Well, we should be okay with this Suburban. Keep your eyes open for Highway 191. Have to turn south there." I stole another glance in the rearview. Cassidy must've seen it.

"Gus?" She turned and looked behind.

"Every once in a while I think I see something, but then it vanishes. If someone's following, they're doing a good job staying out of sight. How far's Rock Point?"

"Maybe thirty miles."

"You have directions to Eddie's place?"

"No. He lives on a small ranch near Rock Point, along the Chinle Wash, they said. We'll have to stop and ask for directions. Better change your watch. It's three-thirty, Central Standard Time. We're out of the Mountain time zone."

I handed her my watch. "You mind?"

She looked at the inscription on the back of the watch. "Who's 'JBI?'"

"My dad."

"Looks like this has been through a war."

"It has. More than one." *Move on.* "We need to get there before dark, Cassidy. Not many motels around here. Hate to drive through these mountains in a snowstorm." We came to the intersection of Highways 191 and 160. Cassidy pointed out the turn. We drove along with a deep ravine on our right—the Chinle Wash.

"Wonder what they do for a living around here?" Tap, tap. "Cassidy?" I repeated my question.

"Wikepedia says it's grazing country—cattle and sheep. Tourism has a small impact. There's a ski area in Mesa Verda National Park. I'd imagine the ski industry is important to them."

"Here's Rock Point. Let's stop at the Amoco station." There was only one set of pumps—Full Service. A fellow in his forties came out and stood next to my window. Navajo, I guessed. He wore a black felt hat, a red kerchief, and a bright red-plaid wool shirt.

"What'll it be, folks?"

"Fill it up and check the oil, please. We need directions, too."

"Let's get the gas started, then I'll see if I can help." He opened the flap and uncapped the tank. Soon the nozzle spilled fuel into the Suburban's thirty-gallon tank. "Now then, what're you looking for?"

"Do you know Eddie Two-Feathers?"

The attendant stepped back and looked in the rear window. "Why?" His eyes pinched. He looked fretful.

"We'd like to talk to him. Can you give us directions?"

"Sorry to sound so gruff, but I'm not sure Nantan wants any more visitors today."

"Nantan?" Good work, Gus.

"No one's called him Eddie in years. Took back his Navajo name when he returned from the service," the attendant said.

I repeated his words for Cassidy.

"We don't intend to cause Nantan any trouble. We called ahead. Spoke to his wife. They're expecting us. This is Cassidy Kittridge. If Nantan knew we were here, he'd want to see her."

The Navajo crouched, studied Cassidy briefly, rose, and said, "Sit tight. I'll make a call." He walked back into the building.

"Do you suppose Knorr got here before us?" Cassidy asked.

"Possible. Could've tracked Eddie down just as easily as we did."

The attendant returned. "Sorry, folks. Nantan had some trouble this morning, and well . . . I'll let his grandson tell you about it. He said 'Nantan would welcome a visit from the granddaughter of his friend, Preston Kittridge.'" He gave the directions.

"Thank you." I handed him my credit card. Once I signed the slip, I drove back the way we'd come. "Must've driven right by their road." Ten Miles outside of Rock Point, we spotted a sign that said Niyol Cha'tima. We tracked a narrow trail in the hardscrabble across the mesa. The trail meandered for a mile or so and soon we came across a large herd of sheep grazing on either side of the road.

I was reminded of some of my favorite westerns. "Boy, if this isn't a throwback to a hundred and fifty years ago."

"These buttes are spectacular. Other than those—with the pine forests and mountains beyond—this could easily be Montana. Feels like home, Gus."

We came up over a small rise. The ranch sat in a broad meadow. The main house was constructed of pine logs and looked hand-hewn. *The genuine article, I bet.* The main house sat among a number of outbuildings and corrals. An ancient dwelling with pine-slab siding weathered to a gray sheen stood off to one side. "Wonder what that is?" Tap, tap. "Cassidy?" I pointed.

"Probably a hogan. And over there on the hill? Bet it's a sweat lodge."

"What's it for?"

"Sweat," she teased and laughed. "Cleansing,"

"Like a sauna?"

"Think so—more for the spirit, though."

We drove around the circular path and stopped in front. A porch ran the length of the house. A small black-and-white dog crept out from beneath and approached our truck. She sniffed all four tires, backed off, and stood wagging her tail.

"Oh, oh." Cassidy straightened. "We gonna have trouble with Sam?"

"Doubt it. He's a wimp. Besides, I think the border collie out there is a female. Nice looking dog. Looks pretty old." I reached for the door handle and hesitated. My heart thrummed against my ribs. It felt like we were about to take a step back in time. I wondered what the next few hours might reveal.

Twenty-Six

WE GATHERED ON THE PASSENGER side. Two additional dogs—younger—darted out from a barn and headed our way. Sammy assumed a tall posture, with his tail arced over his rear quarters. The three smaller dogs checked out his sex, sniffed at his nose, and circled him on tiptoe. None of the four dogs evidenced any sign of aggression and within seconds the juveniles ran back toward the barn.

Sam stood next to Cassidy. The small black-and-white female nestled against her other leg. "You're the Pied Piper of dogs, Cassidy." She was facing the house and didn't hear me.

The front door creaked open. An old man with long flowing white hair stepped out, accompanied by a small gray-haired woman who held his arm. He had on a black felt hat and a bright blue-checked shirt that looked like velveteen. He leaned on a gnarled wooden cane and shuffled to the railing. Hard to tell the age of either one. She wore knee-high moccasins, a pleated white cotton shirt, and a skirt with a concho-belt sash. Numerous strands of beads adorned her slim neck, and her head was covered with a shawl. She was beautiful.

Cassidy stepped forward and approached the porch. "Mr. Two-Feathers? I'm Cassidy Kittridge. It's a pleasure to meet you." She climbed three steps and paused in front of the old man. He looked at her face briefly, then down at her feet.

"I am Nantan, spokesman of the Navajo. Preston Kittridge was a great friend to Nantan. You are welcome here." He stuck out his hand.

Cassidy followed his lead. They did not clasp hands—merely touched palms. She turned slightly and said, "This is my friend, Gus Ivy." She waved me close.

"Thank you for seeing us, Mr. Two-Feathers. I'm happy to meet you." I joined her on the porch and extended my hand.

The old man looked somewhere near my chin. "Welcome." He brushed my palm. "Friend of Cassidy Kittridge is friend of the Navajo."

Nantan nodded to the woman at his side. "Wife, Orenda." We all touched palms. Two men appeared from the barn, both carrying rifles. We watched as they drew near. The taller of the two spoke. "I am Sike, grandson of Nantan. This is my cousin, Bidzil."

We greeted one another. Nantan pointed at Sam with one leathery hand and surprised me with, "Dog. He kill sheep?"

I smiled and replied, "No. He's afraid of sheep, I think."

"Good. This no place for sheep killer."

I glanced at Orenda and noticed she had not broken from a hard stare at Cassidy. The old woman squinted. Worry lines furrowed her brow.

Sike moved to the old man's side. "I apologize for the rude welcome." He showed his rifle. "But, we had other visitors this morning. Had to chase them off."

"Who were they?" I asked, half certain of the answer.

"Don't know for sure. Three men from the city. Nasty. Disrespectful. Said they wanted to buy a book grandfather had. One he received as a gift from Preston Kittridge."

"What happened?" Cassidy asked.

"Sike, this is rude. Please invite our guests inside." The old woman finally spoke, but her eyes never left Cassidy.

"Yes, of course. I'm sorry. Please." He gestured with his arm.

The old woman helped her husband through the door. Cassidy followed.

"I'll be right in. I want to give Sam a little walk first. "Sam. Here, boy." He was reluctant to leave Cassidy's side, but finally edged away as she went toward the door.

"What's the old dog's name, Sike?" Cassidy asked. She made sure she faced him when she spoke.

"Skunky," he replied. "She's too old to work now. Not much room on a sheep ranch for an old dog. I'm afraid her days are numbered."

I didn't like the sound of that, but didn't feel it was my place to interfere.

"You don't mean that this sweet old dog is going to . . . ?"

"Hard life out here, Miss Cassidy. Everyone has to pull his own weight."

Skunky seemed to know that Sike had spoken ill of her; she slithered around behind Cassidy as if to be invisible. "Can she come in the house?" Cassidy asked.

"No. Dogs stay out. Come. Please," Sike offered.

I walked off with Sam. Skunky soon followed. The two old dogs nosed one another, then Sam licked her ear. Skunky wagged her tail, bounded off, and looked back to be sure Sam followed. The two of them played around for five minutes, then Sam was back in the truck. The wind was up and a few large flakes of snow began to fall. "Sorry, Skunky. Guess you're relegated to your nest beneath the porch." She lay down on the steps, and I went in the house.

I stood inside a large gathering room. A huge stone fireplace centered the room. The kitchen lay on my right. Numerous Navajo artifacts hung on the walls. A couch and four overstuffed chairs, covered by colorful blankets, fronted the fireplace. Everyone had gathered around the hearth. Nantan sat next to his grandson. Cassidy on the sofa. Orenda in the kitchen, within earshot.

Cassidy asked, "So, when you refused to sell them the book, what happened?"

"They threatened Grandfather. One of them—tall, skinny guy with a face like a possum—waved a pistol at him."

"Where were you?" she asked.

"In the barn. When I heard shouting, I stuck my head out and saw the guy with the pistol. I ran around back and came through the house with my rifle."

"Did you have to use it?" I asked.

"No. Bidzil was here. He was armed as well. Once they saw us, they backed off."

"Threatened to return," said Bidzil.

"So you'll understand our being suspicious."

"Of course. What were they driving?" I asked.

"Ford Explorer. White. Arizona plates," Sike said.

"And there were three of them?" Cassidy again.

"Yes." He stood and took a copy of the *Cavity* book from the mantle. "Why is this so important?" It still had the dust jacket intact.

"Cassidy, do you want to explain?" I repeated his request after tapping her arm.

"Yes, of course," she replied.

For the next fifteen minutes, Cassidy recounted the history of her grandmother's book. She left nothing out, including the fact that she was Preston's misbegotten granddaughter. "So, we think the book contains a message, a message that when deciphered, will reveal the location of Grandfather's fortune—or a portion of it," Cassidy finished.

My turn. "And we hope Nantan can help us break whatever code Kittridge used. We think it has something to do with Navajo words scattered throughout the text, and may relate to Nantan's service as a code talker."

"And these other guys? How are they involved?" Sike asked.

Cassidy showed them her letter from the bank. "Bailey Greyson received an identical letter. We think he hired these people to find the book. But it's no good without the dust jacket."

"I see. Grandfather? Did you hear all that?"

Nantan sat back and stared at the ceiling. He seemed far away and remained that way for several minutes. The only sound was the crackling of wood in the fireplace. "Preston Kittridge gave me the money to buy this ranch. I will never forget what he did for me. The book was read many times. Your grandmother was a great writer, Cassidy Kittridge, but the words you speak of in the book are not Navajo. They are Lakota."

He might as well have said the words on every page were printed with invisible ink and would vanish at the stroke of midnight.

"Listen to me," the old man said. He took the book from Sike, turned to the middle and read, "*Sung manitu tan ka*. Lakota. Means 'wolf.'" He turned the page. "*Wam Blic*. Eagle. *Tolpa*. Number four. All Lakota. Not Navajo." He closed the book and looked at Cassidy.

"Nantan, do you have any idea what clue my grandfather might've left in the book, or on the jacket that would help us unscramble his message?"

"Maybe. Later. Other things to discuss first." He waved toward his wife.

My mood darkened. I had no idea what he meant and doubted that Cassidy did either.

Orenda approached in silence. Her moccasins whispered across the plank floor. She knelt next to her husband and, once again, looked directly at Cassidy. Nantan flicked his fingers in Cassidy's direction. Orenda crept forward on her knees and sat on her haunches. Her hair had a bright sheen, like the mane of a thoroughbred. She placed both hands on Cassidy's, looked up at me, and said, "What is wrong with this woman?"

Of course. No one had noticed until now. "She's deaf," I replied with a gentle smile.

Cassidy read my reply and tensed as she had read Orenda's lips.

"No. Something else." The old woman rose up on her knees and touched various parts of Cassidy's body.

"Sike? What's going on?" I asked.

"Grandmother is one of our traditional healers. Traditional healing methods are still a strong part of the Navajo culture. She's detected something in Cassidy's eyes . . . maybe her breathing. Tone of her voice, perhaps. Don't know for sure. Grandmother senses something is wrong."

I stiffened at his words. An alarm went off. The old woman had just touched on a fear I had briefly considered and dismissed some time ago.

With eyes closed tight, the old lady hummed. Her lips moved with unintelligible words. She stood and put both hands on Cassidy's head. Slowly, she moved her withered hands down to Cassidy's cheeks, chest, and finally her stomach. She startled all of us with, "Here! It is here, Nantan. Granddaughter Cassidy Kittridge must have *hozho*—tonight." Her voice was loud, commanding.

"Wait a minute. What's going on?" My voice rattled as I knelt in front of Cassidy, next to Orenda. "Does this have something to do with why you disappeared the other night? Are you sick, Cassidy?"

Tears formed and obscured Cassidy's blue eyes as she looked down at me. Her lower lip trembled. She was pale. Her fingers shook as Orenda took her hands and pressed them to her sunken chest.

"Cassidy, please tell me." Only Cassidy and Orenda had the knowledge I sought.

Orenda stood and brought Cassidy's head into her warm embrace. "Shhh. Shhh, child. Orenda will help." She stroked Cassidy's hair and addressed Nantan. "We must get ready for Blessingway ceremony . . . bring her back to *hozho*. She is very sick inside—down here." She pointed to Cassidy's stomach.

My legs buckled as I tried to stand. *Sick with what? How bad?* Concerned, filled with anguish, I reached for Cassidy's hand, anxious to hear the truth and fearing it at once.

Twenty-Seven

ARLIER CONCERNS ABOUT Cassidy's health now appeared to have real merit, and Sam's persistent fawning was meaningful. "Cassidy, please. Is this why you disappeared?"

Through a stream of tears, she said, "Yes. I'm so sorry, Gus. I didn't want you to worry."

I knelt before her once more. "What is it? Tell me. What can I do?"

She gathered herself and said, "I appreciate everyone's concern." She struggled to find the right words. "It's the same illness my grandmother had—late stage kidney failure. I left you the other night to go into the hospital. I have to have dialysis every week or so."

The word chilled me. "Dialysis?" I struggled to think what that meant.

Cassidy sniffed and dried her eyes. "It removes waste from the kidneys. Maintains chemical levels so the body can . . . function."

My breath caught. Words tumbled from my throat. "And . . . how bad is it?"

She smiled bravely. "Pretty bad. My kidneys only remove thirty percent of the waste they should." She held my hand. "Dialysis is critical."

"You could have told me." My heart was pounding. My breathing sped up.

"There was nothing you could do. I was afraid you wouldn't let me come with you. This search for Grandfather's gift . . . it's extremely personal and important."

Reluctant to ask the next logical question, I felt leaden, ten years older in a matter of minutes. "What's the prognosis, Cassidy?"

She considered her answer carefully and nibbled her lower lip. "Unknown. It could progress to an end-stage renal failure. After that, it's a matter of time. I've come to accept whatever happens, Gus."

"But, some people do . . . recover?" This was all too impossible.

"Typically in the end stage, the kidney failure is chronic. It'll never improve. So far, the doctors haven't offered a great deal of hope. Odds of obtaining a donor transplant are long." She spoke very matter-of-factly.

Our fingers laced, and I squeezed tight. "You don't know for sure, though. Neither do they, right?"

She smiled warmly and rubbed my hand. "No, they don't know for sure. Sometimes with proper diet and medication—and help from above—kidney function might stabilize and, well, who knows?"

Orenda had listened intently. "Nantan, we must call the others."

"Yes," the old man said. "Sike, you will see to this and help your grandmother prepare."

Cassidy looked just as bewildered. "What're you talking about?"

"No more talk," Orenda said. "Sike, you will ready supper for our guests." She took Cassidy's hand and pulled her to her feet. "Come with me. I will explain." She led her into an adjacent room.

"Sike? Nantan?" A glance at both revealed little. Afraid for Cassidy's life, I realized how much I cared about her welfare . . . about her.

"You are husband? Lover of Cassidy Kittridge?" Nantan asked me

Was it that obvious? "A very concerned friend, Nantan."

Nantan considered his next words. "Sike will explain after supper. Cassidy Kittridge will not be permitted to eat. She must fast for one full sun. Orenda will ready the herb tea for her. You'll be our guest until sandpainting and Blessingway ceremonies finish. That is all I have to say on that." He motioned for his grandson who helped him to his feet. Together they shuffled off into the kitchen where the old man sat down at the head of a long wooden table.

At Nantan's invitation, I followed and sat down at the table. Sike busied himself with the phone calls, then he and Bidzil prepared supper.

I didn't think I was hungry, but surprisingly enough, I devoured a tasty meal of mutton stew, complete with potatoes, onions, and turnips. A wonderful corn meal pudding followed. Nantan remained silent during supper, but

Sike was gracious enough to answer my questions, and gave a colorfully cap-
sulated history of the Dineh—the Navajo people. He told me that Navajo
beliefs and ceremonies are an integral aspect of their existence. For them, all
creatures are kin—two-legged, four-legged, winged, and finned.

"Everything in nature is imbued with a Spirit. "Guardian spirits
empower, teach, guide, heal, and assist all of us," Sike continued.
"Changing Woman, Asdzaa Nadleehe, is our most powerful spirit. She's the
personification of the earth and the natural order of the universe. She represents the cyclical path of the seasons: birth is spring, maturing is summer,
growing old is fall, and dying is winter."

"What is . . . is it *hozho*? Did I pronounce that right?"

"Yes, Gus. *Hozho* is a perfect state, where everything is in balance; an
amalgam of all that is blessed, beautiful, and without pain. It is harmony."

"And what upsets harmony?"

"Traditional beliefs hold that any act that angers a Holy Person can result
in the loss of *hozho*. For example, it is still believed that killing a bear can cause
arthritis. Killing a sand spider can cause baldness. Watch a dog go to the bathroom and you might go crazy. Kill a lizard and your heart will dry up. Yelling
at a pregnant woman can cause the baby to be deaf." A light smile creased his
lips. "The list is endless. There're hundreds of these taboos . . . and cures."

Indian lore. Wives tales. I wasn't buying it but said nothing. "What is
your grandmother going to do with Cassidy?"

Sike looked to his grandfather, and after a slight nod, answered. "You
must first understand that our ceremonies are sacred—seldom viewed by the
public. For Grandmother to volunteer to help Cassidy is unusual. With
Grandfather's permission, they decided to perform the sandpainting ceremony and Blessingway to restore *hozho*." With his fingers, Sike combed back a
shock of long black hair. "Grandmother is a *Ndilniihii*, a hand trembler; a
special sort of healer. There are also stargazers, herbalists, and crystal gazers.
Each healer utilizes a different set of chants to facilitate a particular cure.
There are many, many chants. Grandmother's chants will attempt to remove
obstacles that block the return of Cassidy's body to health and harmony."

"This is fascinating, Sike," I said. "Thank you for sharing this. Tell
me, where did you get your education?"

He smiled. "Harvard. I have a master's degree in sociology."

"What about your father and mother? Do they live nearby?"

Sadness swept over his face like a cloud before the sun. "Vietnam killed my father. Mother passed away last year."

Does it never end? "I'm sorry. Both losses must have been very painful." *Vietnam. Again, the pain.*

"Yes, it was. Especially mother. Never really knew my father. It was difficult for Grandfather and Grandmother as well."

"Do you mind if I ask the meaning of your name?"

"Not at all. It means 'strong.'"

"And the others?" I asked.

"Nantan is 'spokesman.' Orenda, 'magic power.' Bidzil means 'he sits at home.'" He smiled at the last.

Cassidy and Orenda returned. Cassidy sat down next to me and put her arm around my shoulder. Orenda beckoned Sike for a private chat in the other room.

I twisted to see Cassidy's face. "Are you okay?"

There was a calm, wistful look in her eyes. "Yes. Really. Orenda's amazing. I'm honored to be chosen. Sure like to eat some of what you've had, though. It smells wonderful. Don't look so worried, Gus. I trust these people. I want to do this. Besides, what could go wrong?"

"If it's what you want, then by all me-means . . ." my voice cracked.

Cassidy tilted her head, looked into my eyes, and kissed me on the cheek. "Thank you for your concern, for bringing me here." She rubbed at an invisible spot of lipstick. Her fingers lingered on my jaw line.

My face flushed. Tempted to throw both arms around her and hold her tight, I instead rose. "Time to feed Sam. Probably needs some exercise. Nantan? Is it all right if I let my dog out for a while?"

The old man cranked his head toward me and answered without pause. "Yes. Don't wander far. Heavy snow tonight."

"I'll stay close. Thank you for the wonderful meal."

Without thinking, I kissed Cassidy on the top of the head and motioned to Sike that I was going outside. He nodded his assent. The warmth of the old log house was swept away as a blast of wind struck me full in the face. Heavy snow forced me to duck and turn away. Skunky crept out from beneath the truck. She wagged a friendly greeting.

"Hi there, old girl. Don't you ever get to go inside? Maybe you'd like to spend the night with Sam. What would you think of that?"

I stooped and scratched her ears. She welcomed the attention, and licked the back of my hand. "Come on, let's get your buddy out here." Sam bounded out once the door opened. Skunky greeted him with a playful pose, her head and shoulders lowered to the ground. Sam sidled over, licked her ear, and the two ran off into a wall of thick snow. I grabbed my down jacket and cap and followed.

I leaned into the storm and considered all I had heard. The healing ceremony could prove to be nothing more than hocus-pocus. I doubted that hours of ritualistic chanting would have an impact on Cassidy's dreadful disease. Call me a non-believer. Similar rituals I'd witnessed in Vietnam were equally irrelevant. One thing was certain, however. We had to reach Denver in time for her next dialysis treatment. That would take precedence over everything else. However, if this snowstorm got any worse, our drive through the mountains could be very difficult—maybe impossible. "Sam? Sam! Where'd you go?" Great. Where the hell? I twisted and peered into the blinding snow. "Sam! Sam!"

I slogged through three inches of snow. Fifty yards from the house, I stumbled onto the old hogan. Yellow light filtered through three small windows. Sam and Skunky sat by the front door, both panting in the cold air. "Well, I hope you're proud of yourself, mister." He lowered his head at my scold. Skunky stood underneath his chin to defend him, perhaps deflect blame.

"Come on. I'm not mad. We're not supposed to be here. Let's go."

I snapped my fingers and Sam stood erect. He stole a look at his small friend and when he spotted my wave, trotted toward the house with Skunky. As we neared the front, I heard my name being called. "Over here."

"Gus?" It was Sike. He shielded his eyes as we came to the steps. "Where were you?"

"Looking for Sam. What's going on?"

"Orenda will take Cassidy to the sweat lodge to cleanse her spirit before the ceremony. Cassidy wanted to wait until you returned. You won't see her again until it's over."

"Sike, I hate to shed any sort of negativity on this ceremony, but if she's that sick I need to get her to a hospital."

"It's important for you to cast out all doubts, Gus. You must support her spiritually."

"Look, I understand you folks are fervent in your beliefs, and I don't mean to question your traditions, but Cassidy is a very good friend, and if anything happened because I didn't get her to a hospital . . ." I wasn't handling this well at all. Sike's face darkened. "I'll try my best, Sike, but if Cassidy had told me about her illness sooner, I never would have let her come along."

Sike turned his face skyward. "Well, it looks to me as if you aren't going anyplace tonight, Gus. Why not let Grandmother perform the ceremony and see what happens?"

I nodded. "You're right, of course." Who was I to question their beliefs? Cassidy's vulnerability had gotten to me, however, in a way I hadn't felt in a long time. I didn't know what to think anymore. "I've got to feed Sam and put him back in the truck. Then I'll be in."

"Pull your truck into the barn. It'll be a warmer," the Navajo offered.

"Thank you. Sam and Skunky have become fast friends. Is it okay if she's in there with him?"

"Certainly."

Once the Suburban was in the barn, I filled Sam's food bowl and set it down. Skunky sniffed it and began to eat. Sam sat on his haunches and waited politely. "Good boy. Ladies first." When she was finished, I refilled the bowl. Skunky laid down until he finished. I pulled out his blanket and spread it next to a stack of hay bales. Sam stepped on the blanket, pawed at the fabric to fluff it up, and curled into a clump. He looked at the little dog invitingly. She never hesitated, but trotted over and snuggled against his stomach.

"I'll be damned. You two just met . . . already you're in the sack together." I filled the bowl with water and set it down. "There you go. Snug as two bugs in a rug. Stay here, Sam. And no funny business tonight, you two." Four dark eyes returned my stare.

As I stepped outside and reached to slide the large door shut, another vehicle pulled into the yard and stopped about sixty yards from the ranch house. The truck's lights were extinguished, the motor left running. No one got out. I expected someone to disembark, but whoever was in the cab remained seated.

Twenty-Eight

THERE WAS A FLASH OF LIGHT, followed by a muffled *crack!* Reflexively, I flinched. *Jesus Christ!* A rifle shot. A second shot followed. I slipped back into the barn and dropped the bags. Sam had risen at the sound of gunfire. "Stay." As soon as he saw my open palm, he stopped. I opened the back of the Suburban, unlocked the door in the floor, and raised the lid. *Never get close enough for the shotgun.* Unfamiliar with the Ruger Mini, I opted for the Beretta and loaded it with a full magazine. My heart thumped as I turned from the SUV.

More shots rumbled across the yard, some from the house, others from the darkened vehicle. A yard light above the barn door spelled disadvantage, so I lunged at it with a long-handled pitchfork. *Pop!* The entrance to the barn fell into shadows. Still no cover between me and the shooters, however. I stepped out, closed the door, and ducked around the corner. My mouth had gone dry, while every sense rose alert, alive.

I edged around the east side of the barn, staying in its shadow. This was my only cover. I raised my arm and pointed the Beretta at the truck. Advantage me. *Shooters don't know I'm here.* I held my breath and waited.

"In the house!" someone yelled. "If you want to live, give us the dust jacket. You got two minutes! Then we torch the place!"

I willed my pulse to slow and inhaled—filling my lungs with energy. My heart slowed to a normal beat. The threat thrown across the yard was real. They were serious and had proven their dedication and ruthlessness. Now what? Too far away. I needed to get closer. *But there's no place to hide.*

I lowered myself into the snow to shorten the distance with a belly crawl. As I did, a large group of sheep meandered close to the barn for shelter. *There! That's my cover. Move.* All the lights inside the house flicked off. Where's Cassidy? In the sweat lodge?

The yard was completely dark. Once my eyes adjusted, I could see human shapes near the truck. I counted three heads. Snow swept horizontally, driven by a steady wind. My eyes blurred with icy flakes.

I stuck the Beretta in my coat and got down on all fours. Trembling like paper in a strong breeze, I crawled toward the milling sheep thirty yards ahead. More shots. *Pop! Pop! Pop!* Then a volley of answering fire from the house. Someone yelled, a surprised shout. My pace quickened toward the mobile wall of yarn. Suddenly the area was lit by an orange, flickering torch.

The sheep were upwind of me, but the nearest ones sensed my presence and began a nervous tap dance in the snow—jittery, skittish. *Shit! They're gonna scatter.* I shifted to one knee, inhaled sharply, then exhaled. I aimed at the silhouette with the torch and squeezed the trigger, but the guy moved. A lot of explosive noise but it was a miss. I pulled the trigger a second time. Then a third. And a fourth—the noise deafening to my ears, yet muffled by the storm. Additional shots came from the ranch house. Then popping sounds from the truck.

The shooter with the torch dropped into the snow. The flame burned briefly, then flickered out. The gunman didn't move, when suddenly a slug slammed into the sheep in front of me. She bawled, toppled over, and struggled to rise. The herd scattered. Totally exposed, I plopped down and tried to press my stomach into the thin layer of snow behind the wounded lamb.

Something nicked my cheek and a puff of snow flew up next to my face. A second puff erupted on my right. I raised the pistol and fired three more times, then rolled to my left. Sike and Bidzil fired repeatedly, their shots ringing with a *ping-ping*. Lead struck metal somewhere on the truck.

Someone shouted, "Let's go!" Dome lights flashed from inside the truck. Doors slammed shut. The engine roared to life. The pickup spun in the snow as the truck turned a hundred and eighty-degrees. As the tires gripped solid ground, the truck tore back down the road. I stood up and fired my last two rounds at the dark shape as it passed.

I collapsed into the snow. *Been too many years since a firefight. Jesus Christ! I'm too old for this.* The reality of the event brought a wave of nausea. Panting heavily, teeth chattering, I let the pistol slip through my fingers. I picked it up. The dogs were barking steadily from the barn. My entire body felt as cold as the hull of a Bering Sea crab boat. I had to wonder: Was mine the killing shot?

"Gus! You all right?" Sike called out

"Yes!" I managed "How 'bout you?"

"We're fine."

Sike rose up from behind a clump of low junipers. He edged toward the fallen gunman. When he reached the still form, he kicked the enemy's weapon away, toed the man once, knelt down and felt for a pulse. "He's dead!"

I shuffled over. Bidzil appeared, rifle dangling from one hand. We stared down at the bloody figure in the snow. Sike rolled him over. He was Indian, a surprise under the circumstances.

A bottle with kerosene odor rising off a rag stuffed in the end smoldered in the snow. "Know him, Sike?" I asked.

"Yes. It's Shag. Troublemaker from the Nation. Figures. We have our share of bad apples."

"Recognize the truck?"

"Probably. Shag and his bunch are known to the police. Bidzil, go make the call. Maybe they can catch 'em before they get too far away."

"Has to be Knorr's guys," I offered.

"Appears that way. Hey, you're bleeding. Let's see that." Sike stepped close and turned my head to the light.

I reached up and my fingers discovered the blood.

"Come on. Let's get in the house and take a look at that," Sike urged.

"What about this guy?"

"He's not going anywhere. Let the police deal with him."

"One of your sheep took a round in the side, Sike. I'm sorry about that."

"Don't worry about it. Worst case scenario, we eat lamb for a week. You go on inside." He trudged off toward the wounded animal.

Blood dripped off my chin and left a trail of red in the new snow. I shuffled toward the house. A muffled shot from Sike's rifle sounded behind me. My back stiffened with the realization of what he'd done. I stuck the gun in my pocket and mounted the steps.

Cassidy opened the door and rushed over. "Gus, are you all right?" Her voice shook and her eyes widened.

"I'm fine, sweetheart."

Orenda stepped close and pressed a kerchief against my cheek. "Come," she said, in complete control once again. She led me to the kitchen and pushed me down in a chair. "Hold this," she commanded and took Cassidy's hand to hold over the kerchief. She opened a cabinet and withdrew a leather package with an assortment of medical paraphernalia. Orenda wet a rag and stood before me. Her hands looked like aged paper and felt as fragile as moth wings. She lifted my chin with her free hand, removed the kerchief, and swabbed the wound.

Cassidy leaned forward and examined my face, her brow furrowed as she examined the wound. "You are very lucky, Augustus."

Oh, oh. That's the second time she's called me that. "You think?"

"It's pretty deep, maybe two inches long. You'll have a scar but that will just add to your rugged good looks." She smiled and kissed my ear. Her breath tickled, pleasantly. She straightened a tuft of my hair and stood back.

Orenda finished cleaning the wound and threaded a needle with what looked like cat gut. She dabbed on a poultice that stung like hell, then my cheek numbed. I hardly felt the eight stitches. When finished, she immediately turned her attention back to Cassidy. Then the old woman put a kettle on the stove to heat water, her eyes never wandering far from Cassidy. Within minutes, she had a special tea prepared.

"What is this?" Cassidy inhaled the aroma.

Sike moved in front of Cassidy. "It's sage, sweet grass, and cedar. For your journey. Once you've finished the tea, she'll take you to the sweat lodge for the cleansing ceremony."

I was more than curious. "Then what?"

"Water is poured over hot rocks. The steam will release impurities from Cassidy and send them to the four winds. It's really a rather pleasant experience. Grandmother will chant, and the smudging process will follow. Bundles are lit. Smoke is passed over Cassidy's body. After a while, she'll be led to the hogan for the sandpainting ceremony."

"I'm honored to be selected, Sike," Cassidy assured them all.

The old woman touched Cassidy's cheek. "We must make you well. You have a great and important mission ahead of you. But, you must find *hozho* to complete your journey. Orenda will make this possible." She finished mixing the tea and handed the cup to Cassidy. "Drink," she commanded.

Cassidy sat down at the table, and sipped the tea. She looked like a small girl whose grandmother had just handed her a cup of homemade chicken soup. Small, fragile, vulnerable, but full of trust, Cassidy willingly accepted whatever blessing the old woman had to offer.

Sike brought down cups and set a bottle of Jack Daniels on the table. He moved with the fluid confidence of an athlete or soldier. "Gus?"

"That'd be perfect, Sike."

Soon the whisky slipped past my tongue and lit a warm spark deep in my gut. Not much of a booze drinker, that cup of Jack Daniels tasted like honey.

The front door swung open. A blast of cold air blew in along with two policemen representing the Navajo Nation. The taller of the two said, "Sike, Nantan. Greetings."

"Hello, Hastiin. Thank you for coming."

"Looks like you've had quite a night."

"Indeed."

"Who are your guests?"

Introductions were made. Hastiin said, "We caught up to the others. Chased 'em down 191 and found 'em after they slipped off the road into Chinle Wash."

"Shag's bunch?" Sike asked.

"Yes. One of them was dead—thrown from the truck. The other has a broken leg, but he'll live. Confessed to everything. Said they were paid five thousand dollars to bring back a wrapper for some book. Guys who hired 'em didn't care what they had to do to get it."

"Guessed as much," Sike offered. "Same fellas from this morning. You heard about that?"

"Yes. Our deputies are out looking for that ratpack. Doubt they'll be back. Matter of time before we find the Explorer. Now, what's with this book?"

Sike rose and led him into the living room. "I'll explain everything," he said.

Orenda took Cassidy's empty cup. "Come. It is time."

"Do I need to bring anything?"

"No, I have everything ready for you, Shysie. Say good-bye to your friend." She brought Cassidy to her feet.

Cassidy studied the old woman. "Shysie?"

"Shysie is 'silent little one.' It will be your Navajo name."

Cassidy hugged the old woman tightly. "Yes. Thank you." Tears filled her eyes. Cassidy took my hand and led me into the other room.

When we were alone, I hugged her tightly. I didn't want to let her go. "You sure you want to do this, Cashmere?"

"I do. I think it's important. I'm going to miss you, though." She laid her hand alongside my face, gently fingering my wound. Her eyes studied my own. "I've grown fond of you, Augustus."

There it was again, except when she said it, trouble seemed miles away. The space between us vanished as she folded into me. I didn't want to give her up to Orenda. My legs weakened—like green grass heavy with dew. "Seems like we have something going on here, Cassidy. I'd like enough time to let it play out, you know?"

"Yes. Me too. Don't worry. I'm not letting you get away." She rose up on her toes, ran her fingers through my hair, and pulled my head down. Our kiss was long, intense. When I opened my eyes, she gave me a hug, and we drifted apart. "Bye-bye. I'll be back before you know it."

"I'll pray for you, sweetheart." The words didn't come easily. It had been a long time since my entire body felt so captivated by a woman.

Orenda approached, covered Cassidy's head with a shawl, and wrapped a blanket around her shoulders. Bidzil led them to the back door. Cassidy looked back, wiggled fingers of one hand, and they ducked into the snowstorm, the door beating an anthem in their wake.

With two hefty reservation police in the other room, one dead man in the snow outside, a dead lamb in need of proper slaughtering, all I could focus on was Cassidy and her well-being. When she stepped out that door, I knew it'd be twenty-four hours before I'd see her again. I imagined it'd be the longest twenty-four of my life.

Twenty-Nine

NANTAN STOOD AND MOTIONED for Sike. The old man leaned on his cane and said, "We will talk in the morning, Gus Ivy. Thank you for your help tonight. I will not forget that."

"You're welcome, Nantan. Good night." Sike led the old man into one of the back bedrooms.

Hastiin came over and sat down. "Sounds like you might've helped avert a real tragedy here."

"Looks to me as if Sike and his cousin can take care of themselves," I offered.

"Maybe. Shag and the others are bad dudes. They might've just managed to set the place on fire. Pretty liquored up."

"Anything more about the guys who hired them?"

"No, but there's a report of a second car in the vicinity. Closer look at the accident scene revealed another set of tracks. Truck may've been coaxed into the wash."

"What kind of car?"

"Don't know. Too dark. Passed our witness going eighty. All he could see was a late model sedan."

Hastiin asked about Knorr. I gave him a thumbnail sketch. "They have a copy of the book, but not the dust jacket." Meanwhile, I wondered if Knorr and his gang had split up, why bother to run the truck off the road? And where are they now?

"And this book? Why's it so important?"

I briefly told him why.

"Well, that's between you and Nantan far as I'm concerned. If Knorr gets himself caught, then you can continue your ahhh . . . little treasure hunt without any further interference."

"That would certainly be a relief," I replied. Obviously, he didn't believe anything good had ever come of such a pig-in-the-sky treasure hunt.

Sike returned.

"Have everything I need, Sike," Hastiin said. "If you think these guys might come back, I can leave a deputy behind."

"No. We'll be fine." He nodded toward me.

"Okay. Good luck. Keep your eyes open."

"We will. Take care." I shook his hand and Sike walked with him to the door.

Sike returned. "Hastiin says we owe you a great deal of gratitude. I agree. Thank you for stepping up."

"You're welcome, but I think you and your cousin would've done fine without me."

"Maybe. Those clowns were pretty determined. Weren't thinking too clearly, though. If they'd burned the house down, what did they think would happen to the wrapper?" Sike asked.

"Good point. Say, who're the people in the Hogan with your grandmother and Cassidy?"

"Relatives."

"Relatives?"

"Other healers on hand to help with the ceremony."

I was exhausted, but this was an opportunity to gather more information. "What's the significance of this sand painting, Sike? What's going to happen?"

"Sand painting is sacred to the Dineh. Depending on the illness, there are over five hundred different paintings that can be created. All are derived from chants—or 'ways' used to effect a cure."

"Sounds like an art form."

"It can be, but it goes way beyond that. It's an integral part of our culture."

"And the chants?"

"Each chant has a specific purpose. The Bead Chant cures skin disease. The Night Chant, nervous disorders. We have lots of 'em. Part of Grandmother's art is in the choice of each chant."

I must've let my skepticism show.

"Try and keep an open mind, Gus. Cassidy will sit in the center of the painting facing east."

"What will the painting look like?"

"Hard to say. The principal colors will be white, blue, yellow, and black. All relate to the four sacred mountains, the boundaries of our nation. Sand painting, *iikaah*, means, 'place where gods come and go.' The ceremony prepares the way for the forces of the Holy People to intercede."

"How large is the painting?" I asked.

"Four to six feet. They begin in the center and work outward in a sunwise pattern. The painting will have a protective garland around the perimeter to keep evil away. The actual design utilizes a Sacred Hoop symbolizing the circle of life—the foundation of the universe, and will incorporate the Four Powers represented by the four points of a compass."

"I heard Orenda mention something about a blessing?"

"The Blessingway ceremony completes the ritual. It's a baptism using sacred earth where Cassidy receives a final good health blessing."

I tried to mask the doubt that draped my face, and worked for a look of pure faith. It was a struggle. Weariness distorted the desired image. "What about Cassidy's deafness?"

"Chants are for the gods to hear. Cassidy doesn't need to actually hear what's being sung—she'll feel the words, and Grandmother will sign to her."

If Cassidy had developed a sixth sense over the years, I decided whatever her experience with Orenda might be, she'd likely find it exhilarating. Still . . .

Sike's dark eyes bore into my soul. "It's important that loved ones open their hearts and minds to the possibilities offered by this, Gus. Many medical practitioners have studied our sand painting ceremonies only to conclude that the results defy rational, medically-based explanation. But your support is essential." His dark brows rose like arrows.

"I apologize for my skepticism, Sike, but it's mindful of what I witnessed in Vietnam, and, well . . . most of that was hocus-pocus. However,

I promise to remain open-minded and to pray for Orenda's success. Who am I to question a tradition that has endured for centuries? I care a great deal for Cassidy and appreciate everything you folks are doing for her." My declaration was earnest and if praying would help . . . ?

"Give it a chance. That's all we ask. Now, it's time for sleep. Come on, I'll show you your room."

I picked up our bags and followed Sike to an inviting, clean bedroom with a double bed. He pointed out the bathroom across the hall and said good night.

A trip to the john offered a first look at my face. Gingerly, I washed around the wound, brushed my teeth, and fell on top of the bed. A soft blanket covered my aching body, and after a brief prayer for Cassidy, I slipped into a deep slumber.

I was awakened more than once by a sing-songy hum that went on for hours. I stood near the window. The moon shone swollen and pale and ill-formed just over the hills. The chanting became louder, the words indistinguishable, yet captivating. It was a euphonic song sounding through the cracks in the logs of the old ranch house.

Back in bed, my eyes lifted toward the plank ceiling. A circular web spun noiselessly overhead. About six inches in diameter, it looked like an ethereal spider web. Three small blue feathers dangled beneath the circlet, each feather twirling aimlessly. The web had a hole in the center, and it rotated rhythmically as melodious chants continued to drift into the room. This small wooden hoop was simple but meticulously constructed, a dream catcher as I recalled.

Unable to go back to sleep, I lay awake, studying the movements of this magical ring. Minutes might have passed—maybe an hour. I lost track. My mind felt free, as light as a soap bubble. This strange, peaceful place, although a mere bedroom, transported me to a sense of safety. A thing that hadn't seemed possible.

SOMETHING STARTLED ME early the next morning. My heart thrummed like a baby bird. Once I adjusted to the strange surroundings, everything slowed, and the memory of the haunting chants returned. I longed to return to the placid state I'd found during the night, but concern for Cassidy's health intruded.

She was so fragile, like a Barby Bunny away from its nest. And the real issue settled like a stone deep in my guts. What if she doesn't get any better? What if her condition doesn't improve, and her kidneys shut down? My eyes misted. I sat on the edge of the bed and craned my neck to watch the dream catcher spin one way, then back.

Deal with what you can control, Gus. It's outta your hands. Please, Lord. if anyone deserves to live. Please? Saliva gathered on my tongue. Be there for her. It's all you can do. Let Orenda spin her magic. I sat up and sucked air through my teeth. Still have to get her to a hospital.

I took a hot shower, shaved around the wound, dressed, and went out into the kitchen. The old man was already up. "'Morning, Nantan."

"Good morning, Gus Ivy. Did you sleep well?"

"Yes. Thank you. I heard Orenda and the others during the night. Their singing was beautiful. Did everything go all right?"

"Not known yet. Orenda will stay with Shysie for the rest of this day."

"What happens to the sand painting when they're finished?"

"It will be destroyed."

"That's too bad. I'd liked to have seen it."

"Not possible. Sands are swept away and thrown to the four winds."

"Why is that?"

"Blindness, perhaps even death would befall the transgressor. It is always removed . . . in reverse order."

"I see." Not really, but once again their ways proved puzzling.

"Would you like coffee?"

"Yes, thank you."

Sike came in. "There's a pot on the stove, Gus. Cups are over the sink."

"Thanks. 'Morning Sike. Any sign of Knorr's bunch?"

"No. Spoke with Hastiin earlier. The white Explorer was spotted north of here late last night. Highway patrol gave chase but lost it near Durango."

"Good. Maybe that's the last we'll see of them."

"If I were you, I'd be watchful of their return," Nantan offered. "They are stubborn. I don't think they're ready to abandon the hunt."

"You may be right," I said.

"I'll get breakfast started, Grandfather."

"Time to let Sam out if that's okay, Sike?"

"He's already out. Had to open the barn to get hay for the sheep. He and Skunky have become good friends, haven't they?"

"Yes, they certainly have." Anxious to find out about Skunky's future, I decided to wait. Sike's comment about her had a disturbing finality to it that bothered me. Stay out of their affairs, Gus. "Well, I'll just go and feed him and see how he's doing."

"That's fine. Breakfast will be ready in ten minutes."

I threw on my coat and stepped into a winter wonderland. Sunlight washed the landscape. At least eight inches of snow had fallen. The cedars, willows, cottonwoods, and pines weighed heavy with the thick, white blanket. The sky was bright blue, unbroken by a single cloud. The sun dazzled with a brilliance I hadn't seen in years. The snow sparkled like millions of quartz grains. I inhaled a mixture of mesquite, eucalyptus, and sheep manure. Such a silent land. Nantan and his family were very fortunate.

Mountains in the distance towered over multihued cliffs and buttes. Red-orange outcroppings, veins of yellow limestone, and peaks topped with brilliant pearl-white snow framed patches of dark-green conifers. I tracked the view for a long time, then stepped gingerly into the deep snow. My boots remained in the truck. Fortunately, Sike's footprints led directly to the barn, so I simply followed his path to keep out of the deep snow.

The barn door stood open. As I approached, Sam spotted me and bounded out along with the young pups. Skunky was nowhere in sight. They all danced around as I fought to keep out of the deep snow. "Hey, sport. You have a nice night with Skunky?" Sam leaned against my right leg for a pat. "Come on, let's get you fed."

A hundred or so of the wooly sheep clustered on the south side of the barn, soaking up the morning sun. They munched mouthfuls of green alfalfa. If they held a grudge over the previous night's assault, they gave no sign. I fed Sam, slipped on my boots, and went back to the ranch house. I scanned the yard for Skunky and finally spotted her over by the Hogan; relieved to see she was all right.

Nantan had forked a piece of fried meat as I returned to the kitchen. A wonderful aroma of fried eggs, baked bread, and crackling lard mingled with fresh-brewed coffee. My mouth watered.

"Just in time. Grab a plate," Sike said.

I served myself, then, with a fresh cup of coffee, sat across from Nantan. None of us spoke during the meal. It tasted delicious, and if I hadn't felt it impolite, I'd have loaded my plate a second time. When Nantan finished, we took our plates to the sink.

"Come. We will talk and smoke," Nantan said. He pushed back from the table. I stood ready to help him up. Nantan offered an arm, rose with some effort, lifted his cane, and shuffled with me into the living room.

Sike threw another log on the fire and pulled down a pipe from the mantle. Once it was loaded with tobacco, he handed it to his grandfather. Sike then snapped a pine twig from another log and stabbed it into the fire-box. It flared then caught fire. Nantan held the clay pipe in one hand and guided the flame to the bowl with his other. He puffed four times, inhaled, and handed the pipe to his grandson. Sike took four puffs, as did I before returning the pipe to the old Navajo.

Nantan finally spoke, "You soldiered with my son? Sike's father?"

I hadn't expected that. "We fought in the same war, yes."

He stared at me for a long time, then simply nodded. His eyes teared and he cleared his throat. "I had a vision during the night. I saw the wind moving in a circle. It blew softly upon a blushing flower with spikes like kitten tails. The answer you seek is there—in the wind and the sand, Gus Ivy."

Thirty

ANTAN'S WORDS FLOATED in my head like smoke from the old man's pipe. Wonderfully descriptive, the images evoked were poignant and memorable. Breathlessly, I prodded for more. "Where, Nantan?"

"That is not known," came Nantan's reply. "I heard laughter like many children. I have been thinking on your journey, Gus Ivy, and I've reflected on the Bower book. The answers you seek are elusive. They are humble—innocent, like children's play."

His words confounded me. "Nantan, why is it not possible that Kittridge would have used your language to hide his message?" I had to eliminate this once and for all.

"There is no passage in the book with our words," he said. "Only Lakota words. I'm sorry, but Preston Kittridge used some other method."

"And you have no idea what that might be?" I asked.

"Only what I have already told you. That is all I have to say on that."

Subject closed. Damn. I jotted down his words and realized they could form a Navajo poem or song:

> Wind in a circle.
> It blows softly
> on a blushing flower
> with spikes like kitten tails.
>
> The answer comes
> in the wind and Sand.

Answers are elusive
but humble
Innocent—
like children's play

Nantan said, "I will tell you a story."

Delighted he was not completely finished with me, I replied, "Please do."

"Long ago when the world was young, an old Navajo spiritual leader, high on a mountain, had a vision. In this vision, Iktomi, the great trickster and teacher of wisdom, appeared in the form of a spider. Iktomi spoke to the holy man in a sacred language. As he spoke, Iktomi the spider picked up the elder's willow hoop, which had feathers, horsehair, beads, and offerings on it, and began to spin a web."

I was thoroughly enjoying the old man's fable.

Nantan continued. "He spoke to the elder about the cycles of life—how we begin our lives as infants, move on through childhood, and on to adulthood. Finally we go to old age, where we must be taken care of as infants, completing the cycle.

"'But,' Iktomi said as he continued to spin his web, 'in each time of life there are many forces—some good and some bad. If you listen to the good forces, they will steer you in the right direction. But, if you listen to the bad forces, they will steer you in the wrong direction and may hurt you. So these forces can help or interfere with the harmony of nature.' While the spider spoke, he continued to weave his web."

While Nantan spoke, he made himself a rolled cigarette from crushed tobacco.

"When Iktomi finished speaking, he gave the elder the web hoop and said, 'The web is a perfect circle—attached to the hoop eight separate times, as many times as I have legs. There is a hole in the center. Use the web to help your people reach their goals, making good use of their ideas, dreams, and visions. If you believe in the Great Spirit, the web will catch your good ideas and the bad ones will fall through the hole.'"

Nantan smiled. Sike struck a wooden match and lit the old Indian's cigarette.

"The elder passed on his vision to the people, and now many Indian people hang a dream catcher above their bed to sift their dreams and visions. It is said that the dream catcher holds the destiny of the future."

The old man adjusted himself and continued, "Perhaps the answers you seek are within the dream catcher. Sike will answer your questions now, for I am tired." He stubbed out the smoke and motioned to his grandson for help.

The younger Navajo brought the old man to his feet. "You will receive a dream catcher," Nantan said. "Carry it with you, for it will show you the way." The old man's dark eyes bore into mine "Study the numbers, Gus Ivy, for they are important." His eyes had a mischievous twinkle as he spoke. A slight smile crossed his lips.

He knows the answer! Dammit, the old man knows! "Wait. What numbers?"

Nantan cut me short with a wave of his leathery hand. "You must visit Iktomi at the great Butte to seek your vision. There it will be as quiet as a spider's crawl. Embrace the quiet, for that is when your vision will appear. That is all I have to say on this."

I watched the old man shuffle off to his room with Sike. My head churned with images of spiders and webs and elusive dreams. *Why won't he tell me everything? The old man has the answer, while I'm more confused than ever.*

Sike returned. "How about some coffee after all that, eh?"

We went into the kitchen. "Sike, would your grandfather have given Jack Kittridge a dream catcher?"

"Yes. Grandfather and Jack were very close. He told me that prior to Jack's death, he made a catcher for him; one which Jack carried into battle. After his death, it was sent home to Preston along with Jack's other effects. He included a note explaining the significance of the dream catcher."

"Interesting. What about the one hanging over my bed?"

"That was mine, as a child. Smaller than an adult's, it's made of willow, as most are, but the web is cordage from bluegrass. The owl feather hanging below represents wisdom, the eagle feather courage. Children's dream catchers are not meant to last. Eventually the willow dries out and the cordage collapses. The one in the bedroom survived somehow."

"Does Cassidy have one?"

"Yes. Her feathers are of the bluebird, signifying happiness and singing."

"How are the adult ones different?"

"The web is woven from horsehair and they're slightly larger."

"Your grandfather suggested I should go to Spider Rock?"

He smiled and sipped his coffee. "Ah, yes. You've noticed Grandfather is a man of few words. It's a red sandstone butte almost eight hundred feet tall—in the Canyon de Chelly, twenty miles from here. In the old days, our people would journey there for guidance—to seek a revelation of their destiny. Many still do. Legend says that Spider Woman—one of our most sacred deities—after teaching our ancestors the art of weaving, chose the top of the butte for her home."

"Apart from that, what powers did she have?"

"The elders warned the Dine—the Navajo children—that if they did not behave themselves, Spider Woman would let down her web ladder and carry them up and devour them."

I loved that thought. "That might tend to keep a kid in line."

Sike laughed. "Yes. They were also warned that the top of Spider Rock was white from the sun-bleached bones of naughty Dine. There're hundreds of stories about Iktomi; many times she's found rescuing warriors pursued by their enemies."

"And, your grandfather wants me to visit this place?"

"I think he hopes you'll open your mind to the possibility that by being in the presence of the butte . . . of Iktomi, something might occur to you that will prove helpful in your dream search."

"Hmmm. When will Cassidy be ahhh, purified, finished?"

"Not until the sun sets."

"Kinda hate to leave her."

"You cannot see her until it's over anyway. I'd encourage you to go. I have chores to do the balance of the day, and there really isn't much for you to do around here. But before you go, Grandfather asked me to give you a gift." He left the kitchen and returned with a package wrapped in tanned hides. He set it in front of me. "Open it. Please."

Inside the bag was a dream catcher. Rawhide formed the perimeter and it was encircled with white beads. The web was woven from horsehair and between the eight main strands were hundreds of thinner fibers. A hole the size of a snuff tin lay at the center.

"The four feathers are quail," Sike said. "This is grandfather's way of thanking you for last night."

"It's beautiful, Sike. And the quail feathers mean what?"

"Cleverness."

"It seems to me that it might take a layman years of study to learn your culture." I was beginning to see the depth of the Navajo's spirituality.

He smiled his assent. "Yes. I'm still learning."

"Thank you, Sike. Will I have a chance to thank Nantan before we leave?"

"Of course. Now, let me give you directions to Spider Rock."

I quickly jotted down Nantan's final comment:

> Within the dream catcher.
> Study the numbers,
> for they are important.

I decided this would be a good time to call Bryce and Alison. I stuck my notepad back in the satchel and went into the kitchen to use the phone. Something about numbers . . . but what?

Thirty-One

SIKE AND I WERE LEANING against the Suburban. He had just handed me a package containing lunch along with a thermos of coffee. I cleared my throat. "Sike, I need to talk to you about something. There's no easy way to say this, so I'll just barge ahead. I'm worried about your plans for Skunky." I studied his eyes for a reaction. There was none.

"Continue," he said.

"Well, based on comments you made about her no longer being useful, it sounds like you intend to put her down one of these days. It really is none of my business and if you tell me to go to hell, I'll back off, but I wonder if you've considered maybe giving her to someone else."

"That's not the way things are done out here, Gus."

"I know that, but it's just . . ." *You opened the door, dumb ass, now you have to go through it.* ". . . ah, because of my own experience in the Army, I'm particularly sensitive to the plight of working dogs when they're no longer needed." I waited for Sike to comment. He did not. I was out on a limb. *Careful, Gus. Tricky ground here.* "Here's the thing, Sike. I was a dog handler, part of the Sixty-Third IPCT in Vietnam. Abby was my dog, a yellow lab, and we were part of a five-man combat tracking team. I trained her, and we worked together for over two years. Grew pretty attached to her." I stooped and petted both dogs.

Sike looked puzzled. He crouched down to the window and looked at me. "Gus? Please, go on. What happened?"

"Well, the war ended. Abby could easily've been adopted out but the Army refused. 'Too expensive to ship and quarantine,' they said. Truth was, they didn't want to bother. In the end, a thousand heroic dogs were euthanized. Abby included. She saved hundreds of lives, Sike. Mine included, but when it was over, I was helpless to save hers." My eyes clouded simply telling the story.

Sike laid a hand on my arm. "I'm so sorry, Gus."

I blew my nose. "Anyway, that's the gist of it. Haven't told that story too many times. Skunky's situation brought it all back. Anyway, I do know how things work on a ranch, and if there's any chance we could somehow adopt her, Sam and I would love to have Skunky come and live with us."

"Now I understand your concern. I'll talk to Grandfather. Let's see what he says. Now, go visit Spider Rock. I think it'll do you good."

"Sure." My emotions were raw . . . close to the surface. Being alone with Sam sounded right.

"When you get to the end of our road, turn left. Go six miles to the next crossroad and take another left. Stay on that for twelve miles. You'll run into the Butte. Can't miss it. You'll see a path of sorts. 'Bout a mile in from the road. You bring your boots?"

"Yep."

"Okay. Good luck. See you when you get back."

I reached out and shook his hand. "Thanks, Sike. For everything."

With Sam riding shotgun, I eased away from Sike. The Suburban carefully parted the herd of sheep before us. I turned left at the main road. A pair of bay-colored horses trotted alongside, then darted across the gravel directly in front of the Suburban. Five minutes later, a coyote shot across the road. I threw the steering wheel to the right and braked. *How cool is that?* Everything running free and wild. Talking about Abby with Sike had left me feeling peaceful and content. Probably should have dealt with that mess years earlier . . . seen a shrink or something. I laughed inwardly at myself. *Still haven't faced the other issue though, you chicken-shit bastard. Too busy. No, too much guilt. Never let anyone get close enough to pry— or care.*

I cracked my neck and sat straight. Concentrate on the book. Nantan said the answer was simple. Still need something to get us started, but— what? And those damned numbers.

"That must be it, Sam." A tall butte stood against a palisade of sheer cliffs. We approached the giant red monolith. The closer we got, the higher it seemed to rise into the endless blue sky. "Good Lord, look at the size of that thing." It appeared much taller than eight hundred feet. It was impressive. I spotted the turnoff and left the road.

With the truck in four-wheel drive, we crept onto the path leading to Spider Rock. We had descended into a broad valley. On either side, iron-red rock formations topped with snow formed a perfect swale. We were entering the Lost World—Iktomi's Shangri-La. After a short distance, I stopped. "This is far enough, Sam. Hate to get stuck out here." Once the truck was parked, we got out. The heavy snow from the night before had already begun to melt.

"Come on, Sam. Time for a little exercise." He leapt out and held his nose high, testing the air. Soon he sniffed like crazy and headed into the scrub. "Stay away from the porcupines." I locked the truck, and we set off down the path. Sam trotted ahead, but stopped frequently to check out scraggly yucca plants and withered evergreens. It was very quiet. Too quiet, the air heavy and still—venerable came to mind. We were trespassing in a world that belonged to others.

The only sound was the wind as it caressed through stunted ponderosa pine and worn-out junipers. The stillness felt like an invisible wrap of cellophane. The colors I had seen from a distance now filled my view. Yellowed limestone with many different shades of brown and tan blended perfectly with the bright reds and oranges of the larger rock structures.

I paused every few minutes to take it all in. This was truly a magical place. We could easily have been the first to stumble on the numbing beauty of this quiet valley. Suddenly, a high-pitched screech filled the canyon. A pair of red-tailed hawks, like sentinels, circled high above the tallest buttes. Their voices announced our arrival, reverberating and echoing over this wonderful place. The loud call of the raptors was oddly comforting. Although we had a visitor's pass from Nantan, I felt we were somehow intruding on sacred ground.

It took fifteen minutes to reach the base of the towering pinnacle. The sun burned high, the temperature already oven-lined. I removed my coat. Sammy flopped down and gulped mouthfuls of snow; his tongue lolled and he panted heavily. I found a large flat rock, swiped at the small amount of snow that still clung to the warm surface, and sat down. I craned my neck and leaned back. The butte was awesome. It looked like a Gotham City monolith—without windows.

A sheer rock face from bottom to top, it appeared to be about a thousand yards in circumference. I lay down and pillowed my head on my coat. With the sun slightly behind, I could look straight up into the sky. The hawks continued their play—around and around in endless circles. Every so often they caught a warm updraft and floated ever higher. I thought how marvelous it would be to be able to fly so effortlessly. Before long, the hawks dipped and lighted on a small outcropping near the top. *Wonder if they have a nest way up there?* Probably too early for that—but in a month or so? I envied their freedom.

I shifted my gaze and spotted Sam trotting off into the scrub. He stopped once and looked back. "It's okay, Sam. Go ahead." I resumed my meditative attitude and closed my eyes. A warm breeze slipped over me. The sun crept even higher until it was directly overhead. All sound ceased to exist. I imagined a delicate, finely spun ladder that ascended the face of Spider Rock. A small voice beckoned from above. Barely a husky whisper, I imagined the voice of Iktomi—spider woman, teacher of wisdom. "It is time to trust, Augustus. Open your heart and all pain will go. Then you will know." Her voice faded.

Time passed. It seemed like hours, but proved later to be mere minutes. I could have remained there for the entire day, and might have, if not for Sam, whose wet, slimy slurp woke me.

"Hey, cut it out." I pushed him off with a forearm and opened my eyes. My first thoughts were of hawks, and the wind, and spider webs. There was no connecting thread—no coherent story, just random images that vanished quickly as the fog in my brain lifted. I sat up and rotated my head to release the kinks.

"You hungry, Sammy? Let's see what Sike packed." I opened up the bag and withdrew a lamb sandwich made with corn bread. There were celery sticks and dried chips of some sort. Everything was perfect. I sipped a cup of strong coffee while Sam gobbled up the scraps. A number of small birds appeared, accustomed now to our presence. Black-capped chickadees sang, *dee-dee-dee* in time with their restless movement. A flock of pine siskin chirped and swarmed in collective safety. A pair of nuthatches tipped over on a lanky pena in their upside-down view of the world. Blue jays, meadowlarks, and brown sparrows darted every which way as they located bits of food revealed by melting snow. The entire experience felt wonderful. If I live to be a hundred, I'm certain there will never be another day like this.

And then, as if an alarm sounded, silence fell like a heavy blanket over the neighborhood. I looked skyward. The hawks were up again; this time it appeared as if they were on a different sort of mission. One of the pair—the tercel, broke formation and hovered in one spot. As air released from beneath its wings, he dove toward the earth. His dive continued and just when the bird achieved full thrust—just when I thought it would crash into the rocky ground—it spread its wings. In a brief flash, the hawk dropped its talons and struck. With a chipmunk firmly grasped in its talons, the male alighted in a dead pine tree.

I wished Cassidy could be here to share the beauty of this place; its magic and spirituality imprinted itself on my soul. The thought of her made me anxious to return. "Come on, Sam. It's getting late."

I gathered our stuff and headed back to the Suburban. Far above us, the female had joined her mate on the old tree. He promptly ripped off a piece of flesh to give to her. I looked directly at the male one last time. He returned the stare. We were connected, the hawk and I, but I didn't know quite how. A strange sense of sadness settled over me as I took one last look at Spider Rock. I knew, with absolute certainty, I would never return.

Thirty-Two

WE PILED INTO THE Suburban and drove away from Spider Rock. Halfway to the ranch, I noticed a car following some distance behind. My heart skipped a beat as I tapped the brake. A slash of brown showed, then the car vanished behind a curve. It was the Taurus. I slammed on the brakes and twisted the wheel. *Let's find out who this asshole is.* With the truck in reverse, I backed up, then spun the wheel again.

The Taurus made the identical move and sped off in the other direction. I put the truck in drive and stabbed at the gas pedal. The oversize tires scrabbled for traction, and the SUV fishtailed for thirty yards. The big engine roared. My knuckles tightened on the wheel. Within seconds, the gap closed. I was gaining on the smaller sedan. I leaned over and withdrew the Beretta from the glove box.

Suddenly I heard a loud explosion, and the truck skidded. "Awww, shit!" I fought the wheel as the SUV aimed for the yawning ravine of Chinle Wash. Too late. The canyon was directly in front of us. I cranked the wheel as hard as I could, but the blown front tire wouldn't yield. We were going over the edge.

But then the lumbering Suburban crept away from the precipice and ground to a shuddering halt. My upper body lay draped over the console, afraid to move. My pulse pounded as my ear pressed into the gray leather. *This can't be good. Should I move?*

Slowly, I rose and peered out the window. I gaped at nothing but blue sky, with mountains beyond. We were suspended on a stationary cloud above the gorge. The truck still rocked slightly as it settled on its springs. *If this slips a fraction of an inch, I really will have something in common with that hawk.*

Sammy whimpered and hugged the door, away from danger. The Suburban lurched. I couldn't breathe. The back tire's slipping! Move to the passenger side. My heart wouldn't calm, yet somehow I gained my hands. Gingerly, I unbuckled the seatbelt, crawled across the console, and eased up on the door handle. *Stay here 'til Sam's out—counterbalance.* The Suburban creaked and shifted. I held my breath. Locked in a time warp, I heard pebbles and rock skitter from beneath the rear tire and tumble hundreds of feet to the creek below. I pushed the door open, and Sam tumbled out. I was right behind him, falling out headfirst. I lay still and stared up at the punctured sky. A few high cottony clouds drifted past with the hawks.

A trembling Sam slinked off to the safe side of the road. I got to my feet and backed away. Most of the left rear wheel hung off the edge. Small chunks of road rock continued to break away. "Good Lord watches over drunks and fools, Sam." At the sound of his name, he crept back and lifted his leg against the one rear tire still on solid ground. "My sentiments exactly."

We faced with a long hike back to the ranch, but then a vehicle came around the corner. I leaned in to grab the pistol off the floor. A green pickup approached and stopped in the middle of the road. Air blew from my cheeks. Deputy Hastiin flicked on his warning lights and got out. He smiled and walked over to the edge. "Seems as if you've been living right—or is it wrong?"

"Man, am I glad to see you." I put the Berreta back in the glove box.

Hastiin maneuvered his truck into position, attached a tow strap, and jerked the rear end of the Suburban back onto solid ground. We removed the spare tire from beneath and made the change. Fifteen minutes later we were done.

"Better get that tire fixed first chance you get." He threw the strap in the back of his truck and asked, "Now, what happened?"

I told him about the brown Taurus.

He frowned. "Perhaps you should leave the police work to us from now on." His broad shadow spread on the washboard road. In his reservation uniform, he was the picture of a Tony Hillerman character.

"Wanted to get close enough to read the license plate, but you're right. Sorry to create problems for you, Deputy."

"That's all right. Nantan and his family asked that I watch out for you, Mr. Ivy. Can't come down on you too hard."

I nodded. "We'll be leaving tomorrow."

"I won't see you again, then," he said. "Have a safe trip. Come back and visit, all right?"

We shook hands. The chance of a return visit seemed unlikely at that moment. "Think I'll stick to the flatlands."

He laughed. "Yeah, hard to fall off a cliff out on the prairie."

"There's truth in that."

He drove off and waved.

We were back at the ranch by four-thirty. Sammy hopped out and bumped into Skunky as she trotted toward him. They yipped and squealed like young pups, then ran off toward the barn. Sike rode up on horseback, dismounted, and waited for me to climb out, sore, tired and sunburned.

I walked over and patted the tall roan. "Spider Rock was spectacular, Sike. I'm glad Nantan suggested it."

"Worth the trip?"

"You bet." I then told him about our encounter with the brown sedan.

"Good thing Hastiin came along," Sike said. "You'd have had a long walk back."

"We'd still be walking. That valley was magical, Sike. I fell asleep in the sun. Might've stayed there 'til dark if Sam hadn't woken me up."

"It's a great place for reflection."

"It's more than that. I found it to be quite . . . spiritual." I swiped my face, knowing I hadn't done justice to the place. "How's Cassidy doing?"

He turned toward the Hogan. "Sounds like the Blessingway's winding down. Grandmother will be exhausted. We hoped you'd spend another night with us?"

"Certainly. That's very kind of you. Rather not drive through the mountains at night."

"Good. Typically after one of these ceremonies, we celebrate with lots of food and drink. Grandmother's helpers will join us."

"Sounds terrific. In that case, I'd like to talk to Nantan again. This may be my last opportunity."

"I'm sure he'd like that. I'll put Jessie away and meet you in the house." He led the horse away.

Nantan was dozing on the front porch. The late afternoon sun had soaked into his dark jean jacket, and he looked quite comfortable. I picked up his hat from a chair next to him and studied the sweat-stained brim. What did Grampa say? Oh yeah, "The smell of an old man's hat is like the nostril of a horse—breathing in what something ancient and beautiful has breathed out." I sat on the chair with the hat in my lap content to be in Nantan's company.

The old man sensed my presence. "You are back, Gus Ivy." He opened his eyes and raised his head.

"Yes." I handed back his hat.

"And did the spirit of Iktomi make herself known to you?"

"I don't know, Nantan. Perhaps. Spider Rock is truly a place of great energy and wonder. A pair of red-tailed hawks appeared, scouring the sky above. I thought an image appeared during my nap, but I'm not aware what that was." Strangely, I felt no shame in admitting to the dream.

"You are not one of the Dineh, Gus Ivy, but that should not matter if you believe." His eyes angled at the worn planks on the porch.

"Believe in what, Nantan?"

"Of a spirit greater than you. Did the hawks appear in your dream?"

"No. They were actually there. They were real."

His dark eyes bore through me. "Tell me of your dream."

I thought back to my brief sojourn. "I saw a ladder spun from fine threads, and what you call Iktomi appeared, I think. She said, 'It is time to trust. To open you heart, and the pain would go.'"

Nantan shifted and looked directly at me. "I know why you hide."

"What?"

"You fought well as a soldier? With honor?"

Back to my soldiering again . . . "I hope so."

"And you lost good friends in battle?"

I hesitated. Images of Maxie and Tyler appeared. "I did."

The old man leaned over, placed his palm against my chest. "Now I know your heart. Acknowledge their importance. Stop hiding from the pain."

His words struck like a clap of thunder. "How . . . ?"

He withdrew his hand and flicked his fingers meaning, "Subject closed," then rose from the chair. "When you find yourself in a spiritual place, Gus Ivy, open your soul. When the wind whispers to you through the cedar boughs and the cry of the hawk beckons from above, listen and observe. Our Sacred Text teaches us there is another place we seldom visit. It is the skyworld of spirit and peace. I believe you were at this place on the rock."

"Were the hawks real, Nantan?"

"They were for you. That is all that matters. Stay in touch with that place, Gus Ivy. Remember Iktomi's words and the dream you chase will be realized. That is all I have to say on this."

Sike returned and helped his grandfather into the house.

I stood and stared at the hunched back of the old man as he shuffled into the house. His words echoed in my head: the hawks were for my eyes alone. But, why? What's their significance? And what about Iktomi? And, how did he know about Tyler and Max?

Sike returned. "What did grandfather say?" After I told him, he smiled and nodded. "That is a good thing."

Supper was delayed until the sun went down. Neighbors and relatives arrived. Soon the yard was filled with cars and pickups. A rosewater light seeped through the west windows of the old ranch. I stepped outside as the sun melted into a splash on the horizon. I compared it to a typical sunset in Minnesota, where a sky pool of cyan, magenta, and deep maize spreads and lingers for a long time. A desert sunset is unlike any other. There are no sluggish evenings in the desert as darkness falls quickly. The orange sphere plunges and simply disappears. The hush of night is sudden. In the desert, the sky darkens in minutes, and soon the first stars appear. I imagined the artist must be particularly swift to catch a desert sunset.

After the last glimmer of the setting sun stole below the horizon, the show was over. I went back inside. The house began to fill with people, and I shuffled from one group to another as Sike introduced me. Cassidy was brought to the house shortly after. She looked at peace and immediately folded into my arms. Our embrace was more than it appeared. She smelled of sage and pine. When we broke, she held my hand and wouldn't let go. She smiled at the crowd gathered around her. Cassidy looked tired, but that was expected. What surprised me was her total inner peace. She looked both refreshed and wonderful.

"How do you feel, Cassidy?"

"I feel terrific, Gus." Her broad smile was as pure and clean as an apple slice. "Apart from being extremely hungry, I think the experience did me a world of good." She was glowing.

"Come on, let's get some food in you before a gust of wind blows you away." I steered her toward the enticing banquet.

We feasted for two hours. Traditional Navajo songs were sung, prayers to various spirits offered, and when we couldn't possibly eat another bite, Nantan passed the pipe. Conversation hushed as the men gathered before the fireplace. I took the requisite four puffs and handed the pipe off to Sike. When the smoking ended, Orenda led Cassidy over and centered her in the group.

Sike brought a chair and motioned Cassidy to it. Orenda knelt at her side. "Cassidy Kittridge has found *hozho*." The old woman dug a withered hand into her skirt and withdrew a handful of small black stones. "The sacred stones have rubbed against her belly and chased away the evil spirits." She held both hands high, closed her eyes, and began a barely audible chant. When Orenda finished, she handed the stones to Cassidy. "Take the stones. You have been told what to do with them."

"Yes. Thank you, Orenda." Cassidy's eyes glistened.

"I will tell a story," the old woman said. She looked into Cassidy's eyes.

"Now, one day the Creator was sitting and watching the children play. She saw their joy and youthfulness. She saw the beauty of their surroundings and the fresh fragrance of the trees and flowers. She saw their beauty and the sunlight in their hair. These were wonderful things.

"But then the Creator realized that all things change. Children grow old and gray and their skin wrinkles. Beautiful women grow fat and ugly, and their beautiful black hair goes gray. Leaves turn brown and die, and beautiful flowers with wonderful smell fade. Creator's heart grew sad and troubled. It was autumn and times would be hard.

"Creator decided she must make something that everyone can enjoy. Something to lift hearts and spirits. So she took out her bag of Creation and began to gather some things together. She took blue from the sky and whiteness from the cornmeal. She gathered some spots of sunlight and the blackness of a woman's hair. She took the yellow of the falling leaves and the green of the pine needles. She gathered the red, the purple, and the orange from flowers. And last, she added the music of the songbirds. All of this she placed in a bag.

"When she had finished her gathering, she called the children together. She told them to open the bag and there would be a surprise for them. So they opened it. Out flew hundreds of beautiful butterflies! They flew all around the happy children and played in their hair. They fluttered around and sipped nectar from the flowers. The hearts of the children and the adults soared. Never before had they seen such wonderful, happy things. The butterflies began to sing their humming songs as they flew.

"But a jealous songbird lit on Creator's shoulder and scolded her. He said, 'It is not right to give our songs to these pretty things. You told us when you made us, that each bird would have his own song. These pretty things have all of the colors of the rainbow already. Must they take our songs, too?'

"Creator said, 'You are right. I made one song for each bird, and I must not give them away to any other creature.'

"So butterflies were made silent, and they are still silent to this day. But their beauty brightens the day of all people and brings out songs from their hearts."

The old woman finished the telling, and looked up at Cassidy. "You are now Shysie, the silent butterfly." Orenda's eyes teared, her aged hands trembled.

Cassidy remained frozen in place. She threw both arms around Orenda and whispered something in her ear. The old woman stroked her back and nodded at Sike who presented Cassidy with her own dream catcher. It was perfect—all white with brilliant pearl-colored feathers that dangled from the willow. It took a moment for Cassidy to collect herself. She stood, walked around the room, hugged everyone in turn, and thanked them for their prayers.

Cassidy returned to Orenda. "I can never repay you kind people for what you've given me. I will never forget your love. If Gus and I are fortunate enough to find grandfather's legacy, we intend to share it with the Dineh." She looked at me, and I nodded my assent.

Orenda gave Cassidy a last hug. "Sike will prepare a cup of tea for you, Shysie. Then you will sleep like a lamb by its mama's side." She turned to me and finished with, "You must be with her tonight, Gus Ivy."

Cassidy read the old woman's words and smiled.

I blushed but thought it a terrific suggestion. This remarkable evening ended abruptly; as if Iktomi herself entered the room and laid a web of gossamer over the crowd. The guests departed, and Orenda escorted Nantan to bed. It had been quite a day for everyone.

Once Sam and Skunky were shut in the barn, I returned and escorted Cassidy into the bedroom. She slept in my arms that night, her head nestled against my neck. I stayed awake for quite a long time and thought of how everything had changed. It'd been a very strange, eventful day. I stared up at the dream catcher and fell asleep.

Thirty-Three

RIDAY MORNING I was up early, anxious to continue our extraordinary odyssey. Cassidy remained in bed, so I left to feed Sam and his new friend. An overwhelming sadness clouded the moment, as I knew we'd be leaving Skunky behind in a short while. Joined by the other two pups, the five of us walked and played for twenty minutes.

By the time I returned to the house, Cassidy was up helping Sike in the kitchen. She came close, and after a meaningful kiss, she whispered, "Next time, keep me awake." Her eyelashes fluttered against my ear as gently as a butterfly. My pulse raced as I considered her admonishment. She pulled back and winked.

Before long, Nantan joined us. Once Sike had breakfast prepared, we sat down to eat. Everyone ate sparingly, however, as the feast from the night before lingered. Orenda hadn't appeared by the time we finished. "Grandmother is tired," Sike offered.

"I'm not at all surprised," Cassidy pushed her plate away. "She's a remarkable woman, Nantan."

"Yes. I think she may sleep all day," the old man announced.

Cassidy frowned. "I'd hoped to thank her and say good-bye."

"You already have, Shysie." Nantan waved his hands for emphasis. "Orenda say you are Dineh. She say your heart is big, the spirits are all around your soul. Live well, Cassidy Kittridge."

"I will," she choked out. Cassidy stood, went to Nantan, and hugged him tightly. "Thank you."

Nantan looked at me as Cassidy returned to her chair. "Remember my words, dream hunter."

"I will. You and your family have been wonderful, Nantan. I'll never forget our time here." I pushed back from the table. Emotional moments such as this made me uncomfortable. "We have a long way to go. We should be going. I'll get the bags."

When I returned, Sike, Nantan, and Cassidy were gathered outside the front door. The sun had reduced the snow depth considerably. It looked like another glorious day.

Nantan looked up. "I've thought on Skunky. She's happy with the big tan dog. She should spend her last years with Shysie, Gus Ivy, and her new friend."

I was moved beyond words at the old man's gesture. And then, he said something very strange. "She has more work to do, but it is not here—it is with you." The old man's sensitivity touched me deeply. But, what did he mean by, "more work'"?

I kneeled and frisked Skunky. "Are you certain about this, Nantan?"

"Yes. Orenda said the little dog would be a reminder from our place—a totem for Shysie."

Cassidy was crying now. "Nantan, that is so kind of you. We'll take good care of her. Thank you. And please thank Orenda."

"Yes, I will. Come, it is time," Nantan said, and nodded to the little dog. Sam and Skunky were lying together in the sun on the far end of the porch. Both rose and trotted over at Nantan's unspoken command. I left to retrieve the Suburban from the barn. Upon returning, I loaded the bags and stood by the truck.

Nantan leaned on his cane and clucked at the small dog. Skunky stepped close and looked up at the old man. With some difficulty, Nantan knelt down and nuzzled the small dog. I could see his lips move but the words were indecipherable. The old man next laid a large hand on her head, stroked her gently, and looked beyond to the distant hills. After thirty seconds, Sike helped him to his feet, and Nantan waved the dog away. Skunky slipped down the steps and looked back at her master one final time. Sam followed, and the two stood side by side next to the truck.

"We'll take good care of your dog, Nantan." I went and brushed his palm with mine.

He looked into my eyes. "Yes, I know." There was sadness couched there.

The creases in his mahogany face deepened. "You are a good man, Gus Ivy. Listen to the good forces of the dream catcher. Hear the quiet wind. Learn to share your soul." His eyes went to Cassidy, and I understood. "There are important things you must still attend to. Remember your time at Spider Rock . . . the words of the spirits."

I looked into his eyes. There was something else, hidden. "The numbers. You know what they mean, don't you, Nantan?"

A brief smile creased his lips. "Perhaps. Know this, Gus Ivy. If your heart is pure, the spirits will guide you to your dream. It is not for me to intrude more than I have. Go now, for the laughter like children will be gone soon. Perhaps we will meet again, Gus Ivy . . . in another life."

My eyes clouded unexpectedly. Without proper words, I couldn't speak. I simply nodded, brushed his palm again, and turned to Sike. We touched palms briefly. He too understood the significance of that moment.

Cassidy hugged both in turn, and climbed into the Suburban.

"I will return, Sike." This surprised me. I thought I'd never see this place again.

"I know. Good-bye." Sike said.

Skunky took one last, over-the-shoulder look at Nantan and followed Sam into the Suburban. I climbed in and waved as we pulled out of the yard. Even if we never found Preston's fortune, something valuable had transpired here; something important and necessary. I watched the rearview until the old man on the porch was gone from view.

As we drove north, neither of us spoke for a while. One of Nantan's last comments stuck in my mind: the laughter of children will be gone soon. I glanced out the window and wondered what he meant. Sam and Skunky sat together on the back seat. The little dog appeared quite content with her new lot. She snuggled close to Sam; her small black-and-white head perched on Sam's rear flank. Unlike when we first arrived—neither dog now seemed as protective of Cassidy. They both still stayed close to her side, but their purpose had shifted somehow. I wondered if it had anything to do with the sand painting ceremony.

"Cassidy?" Tap, tap.

She turned her head. "Yes?"

"You want to talk about the ceremony?"

"Hmmm. It all seems a blur, Gus. Maybe someday I can describe it in detail, but not right now. I can tell you that it was the most emotional, inspirational event I've ever experienced. I came away feeling that somehow my life has changed. Orenda signed to me the entire time. I missed some of her words, but every chant, every song, was accompanied by her signing. She's amazing, Gus." She paused. "And, what about you? I gather you had an awakening of your own out at this place called Spider Rock?"

I tried to describe what had happened on the rock but failed miserably. "Something about Nantan touched me here, Cashmere." I laid my hand across my heart. "Never much for religion, I felt as if I'd been to a communion service and made clean. It was weird. My conversations with Nantan most certainly left a profound impression. Don't know how it all relates to our mission, but it was all to the good." She caught me off guard with her next question.

"Then, are you ready to tell me what happened in Vietnam?"

I hesitated. *Shed the pain in your heart*, he'd said. *Not sure I'm strong enough*. My voice was barely a whisper. "I, ah, I don't know Cashmere . . ."

"Stop the truck, Gus."

I pulled alongside the dusty road, put the truck in park, and stared out the windshield. My heart was pounding . . . this was unfamiliar territory. "War breaks men apart, Cassidy. When I finally came home, all I wanted was to be left alone. To use my hands. Stay busy. Took the first job available as an apprentice carpenter working for an old Swede, named Christian Swedenborg. Many years later, I realized that was how I rebuilt my life and myself."

Cassidy reached over and stroked my arm. Her touch was gentle but prodding. "Can you talk about what happened?"

"I don't know. No . . . I can't." Too choked to breathe or talk, I got out of the truck and walked away. Five minutes later, I returned. Cassidy was out of the SUV, waiting.

"Sorry, Cassidy. Cesspool's pretty full."

She nodded knowingly. "Talk to me."

What the hell. "It was my second tour," I began. "Last year of the war. Our company was sent to the A Shau Valley . . . a fire support base called Ripcord. In '68 it'd been a Special Forces camp, but after a particularly bloody battle, it became the Valley of Death. First Cavalry was sent in to push the NVA out. Our CTT team went ahead. I'd put Abby on a scent, and we followed Charlie at speed. But nothing felt right that morning." I watched her eyes to be sure she understood. "Two of my friends, Tyler Gruber and Max Nagel died shortly after we left camp. It was all my fault."

She inhaled sharply. Her eyes misted. "Why . . . why do you say that?"

Keep going. You have to. "Abby was trained to see, hear, and smell the enemy. She could detect mines, tripwires, stake pits. Many times she found bad guys buried in the ground—waiting to attack. She never missed a signal. Never. She'd stop, point with her head, and raise one paw. That's what she did that morning, but I ignored her . . . pulled her back to the rear. We were twenty yards behind when the VC opened up. By the time I got back, Tyler and Max were dead. Joe and Ed Tom seriously wounded. It was a slaughter. They never had a chance."

"I don't understand. You must have had a good reason for pulling Abby back."

Looking out over the vast mesa, I tried to explain. "She'd been sick. Company vet loaded her up with antibiotics and sent her back to me. Said she wasn't ready, that her nose might be affected, but they sent us out anyway." I looked over at Cassidy. "I didn't trust her. She knew Charlie was there and I didn't trust her."

"It wasn't your fault, Gus."

"I could have declined the mission."

"Would the others have gone without you?"

"Probably."

"Then you know why you went out, don't you?"

"Thought I did. Thirty-five years later I'm not so sure."

"Because you had to. It was your job . . . yours and Abby's. Without the two of you, your team wasn't complete. You had to go, Gus." Moments passed. "What about the other two, Joe and Ed?"

I cleared my throat. "Ed Tom . . . southern boy from Georgia . . . lost a leg. Joe suffered a serious head injury. Once they were airlifted out, I never saw either of them again." Now the pain was excruciating. I couldn't breathe. My chest was in a vise.

"After the war, did you contact them?"

"No. I didn't. Couldn't face 'em. On top of everything else, I'm a coward. Don't know what happened to them."

"Good Lord, Gus. You've been carrying so much guilt."

Her words helped some, but the pool was too deep. We talked for another twenty minutes, walking up and down that dusty road. In the end, I told her how I had to abandon Abby. "The Army killed her, Cassidy."

"I'm so sorry, Gus. My God, what a waste. How could they be so heartless?" She was crying along with me now.

"They lied to us. Army never intended to place the dogs. Only a very few were ever placed and those were adopted out by their handlers. That's what I should have done . . . maybe Abby would have lived. I trusted those bastards and they betrayed me . . . my own country. We did our duty. So did those wonderful dogs. And in the end, the Army treated us like dirt. I'll never forgive them for that. Abby deserved better. They all did." The ache in my chest slowly eased.

Cassidy leaned over and kissed my cheek. "Thank you." We hugged and together gazed at the brilliant sun as it brightened the distant peaks.

No further words were required. She stroked the back of my neck, and I the small of her back. We were two souls now united by a common thread—the shared knowledge of pain and guilt. I should have felt exposed by the unburdening, but did not.

We stood silently absorbing the morning rays. I took a deep breath of the clear air. "Let's go, Sweetheart. Denver's a long drive."

"Okay."

We climbed back into the Suburban and drove away. Our original mission remained before us. Nantan's words had given me new confidence that something important awaited at the end of Preston's rainbow.

Thirty-Four

I THINK NANTAN KNOWS where the treasure's hidden, Cassidy?"

"What? Are you serious?"

"Yes. But, for some reason, he felt it important that we discover the answer for ourselves." I told her what he'd said while checking the rearview out of newfound habit. "Let's go over my notes. Maybe we're over-thinking this whole affair."

She studied my list, opened her laptop, and read my notes out loud. "'Wind moving in a circle. It blew softly upon a blushing flower with spikes like kitten tails. Answers are elusive, but humble. Innocent—like children's play. Within the dream catcher. It is in the wind and the sand. Study the numbers for they are important. The laughter of children will be gone soon.'" She paused before asking, "What's the common denominator here?"

"I don't know." My eyes ached "The key's missing. If we find that then Nantan's words might make sense."

OUR DRIVE NORTH TOOK us up Highway 160 to Cortez. We selected the southernmost route to Denver to avoid the treacherous mountain passes. By the time we stopped for the night in Alamosa, Colorado, we had covered more than half the distance to Denver.

"That's enough." A Super 8 Motel beckoned. I pulled in and stopped in front of the lobby. "I'll get the rooms if you want to walk the dogs."

"Deal. Come on, Sam. Roust your little friend," Cassidy said.

Cassidy took the dogs over to a broad meadow adjacent to the motel.

After registering, I came out and joined Cassidy and the dogs. Then I saw the Taurus. "Look." I nodded in the direction of a car parked some distance away near the entrance to a neighboring gas station. "Same car as before."

"Where?" She followed my nod and stared. "Oh, I don't think so. That's a different color."

"You sure?" I was a bit colorblind, but it looked brown to me. "Guess my eyes are tired. Come on, let's get settled and find a place to eat." I took a last glance over my shoulder as I guided Cassidy to the motel. "Sammy. Skunky. Let's go." Both dogs bounded over and trotted ahead.

I had taken a single room with two double beds. If my choice proved presumptuous, I'd feel like a boob. The manager said both dogs were welcome, as long as they didn't disturb the other guests. I assured him they wouldn't. We brought the dogs into the room and closed the door. Cassidy looked around the room. I stood and fidgeted. Skunky jumped up on the nearest bed and flopped down. For an outside dog, she adapted quite readily to life on the inside. "Guess we have to sleep together again, Augustus. Do I have time for a shower before we eat?"

And that took care of that. "Sure. I'll feed the dogs."

She opened her suitcase, removed what she needed, and slipped into the bathroom.

As the dogs ate, I lay down and thought of Nantan's words. My brain grew weary as I considered all the possibilities. A swirl of warm, moist air settled on me.

"Augustus?"

I propped myself on both elbows and looked past the tops of my feet. Cassidy's hair was damp, and she had a large towel wrapped around her slender body. She stood with one hand on her hip in a very provocative pose. "Your turn, Gus. I like the men I sleep with to smell pretty."

I rolled off the bed and managed a weak, "Okay, then. Hang on to that thought."

When I came out of the shower, Cassidy was dressed in jeans and a sweater with T-shirt beneath. She looked and smelled fantastic. We kissed. Her eyes sparkled with promise.

We ate at an Applebee's next door. As we left the restaurant, there was no sign of a brown car. It was late, and we decided we were too tired to wrestle with Preston's puzzle. At least that was our excuse.

When I came out of the bathroom, she was already in bed. I craved her warmth and now familiar, comforting smell. My longing at that moment could have fueled a furnace. She threw back the covers and waved me close. She was naked. With a wry, seductive smile, she whispered, "Hi there."

"Hi, yourself."

I undressed and slipped into her arms. Lilacs filled my nostrils. It was the perfect aphrodisiac. Her body was as I imagined it to be—lean, soft in all the right places, taut in others. A novelist would have described her breasts as, "pert and upright." She was extremely sensitive to my every touch. Our lovemaking proved ardent and energetic, as if each had been waiting for the other for a long time. I couldn't get enough of her. She was enthusiastic and unselfconscious.

Whispers in her ear were for my benefit only. She couldn't hear my groans of delight, but that was a minor inconvenience. It was a honeymoon night of sorts and I didn't want it to end.

Much, much later, we fell asleep in a tangled, sweaty heap.

THE NEXT MORNING, I gave Cassidy a sleepy kiss and headed for the shower. Once dressed, I took Skunky and Sam out for a walk. When I returned, Cassidy was ready, and we headed for the motel's dining room.

I looked at Cassidy across the small table and asked, "We weren't too noisy, were we?"

She laughed and replied, "How would I know?"

"Oops." My ears burned a bit as I said, "Yeah. Right."

"Was I moaning too loudly, Gus?"

"Just a bit. No more than me."

"I'll try to be quieter next time."

"No. Don't. I loved it."

Once we were back in our room, we packed our bags. I watched as Cassidy applied a small amount of rose-colored lipstick. She required little embellishment; her beauty was genuine. She caught my stare. "Approve?"

"Sorry. You're just so damned pretty, is all." I probably sounded like a pimply teen, but she only smiled.

She jumped into my arms and wrapped both legs around my waist. "What a perfectly wonderful thing to say to a girl you've just ravished." She kissed me long and hard. "Ouch! What did you do to me last night, Gus? I'm sore all over. Even my lips ache." She fingered her slightly swollen upper lip. "However, if you're at all interested in another round . . ."

I stroked her hair and chuckled. "I'm an old man, Cashmere. Certain body parts are a bit tender this morning."

"Oh. I'm sorry. Anything I can kiss and make better?" She slid off and slipped her fingers beneath my belt.

"Maybe tonight," I mumbled.

"It's a date." She winked. "I'll get my bag."

"We'd better get that tire fixed before we leave town."

"What tire?"

"Oh, geez, that's right. I forgot to tell you. I ran into that Taurus yesterday on the road."

Naturally, she wanted to hear every detail.

We purchased a new tire at a local Goodyear store, remounted the spare underneath the SUV, and were back on the road by nine. Our trip took us to Durango, Colorado, where we picked up Interstate 25. We were in Colorado Springs by two that afternoon and reached Denver at five. Because it was Saturday, traffic was light.

I found a Motel6 that welcomed our four-legged companions. The motel was situated adjacent to a park with a broad expanse of grassland. "This is perfect. We can run the dogs in the park." Once the dogs were out, they immediately spotted the grassy park. "Go ahead, Sam. Take your lady friend over there and take care of business." I waved him off.

Cassidy and I followed, and for the next thirty minutes, we tossed a tennis ball for them. Sam knew what he was about and Skunky soon caught on. Once he had the ball in his mouth, she'd sneak up and snatch it loose. He didn't seem to mind and chased after her with delight.

I studied Skunky. "How old do you think she is?"

"Sam is nine, right?"

"Yes."

"Skunky must be older—maybe ten or eleven? She seems to be in wonderful condition."

"Sike gave me a few tips on how to work with her. Her herding instincts are very strong, and he told me that border collies love to gather anything that moves—including people."

"Let's try it," she said.

"Okay. Call her to you."

"Skunky. Here," Cassidy called. The little dog immediately stopped and trotted over to Cassidy's side.

"Now, I'll take Sam over there." We walked off about thirty yards. "Hold your arm alongside her head. Now point at us, and say, 'Away!'"

She held out her arm and repeated the command. Skunky darted over and skittered behind us. She dodged back and forth and nudged my legs.

"She's wearing now, Cassidy. Tell her to, 'gather!'"

The dog edged toward us as Cassidy gave her the command. Sam and I walked toward Cassidy. "Now the command is, 'come by.'"

"Come by!" Cassidy called. Skunky kept up a steady back and forth weave and brought us back to Cassidy.

"That's wonderful! She knew exactly what I wanted," Cassidy said. "Good girl, Skunky." She leaned down and stroked the dog's head. "I'd love to see her work a herd of sheep someday."

"Don't see why you couldn't," I offered. "Plenty of places for that sort of thing in Montana. Have you thought about going back?"

"I have. I'd love to, but . . . well, we'll see what happens."

I didn't press it. "Let's go." On the way back, I picked up a copy of *The Denver Post*. Reading the front page, I was startled by the headline. "You won't believe this." Tap, tap. "Cassidy, look at this." The caption read: "LOCAL MANUFACTURING COMPANY TORCHED."

Cassidy eyes focused on the sub-titles that read: Montana Minerals Burned to the ground. Arson suspected. She then said aloud, "A body was found inside, Gus. Listen to this: 'One of the company's oldest employees, Jason Schmidt, was found strapped to a chair when firemen entered the building.'" She watched my lips.

"Shit. Sounds like Micah Knorr," I said. "So, we have to ask, what did they find?" I opened the door and the dogs darted in. "What else?"

"'Timothy Stevens, CEO said, Jason came to Denver when the company moved from Montana. An employee for over fifty years, his death is a shock to all of us. Stevens was unable to speculate on the motive for the fire or about why Schmidt was killed.'" She laid the paper on a chair.

"Maybe this Stevens can give us some insight into what Knorr might've found." I said. "They've got a head start on us, Cassidy. We might be too late." We had no time to waste. "I want to call this Stevens."

"Good idea."

I picked up the phone and dialed information.

"What about dinner?" Cassidy asked. "How about takeout? Chinese?"

"Perfect."

"I'll be right back."

Thirty minutes later, she hadn't returned. I'd finished speaking with Stevens and made a few notes. Worried about Cassidy's delay, I paced and peered past the curtain. Fifteen minutes later, she returned. "What took so long?"

"Sorry. Busy night." She fumbled with the containers, and soon we ate in silence.

We finished eating. I told her about the phone call. "Stevens told me that the offices had been ransacked. He had a pair of visitors earlier in the day."

"Knorr?"

"Sounds like it. Presented themselves as members of the local historical society—researching World War II defense contractors."

"Clever. Did they ask about the book?"

"Not directly. Mostly interested in company records from that period."

"What else?"

"Stevens told them he had blueprints for the authenticasts and an album of the company's monthly newsletter, *The Mineral Spirit.*"

"I never knew that," Cassidy said. "I'd love to see those."

"Not possible. All destroyed in the fire."

"What a shame."

"They wanted to know if any employees from Billings still worked there. Stevens gave them Schmidt's name—the dead guy, a night watchman. Stevens feels pretty bad about giving out that information."

"Schmidt. I thought that name was familiar. He was the only other survivor of Charlie Company I didn't contact. He must've had a copy of the book, Gus. That poor man," Cassidy said.

"Bet you're right. Stevens thought Schmidt was involved in the casting process for the authenticasts. My guess is Knorr came back later, tortured the old man, rifled the office, and torched the place. So we can eliminate Montana Minerals from our list of sources."

"And if Schmidt had a copy of the dust jacket?"

"Then Knorr has everything we have."

"Except for Nantan's vision," she offered. "We need to get to work. Where should we start?"

"Let's go back through my notes . . . see if anything jumps out. Work back from Nantan's words."

"It's all in my laptop." She plugged in the computer. Soon we were looking at the old man's words again. "'Wind moving in a circle. It blew softly upon a blushing flower with spikes like kitten tails. Answers are elusive, but humble. Innocent—like children's play. Within the dream catcher. It is in the wind and the sand. Study the numbers for they are important. The laughter of children will be gone soon.' Any ideas?"

"Tornado? Dust storm?"

"The second sentence refers to a rose, I think." Cassidy said. "I picked up on that during the sand painting ceremony. A 'blushing flower' is a common Navajo symbol for rose."

"I'll buy that. How about 'children laughing'?"

"A playground? School? Maybe we should be looking for Grandfather's childhood schoolhouse."

"An intriguing idea. Nantan said we had to hurry, that 'the laughter of the children will soon be gone.' You said Preston was from . . ." I riffled through my notes. ". . . Wolf Point, Montana, right?"

"Yes. In the northeast corner of the state."

"List that as an option. There's another reference to children, 'innocent and humble.'"

"Well, children are simple, uncomplicated, I mean," she replied.

"What if Nantan meant the answer is not very complex? Something in his voice intimated the code might've been very simple. Let's move onto notes about the book."

We spent the next two hours tossing ideas around. By eleven we were exhausted and decided to call it quits. I walked the dogs and then joined Cassidy in bed. I propped myself up so she could see my lips. "We have to find Bailey Greyson tomorrow, Cassidy."

"You think he's behind this, don't you?"

"I do. I want to lean on him. See what happens."

"Remember, I have to make an appointment for my dialysis treatment?"

I nibbled on her lower lip and said, "We'll take care of that first thing. I'd like to be there with you, Cashmere."

"They won't permit that, Gus. It's a sterile environment. You'll have to wait outside."

"Then I'll wait."

"Now, it seems to me we made a date this morning for another 'getting to know me' session." She rolled over and leaned back with both arms extended. Her eyes sparkled. "Remember this?"

Thirty-Five

O N SATURDAY MORNING we woke early, and brainstormed our plans for the day.

"Do you suppose Bailey Greyson works on Saturdays?" I asked. "It's March . . . tax season. If he's a CPA he'll be there."

"Good point."

Cassidy's face darkened. A slight frown creased on her forehead. "I have to call the hospital." She had on the same beige cashmere sweater I had first seen her in. Soft wool suited her.

My blood chilled, and I leaned close. "You feeling sick?"

"No, no. I'm fine. But, I'm overdue for my treatment, and that always makes me a little jumpy." The apples of her cheeks were pink. Her pale blue eyes stood out against her soft white skin. I thought she looked like a million dollars. Not at all like a woman with failing kidneys.

"Well, let's get it taken care of. Do you know who to call?"

"I have a list of hospitals." She rose and stepped over to the small desk.

She opened her purse, attached her TTY, and dialed a number. After five minutes she was finished. "I can get in this morning."

"Good. What time?"

"Ten thirty. St Joseph's. I have directions."

It was nine. "I still want to be with you, Cashmere."

"I'd like that, Gus." She smiled warmly. "Let's get going. We can be at Greyson's office by noon." She gathered her things and handed me a slip of paper. "Here's the address."

"Is your computer still on?" I asked.

"It is."

I went to Map Quest and pulled up directions to Greyson's office. "Got it. On Division Street. We gathered the dogs and left. When we arrived at St Joseph's, Cassidy held my arm as we entered. When we reached the dialysis unit on the second floor, she stopped just outside.

She laid her fingers on my cheek as she spoke. "This will take a couple of hours, Sweetheart."

I was trembling. Something about hospitals . . . the pervasive smell of antiseptic, body odor, food, and floor wax. The incessant monotone from the intercom grated—doctor this, doctor that. I hated hospitals. "I'll wait over there." I nodded at the small waiting room.

"Go down to the cafeteria, buy a magazine, and eat breakfast. You look kind of peaked. Last night too much for you?" She kissed me and flicked her tongue out.

"Maybe." She always managed to raise my spirits. "'Bye, Cashmere."

"'Bye, Gus." She wiggled her fingers as the door swished open and she disappeared from view.

Two hours later, I returned from the cafeteria and headed back to the waiting room. As I exited the elevator, an older gentleman passed by coming from the dialysis unit. A hand covered his face, so I couldn't get a clear look, but something flashed as familiar. I turned and watched him hurry away. He didn't stop at the elevators, but continued around the corner toward the stairs. I was just about to follow when Cassidy called my name.

"Gus?" She was talking to a doctor and waved.

The doctor smiled, patted her shoulder, and went through the pneumatic doors. I darted forward. "Cassidy? Everything all right?"

She was beaming. "Yes. Fantastic."

"What?"

"My blood urea level is down. Same with creatinine." She was effusive, animated, but might have been speaking in tongues.

I squinted and nibbled my lip. "And that's a good thing?"

"Very good. The kidneys filter urea and creatine. When unable to filter, dialysis takes over."

"Why the sudden change?"

"The doctor couldn't explain it." Her eyes sparkled. "He said if these measures continue to decline, I'd only have to come in once every four weeks. Isn't that wonderful?"

"That's great news, Cassidy. Best we've had since we began this odyssey. Did you tell him about the sand painting ceremony?"

"I did. He knew about Navajo healers and didn't scoff. He's seen cases where recovery from certain illnesses couldn't be explained."

"I'll be damned. Maybe Orenda's techniques have merit."

"Oh, I think so. I'm so excited about this, Gus." Cassidy squeezed my hand as we walked to the elevator.

When we reached the SUV, I scanned the area. No sign of either the Taurus or the old man in the hall. "Check that map on the dash, Cassidy." As I drove, she gave me directions.

We arrived at Greyson's office and parked in an adjacent ramp. "How do you want to do this?"

"I found Bryce's old badge in the glove box. I've thought about this and decided we should probably not admit who we are until we see what he says. I'll flash the badge, make him squirm a bit."

We walked across the street and entered the building. We found Greyson's office listed as Suite B—second floor. We took the elevator.

A sign on the door read Bailey Greyson, CPA. I turned the handle and let Cassidy through ahead of me. It was a small suite of offices with a reception area. A studious looking young man stood next to the receptionist's desk.

"Bailey Greyson?" I asked.

"No. Bailey is out of town. Did, uh . . . do you have an appointment? I'm not aware of any appointments on the calendar. Let me check—"

"And, who are you?" I interrupted, with a sharp edge in my voice.

"What? I'm Michael Keefer, Bailey's assistant. How . . . how can I help you?"

"By telling me where Greyson is."

"She's out of town on business."

The look of surprise on Cassidy's face mirrored my own. "She? Bailey Greyson's a woman?"

"Yes, of course. Oh, I see. That's a common mistake. Now, what was it you wanted?"

I reacted quickly. "We're with the SEC, investigating a securities violation. We've a number of questions to ask Miss Greyson. When will she be back?"

"Uh . . . to be honest? I dunno." The young man rubbed his chin, unsure about us now.

"Look young fella . . . Michael. Greyson's in a great deal of trouble. We've proof she's involved with one of her clients in an insider-trading deal. If I were you, I'd be as forthcoming as possible." I stepped over to Keefer's desk and sat down. "You remember what happened to Martha Stewart? Jail time."

"I don't know anything about . . ." the young assistant looked doubtful and chewed his lower lip.

"Bullshit! You're her associate." I pointed my finger. "You know plenty. She's dirty and if you don't cooperate, you'll spend ten years in a federal penitentiary. You know what they do with young guys at Florence?"

Keefer threw his hands in front of his face. His eyes widened, and he sucked against a full set of bright teeth. "Hey, I've only been working for her for six months. I just answer the phone and run errands and stuff."

"Really. Then here's what I'd suggest you—"

"What's that?" his voice trembled. He sounded anxious to help himself out.

"—you take your lunch break—now. Get a nice reuben across the street at the corner deli. Order a piece of pie. After thirty minutes, come back here. How's that sound?"

A light went off in the young man's head. "Oh. Okay. I am kinda hungry." He made one last attempt to defend Greyson. "Uh . . . don't you have to have a subpoena or warrant or something?"

I tried for a leaden face; like the sky before a cyclone. I stood tall, creaked my neck, and said, "Listen, pal. It's Saturday morning. The judge is playing golf. He'll be pissed as hell. And you know what they say about shit flowing downhill? That means when I come back, I'm not going to be as accommodating as I am now." My eyes bore straight through him. "Is that what you want? You want a glimpse of my darker side?"

Truly frightened, Keefer stammered, "Uh-Uh, no. I'm going to go get something to eat. Will you—"

I interrupted before he could blink. "We'll lock the door. Don't worry. Now scoot." I took Keefer's arm, marched him over to the door, and opened it. "Got your wallet?"

The young man looked as if he might change his mind. "Yes, but—"

"Good. Wise decision. We'll be sure to make a note of your cooperation in our report to HQ."

After nudging him out the door, I quickly closed it. "How'd I do?" I smiled at Cassidy.

"HQ? The judge and his golf game? Nice touches." She laughed lightly. "Didn't know you had it in you!"

"Me either. So, where do we start? Her office?" I pointed at a door marked PRIVATE.

Greyson's office was surprisingly spartan. Other than a wall of books and a couple of filing cabinets, very little in the small room revealed a clear picture of the woman. It appeared the CPA was seldom here. We dug through the desk drawers and rifled the cabinets. After fifteen minutes, we'd come up dry. "Nothing on Kittridge, nothing on Knorr." I paced the small office.

A corner of the desk pad showed a couple of pink phone messages tucked beneath. "Oops. What's this?" I fingered two square slips. "Bingo."

Cassidy read the scribbled messages. "'Please call Micah Knorr at your earliest convenience.' Looks like a cell number."

I studied the second one. "This says, 'L.S. returned your call.' Wonder who L.S. is?" Something tugged at my memory. I rubbed my temples in a circular motion but couldn't make a connection.

"I don't know," Cassidy handed me back the second slip. "Now that we know she's tied in with Knorr, what's next?"

"Let's shake their tree and see what kind of nuts fall out." I picked up the phone, punched the number on the slip, and leaned back. It was answered immediately. "Mr. Knorr?"

"Yeah? Who's this?"

"It's Michael Keefer. Ms. Greyson's assistant." I added a bit of lilt to my voice.

"How'd you get this number?"

"Ms. Greyson left it with me. The other numbers she left went unanswered."

"What do you want?"

"I have a message for her."

Silence. Knorr came back on the line. "Go ahead. Haven't seen her, but if she calls, I'll pass it on."

"Oh, good. The message is from a Mr. Ivy. He said, 'You're too late, and you can stop the search. It's over.'"

"Who? Ivy? What the hell's that supposed to mean?" Knorr asked.

I smiled at the alarm in his voice. "Said to tell you that quote, 'Messed up down at the Navajo Nation. Your hired help spilled the beans, and you might as well catch the next plane to Venezuela, because every cop in eight states is on your tail.' Unquote."

"Who the hell is this?" Knorr had clearly sensed the scam.

I imagined gobs of spittle flying from Knorr's lips and enjoyed the byplay immensely.

"It's Ivy, pecker-head. You kidnapped my sister and threatened my friends. I owe you."

"You sonofabitch!" he sputtered.

"You messed up, scumbag. Payback time. The feds said to keep you on your cell for a full minute. My watch says we've had our little chat for well over a minute. Wouldn't be surprised if they're headed your way right now."

"Boris! Take a look—"

"Better book that flight real soon, sport. Sleep tight, dip-shit."

Click. The line went dead.

I leaned back and replayed the conversation for Cassidy's benefit.

"What did you just do?"

"Gave 'em something to think about. Come on, let's get out of here." We left the office and returned to the Suburban. Sam and Skunky wagged their collective greetings.

"Don't worry, Cashmere. They've got to wonder what we found in her office that would send the cops their way. If they're ahead of us . . . well, maybe they'll do something stupid. I wanted to slow them down. Now we have to unravel your grandfather's message."

"Where do you suppose Greyson is?" Cassidy asked.

"Doubt she's at home filing tax returns," I offered. "And probably not lying on a beach somewhere. I'll bet she's not far from Knorr."

Thirty-Six

WHEN WE GOT BACK to the motel, Cassidy and I took the dogs for a romp in the neighboring park. Sam and Skunky had been cooped up and were full of energy. A group of six kids and their mothers were in the play area about fifty yards away.

Suddenly, Cassidy grabbed my arm. "Oh, my God!" Her face turned white. Her hand flew to her mouth.

I spun around and looked at two toddlers who had wandered away. They headed for a fast-moving creek fed to overflow with spring melt. The children were already dangerously close. The mothers were oblivious to their children's plight. We were two hundred feet away—too far to stop the tragedy about to unfold. The mothers would never react in time. My heart thumped against my rib cage.

Cassidy never hesitated. "Skunky!" she called.

The little dog stopped and focused on Cassidy's raised arm. She lowered her arm and pointed at the toddlers. "Away!" she commanded.

Skunky turned, spied the kids near the creek, and sped away. She tore across the broad expanse of grass, a blur of black and white, covering the distance in seconds. The toddlers had reached the edge and teetered on the slippery brink. One little girl waved her arms as if she was losing her footing. The swollen creek would surely sweep her away. Skunky skidded to a stop near the children and looked back.

Cassidy shouted, "Gather!" Her arm flew out to one side.

Time stood still as Skunky inched toward the children, both of whom had frozen at Skunky's appearance. She stopped, and with her head lowered, crept behind the girl closest to the creek. But then, Skunky's hind legs slipped. She clawed at the muddy bank and slipped below the crest. The little girl toppled above her.

"Oh no!" Cassidy grabbed my arm.

Suddenly, the little girl's head reappeared. She had fallen on top of the little dog. Skunky scrabbled for traction and powered back up. The child rolled off Skunky's head and neck. The little dog regained her footing and stood firmly planted between the creek bank and the toddlers.

The kids were truly frightened now and backed away. Skunky rose from her crouch and nudged the children away from the creek.

Both mothers had witnessed the entire episode and had run over to swoop up their children. Once they had them in tow, Cassidy called out, "Skunky, here." The dog hesitated, then sauntered back to Cassidy's side. She stood quietly, her tail swishing gently, ready for more work.

We walked over to the creek. The mothers were frantic. One blubbered, "They slipped away so fast. Thank you so much."

The second had her hand to her mouth, her child's face buried in her ample thigh. "I knew we shouldn't have brought 'em here." Her face was void of color.

"That's a wonderful, brave little dog you have. I think she . . . " The little girl's mother was too distraught to finish.

"Yes, I know. Are your children all right?" Cassidy asked.

"They're fine. How can we ever thank you?" one of the mothers asked.

"I'm glad we were here. Come on, Skunky." We waved good-bye and headed back to the motel. The two dogs trotted in and headed for their bowls. Cassidy was trembling.

"That was pretty quick thinking, Cassidy."

"I'm so glad you showed me those commands, Gus. Otherwise . . ."

I had a thought. "You don't suppose that was Nantan's vision do you?" She wasn't watching, so I had to repeat myself.

"What do you mean?"

"Children playing? Laughing? He said we had to hurry. Could he have foreseen that entire episode?"

"Yes, of course. He did. That's why he sent Skunky with us. What a frightening premonition for Nantan." Her face blanched.

Then, what about our quest? Were all his visions as well founded? "Nantan's vision will only make sense once we decode Preston's message. He wouldn't show us how to unravel the cipher. Merely confirmed that we were on the right track."

"So, we really need to dig into the book," she said.

"Yup. Let me ask you something. When Orenda finished the sand painting, did you get a good look at it?"

"No. They hustled me off and immediately brushed it out."

"Hmmm. There goes that theory. Okay, let's start with Preston's initial clues. "The letter and the dust jacket."

"Go on."

"We agree that this—" I waved the letter—"Is an invitation to search further, and the Shakespeare quote is a tease, right?"

She opened her laptop. "Yes. Continue."

"Kittridge wanted them to band together and, what did he say?"

Cassidy looked at her screen and read: "'Draw strength from your friendship. There is great wisdom and knowledge to be had from sharing. Open your eyes, study the signs, catch a dream, and enjoy the fruits of your labor.'"

"That's it. Catch a dream—a dream catcher. Now, on the last page of the book . . ." I picked up the *Cavity* book and read, "'There's More to Follow.' Here we're directed to the wrapper—to the bogus list of Bower's books. It talks about 'valuable, important fiction. Every letter, every word, every paragraph, every page has been carefully constructed by the author to present for you a truly memorable and worthwhile journey.' The final sentence says, 'It will pay you to look on the other side of the wrapper.' And at the bottom is the address of Franklin Press. 1611 Liberty Bell, Franklin, Pennsylvania." Suddenly a spark arced. Everything fell into place and blood rushed to my head in a whirl.

"Gus? What's wrong?"

My heart raced. "Where's the wrapper?" She uncovered her folder and handed it to me. The hair on my arms tingled. The clouds parted, and I stepped into bright sunlight. "The address is phony. That's why I couldn't find out anything about Franklin Press." I waved the jacket at her. "Do you remember which of Mary Beth's titles were bogus?" My voice raised a fraction.

"Yes. Numbers one, six, and eleven," Cassidy said. Then she got it. "And the address for Franklin is 1611—one, six, and eleven."

"Bingo. Liberty Bell. Task Force Liberty Bell. There's no such street." I handed her the wrapper.

"And the first title was, *Message to the Angels*," she read.

"Yep. Every hint, every clue, every message that Kittridge left was cleverly written for the boys of Charlie Company."

"Their division was called, the Angels." Cassidy said. "And the phony address represents the Sixth Army, Eleventh Airborne Division, First Squad of Charlie Company."

"Open Google and see what you can find on codes and ciphers. Nantan may have been right. We're over thinking this. 'Humble,' he said. 'Uncomplicated.' That means simplicity. Let's see what happens if we find a simple, uncomplicated cipher." I stood behind Cassidy with both hands on her shoulders as she began her search. Before long, the possibilities popping up on the screen mesmerized us. Cassidy discovered many variations of codes; the oldest one used by the Greeks in 480 B.C.

She read from the screen. "'Steganography—concealed writing. A classic technique that included tattooing a message on the scalp of a messenger.' They let his hair grow out and sent him on his way. When he arrived at his destination, they shaved his head to read the note."

"So they had to wait for his hair to grow before getting a reply!"

We chuckled at the image.

"There," I pointed. "Read that bit about transposition." I squeezed her shoulder and repeated my request. The examples given seemed extremely complicated, however. The more we dug, the more confused we became.

"There are mono-alphabetic substitution ciphers, cryptography, code numbers." Cassidy tilted her head back. "I don't know, Gus. The methods are infinite, with hundreds of variations."

We spent over an hour testing many of the examples, but nothing made sense. At six o'clock we stopped. The dogs were restless, and my brain had numbed. As we left the room, it seemed as if we were no closer to a solution. Our moment of joyous discovery faded to a complex, stupefying vortex of incalculable possibilities. "It just can't be this difficult, Cassidy. It can't."

WE RETURNED TO OUR ROOM at eight. Sam and Skunky showered us with sloppy kisses. So far, they'd both been perfect guests—no accidents, no complaints.

I took them for a walk but cut it short when a weird idea occurred to me. I marched into the room and said, "Ovaltine!" Cassidy was looking at her computer and hadn't heard me. Tap, tap. "Ovaltine."

"What about it?"

"Ovaltine sponsored the Captain Midnight Show. They hawked a Secret Decoder Ring. I took the coupon from the Ovaltine jar, taped a nickel on a card and sent it in. After an eternity, a little package arrived with the Captain Midnight Secret Decoder Ring." My mind traveled back in time. "As a kid, I sent away for all sorts of stuff. Every comic book and radio show solicited readers or listeners to send for what inevitably turned out to be junk. "*The Green Hornet*," I said. "*Jack Armstrong*. My favorite radio shows."

Cassidy shook her head. "All before my time, I'm afraid."

"The Secret Decoder Ring worked, Cassidy. Sort of."

"How does that relate?" Cassidy remained confused.

"Stay with me here. The ring was pretty chintzy—made out of plastic with a rotating dial. There were two sets of letters from A to Z. The one on the face of the ring was stationary, the other hidden beneath. You created your own secret code by moving the second set of letters on the dial."

"And?" she insisted.

"Well, depending on where you set the dial, the A on top might match up with the D below, and so on."

She shook her head.

"If I wanted to send a message that said, 'Sally is ugly,' I'd write what looked like gibberish: 'xcddef ot erdf.' My friend had to have a ring of his own, of course. He'd look at his and match each letter on his stationary dial, and the letters below on the secret dial revealed the message. After a lot of fiddle-farting around, he'd decode the message."

"Okay, I think I understand, but what's your point? That Grandfather used one of these Secret Decoder Rings?"

"In a way, that's exactly what I mean."

Thirty-Seven

I JUST RAN ACROSS SOMETHING," Cassidy said as she scrolled to a link. "A web site called Cipherspace. It says, 'A simple cipher is the easiest of all. Similar to a transposition code, but much less complicated.'"

"Like my decoder ring."

"Sort of. If the message is embedded in text, they suggest that 'The key is a series of numbers representing characters—letters of the alphabet, words, and paragraphs.'"

"Numbers. That's it. Nantan said, 'study the numbers for they are important.' The only numbers we've seen are 1611, the Franklin Press address—the list of bogus book titles."

"Yes," Cassidy said. "And one, six, and eleven are imaginary titles." She chewed on the end of her pen for a bit. "What if the first number—one—is supposed to represent, uh . . . what? The first letter of a given word?"

"That's beautiful, Cassidy. The first bogus title is *Message to the Angels*. The sixth is *Journey North*, and the eleventh, *Crossing on the Prairie*. One, six, and eleven. 1611."

"Start with Chapter One, Gus."

I picked up the book. "Now what?"

"Look at the sixth word in the first sentence." Cassidy suggested.

"What about the number eleven?"

"Hmm." Cassidy leaned back and stared at the ceiling. "How about the eleventh page—first letter of the sixth word on say . . . every eleventh page?"

I went to the sixth word on the first page, found the first letter, and then repeated the exercise on every eleventh page. "Nope. Gibberish."

"Reverse the order. Eleventh word, sixth page, first letter," she suggested.

After giving this a chance, I had to shake my head. "Uh-uh. Doesn't work."

She nibbled the pencil. "Think about this: every word has at least one letter in it, right?" Cassidy asked.

"Yes. That narrows the choices considerably. If I use the first letter of the sixth word in every combination . . . Wait. Let's try the eleventh paragraph. The first letter of the sixth word is T, so now what?"

We were both looking at the text. Cassidy pointed to the sixth sentence of the eleventh paragraph: "Sheepmen have moved into the Tonto." She pointed to the letter, T.

"Let's count another eleven paragraphs. The first sentence begins, 'No ties bound him in Oregon.' The first letter of the sixth word in that paragraph is O," Cassidy said.

We went to the thirty-third paragraph and found, "Colter had a hard face, The," "The first letter of the sixth is another 'T,'" I said.

After another eleven paragraphs, we had, "But, this band of sheep Had." "H" was the letter. Then, "the plaintive uproar was not Expected." "E, Cassidy."

"Yes. We have just spelled out, 'to the.' I think we have it, Gus."

As my heart stopped, her excitement matched mine. "Keep going, kiddo."

She counted another eleven paragraphs but found the sentence to be a short four-word phrase. "Buck stared in disbelief."

Me too. "That doesn't work, does it?"

"Not without a sixth word. Now what?"

"Go to the next paragraph . . . one that has at least a six word sentence."

She did that and found a B. Eleven more paragraphs and we had "V." Next came "A," "R," and "E."

"We now have 'to the bvare.' Something's wrong. The last word isn't spelled right."

Our moods soured a bit. "Stay with it," I offered. Ten minutes later and we had a very strange first sentence: "to the bvrae men of cliarhe cpmnaoy." Capitalization was impossible, of course. Of greater concern, how-ever, was that every word with more than three letters was misspelled. "This can't be right. It's nonsense."

Cassidy typed our peculiar first sentence into her laptop. When fin-ished, she looked up. Her eyes sparkled and her mouth flew open. "I know what she did! I can't believe it. This is so exciting. Please continue, sweet-heart." Her knees bounced as she waited for me to recite.

It was soon apparent that correct punctuation hadn't been a concern. It didn't matter—at least to Cassidy. Within an hour, we had the first portion of this improbable code unscrambled. It didn't look like much, but Cassidy was delighted with it.

"It doesn't make sense," I complained.

Cassidy's voice cracked like fine crystal. "Yes it does. Columbia University published a study I was going to use with my students." She was quite animated now. "It determined that it doesn't matter what order the letters in a word are in; it's only important that the first and last letters of each word be in the right place. For deaf people, this seemed to have merit—at least I wanted to experiment with the concept. Anyway, Columbia proved that the human mind doesn't read every letter by itself. Instead, we read the word as a whole." She waited for my response.

"Only had two years of college, Cashmere. Sorry." I threw up my hands.

"Here's the entire message—at least what we've unscrambled so far." She beckoned me to the computer screen. "Read it and ignore the mis-placed letters—just look at each word."

I read, "to the bvrae men of cliarhe cpmnaoy the rnurmebs one and six and eeveln wree stleceed to rinmed you of yuor bthorers who did not rruten hmoe wtih you my son skpoe wlrmay of you his borhters he will not ctcah his draem but you have mgnaead to ucolnk a door to ahtneor daerm taht will cgnhae the csuore of yuor lfie the jnoeruy may be lnog it will ruierqe cferual sduty the rrwaed for yuor erfoft is stuisbnatal we wsih you mcuh lcuk taverl wlel lvie wlel be hppay form the esat the wset the ntroh and the stuoh it is hlaf of ecah you msut biegn at the ctener the pcale you seek is not oevr terhe it is hree."

And then I understood. "You're right. It's a brain teaser."

"Grandmother must have come up with this—well before the brain wizards at Columbia ever thought about it. Remarkable, isn't it? It would have made her job quite a bit simpler. She only had to worry about getting the first and last letters in the correct place. The rest didn't matter. That's why we thought her writing was stilted and—I think you said—'choppy.'"

We had the code: the first letter of the sixth word of the eleventh paragraph. The sentence had to have at least six words to qualify. We had uncovered a message hidden by Preston and his mistress more than sixty years earlier. The realization was electrifying. "Do me a favor? Rewrite it in plain English?"

"Of course." Cassidy reshuffled the letters and typed the translated version:

> "to the brave men of charlie company the numbers one and six and eleven were selected to remind you of your brothers who did not return home with you my son spoke warmly of you his brothers he will not catch his dream but you have managed to unlock a door to another dream that will change the course of your life the journey may be long it will require careful study the reward for your effort is substantial we wish you much luck travel well live well be happy from the east the west the north and the south it is half of each you must begin at the center the place you seek is not over there it is here."

Cassidy said, "The thought of the two of them working on this is . . ." She sniffed and wiped her eyes. ". . . really quite remarkable."

I focused on the last couple of sentences, repeating them aloud. "'Half of each? The center? Not over there?' What the hell does that mean?" We'd reached the end of the first chapter, a long one at that. "This must have been terribly difficult for your grandmother." I admired her effort and wonderful creativity. Like Cassidy, I pictured the two of them hunched over an old desk with a single lamp as they struggled to bury Preston's message. It was an enduring image.

By midnight we were worn out. I was anxious to continue, but Cassidy was absolutely exhausted. "Why don't you get ready for bed?" I suggested. "I'll keep working on this a while longer."

Cassidy took Skunky and Sam outside, and when she returned, she crawled into bed. My attention was focused on *The Cavity Lake Gang*. I was struggling with the start of Chapter Two. Something was drastically wrong. I used the same system as before—first letter of the sixth word of the eleventh paragraph— but what it revealed made no sense.

Maybe he changed the code? I tried different sets of one, six, and eleven but nothing worked. A dead end. *What'd you do, Preston? Skip a chapter?* I applied the same formula to the third chapter, then the fourth. Nothing. Frustrated, I closed the book. Enough. Cassidy was asleep. I undressed and slid into bed.

Sleep eluded me. I tossed from one position to another, mind racing. First too hot, then too cold, I rolled to the edge and sat up. *What am I doing wrong?* I imagined the *Cavity* book lying in the dim light like a beckoning siren, "Come closer. It's all here." A draft of chilled air wafted over my exposed skin, as if a door had opened to the cold night outside. I crawled back into bed and pulled the covers up to my chin.

Preston's motives may've been commendable, but truth be told, the book had caused a great deal of heartache. Was there more to come? And if we solve the riddle? Then what? What if Knorr beats us to it? Or, what if we meet them again? It hadn't all been bad, though. Without the book, I wouldn't have met Cassidy. And that's a good thing, I kissed her forehead and closed my eyes.

I slept but didn't rest. Fragmented images of guns, spiders, ladders, Abby, cowboys, and Indians evolved into a bizarre, convoluted jumble of images. I woke with a screaming headache; a jackhammer worked its way around the interior of my skull. My mind was mush, a tangled mass of pick-up sticks. Everything I had experienced over the past week fell off the shelf that was my brain and landed together in one huge muddle of muck.

The clock radio said 5:00 a.m. I went to the bathroom, threw cold water on my face, and decided to forgo further attempts at sleep. I dressed, gathered the dogs and left the room. With my heavy coat zipped tight, I stepped out into the cold early morning. We hiked over to the park.

A pink-hued, violet span of daylight appeared just over the eastern horizon. Anvil-shaped cumulonimbus clouds rolling from the west would soon obscure this brief opening in the day. *The hole in the sky is the void in my brain*, I thought.

Sam and Skunky finished their romp, and we returned to the motel. We rounded the corner and threaded our way through numerous cars and trucks. As I edged between the vehicles, something caught my attention. I stopped and turned. Fifteen feet away was an apparition, a ghostly reminder of the dark side of our odyssey. In the first half-light of the chilly dawn, I stared at a brown Taurus.

Impossible, I thought. They couldn't know where we are. I stepped closer. It was difficult to see the true color of the sedan. Covered with dust and mud, it was definitely a Taurus, but brown? The plates. Check the plates. Three steps closer, I crouched and wiped away a cover of mud from the metal plate. Arizona. Every nerve ending in my body tingled.

I straightened and looked around. No one in sight. I moved to the passenger side and looked into the window. A tangle of road maps, empty Burger King bags, a box of Kleenex, and a pair of leather gloves littered the front seat. The back contained a metal case and a pair of muddy boots.

Sam and Skunky wandered over, waiting. A slight breeze blew across the lot as dawn broke. I was exposed. The hair on my neck stood up. Goose bumps erupted on each arm. I backed away and snapped my fingers for the dogs. Back in our room, Cassidy was dressing, and she saw my image in the mirror. "Gus? What's wrong?"

"Remember the brown Taurus?"

"Yes, what about it?"

"It's parked outside. It's definitely the same vehicle." I stood shifting from one foot to another for a moment before going for my bag.

"What are you going to do?"

"Find out who it is." I dug in my bag, pulled out the Beretta, and threw on my coat

"Gus? Please don't . . . do anything foolish." Her face paled. Her eyes misted. She looked as if she had more to say, but held off.

"Stay here. I'm going down to the office to find out what room they're in. Don't worry. I'll be fine. Lock the door and don't open it. I have a key. If I'm not back in ten minutes, call the police." I didn't wait for her objection, but cracked the door and stepped out. Early risers were out, anxious to be on their way. I wished now that we'd left hours before.

Thirty-Eight

B Y THE TIME I REACHED the lot, the Taurus was gone. I scanned the
area but saw nothing. I hurried to the office, and as I rounded the
corner, found the Taurus idling outside the lobby. I ducked down
on the driver's side and looked into the interior of the office. One
person other than the clerk was visible—an older man near the
coffee urn. I hefted the Beretta and waited for Knorr or his men to appear. No
one else showed inside. The old man poured a travel mug, waved at the clerk,
and headed for the door. When he passed through the glass door, he raised his
head and looked around.

This can't be! Impossible. I stood and pocketed the weapon. "Limas?
Is that you?"

Startled by my sudden appearance, the old man's coffee spilled. He
held it out away from his body and finally spotted me behind his car. "Jesus
H. Christ! You scared the hell out of me, Gus."

Ten minutes later, I reached in my pocket for the room key. Once the
door was unlocked, I stepped in and waved to get Cassidy's attention. She
was sitting on the bed with Skunky. Sam lay at her feet.

She stood and ran over. "Gus? Thank God! What happened?"

"I have someone with me you may remember."

"What? Who?" I stepped aside and opened the door wider. "Limas!"
She ran over and threw her arms around him.

"Hi, there, Cassidy."

Limas had explained that he and Cassidy were old friends, that he followed us out of a sense of concern for her safety. Beyond that, my mind
was on holiday and having trouble catching up.

Cassidy smiled sheepishly. "Gus, we owe you an explanation—and an apology."

"An explanation would be appropriate," I said stiffly.

Smead held Cassidy's hand and explained. "When I first heard what Cassidy was up to, I flew to Phoenix and offered to help her."

"Help how?"

"Why, to get a read on you, Gus. Once she was convinced of your, ah . . . veracity, I meant to go home." He looked at her, patted her arm, and continued. "But then, when I heard about the barber and then Manny, I decided to hang around, just in case."

"How do you two know each other?" I asked.

"Kind of a long story, but I was hired to watch over the family many years ago," Limas said.

"By?"

"Preston Kittridge."

"Wow. Guess there is more to this." It took a while to assimilate this new development—the gambler from Havasu. Surprised by his sudden appearance, I was curious about his relationship to Cassidy—and Kittridge. "Did you know he was following us, Cassidy?"

"Yes, I did. Limas made me promise not to tell—until he was convinced you could be trusted."

I threw my hands out. "How?"

"We've been text messaging. With cell phones." Her eyes pleaded for forgiveness. "Please don't be angry with me, Gus."

"It's okay, sweetheart. I'm not angry. A little confused, maybe. You managed to dodge my concerns about his Taurus, but when were you guys going to clue me in?"

"This morning, actually," Cassidy offered.

"Just about to come knock on your door, Gus."

I wanted to know more about Smead but needed to focus my thoughts. "How about some breakfast? We can talk over a stack of pancakes."

"Great idea." Smead petted Sam.

"My treat." Cassidy took Limas by the arm.

"Who's your little friend, Cassidy?" Limas nodded at Skunky, who stood near Cassidy's side.

"Isn't she beautiful, Limas?" Cassidy told him about Nantan's gift.

I looked down at both dogs. "You guys stay." Sam had already assumed an attitude of indifference and flopped down with his head on his front paws. Skunky huddled close to his flank.

We hiked across to the restaurant and settled in a booth. Cassidy and I on one side, Limas on the other. A waitress took our order.

"Okay, Limas. You were at the craps table to check me out—that much's clear. Was that you I passed at the hospital?"

"Yep. Thought you'd flag me down for sure."

Cassidy leaned over so she could see my mouth. "Limas retired a couple of years ago. We talk on the phone every so often. He suggested I might need his help."

"Sorry for the subterfuge. Don't blame Cassidy, though." He sounded genuine. "You see, I'm suspicious by nature. Kittridge hired me to protect Mary Beth and her family. Over the years, I've become paranoid about anyone Cassidy associates with. Sometimes she's a little too trusting for her own good."

"That's fine," I said sincerely. "But, how'd you manage to stay with us?"

He laughed at that. "Cassidy kept me apprised of your destination. You certainly haven't made it easy, though—especially when you reached the Nation."

"Did you take Cassidy to the hospital in Phoenix?" I asked.

"Yes. Then, once you started north, I thought more than once you'd spotted me."

"I did—spot you, that is. Pretty certain you belonged to Knorr's gang."

"Knorr. Right. Another of my concerns. Heard the gunfight at the ranch and almost came in then."

"Cops said it looked like someone ran those guys off the road, Limas. You have anything to do with that?"

Cassidy straightened. "Limas?"

Limas looked into her eyes. "Not directly. They sideswiped me, lost control, and pitched over the edge. Can't say I felt too sorry for those fellas. Cassidy said you'd stay for a couple of days, so I got a room in town."

She nodded and watched him speak.

"Anyway, I just kinda hung around 'til you folks left. Drove around and checked out the scenery. Then I ran into you on the road."

"Almost bought the farm there, Limas," I said. The remembrance made my knees wobble.

"Sorry about that. Waited to make sure you were all right, then left when the cop showed up."

"No more secrets." Cassidy shifted her gaze to me. "He's been like a father to me, Gus, especially after mom and dad passed away." She smiled and patted his arm lovingly.

"You up to speed on what we've learned, Limas?"

"Pretty much. "How close are you to finding Preston's message?"

"We've unscrambled some of the text, but haven't been able to go any further," Cassidy said.

"That's mostly good then. When Cassidy first told me about all this, I had my doubts. But it surely seems Preston hid something of great value."

"We could use a fresh viewpoint right now, Limas. Unfortunately, Knorr has a jump on us." I told him about the Montana Minerals fire and the horrendous fate of Jason Schmidt.

"Hmmm, don't know what help I can give, but I'll do what I can. Kinda tired of eatin' your dust."

"What was your arrangement with Kittridge?" I asked.

"My contract with Preston's estate expired when I turned seventy-five. Spent all but eighteen years of my life watching out for Mary Beth, Ramsey, and his wife Elizabeth. When Cassidy came along, kept an eye on her too. Preston thought someone might take advantage of the family—what with Mary Beth's deafness and all. I was hired for protection. To check on folks who need checkin' on. Preston's estate was sizable, and Mary Beth was wealthy in her own right."

"Did you ever have to . . . intercede?"

The old man never blinked. "Couple times."

Satisfied I said, "Okay. Let's talk about the book."

"Did you try different combinations last night?" Cassidy asked.

"Yeah, but ran out of ideas. We're stuck, Limas. Could only get through the first chapter. After that, nothing's worked. Almost as if Preston lost interest, or decided to make it so difficult no one could unravel it."

"Doesn't sound like Preston," said Limas. He fell silent while the waitress set our plates down. "Wouldn't've created anything that vague. Never left things to chance. Nope, once Preston started something, he generally finished it."

I swallowed a forkful of eggs. "What kind of man was he?"

"A kind, generous man. Great friend. Tough old buzzard. Not a mean bone in his body—'cept if he felt someone wasn't truthful. He truly disliked Roosevelt and made no bones about it."

"Why?"

"Had something to do with Roosevelt meddlin' in his business. FDR's mandate about wartime profiteering, and such. Always thought Preston stashed away most of his fortune just to spite Roosevelt."

"You know that for a fact?" I asked.

"Nope, just a guess is all."

"How'd you meet? You and Kittridge."

"I applied for a job at the plant. He interviewed me. I was seventeen—too young to enlist. War was just about over. He saw something in me that . . . well, I fit a profile he had of someone who could take care of himself. He wasn't well and wanted to make sure someone looked after Mary Beth and Ramsey."

We watched as Limas ate his breakfast. "Good pancakes," Smead commented. "Cassidy, you should have some of these. Look like you've lost a little weight."

She laughed. "See what I mean? He's always worried about me. I had to fast for twenty-four hours, Limas. Remember?"

"Hrrrmph. You eat like a bird," he replied gruffly.

We finished eating without further discussion.

On the way out, I asked, "Limas? You carry a weapon?"

"Yessir, I do. Colt .45 Auto. Range isn't much, but it's guaranteed to stop a bull at twenty-five yards," he stated without pause.

I lagged behind and watched the old man walk with Cassidy. She looked over her shoulder at me, then turned back. I was ready to accept Limas as a potential asset. I'd instinctively liked him from when we first met at the casino, and obviously he cared a great deal for Cassidy, his ward. And if my premonitions about Knorr proved correct, we certainly could use his help.

Back in the motel room, Limas sat next to Cassidy and studied Preston's opening message. "I agree with your assessment. This first part's a thank you—a heads-up that the hunt will be challenging."

"What about the last couple of sentences?" Cassidy asked.

"That does sound important doesn't it?" Limas read aloud: "'From the east the west the north and the south it is half of each. You must begin at the center.' Let's see, if you drew a line from north to south . . ." Limas grabbed up a pencil and scribed such a line on the notepad. ". . . then if I draw another from east to west, the center of those intersecting lines is exactly half of each." He looked in the mirror until Cassidy caught his gaze. "That's where he wants you to start, Cassidy—in the center of these two intersecting lines."

"The center of what?"

He answered with a quote. "'The place you seek is not over there . . . it is here.' It's a starting point—the center on the north-south, east-west axis."

"If Grandfather wanted to provide a fair chance for all the soldiers, no matter where they lived, then maybe . . . "

I jumped in with, "He would have wanted to start in the middle of the United States."

"Yep. Think so. Anyone know the geographic center of the U.S.?" Limas asked.

Cassidy went to the Internet. "Lebanon, Kansas. 'Is not over there, it is here.' It's Lebanon, Kansas—not Lebanon, the country."

"Good," I exclaimed. "That's it, then. Hell, a treasure hunt has to begin someplace, right? Log on to Map Quest, Cassidy."

She hadn't heard so Limas tapped her arm and repeated my request.

Soon she had a map of Kansas. "Lebanon's just south of the Nebraska border."

"That's where we have to start. Let's pack up, check out, and drop Lima's rental car at the airport." I was anxious to get moving. "Then we have . . . what? Four hundred miles to figure out the rest of the message. Sooner we get to Lebanon, the sooner we'll know where to go next."

Cassidy nodded in agreement, logged off, and unplugged the laptop. "I'm so happy Limas is here." She stood, put an arm around my waist, and smiled at her lifelong protector.

"Yeah, and I can stop looking over my shoulder." I rubbed her back and looked at Limas.

He observed my affectionate gesture without comment. "I'll meet you out front."

Within twenty minutes, we were ready to leave. "We need Interstate 76. Airport is on the way. We'll follow you, Limas," I said.

"Fair enough. Cassidy, you wanna keep me company?"

"Yes. I'd like that. We can chat and get caught up on a few things." She kissed me and slid into the Taurus with Skunky. By now, she and the little dog were inseparable. Our caravan headed for the Denver International Airport. With luck and fair weather, we'd be in Lebanon, Kansas, by nightfall.

Thirty-Nine

I CONSIDERED THE IMPLICATIONS of all that had happened. While my trust in Cassidy had grown with each passing day, the sudden appearance of Limas cast a slight shadow on everything. I was conflicted about my initial assessment. Limas had spent many years watching over Cassidy, so on the surface, his behavior seemed reasonable. Additionally, I'd spent time with him at the craps table and had come away liking the old guy.

On the other hand, his motives could be construed as a bit more mercenary. Limas might be tempted by the prize beneath Preston's rainbow, and want a cut for himself. He was a gambler, after all, presumably on a fixed income. Watch and listen. That's all I can do. His affection for Cassidy was genuine, that was pretty clear. He'd been a major part of her life for forty-some years. *Did I trust her? Yes.* Then I had to trust her judgment as well. Didn't I?

As Limas turned in the Taurus, Cassidy and Skunky strolled over and climbed in the front seat. I opened the back of the Suburban to load the old man's bag and noticed the sky darkening in the west.

Limas followed my look. "Big storm on the way. Down over the Rockies. If we're lucky, we'll outrun it." Limas climbed in back with Sam. Cassidy sat in front with Skunky, who curled up on the floor at her feet. She opened her laptop, and we headed east on the interstate. Limas studied the titles on the back of the wrapper. "*The Long Road Home*," he said as calm as could be.

"What?" I looked at him in the rearview.

"The sixth title. Each of the three bogus titles is significant. They mean something specific—beyond their importance as keys to the code. The first one, *Message to the Angels* was an invitation. The sixth implies that the end is a long way from the starting point." Limas was pretty convincing.

"What about the eleventh, *Crossing on the Prairie?*"

"Well, we're heading across the prairie, right? Let's try your decoding system on Chapter Six," Limas suggested. He turned to the sixth chapter, found the eleventh paragraph, and soon tapped Cassidy to give her the letters.

After a while, Cassidy read, "'Cnuot the lges of a sdepir. Dvdiie in hlaf.' Translated? Count the legs of a spider. Divide in half."

"Eight," I said. "Spiders have eight legs—same number as the web strands on a dream catcher. So we have half of eight, or four. What do we think that means?"

"Back to the north/south, east/west axis?" Cassidy offered.

"Maybe," Limas said.

Soon they revealed more. Cassidy read the translation: "'Divide in half again. Then once more. These will guide you after this. Horace Greeley counsel is correct. But first travel toward the scarlet songbirds zero point. This is not where you are.'"

She turned. "Any ideas?" She chewed her lower lip. "Me either. Perhaps there's a landmark in Lebanon—you know, like a statute or monument."

"Possible." We were stumped. The last few sentences confounded all of us. "Must be some sort of geographic directive."

"If so, it's pretty ambiguous," Cassidy countered.

I set the speed control at ninety and we barreled across Kansas.

For the next couple of hours, we bandied ideas around but came up with nothing of substance. Tired of the mental masturbation, I studied the view through the windshield. These were the true western flatlands. Buffalo grass growing no more than two feet in height, but sending roots deep into marginal soil for life-giving nourishment. A constant force on the prairie, the wind only ceased at sunset. The highest point in any direction proved to be the occasional overpass that swept up above the surrounding grasslands. A huge fan of Willa Cather, I recalled something she'd said about the prairie: "Elsewhere the sky is the roof of the world; but here, the earth is the floor of the sky."

On other trips I'd had across prairies of the Dakotas, late in the day—with the sun at my back—the car's shadow grew like an oil spill. It was a land without definition. A few grain silos in the distance and all these anomalous wind turbines sprouting like giant beanstalks. Each machine was identical—pure white with three huge fins that slowly rotated and mark time with the endless wind. They were an ugly blight, constructed in clusters of eight, spaced a couple of hundred yards apart, but oddly seductive, like soundless metronomes. And then I had an idea. It was absurd, but maybe. *Why not? Wind in circles?* I decided to keep my wild hunch to myself for now.

We pulled over at a rest stop just outside of Ogallala, Nebraska. As I let the dogs out for a much needed break, I heard a sound that sent a shiver down my spine. At first I couldn't identify what my ears had picked up, yet I sensed a familiarity somehow. The noise came from the north. It was raucous, orchestrated. What had Nantan said? "Listen."

Then I knew what it was. I'll be damned. I touched Cassidy's shoulder and turned her toward me. "Cassidy. I'm listening to . . . to the sound of children laughing."

She was predictably confused. "I don't understand."

"'Like children laughing.' Nantan said—'children laughing.' Look!"

And then we saw them. Thousands and thousands of sand hill cranes lifted from the shallow reaches of the Platte River and clouded against the horizon. The sky soon grew black as they rose and circled up in apparent confusion. They rotated into and out of the wind, an aimless flight that looked and sounded like pure enjoyment more than anything else. If they had a purpose, it was impossible to determine what it might be. The noise proved deafening. I regretted that Cassidy couldn't hear their calls, as it was truly a remarkable sound—like thousands and thousands of children at play, as only the innocent child can laugh and giggle.

Limas stood with and observed the spectacle. "I've heard about this. It's a staging area. Stopped here on their way north for hundreds of years. It's marvelous, isn't it? Saw a *National Geographic* special once. Many as a million rest here before they continue on."

I had to shout to be heard now, as each kettle of soaring cranes redirected and flew overhead. "Heading out to feed, I imagine." More of Nantan's message echoed through my head. "In the wind and sand," he had said. And, "You must hurry, for the laughter of children will be gone soon." I thought he meant the children Skunky rescued, but maybe it was also the cranes. It all made perfect sense. We were on the right track. I was sure of it now.

I reminded Cassidy of what the old Navajo had said. "Of course. They're only here for a short time, and then they're gone," she agreed.

Limas offered, "Sounds like Nantan's vision has legs."

"Something about him was almost reverential, Limas. I actually think he knows where the treasure's buried but left it to us to find it for ourselves." I repeated everything for Cassidy's benefit. "He sent Skunky with us to fulfill her destiny. He saw all of it. We have to be getting close." My blood churned. I had to catch a breath.

"Gus? Can you describe the sound for me?" Cassidy looked skyward.

"I'll try, sweetheart. You remember as a child when the schoolyard filled at recess? Kids screaming and laughing?"

"Yes, I think so."

I lowered my gaze and faced her. "Try to imagine that same sound multiplied by a million. It's musical and heavenly, actually." I stepped to one side and put an arm around her shoulders. It hurt to realize how much she missed every day of her life.

"Thank you, Gus." Her eyes misted but continued to watch the cranes as they slowly worked their way into the wind. Soon we could see flock after flock spiral down in a crazy freefall as they dove to feed on the grain stubble south of the interstate. The gawky, stick-legged birds grazed without fear among a herd of Black Angus—neither species giving the slightest heed to the other.

Limas broke the spell. "Anyone have any ideas about Horace Greeley?"

It took a moment for me to understand his question. Oh, yeah, that last line. "No. But isn't he the guy who's famous line was 'Go West, young man'?"

Cassidy faced him. "The battery in my computer died. I'm afraid my laptop isn't going to help us now."

"Be right back. Gotta check the line on the Final Four." Limas strolled off punching numbers into his cell phone.

"Maybe there's a statue of Greeley with an inscription," Cassidy offered.

"Might be all we've got to go on. But we're going east right now. Does that mean we turn around and go west from Lebanon?"

"Could be. Need to cogitate a bit on that," Limas had returned and sounded like he had the nut of an idea.

We picked up a sack of burgers at a McDonald's in Ogallala. I gassed up the Suburban, and we were back on the road in no time. There was little traffic, and the weather system we had been concerned about stalled. We passed through North Platte, and heard on the radio that the snowstorm would reach the central plains sometime Tuesday. I felt certain we'd be long gone by then.

Once we drove through Lexington, we turned south at Kearney and reached the small village of Lebanon at four thirty in the afternoon. There was no statue of Horace Greeley. As a matter of fact, the only landmark of note was a bank of eight large grain silos that stood out on the horizon. We poked around until we stumbled across a small brass plaque on a rock that proclaimed this to be the precise geographic center of the United States. We should have felt something more than mere indifference.

Sam sniffed the monument and lifted his leg on the plaque. We chuckled at his impropriety but stood fixed in place, with no idea where to turn next.

Limas laid the notepad on the hood of the SUV. "Preston said, 'but first travel toward the scarlet songbird's zero point.'" I watched Limas underline west from the Greeley quotation.

"What's a scarlet songbird?" His bushy brows rose as one.

I knew that. "A cardinal."

"Very good." Limas said. "Before I went to work for Preston, I worked for an old German on a survey crew. Hans Hagen drilled words and symbols into my head all day long. One that stuck was 'cardinal point.' It's any of the four major points on a compass: North, South, East, and West. The cardinal point of zero degrees is north. I think we have to go north and west: Northwest."

I considered that as I studied the map. "I'll buy that. Hell, we don't have any other ideas." I looked to be sure Cassidy was with us. "What were the next few sentences, Cassidy?"

She showed us what she had written. "Translated it reads, 'Find a color of the rainbow in the sky. This is not where you are.'"

"And that earlier message said something about the eight legs of a spider—'divide in half, then half again, and once more.'" Limas offered.

"Yup, numbers," I said. "Nantan's numbers, again. It's a reference to the numbers eight, four, two, and one—right?"

"Yes. Think so. Lemme look at that map." Limas was in control now. "Here, look—Red Cloud, Nebraska. Red's a color of the rainbow. Clouds in the sky?"

We were on a roll. "Could eight, four, two, and one refer to highway numbers? Or some combination?"

Limas scratched his head. "They'd have to be state or county highways in use sixty years ago."

I looked at the map. "Highway 281 will take us to Red Cloud."

Well, it's a start," Limas said. "I've a hunch that old Preston didn't make this any easier from here on. But, we agree we have to work our way northwest?"

Cassidy and I nodded. "Let's go." We piled into the Suburban, turned north on Highway 281, and we left Lebanon behind. Once we crossed the border, we passed through Red Cloud and continued north.

Forty

CASSIDY WORKED ON Chapter Six without benefit of her laptop. She read us the clean version. "'Your next stop is fast.'" She pointed on the map to the town of Hastings and smiled. "That's pretty simple."

The next clue was more difficult. Cassidy read, "'If your path is true, search for a great land mass without water.' Any ideas?"

We puzzled over that for a bit, and Limas said, "Grand Island is north of here."

I sensed we might be nearing the end of our quest. My rear end had numbed from too many hours in one position, but my excitement grew with each new revelation. I glanced at the map. "Highway 2 runs northwest from Grand Island. Two is one of the numbers in the riddle. Looks pretty desolate up there." I checked my watch. "Getting late. Might want to find a motel and continue on in the morning."

"Not a bad idea," Limas said. "Been a long day."

"Yeah, let's stop. Skunky's restless. Need to eat anyway. Cassidy?" I tapped her knee. "We think we should stop for the night."

"That's fine. I can charge my laptop during dinner."

We pulled into a Super 8 motel lot outside of town overlooking a broad expanse of knee-high grass—a great place for the dogs to run. Once we unloaded and checked in, Cassidy and I took the dogs for a romp over the adjacent grassland. Sam kept his nose to the wind and before long quartered a strong scent.

"Watch this, Cassidy." I whistled and raised my hand over my head. Sam sat down to take my direction. "Back!" He jumped up and dove into the taller grass beyond where he had been. All at once, a covey of quail burst skyward from a thick clump of bluestem. Sam stood and watched while Skunky bounded after the small birds. We followed the dogs to the next crest.

"That's almost the same signal we learned for Skunky."

"Pretty much the same idea, except he's chasing birds and she's rounding things up." Cassidy took my hand. Her touch was welcome, a reminder of our new rapport. Our arms swung naturally as we walked shoulder to shoulder. At that moment, I believed that even if Preston's treasure turned out a colossal hoax, something wonderful lay ahead for the two of us.

Sam caught up to Skunky on a small bump that rose above the prairie. The sun broke through the heavy clouds at that moment and appeared as an orange ball beneath an overhang of gray-violet clouds. The view was memorable. On the way back, our shadows spread before us as long willowy shapes creeping over the sea of grass. We were silent until we reached the edge of the field.

"You don't think those horrible men are going to find Grandfather's treasure before we do, do you Gus?"

"Dunno. They're working from the same information we are. Depends on how smart they are. We know they're dedicated and devilishly persistent." I shuddered and blew sharply through both nostrils. Every time I thought of Knorr my guts churned.

Cassidy and Limas went over to the restaurant while I phoned Bryce. Ten minutes later, he was up to speed.

"You sure you can trust either of 'em, Gus?"

"They're not involved with Knorr, if that's what you mean."

"Yeah, but what if they have their own agenda? Other than what they've confided, what do we know about either of them?"

"I'm pretty close to Cassidy, Bryce." My face flushed as I spoke. "I can't believe I'm missing anything, and Limas really seems concerned for her safety."

"You may be too close. Remember, a hard-on has no brains, Gus. Anyway, I was there to watch your flank. Just be extra careful. Pay attention to anything that looks out of place, okay?"

"I will. Look, I've gotta get dinner. I'll call when I know more."

"Take care. Watch your back."

We dined on Nebraska's famous beef at a local steakhouse. As the meal settled, I grew weary and yawned continuously. Most of the conversation had been light and cursory, but we did discuss Cassidy's remarkable recovery. I was becoming more comfortable with Limas, and had begun to accept him for what he was—an old friend and confidant of Cassidy's. My initial concerns were moderating.

Nantan's words intruded and danced around the edges of my brain. "Listen to the good forces. Time to trust. Open your heart. It's in the wind and sand." *Or, were those Iktomi's words? I shook my head.*

"Gus?" Cassidy had noticed my introspection. "Are you all right?"

"Yeah. Just thinking of something Nantan said."

"Like?"

"Well, sand for instance. Did he mean sand hill cranes?"

Limas wiped his mouth and said, "I'd say not. Probably his way of telling us that we're in the right neighborhood. If we continue northwest, know what we'll run into?"

"What?"

"The Sand Hills."

"What's that?" Cassidy asked.

"Well, it's something I know a little about—a huge area of mixed-grass prairie and sand dunes, all anchored by some of the toughest plants on God's green earth," Limas offered. "At one time it was considered irreclaimable desert, but in the mid 1800s, settlers discovered it to be wonderful rangeland."

"Are they like dunes in the desert?" Cassidy asked.

"Pretty much. You'll see some of the most amazing hills and mounds, some as high as six hundred feet. Why, you'll swear you're someplace in Egypt. Nothing like it anywhere else in the U.S. A harsh environment— bleak and dreary, but at the same time delicate and fragile. Indians thought the land was sacred—a final home for departed spirits." He paused and looked out the side window. "Often thought that this might be where Preston's ranch was—the Circle MB. Never knew for sure, though."

"Makes sense," I said. "Drivable from Billings. Sure as hell remote." My next question caught as I spoke it. "You think that he might have hidden his treasure on the ranch?"

"Hmmm. Now that's an interesting idea. Never had reason to think about it until now. Possible."

An electric charge pulsed steadily through my body. "It's logical. He'd have had plenty of time to find a good hiding spot. Whatever happened to the ranch, Limas?"

"After the war—after Jack died—Preston was pretty depressed. Had his foreman torch the place. He and Mary Beth never went back."

Cassidy had been watching our conversation intently. "How sad. I always wondered what'd happened to it."

"If I was a betting man—which I am—I'd say that's where we're headed," Limas offered.

"Come on, let's get back." My head ached. I needed a handful of ibuprofen.

It was eight-thirty when we got back to the motel. I laid on one of the two beds and waited for the painkillers to take hold, while Cassidy fiddled with her laptop. A line from a Shelley poem came to mind. "The lone and lonely sands stretch forever." Images of windswept, sandy plains eased my throbbing head.

Cassidy and Limas went to work on the text and soon were discussing newly revealed clues.

"This is a tough one," Limas said. "We already have 'it is more difficult now,' but this next one's a doozy. Have it translated yet, Cassidy?"

"Yes. 'There is a meander you must find like a fine thread gently laid with eyes closed. Then on to the honeyed standard. Not dry but wet.' Any ideas?"

"Nope. Told you he wouldn't make this easy." They gave up after an hour and Limas waved good night, going for his room.

While I waited for Cassidy, I tried to imagine what thread Kittridge had in mind. I drew a blank. My brain was loose sand. Then, my new best friend slipped into bed—naked. Once again, she crawled on top of me. She posed just above my face—her weight on her hands. Her breasts hung tantalizingly close.

"Are you going to tell me what happened in the elevator with Doreen?"

My lips were occupied, but I managed to mumble, "Nothing to tell."

"I can't see you, but I'll assume you're not going to tell me. Did she try to seduce you again?"

"Sort of." I didn't bother to look up.

Cassidy straightened her arms and frowned. "Nod your head if you turned her down."

I nodded vigorously. "Yup."

"Hmmm. Why?"

She could see my mouth now. "Look, I'm no Boy Scout. Far from it, but it didn't feel right. Far as I know, she's a pro. Never been with a whore before and I'm kind of proud of that." That seemed to satisfy her. I touched a recently discovered, extra-sensitive spot that sent a shiver through her body, and we were off to never-never land.

Her energy was amazing. We swung into a two-person concert—she the conductor and I the fiddler. She threw her head back and rocked and heaved and smiled with every thrust, while I studied her face. Her excitement and ardor only added to my already heightened lustiness.

The bed groaned, but I didn't care, and she couldn't hear. Finally, the moment arrived when we truly came together. Our mutual release went on forever.

I was deliriously happy. "Cassidy, you have no idea how good that felt," I panted. "God, I love being with you."

She collapsed on me and whispered, "Me too, Augustus. I've had a few lovers before, but no one ever made me feel like this." She kissed me and remained on top of me for a long time.

Finally she rolled off, inhaled sharply, and said, "When can we go again?"

"Geez Louise, woman, you're insatiable. I'm a doddering old man, remember? Gimme a couple of hours, okay?"

"Oh, all right. I'm going to set the clock, then I'm coming back and this time *I'll* be tapping on *your* shoulder."

EARLY TUESDAY MORNING, Sam laid his heavy paw next to my face. He patiently waited for me to respond. Cassidy was into a slight snore, so I slipped out of bed, dressed, and took the dogs outside. The first long panes of light fanned over the flatland. Daylight broke, but the sun remained locked away behind a thick bank of clouds.

The dogs headed for the grassy flat next door and waded into the silky meadow. When we reached the same crest as the evening before, I stopped and scanned the expanse. Somewhere out there lay Preston's hoard—but where?

Sam returned, wet with dew. I plucked a long, sinewy strand of dead grass from his head, and studied the pattern it made in my palm. It twisted and drooped. The back of my neck itched. I folded the length of grass in my palm and hurried back.

Once in the room, I opened Cassidy's computer and went to work. Cassidy woke up just as I finished. "Check this out, Cashmere."

She padded over and sat on my lap, her nakedness intoxicating. The nape of her neck tasted salty. She read, "'There is a meander you must find like a fine thread gently laid with eyes closed. Then it is on to the honeyed standard. Find the not dry but wet sweet flag.'"

"You've added a couple of sentences. Good job, Gus." She twisted to face me.

I laid the strand of grass over her right breast and let it fall off to one side.

She giggled and looked down. "That tickles. What are you up to?"

"The honeyed standard." I retrieved the slip of grass, let my fingers wander a bit, and said, "Come on, kiddo, get dressed and I'll show you what it means."

I knocked on Limas's door while Cassidy showered. "Do you have that map handy?"

"Yes. I'll get it."

"I think I know where we have to go."

We gathered in our room. I let the strand of grass drop carelessly on the bed. "What meanders?" I pointed to the wilted piece of blue stem.

"A drunken sailor," Limas answered.

I grinned. "Yeah. What else?"

"A river," Cassidy offered.

"Correct-o-mundo. And the Loup River is northwest of here. It's spelled with a U, but loop describes the shape it carved across the landscape."

"And the rest?" Cassidy's voice rose. "'A honeyed standard?'"

"That one threw me at first. With the help of your laptop and its thesaurus . . ." I read out loud, "A synonym for 'standard' is flag. And 'honeyed' can mean sweet. Sweet Flag is a common flower in Nebraska. The clue said, 'find the not dry but wet sweet flag.' I Googled sweet flag and learned that calamus is the root of sweet flag." I pointed at the map. "What we have here is the Loup River. Notice how it flows from the Calamus Reservoir up here." I stabbed my finger at the map. "That's northwest of us, and we have to take Highway 2, another of Preston's numbers"

"I can't believe it," Cassidy said.

Feeling rather good about myself, I said, "It's off to see 'The Calamus.' Let's grab a bite here at the motel."

"I've a few more pages to translate in Chapter Six," Cassidy said. "Bring me back a bagel?"

"Will do." We left Cassidy hunched over her laptop and made our way to the motel's lounge.

Forty-One

CASSIDY HAD FINISHED her work when we returned, so we checked out, collected our gear, and piled into the Suburban. Highway 2 paralleled the meandering Loup River. The air in the SUV was charged with a new energy. We tracked the Loup toward the Calamus Reservoir. "'It is the nature of water to be someplace else,'" I exclaimed.

Cassidy chuckled. "Now, where did that come from?"

"Can't remember." I glanced at the map and considered the source of the Loup. Rivers did always seem to be restless, and certainly out here, they ran nowhere from nowhere. Much like my own life. I threw the map on the dash and glanced at Cassidy.

We were being led into the heart of the Sand Hills. Even at this time of year, the landscape was inspiring. It was like looking out over a broad, brown sea scattered with tufts of grass. High, massive dunes like crested waves dotted the plains. They were vast and undulating—majestic, serene, and primeval.

"Reminds me of the top of a thick meringue pie," Limas offered.

"What are those wind-swept hollows?" Cassidy asked.

"Blowouts. Kinda like bomb craters, aren't they?" Limas answered.

I was surprised by all the small potholes. "Thought this'd be totally arid." Every small pond held clusters of waterfowl. "I've never seen anything like this."

"Heard some say it's like the surface of Mars," Limas said.

"Oh, no. That's unfair," Cassidy countered. "It's beautiful. Haunting, really."

April was a couple weeks away, but it was apparent that once everything was in full bloom, a verdant coat of green would rival that of the best Minnesota spring.

Cassidy was back at work. "'In one sense alone you must now rely, but beware of a second that will tempt.'" She pivoted, her brow furrowed.

"What's the key word there, 'sense'?" I asked.

"Sounds like it."

"He's talking about two of the five senses," Limas said. "Can I see the map?" He studied it for a bit and declared, "Rose. Small town about fifteen miles from here."

"I missed that, Limas," Cassidy said.

He repeated himself.

"Yes. Rose—smell. A rose has thorns. Touch refers to the second sense. It fits," she said. "And, remember what Nantan said about the blushing flower and kitten tails. Okay, that's the end of Chapter Six. Should I jump to eleven?" She paged ahead. "Crossing on the Prairie?"

"Yes. Go ahead, Cassidy."

By the time we reached the town of Rose, she'd managed to reveal more from Chapter Eleven. "Here's what I've got. 'You are close but not yet there. Still northwest but a choice must be made. Look where the wind blows and little grows. Where sand and water cloud your eyes. Erg is abundant in this place.'"

"Erg?" There's a new one. What the hell's an erg?"

"I'll look it up." Cassidy tapped the keys and soon came back with, "Sand sheets. Large sandy deserts."

"Sounds to me like we have a decision to make," Limas said. "If we continue on Highway 2, we come to an intersection at the town of Mullen. It's about twenty-five miles."

"Maybe there's a road that turns off before then," I offered. "Better stop and think about this." I pulled over outside of Rose.

We all got out and stretched. Sam and Skunky wandered off into a sandy area and took care of their business. It wasn't long before both hobbled back—each dog lifting one leg at a time. It was as if they both had just run through a bed of hot cinders.

"What happened?" Cassidy knelt next to Skunky. Concern filled her voice.

"Sand burrs." I plucked the nasty, thorny balls from between Sam's toes, and motioned for Cassidy to watch. "Hate these things. They'll spoil a pheasant hunt quicker'n snot on a cold day." Sam licked my hand in gratitude as I rolled him over and removed each tiny, briary orb. "Nature's perfect conveyance."

Cassidy finished and climbed back in the front seat. Her grateful little dog hopped up, curled at her feet, and licked her sore paws.

I leaned against the SUV and admired the scenery while Cassidy toiled over the book. After ten minutes, she called out, "See what you think of this. 'Find the anger of four lines. One is to fish. Two is a president. Three is empty. And four has little merit. X almost marks the spot.'"

"Look up, 'anger' in your thesaurus, Cassidy." I leaned in and repeated my request.

After twenty seconds, she said, "Anger is resentment; a strong feeling of displeasure or hostility. It can be a noun or a verb. Rage, fury, wrath. Wait a minute. It also means irritate or annoy."

I had an idea. "Find the anger of four lines. You think instead of anger it means angle? Could Preston and Mary Beth have made a mistake?" I didn't think so. We were at a dead end—in the middle of nowhere—just outside of Rose, Nebraska. And if we remained here much longer, our dogs would be crippled with bloody feet.

No one said a word. There was nothing to say. At the moment, anger was the appropriate adjective to describe my mood.

"Consider this: in its simplest form, anger means to be cross, correct?" I waited.

Cassidy's chin rested on the backrest. "I think I know where you're going, honey. If cross is the synonym, then it could mean crossing, or intersection."

"Right. So, if anger actually means to intersect, then that's what we ought to be looking for. The intersection of what? Couple of roads? Hell, sixty years ago most of these roads didn't exist."

Cassidy was undeterred. Her enthusiasm unwavering. "Why don't I keep translating? I'm sure we'll figure it out sooner or later." She turned back to the book.

I studied the road atlas, hoping something would jump out. Tap, tap. "Do me a favor and log on to Mapquest."

She laid down the book and went to a new screen. "Okay. Now what?"

"Find a map for Nebraska and zoom in on the area around Rose."

She had the map in seconds. "All right. We are here."

"You see anything that shows an intersection of four lines—like four counties that meet with a common corner?" It's a stretch, but what the hell.

My request drew Limus's attention. He pocketed his cell and leaned over to look at the screen.

"Oops. Wait a minute. You may be onto something, Gus. Jot this down. Barron, Dismal, uh . . . Washington, and Hooker." She looked over at me.

"What's that?" I asked.

"Four counties with a common corner." She smiled.

"Has to be it, Cassidy. Anger is an intersection," I said. "One of the clues said, 'one is to fish.' Fish. Hooks. Fishing hooks. Hooker."

"And another was a president—Washington," Limas exclaimed.

"And then we have 'three is empty.' Barron," Cassidy exclaimed. "The last one says 'four has little merit.' Dismal. That's it. Those are the four counties."

"Where do they meet?" I asked.

"Let's see . . . north and west of here—about twenty miles or so."

"Then that's where we're headed." I was as excited as a small boy with a new puppy.

"If you folks don't mind, my bladder has to be emptied," said Limas. "Such is the plight of an old man." He slipped out and walked behind the SUV.

"You think we're really that close, Gus?" Her blue eyes sparkled. She pressed her hands together in anticipation.

"Maybe so."

When Limas returned, we left Rose and the sand burrs in our wake.

"When you get to Mullen, turn left on Highway 20, Gus," Cassidy suggested.

"Got it." We tore down the deserted blacktop.

Cassidy continued to work on the book, and by the time we reached Mullen, she had more. "This is getting even more difficult. What does this mean, Limas?"

He leaned forward to look at the screen. "Latitude and longitude coordinates," Limas declared.

"Cassidy, see if you can find a Web site that'll help identify those coordinates."

"I'll try Google. Just a minute. Darn, looks like the batteries are almost gone." The alarm in her voice hung in the air. Without her laptop, we were screwed. There was no way we could locate map coordinates without a GPS or computer.

"I'm at WorldAtlas.com," Cassidy declared. "They have a link for this sort of thing. If I type in this data . . ."

I pulled over to the side of the road and held my breath.

"Here it is. Got it," Cassidy declared. Her eyes wide, she clutched my arm. "Look." She pointed at the screen.

"The image is fading. What am I looking at?"

"Right there. Near Rosewater Lake. It's getting us close, but we're missing the seconds value for both the latitude and longitude. They can only give an approximate location without the seconds."

"How close?" Limas asked.

Cassidy stared at the screen. "Let's see. Every degree of latitude equals sixty-nine miles, and every minute is 1.15. A second is .02 miles. So, a rough guess? Little over a mile."

"What about longitude?" I asked.

"Hmmm." She silently computed the difference. "Pretty much the same as latitude." She looked up.

"We could still be off by as much as a mile in any direction, maybe more," Limas said.

"That covers a lot of ground." I emptied both lungs through my nostrils with a loud whistle.

"Yes, but we're close, aren't we?" Cassidy's eyes were wide with hope.

"I think so." The mistress reappears. "Try and decode the rest of the chapter before your computer shuts down."

She turned back to the laptop. "Too late. Batteries just died. I'm sorry."

"That's okay, sweetheart. We'll do it by hand. Limas can write while you read. I'll drive toward this Rosewater Lake area. Then we'll at least be in the right neighborhood."

We continued west, passed through Mullen, and turned south on Highway 20. Immediately after turning left, I hit the brakes. "What the hell?" I backed up to a sign that faced the corner. I pointed through the windshield. "Check it out."

We all stared at a green and tan sign.

"Sand Hills Golf Club," Cassidy read out loud. "Private. Golfers welcome by invitation only."

"Well, if this don't beat all," Limas said.

"Is this a joke? A golf course out here?" Cassidy raised her hands with palms upraised.

"Nope, it's for real," I answered. "I've heard about this place. Built a few years ago by some local guy who loved the game. Got a big write up in *Golf Digest*. Course was constructed fairly inexpensively—designed as a links-type course. Didn't have to move much dirt—just built it between the dunes."

Cassidy shook her head. "But, it's in the middle of nowhere."

"It's an exclusive destination course. People with money will travel all over the world to play a great golf course. Apparently this ranks pretty high."

"Let's hope they didn't build it on top of Preston's treasure," Limas muttered.

"What did you say, Limas?" Cassidy asked.

"He said, if they built the course on Preston's treasure we are up the proverbial creek without a paddle."

"Never did understand the attraction of that game," Limas added.

"Okay, Cassidy. Let's keep working on the translation." We had to remain focused.

"That's it, Gus," Cassidy declared. "End of the chapter." Her voice fell off a cliff and the sparkle vanished from her eyes.

"Read it out loud." I pulled into a small park beside Rosewater Lake. Sadly, it seemed we were no closer to Preston's treasure than we were back in Chandler. My heart skipped a beat as I wondered if Kittridge had led us on a wild goose chase.

Cassidy read, "'Seep and you shall find. Listen to the twist of the wind. A dream catcher beckons as it creaks and groans as an engine of the firmament. Congratulations my friends. Remember those less fortunate than you. Preston Kittridge.'"

"That's it?" Limas asked. "You sure there isn't more? Perhaps you missed something." His eyes pleaded for answers.

"No, that's it. Must've misspelled seek," she said.

"Well, shit on a shingle," Limas said. "The latitude and longitude coordinates aren't any good to us without a map to pinpoint the location."

"Yes, and without the seconds value," Cassidy said, reading his lips.

"We need a GPS. Or a computer," I offered.

"Unless one of you has such a device tucked away someplace, we're dead in the water," Limas whined.

"Wait a minute!" I had an idea. "A lot of golf courses have GPS devices on their golf carts. They used to give you the distance to a particular flag from any point on the course. Everything's calibrated from the tee box to the pin. What if they have those at this Sand Hills Golf Club?" It was a long shot

"Doubt they'd do us much good, but they might have a mapping device—or at least a computer. Then we can dial in our latitude and longitude and get a starting point," Limas offered.

"Well, unless someone has a better idea, let's drive to the golf course," I suggested.

"We'd better invent some sorta story," Limas offered.

"Why?" Cassidy asked then quickly followed with, "Oh. I see—don't dare tell them the truth, do we?"

"What if we say we're checking out a piece of land for sale and lost the directions?" Limas offered.

"That should work."

"Okay, that settles it," I said. "Has to be someone around. Should be just about ready to open the course." The clubhouse was only a mile away. We pulled into the parking lot of the golf club. Half a dozen cars and trucks were parked in the lot. I scanned the area but didn't see anyone.

The clubhouse and lodge were built of logs, much like Nantan's place but much larger. It sat on a broad hill thirty feet above the surrounding landscape, like a wooden ship riding a crested wave, the view like looking out over a stormy sea.

The area around the lodge had been meticulously planted with dogwood, spirea, low-spreading junipers, and numerous spruce trees of varying sizes. Each was carefully positioned, but unnatural in that environment. Nothing in the Sandy Hills inherently grew taller than a few feet, I'd observed. The first tee was laid out between two sandy embankments of modest height. The fairway snaked around additional mounds and vanished over a narrow ridge. What I could see of the course indicated a tough track, with little room for error.

I turned off the truck, but made no move to get out. "This place should be a beehive of activity, Limas. Where is everyone?"

He looked at his watch. "Don't know. Only two thirty—too late for lunch."

I scanned the grounds and fixed on a large green pole barn tucked behind a group of evergreens. All the doors appeared closed. That seemed peculiar.

Limas was impatient. "Come on, we're wasting time." He reached for the door handle.

Forty-Two

I LET SAM OUT, and he wandered over to the other vehicles and sniffed each with interest. Skunky ran over as if to play, but Sam had other ideas. His tail rose, and a clump of hair behind his head lifted.

"Sam? What's got your dander up? Come here. Sam!" He looked at me and slowly retreated. "Stay. You, too, Skunky." They sat next to the truck. The air in the yard was charged. My scruff was up as well. I went around to the passenger side, leaned over Cassidy's knees, opened the glove box, and retrieved the Beretta.

She inhaled sharply. "Gus?"

I shook my head and backed out. I tucked the pistol down my back, flipped a hand back and forth, and mouthed, "Something's wrong here." An old, but familiar itch began at the base of my neck and crept into my scalp. *We're being watched.* My arms fell to my side—tense and twitchy.

I started off and motioned Limas to follow. We crossed to the walkway and approached the clubhouse door. Cassidy lagged behind. A large double door halted our entry. I reached out for the handle. Suddenly the right hand door swung toward me. As it cleared, a double-barreled shotgun stabbed the air fronting my chest. My heart landed somewhere near my scrotum. The man on the other end looked familiar.

"One false move and I blow a hole in your chest," the man said. "Hands behind your neck—now!" he commanded.

The second door opened. Two others stepped forward. Each with a pistol. One aimed at my head. I folded both hands behind my head.

"Step back and join the old man and the dummy," the tallest of the three instructed. I bristled at his reference to Cassidy and made a move toward the door.

Limas grabbed my arm and pulled me back. "Don't," he whispered in an urgent tone. He tugged at me, and together we backed until we stood next to Cassidy. Sam's barks echoed through the property. He was stiff-legged—as upset as I'd ever seen him.

"Well, well, aren't we a happy little group?" the taller one said. "Permit me to introduce ourselves. The irascible gentleman holding the shotgun is Boris Lesard. My other companion here, the large one, is Edwin Prittie. He likes his nickname—Hardboiled. I believe you two have met before. That right, Ivy?"

"Last time I saw him, he had a cornstalk in his mouth. Bad choice for a toothpick, Mullet." I was stuck in concrete. *How in the hell did they get this far?*

Prittie's jaw hung to one side. His tongue lolled a bit, but his eyes were murderous. He lurched at me. "Now, now, Edwin. Plenty of time for that later. I am Micah Knorr. You've caused us an endless amount of trouble, Ivy. But alas, your odyssey has reached an end. Keep a close eye on him, Boris." Knorr stepped closer. "We know the deaf broad, but who's the old man?" He pointed his weapon at Limas.

"Names Smead, jerkwater. Limas Smead."

"Smart ass, huh? What's your relationship to these two?" Knorr's face and neck were scarred with deep pockmarks. Each fissure rippled as he spoke. Beyond homely, he was so gap-toothed that if he'd been an electrician he could have used his front teeth as a wire stripper.

"Hired to protect Cassidy," Limas replied.

"I see. Not doing such a great job, are ya?" Knorr laughed.

"Not yet," Limas replied. His lips tightened and his eyes blazed.

Cassidy understood everything Knorr had said. I could feel her tremble as she leaned close to my side.

"Walk toward us . . . all three of you." We shuffled toward the doors. "Shoot the dogs, Boris," Knorr stated in a flat, matter-of-fact tone.

Lesard raised the shotgun and aimed it at Sam. Without thinking I turned, whistled and raised my arm. "BACK!"

Sam came to attention and immediately tore off toward the brush beyond the SUV. Skunky raced alongside eager for a romp.

The first blast from the double-barrel kicked up dust and gravel behind the retreating dogs. The second shot resulted in a sharp yelp. One or both had been hit. If the shotgun had been loaded with buckshot, the damage could be severe. If bird shot, the damage would be less. Both dogs tumbled into a trace leading to heavy cover.

A white-hot rage unlike anything I'd ever experienced now controlled my body. Killing Prittie with my bare hands would be pleasurable. I might prolong Lesard's death by a few hours, however. I lunged for the weapon. *Too far away!* With time to react, Lesard swung at my head. I heard a loud, thump! I landed on my back, and the wind escaped my lungs in one sudden rush. Time passed, maybe hours. I looked up at the darkening sky.

Mullet interceded and stood over me. "Gedd aap." His grotesque, pretzel-like half-smile was hideous. His jaw wasn't working as it should.

Cassidy and Limas helped me to my feet. My head spinning, both legs had become leaden. Everything was a blur. McDonald's double cheese crept up my throat.

"Enough. Everyone inside." Knorr stepped back and gestured broadly with his free hand. We were marched up the steps into the foyer. "Straight ahead . . . into the grill."

We left the entryway and were ushered through a set of French doors into a large room with a bar and a number of round tables. My head hurt like hell. I prayed for Sam and Skunky and hoped they'd stay hidden until . . . what? I still had the Beretta, that's what.

I looked around the clubhouse. The wood paneling looked like expensive cherry and the lush carpet absorbed our footsteps. Every flat surface held a quarter-inch of gritty dust. I imagined numerous, serious dust storms over the winter months casting airborne sand particles through cracks around the many windows. The room smelled like a seldom-opened storage closet. Cassidy coughed and sneezed three times in rapid succession.

"Sit at the table near the window," Knorr commanded.

As we sat down, the two stooges stood on either side fifteen feet away. Knorr pulled out a chair and sat across from us. He didn't look as I pictured he might. Tall and slender, his stringy brown hair dove over each ear. I'd never seen eyes as gray. Wire-rimmed glasses sat crookedly astride a bulbous nose. Not the greasy hood I had envisioned.

Prittie was a hulk with a fat head and a twisted mouth. His stuccoed face looked even more pathetic up close. Well over six feet, his upper torso was as wide as a Kelvinator.

Lesard, the wedge head and acknowledged sadist, had a face the color of concrete, and a pair of hands that resembled baseball mitts.

"What'd you do with the owner?" I asked.

"He's tucked away with a few others out in the equipment shed. Now, let's get down to business, shall we? You've been a pain in the ass, Ivy. Frankly, if we didn't require one last bit of information, you'd all be dead by now." Knorr's eyes dulled. He might as well have been the Orkin man talking about termite eradication.

"We don't know anything more than you do," I said, surprised to have found my voice. I swallowed hard.

"That so? And what're you doing here? Gonna play the back nine?"

"We know we're close, but don't have an exact location."

"Really. Why don't I believe you? Perhaps a demonstration of our zeal will encourage you to share with us . . ." He nodded at Prittie who then lumbered from the room. In seconds he was back, and not alone.

A second person, smaller and dwarfed by the slack-jawed goon, received a rough shove, stumbled ahead, and fell to the dusty floor.

My mouth dropped wide. Cowering beneath a towering Prittie was a ghost.

Forty-Three

DOREEN SHOULD HAVE BEEN dead. Instead, she was sprawled on the floor in front of us—terrified and disheveled. With her hands bound behind her back, kneeling as if in prayer, her chest heaved with each frightened breath. Duct tape covered her mouth. Her eyes bulged as tears streamed down her pale cheeks.

"What the hell have you done to her?" I pushed my chair back and stood.

Cassidy rose to go to Doreen's aid, but Limas stuck an arm out and restrained her.

Doreen whimpered like a lost kitten. Her nostrils flared as she sucked for air. A distant memory, I assumed she had been killed and her body dumped. I shook my head to clear the fog. It was all slowly registering.

"You all know Doreen Leaper?" Knorr said. "Of course you do. Unfortunately, Doreen failed a simple task and reluctantly accompanied us on our journey across the prairie. She's been busy entertaining my two friends; however, they've grown bored with her lack of . . . enthusiasm. Therefore, she's quite expendable." Knorr nodded at Prittie.

Mullet bent low, grabbed a handful of Doreen's hair, and yanked her upright. The blonde temptress yelped. The tape bulged like an inflated baggie. She caught her balance and stood. Prittie raised his shotgun and pointed it at her right breast.

"Be a shame to blow apart those beauties, don't you think?" Knorr asked. "However, if you aren't completely forthcoming in a matter of seconds, Edwin will shoot. As you have certainly ascertained that neither of my associates is averse to killing. Actually, I think they rather enjoy it." He looked from Doreen to me.

He was serious. Doreen didn't deserve their tortuous abuse. "The notes," I blurted. "Everything we've learned is in our notes." My heart thrummed steadily.

"And those are where? In the Suburban?" Knorr's one eyebrow rose and settled.

"Yes. Take 'em . . . take 'em all. Just don't kill anyone else," I pleaded.

"Boris, escort Ivy to the truck and retrieve his notes."

Lesard took four steps and yanked me from my chair. "Move," he commanded. A cloud of rank body odor and cheap cologne trailed the goon.

"Don't be a hero, Gus." Limas muttered.

"Sound advice," Knorr echoed. "Please hurry," he waved us away. "I'm anxious to complete our business here and return to civilization."

Lesard followed me out to the Suburban. I looked around for the dogs. A pair of red-tailed hawks shrieked directly overhead. They flew off to the west a short distance, called again, and resumed their endless orbit. When we reached the SUV, I stole a quick glance at the ground below the birds and thought I saw movement beneath a thick juniper.

I went to the driver's side and opened the door. Before Lesard could react, I turned, held my palm out toward the juniper, and yelled, "Stay!" I prayed Sam and Skunky were all right. I leaned in and grabbed my notebook, then stepped back.

Lesard blubbered, "What the hell ya doin?" He looked around and understood. "Dogs are dead, Ivy. Let's go."

He took the notes and waved me inside. Once we returned to the grill, I went to my chair and sat down. Cassidy looked at me, her eyes filled with concern. "The dogs?" she whispered.

"Don't know," I mouthed. My head was turned so Knorr couldn't see us speak.

Lesard handed the notes to his boss like a dutiful hound. "That's better. See how smoothly everything flows when you cooperate?" Knorr turned and looked at Mullet, who had his arm around Doreen's neck.

Doreen shook her head at Knorr, rolled her eyes, spun around, and flapped her hands like a wounded gull. Knorr nodded in reply.

Mullet laid the shotgun down and untied Doreen's hands. Once her hands were free, she carefully removed the gray tape from her mouth, rolled it into a ball sticky side out, and jammed it into Prittie's mouth. Then she backhanded him across the face. The sound like a gunshot. Prittie never moved. Confused, his eyes fell and stared at the tops of his dirty sneakers.

"That's for pulling my hair, you moron!" Doreen said. She fingered her golden tresses, turned, and stepped toward our table. She leaned both hands on the table and said, "Let's cut out the horseshit, shall we?"

I glanced at Limas and Cassidy. Both looked as confused as I felt. No one spoke. The room collapsed as if all the air had been drawn out.

"Doreen? What's going on?" I asked.

"Name isn't Doreen. It's Greyson—Bailey Greyson."

It took a few minutes before everything fell into place. Her presence at the craps table. The way she corrected the dealer. Her frantic attempt to gain access to my room. The unlikely encounter at the airport and her attempt to slow me down. Her decision to stay behind at the Pima Reservation. And finally, the revelation that Bailey Greyson was a woman. I was glaring at the ringleader—a black widow spider responsible for the deaths of Frank, Manny, and an innocent night watchman.

"Nice trick you pulled back at my office, Ivy," the maleficent blonde accountant said. "Almost had us convinced." She stood to her full height and took control. "And the can of red paint was particularly clever."

Knorr smiled. Their subterfuge had been successful. "Yes, you folks have been worthy adversaries. Now, however, the chips are stacked on our side. Ya crapped out, I'm afraid."

The odds were seriously out of balance—I knew it and so did they. Our only hope of surviving this nightmare was to acquiesce—tell them everything to buy some time.

"All right," Greyson said. "It appears you've come to the same conclusion we have: Kittridge's treasure does indeed exist, and it's someplace close by. But where?"

"What was your relationship to Kittridge?" I asked.

Greyson waved her hand as if dismissing class. "My grandmother was the old man's sister-in-law. Makes me cousin Bailey."

"Why didn't you just get together with Cassidy? None of this had to happen. No one had to die."

"Same reason she didn't contact me. Greed. Look, no one was supposed to get hurt. If it wasn't for these nincompoops." She gestured at the two gorillas. "I'm sorry about Manny and the barber, but what's done is done. Now we move on. I hope you're convinced of our resolve. If you continue to impede our progress, well, the consequences will be on your conscience, Gus."

"How did you get this far without the dust jacket? Or did you get one from the night watchman?" I looked directly at Knorr. His eyes were blank behind the glasses.

"No. 'Fraid not," Knorr replied. "Night watchman was no help." A cruel smile followed. Let's just say our resources are limitless, Ivy. We have our ways."

Images of Frankie and Manny flashed. *These guys'll kill us in a heartbeat. Stall. Play the game. Once they've got what they want . . .*

Bailey drew up a chair and sat down. She lowered her head and studied my notes. "What have you concluded about these last few sentences . . . this nonsense about a 'dream catcher.' An 'engine of the firmament?'"

"We haven't," Limas offered. "Latitude and longitude coordinates are incomplete. Without a GPS or computer, we couldn't go any farther."

Greyson countered. "There's a computer in the office. Let's go and see what we can find. Gus? You the computer whiz here?"

"No. Cassidy takes care of that."

"All right. Bring her along and follow me. Micah, can these two boobs be trusted to keep an eye on the old man?" Bailey asked.

"I'm certain they can," he replied.

"Really." She stood up. "Have you searched them yet?"

Knorr shot a look at Lesard, who shook his head. "Goddammit, Boris. Do it. Now!"

It took only seconds for Lesard to discover my weapon. He held it high then tucked it in his trousers.

"Honest to God! What am I paying you for, Micah?" Greyson asked.

Knorr stiffened. "Need I remind you, my dear, that so far you haven't paid us diddly-squat? Frankly, I've grown impatient with your promises about this pie-in-the-sky venture." He stared her down, then turned away. "Boris, you've disappointed me."

"Sorry, boss," Lesard muttered. He sidled away like a shamed child. Knorr and Greyson rose and huddled near the bar.

I nudged Cassidy's elbow, then waved and waggled my hands as if signing. I dropped my right hand and scribbled in the table dust, "Deaf. Don't talk."

She glanced down, nodded, and wiped away the message. We needed an edge. If they weren't aware of Cassidy's ability to speak—to read lips, maybe it would prove useful somehow.

Their whispered conversation ended. "Gus, get up and bring your lady friend," Greyson said.

I motioned to Cassidy. It crossed my mind that Limas could ruin our little deception, and prayed for his silence. Cassidy stood. I turned and faced her. She looked irascible. Her cheeks reddened, and her nostrils flared. She was animated, eager to bring an end to our nightmare. I feigned more signing and led her from the table.

Greyson stepped close to Lesard, plucked the Beretta from his belt, and socked him in the gut. Then she marched over, and with her free hand, picked up the notes.

Knorr prodded us to a small office near the front entrance. We entered and walked over to the desk. I faced Cassidy and again flashed hands and fingers against my chest. "Cassidy, start the computer. Go to that last Web site we used to find the coordinates."

She nodded and sat down at the desk. She picked up a pen and scribbled, WorldAtlas.com. I let out a rush of air. So far our ploy was working. We waited for the computer to warm up. Without DSL, it took a while to connect.

"Can I see the coordinates?" I asked. Greyson handed me my notes. I laid them before Cassidy. Knorr's gun was trained on Cassidy's back.

"Remember the old man's advice, Ivy. Don't be a hero," he intoned.

Cassidy typed in the coordinates. After a couple of nervous minutes, she reached over, turned on the printer, and hit the print key. Greyson and Knorr leaned close as the printer spat out the data. Knorr ripped the sheet from the tray, but Greyson snatched it from his grip. They now had a map they believed would lead them to a buried fortune.

Forty-Four

CASSIDY LEANED BACK and scribbled, "According to this, Grandfather's treasure might be buried someplace on this golf course."

I read what she had written and handed it to Knorr.

"What? What does she mean, *might be?*" A gob of spittle escaped his lips.

"Let's see that map." Greyson grabbed the paper from Knorr.

I looked at the screen. A bright red star stood out against a backdrop of red, blue, and green lines. What if my hunch was right?

"You didn't decide to get cute did you, dummy?" Knorr asked. Air whistled through his nostrils. His lips compressed, and the pistol rose to a level with her head.

"She understand me?" Knorr asked. "Course not. Make sure she knows that I'll shoot you first," he said.

I waggled, waved with my hands against my chest, and said, "He wants to be sure we aren't holding out on him, Cassidy. You did type in the same coordinates, right?"

She nodded, licked her lips, and pointed to the coordinates scribbled on the yellow pad.

I had to convince them of our veracity. "One concern we had as we approached the golf course was if Kittridge hid his treasure on the property, it might've been discovered during construction. Or, it's buried under tons of earth." I raised my shoulders and blinked.

"Listen, Ivy!" Knorr shouted. "I didn't come all this way to have your dumb-ass friend tell me the treasure can't be found. It's around here, and we're going to find it. And you're going to help 'cause if we don't, you'll all rot out here in the boonies." Knorr's face turned purple. He was panting like a rabid dog.

Hands gummy with perspiration, I was numbed into silence. My heart pounded as his words registered. *We have to find it . . . have to help 'em look . . . buy time.* "Listen. I think there's a landmark still around, and when I see it, I can show you where the treasure's buried. Get some golf carts, and let's check it out."

Knorr didn't respond. He was seconds from a blown fuse. Greyson remained mute, lost in some private thought. "Why do we need you for that?" Knorr asked as the pistol inched higher, level with my mouth.

"He has a point, you know," Greyson concluded. "If you've told us everything, then you're of no further use to us, are you?"

I felt helpless and small. I couldn't think. End of the road. I had one shot and only one. "Because you won't find the treasure without my help. There's one last bit of information I've left out."

"That right?" Greyson asked. "Sound pretty desperate, Gus."

"The old Navajo knew where it's hidden," I declared.

"Who?" Knorr asked.

"Nantan . . . Eddie Two-Feathers. He read the book and had a vision." My declaration sounded weak, without substance.

"A vision, huh? And what did this vision tell him?" Knorr smirked.

Never too skilled at poker, I had learned something over the years about laying down a bluff. If you did it too often, it seldom worked. The best time to throw it out was when you were holding absolutely nothing. When the stakes were greatest—time to go for broke. The stakes couldn't get much higher.

I inhaled and boldly claimed, "Nantan told me what to look for, precisely where the treasure would be buried from that landmark," I lied. "I'll take you there only if I'm certain my friends won't be harmed." I stared directly at Knorr. Maintain eye contact.

Knorr smiled wickedly, then looked at Greyson. They considered my response. Images of what they'd do next hopped about like beads of water on a red-hot skillet. They were everywhere and nowhere. I couldn't guess what they thought of my revelation.

"Here's what we're going to do," Greyson said. "We'll load everyone into golf carts and follow you out on the course. Keep this in mind, though. I've nothing to lose at this point. Boris and Edwin are itching to do things their way." She tilted her head toward Cassidy and continued. "First time we sense any sort of deceit, I can't be responsible for what happens to her."

Knorr added, "And I'll make sure you get to watch, Ivy."

My blood thickened. "I'll help you as long as I know my friends'll be safe."

"There'll be no unnecessary killing . . . unless you fail to deliver," Greyson said. "That clear, Micah?"

Knorr grunted and motioned for the two of us to move away from the desk. "Let's go."

We returned to the grill and sat down with Limas. Knorr and Greyson waved the two henchmen over to the bar.

"Cassidy," I nudged her until she faced me. "Can you read their lips from here?"

"They're arguing," she whispered. "Other two want . . . uh, to kill Limas and me. They don't need us. Greyson's arguing against it." Her voice cracked, and she grabbed my hand as she spoke.

"Limas." My voice was barely audible. "I told 'em I know where the treasure is but would only lead them to it if you two were safe. They don't think Cassidy can speak."

"Gathered that."

How can I pull this off? My hunch's just that—a hunch. And if I'm wrong? *Get out in the open. It's our only chance.*

Cassidy exhaled. "Okay. They've decided."

Knorr and Greyson separated. Lesard left the room while Prittie remained, his double-barreled pointed at Cassidy. The grill crackled with tension. Limas hadn't said much, and now he glared at Knorr—as if he might do something regrettable.

"Limas? You all right?" I asked.

"I'm fine. Everything'll work out, Gus. Be patient."

"Everyone up," Knorr said. He waved the .44 Magnum with authority. "This way. We're all going to take a tour." We were herded into the foyer, then outside. Lesard vanished through a small door in the pole barn.

"Walk toward the shed," Knorr commanded.

We drew close to the large green building and watched as one of the overhead doors opened. Lesard stood to one side then retreated into the gloomy interior.

"Inside." Greyson led the way while Knorr waited for us to pass by.

We walked into the cavernous building. The barn smelled of a combination of oil, gas, and fertilizer. Once my eyes adjusted, I saw five men huddled in a far corner, mouths taped, hands and feet bound. Their eyes were wide—fearful.

Greyson glanced at the men piled in the corner. "Bring the owner over."

Knorr and Lesard marched over, pulled an older man from the pile of bodies, untied his feet, and shoved him back toward the rest of us.

My heart sank as I realized what Greyson was up to. I had to give her credit—she was sharp. I knew what she was going to ask him and dreaded what he might say.

"Take the tape off," Bailey said.

Lesard ripped the tape from the old man's mouth. He jerked as the fabric ripped his skin.

"What's your name?" Greyson asked.

"Luke Dalton," he said. His voice was dry, raspy. His eyes darted from Greyson to Knorr. He looked to be about sixty. His face had been exposed to years of sun and resembled the bark on a darkened oak tree. If he was frightened, he hid it well.

"Did you build the golf course?" she asked.

"Yes. That is, I had it built."

"Tell me, when the course was being constructed, did you uncover anything . . . unusual?" Greyson's eyes bore into Dalton.

"Like what?"

"Anything of value?"

"No. Why? That why you're here? You think something's hidden around here?"

Greyson didn't respond right away. "Have you always owned this land or did you buy it to build the course?"

"We've always owned it. Used to be a working ranch. Father was the foreman, and he purchased the land from the former owner . . . man named Kittridge."

And there it was. The confirmation we all had sought. We were standing on the original Circle MB ranch property. I exhaled sharply.

No one said a word.

Cassidy gasped and tried to cover it with a cough.

Knorr looked at her queerly and was about to say something, but I maneuvered in front and signed to her. "This is Mary Beth's granddaughter, Mr. Dalton," I blurted out. I nudged her forward and continued to wave and waggle my fingers.

His faced registered great confusion. "What exactly is going on here?"

Forty-Five

THIS IS ALL VERY TOUCHING," Bailey Greyson began, "but I've heard enough. Seems we're in the right place, but time's wasting. How many acres was the ranch?"

"Originally six thousand," Dalton said, his eyes never leaving Cassidy's face. "My dad worked for Preston for many years—ran the place for him. When Preston's son died, and with his health failing, he and Mary Beth decided to sell it to Dad for a tenth of it's worth. Your grandfather was a kind and generous man, Miss Bower."

My hands flailed. Cassidy's eyes filled as Dalton's words struck.

Knorr grew animated—anxious to begin the search. "Everything's falling into place, Bailey." He rubbed his hands together. "You better find that treasure, Ivy, or you and your friends are buzzard bait. Come on. Let's get going. Boris, cover Dalton's mouth and stash him with the others." Knorr directed us over to a line of electric golf carts. "How you want to do this, Bailey?"

Greyson studied the group. "Put the old man in a cart with Prittie." She hesitated, a frown creasing her forehead. "Wait a minute. What if someone drives in while we're gone and discovers this bunch?" She waved toward the group huddled in the corner.

"That'd be a problem," Knorr answered. "Better leave someone behind, just in case."

"Can we trust either of these two pea-brains with that?" She nodded toward the henchmen.

"Hmmm." Knorr licked his lips and considered her question. "Boris. Stay here. Keep an eye out."

"You sure?" She sounded doubtful. "Maybe you should stay."

"No way. I want to be there when we find the treasure."

Greyson faced Lesard. "Listen carefully. Stay out of sight. If some-one drives in, tell 'em everyone else is out on the course. Got it?"

"Think so," Lesard replied.

"I'll ride with you, Micah," Bailey said. "Put Ivy and the deaf woman on another cart. Ivy can lead the way, seeing as how he has all the answers."

She peered into the gloom. "Wait. Have Edwin drive one of those mini-trucks over there. It's got a all-wheel drive and bigger engine. If Ivy bolts, Edwin'll run him down." She pointed to a small four-wheeled turf truck with a utility box on the back. "Gator" was printed on the side.

Knorr steered us to a cart and motioned for Limas to go with Prittie in the Gator.

Once everyone was loaded, Knorr asked, "How do I run this thing?"

"Turn the key, flip the switch on, press forward, and step on the gas," Greyson said. "They're electric."

"Let's get going." Knorr turned the key. "Lead the way, Ivy."

I stepped on the pedal and darted out of the shop. The hawks were circling above us, but at a higher altitude. The sun had vanished and a thick covering of heavy gray clouds spanned the broad sky. The temperature had dropped. Snow was imminent.

I stopped in the parking lot. "Mind if we grab our jackets? Looks like snow."

Greyson studied the sky. "Go ahead. Micah, get my coat for me?"

Knorr muttered, "Shit. I hate snow." He hopped out and went to retrieve heavier gear.

My thoughts about the approaching storm were exactly the opposite. Inclement weather might prove a blessing—a diversion, an opportunity to escape. I drove over to the Suburban, climbed off and opened the back. I stole a glance into the thicket of junipers and thought I detected movement. *Maybe they're both okay. God, I hoped so.*

"Keep an eye on him, Edwin," Knorr commanded.

Prittie maneuvered the Gator close. I dug beneath our luggage and unlocked the floor panel. I flipped coats over my shoulder to hide my pri-mary mission—to retrieve the other Beretta. My fingers closed around the gun. I slipped it into my jacket pocket and backed away with an arm full of clothing. Once we were jacketed, we climbed back in the carts. My right pocket sagged with the weight of the gun. Certain Prittie would spot it at any moment, I was anxious to get moving again.

We zipped out of the lot onto the course. I was filled with concern for Cassidy, Limas, and the two dogs. With no real idea where to go and no brilliant ploy to shake our adversaries, depression threatened to settle; I had gambled our lives on a bluff. All I had was this vague notion about something I'd seen back in Kansas. *Look for something on the course. Remember the old Navajo's words. Think.* With no better play in place, I steered the golf cart toward the first tee. A small sign announced the first hole as Blowout.

"Were you serious about knowing what to look for?" Cassidy asked as we drove down the first fairway.

I tilted forward and turned my head. "Sort of. More of a hunch, I'm afraid. Bought us some time, 'til something better comes along." I glanced back at Knorr and Greyson. "How do you suppose they got here without the wrapper?"

She shrugged beneath her heavy coat. "Good question."

I was bothered by the knowledge that our adversaries had some other resource I knew nothing about. Time to think about making a move. I can take Knorr . . . and the blonde. *But what about Prittie? Got to get Limas involved.*

Knorr pulled up on the other side of us. "What's going on?" As a mist had begun to fall, his glasses had clouded over. He had to peer over the top for a clear view.

"I'm looking for anything that looks out of place—an unnatural structure or landmark," I offered.

"Such as?"

"I'll know that when I see it." I sped away as the first flakes of snow drifted down. I worried about Sam and Skunky and envisioned both seriously wounded and alone. I scanned the brush on the fringe of the course. Every now and then a fleeting shape would appear but quickly vanish.

I considered the design of the course, wondering what I was looking for. The Sand Hills Golf Club had clearly been modeled after seaside courses found in the British Isles. The architect incorporated many natural landforms into the design. The massive blowout areas guided the designer in his placement of hazards and bunkers. Every hole had a natural flow and rhythm. The architect simply let the undulating landscape dictate the shape of each. It was a spectacular course; unfortunately, our dreadful situation trumped its charm. We reached the fourth tee, Goldenrod, and I still hadn't seen anything promising.

Greyson drove alongside. "Well?"

"Not yet," I replied. "Let's keep going." I goosed the cart and shot off down a long par-five. It ended with an elevated green surrounded on all sides by deep sand bunkers, each one framed with sharp, vertical, edging. *God help the golfer with a buried lie in one of these,* I thought. I paused and looked for something out of place. Nothing. The redtails were back and flew off to the south. I drove toward the fifth tee—Bluestem.

As we traversed the next fairway, Prittie darted back and forth in the Gator. Any thought of dashing away over a hill was foolish. Besides, I couldn't leave Limas behind. How ironic if my last moments on earth were spent on so splendid and fabulous a golf course and me unable to play.

Forty-Six

BY LATE AFTERNOON, we had managed to cover the entire course except for the last three holes. I had seen nothing unusual other than a couple of small weather shelters and a pump house near Rosewater Lake. The shallow lake touched the course on only a few holes—including number sixteen, Whaleback, a par five. I was desperate and had only a glimmer of hope that something would show itself. We were about to run out of holes and time.

Snow fell at a constant pace, and soon the course lay covered with a slick half-inch of it. Golf carts were not built for traction; the small tires spun as they fought even the slightest incline. Only Prittie in the four-wheeled Gator had positive traction. Knorr and Greyson pulled close as I peered into the blowing snow. We were perched on an elevated tee, huge sand mounds spread out on all sides. I anticipated Knorr's cryptic comment.

"Running out of time, Ivy. You b-b-better come up with something f-f-fast or you and your f-f-friends're gonna be b-b-buzzard food." Knorr collapsed into his sodden coat and huddled with his hands between his legs for warmth.

Greyson looked every bit the fashionable westerner in her fur-collared down parka. Her cheeks were red and matched her lips. "He's right, you know, Gus. I've done my best to keep you from harm, but Micah's losing patience."

I didn't respond. I couldn't. My heart felt as cold as my hands and feet. The blowing snow stung my cheeks. I stomped on the pedal and fishtailed ahead. I fingered the Barretta and wondered if it was time to make a move.

Cassidy shouted into the wind. "What was in his vision? Maybe I can help."

I looked at her and pointed to the pair of hawks as they hung against the wind on an adjacent fairway.

She craned her neck. Snow had now given way to sleet, and Cassidy shielded her eyes for a second look. She looked at me and said, "I don't see anything."

"The hawks. Can't you see the hawks?"

She tried once more. "No. He told you to watch for a pair of hawks?"

At that moment we approached the sixteenth green. I carved a meandered path up and around the snow-covered green. *Damn.* Another blank. Two more holes. There's got to be something. I maneuvered over to number seventeen, Rosewater Seep. Wait a minute! Seep. What was that clue? "Seep and you shall find." I thought they'd misspelled seek. *What the hell's a seep?* "Cassidy. What's a seep?" I was about to repeat my question but she was pointing at something at the far end of the fairway. And then I saw it—Nantan's vision—far down the seventeenth fairway adjacent to the green. "Wind in circles!" I shouted. We looked at each other and in spite of our circumstance, smiled. My hunch had been right.

It stood like a silent sentinel, barely visible through the falling snow. "A dream catcher that with a twist of wind creaks and groans," Nantan had said. My blood churned. Every nerve in my body came alive. We had found it. My brief moment of joy was short lived, however. If I was right, in a few moments we could be dead.

I looked over at Cassidy, pointed down the fairway, and shouted, "That's it. The windmill. Has to be."

She shielded her eyes and peered into the gloom. "You sure?"

"Remember Preston's last clue—'it groans and creaks.' Nantan said the wind was moving in circles," I shouted. "See how it sits down in that valley? That's why we couldn't see it before."

"And, 'the engine of the firmament'?" she shouted.

"Don't know. Come on." I motioned for Knorr and Greyson to follow and raced down the hill onto the snowy fairway.

It took a few minutes to reach the green. It sat in a broad grassy hollow. Two massive dunes sprawled on either side, separated by a few hundred yards. A small pond sat between the green and the windmill. A creek wound away, presumably toward Rosewater Lake. Then I had it. A seep is a spring. The pond was spring fed. Kittridge had the artist draw us a picture on the dust jacket. He showed us where it was buried but we never considered that. It was all there right in front of our eyes: cowboys, an Indian, the ranch, the pond, and the windmill. *My, my.* The cover! I imagined Preston's ranch buildings spread out beneath the windmill. With a spring-fed pond, then the windmill was built purely for effect—or to hide something.

We had been driving downhill ever since we had left the tee box. The green was protected from the wind on two sides by massive dunes. We had to negotiate one final down slope to reach the base of the windmill. I stopped at the crest and waited for the others.

The structure was constructed of wood. Thick, blackened, weathered uprights stabilized by diagonal braces and cross-members of the same wood. The fins looked to be from light-gauge metal and spun wickedly in the stiff wind. A high-pitched *whirrrrr* sounded over the pond. A large tail that served as a rudder had the manufacturer's name printed in large white weathered letters—AERMOTOR. "'The engine of the firmament,'" I smiled at the last clue. Preston's windmill looked solid . . . had to be to withstand over sixty years of wind and sand.

"Is this it?" Knorr called out. He lowered his glasses.

"Think so, yes. The windmill." I pointed. "Has to be somewhere near that." The hawks ceased their vigil and glided down toward the windmill. Both sailed beneath the rotating blades and landed on one of the heavy cross-members.

"Thank you," I whispered. Nantan knew the raptors would be with me until the end. And was this indeed the end?

Prittie pulled in directly ahead of Cassidy and I. He parked the heavy Gator at an angle to the hill. Limas climbed out and walked over to stand next to Cassidy. I studied the Gator.

Prittie sat on the downhill side. His bulk threatened to tip the small utility cart once Limas got out. If he leaned too far to the left . . .

"Guess the old Indian's vision had substance after all," Limas called.

It has to be now! I threw an arm over Cassidy's chest and stomped on the gas pedal. We scooted over the crest and rammed the uphill side of the Gator. Prittie grabbed the steering wheel in desperation as the cart first slipped downhill then rose on two wheels. He had no chance to jump clear.

The cart rolled and slammed him to the turf. The metal frame of the windshield drove his fat head into the soft ground. The cart landed with a heavy *whumpf!*

I glanced at Knorr. He scrambled for his weapon, but before he could find the .44, I pulled out the Beretta and shouted, "Don't move!"

He turned and stared at the gun. "Whaaaa?"

"Go ahead. Let's end it right here, you sonofabitch. Drop it!" I shouted. "Limas! Check on Prittie!"

Knorr laid the .44 on the floor of the cart and raised his hands. I jammed the brake and watched Limas slide down the hill. When he reached the overturned Gator, he knelt down and nudged the body with his foot. He shook his head, picked up the shotgun, and crab-crawled back up the slope.

He wheezed as he stood next to Knorr. In between gasps, he managed to shout, "Search 'em, Gus."

I hopped out, pulled Knorr from the cart, frisked him, and picked up the Magnum. "Move, Greyson." I waved both guns at her then handed the heavier weapon to Limas. "Over here."

Greyson walked around the cart, hands in the air. "Cassidy? You want to do the honors?" I asked.

"My pleasure," Cassidy replied.

The accountant's green eyes widened, in spite of the blowing snow. "Huh? I thought she couldn't hear?"

"Read my lips, bitch!" Cassidy answered. She spun Bailey around and ran her hands up and down her slender form. She patted one pocket and withdrew a small caliber pistol.

"Stick it in your pocket, Cassidy," I said.

She did. Cassidy stepped over to Knorr, spun, and hit him on the jaw with a powerful right hook. Knorr staggered and banged his head against the roof of the golf cart. His glasses flew over the top, slid along the icy surface, and fell to the ground on the far side. His eyes dulled, his legs buckled, and it seemed as if he might collapse. "That's for calling me a dummy," Cassidy declared. She marched back to our cart.

"Remind me never to get you mad."

She rubbed her knuckles and smiled.

"Let's get down to the windmill and see what we can find," I suggested. "We've got about an hour of daylight left, and we still have to deal with
that other goon back at the barn." I waved Knorr and Greyson into their
cart. Knorr retrieved his glasses and sat behind the steering wheel. Greyson
remained silent. Limas stood on the rear and hung on to the roof.

My heart raced. We were so close. I gripped the steering wheel with
whitened, numbed fingers and tried to imagine what we'd find at the bottom of the hill. I felt excited but it was tempered by worry about Sam and
Skunky lying mortally wounded somewhere. "Limas, stay here with these
two. I'm going to drive around and look for the dogs." Tap, tap. "Cassidy,
did you read that?"

She nodded as I released the brake, and we slipped past the overturned Gator. Prittie's head was turned toward me. His eyes were closed.
Flecks of cardinal-red blood melded into the fresh snow. Good riddance.
We drove off into the gloaming. For the next twenty minutes, we searched
and called and whistled. As we came back to the seventeenth tee, a small
shape appeared from behind a juniper bush. Skunky hobbled out and stood
in front of the cart.

"Skunky!" Cassidy called. She jumped out and ran to the dog. But she
was alone. Sam was not with her.

Forty-Seven

THE LITTLE DOG SLITHERED over to Cassidy and collapsed in her lap. I strained to see Sam. "Where's your buddy, Skunky?" My heart sank as I realized what must've happened.

"She's bleeding, Gus." Cassidy's voice caught in her throat.

I crouched. Blood oozed from two holes on her rear flank. She slapped her tail against my leg as I probed for additional wounds. I turned to face Cassidy. "Buckshot. Not too deep. She'll be all right."

"What about Sam?"

My blood chilled at the thought of Sam lying somewhere seriously injured, or worse. "He probably took most of both barrels. Too dark to look for him now. When we get back to the lodge, I'll take the Suburban out. Come on, Skunky." I lifted her into the cart and set her at Cassidy's feet.

Cassidy looked at me. Tears formed. "Gus? You don't think . . ."

I couldn't answer. The truth was too hard to swallow. I drove over to Limas and the other two.

"Any luck?" Limas called.

"Found Skunky, but . . ." I shook my head and waved them to follow us down the hill to the windmill.

I know there's a God. Has to be. Otherwise what's the point of suffering through the pain? *Please, don't take him like this. Don't let him die alone. Not Sam. Please?* Cassidy saw the tears and stroked my cheek.

"Don't give up, Gus. There's still a chance," she reassured me.

I nodded, blew my nose into the dark, and took a deep breath. "I'll be okay. Let's go see what your grandfather buried, Cassidy."

"Yes. Let's do that," came her gentle reply. She squinted through the veil of snow at the forty-foot dream catcher and tugged at her cap.

When we reached the bottom of the hill, I bypassed the green and skirted Rosewater Seep. As I crept close to the windmill, my hawks lifted and vanished into the snow-laden sky, their job completed.

Limas had Knorr stop next to our cart. "Somebody needs to keep an eye on these two," he said.

"Good idea. You've got the .44. Don't hesitate to shoot, Limas," I said.

Cassidy and I looked into the gloaming, each caught in our own thoughts. "Come on, Cashmere. Let's see what Preston left behind. We'll start at the windmill. There's some sort of cover at the base. Probably an access panel for the machinery." I walked over to the windmill, laid a bare hand on the sandblasted gray wood, and shook it. "Plenty sturdy. Hard to imagine how this could have survived so many years of brutal weather." Maybe it's reinforced with steel. I ducked beneath a cross-member and stooped over a series of heavy planks that covered a pit beneath the peak. The drive shaft disappeared into an eight-inch hole in one of the planks. I stuck my fingers in and pulled. The heavy board didn't budge.

Tap, tap. "I need Limas over here, Cassidy. Can you watch those two?" I nodded toward Knorr and Greyson."

"I've handled guns before. Limas showed me how," she replied. Cassidy withdrew Greyson's pistol. Close up, it looked like a .38. She and Limas exchanged places. I had Greyson and Knorr sit on the ground against the golf cart.

Limas and I pried the plank loose. It was twelve inches wide and six feet long. We tossed it aside and pulled out two more, then stuck our heads beneath and peered into the dark pit.

"See anything?" Limas asked.

"Too dark. How deep do you think it is?"

"Has to be below the frost line. Maybe five or six feet?"

"Grab one of those boards and slide it down there. See if it touches bottom." I had another idea. "Wait. You want to drive back to the Gator and see if there's a flashlight in the tool box?"

"Good idea. Be right back." He hefted himself up and ran over to the cart.

"Keep an eye out for Sam, Limas. And bring some tools with you—maybe a shovel."

Knorr and Greyson huddled quietly, watching us. Knorr rubbed his chin while Bailey tracked Limas. Cassidy stood off to one side with the pistol.

My eyes had adjusted a bit, so I grabbed the plank and slid it into the hole. My guess about the depth had been right—five feet. I wiggled the board and struck metal. Something was down there, but it could easily have been the original water pump. There was nothing more I could do, so I whistled for Sam. After five minutes there was no sign of him. My heart ached, as I feared the worst. Badly wounded, disoriented, he could have wandered in any direction. My heart stopped as I thought of what he'd encounter during the night. Coyotes traveled in packs. I shook my head. The snow continued its relentless pace.

Limas returned with a pair of long handled shovels, a toolbox, and a crow bar. He stepped close. His face darkened. "We've got a problem, Gus."

"What?"

"Prittie's gone."

"Gone? How?"

"Managed to slip from the Gator somehow. Must be strong as an ox. I followed his tracks, but couldn't find him. Sorry, Gus. Thought he was dead for sure."

"Damn! Guy's impossible to kill. Have Cassidy keep her eyes open. Let's hope he went back to the lodge."

Limas dropped the tool kit and went over to talk to Cassidy.

I withdrew a flashlight from the toolbox and aimed it into the pit. Limas returned. "You want to go down there, or should I?" I'd been in a narrow, dark hole once before, and the memory still terrified me.

Seeing that I wasn't too anxious to crawl down, Limas bailed me out. "I'll go." He grabbed the flashlight and edged over the side. His feet landed noisily in the muddy pit. The beam played around the cold interior of the hole.

"See anything?" My voice cracked, and I held my breath.

"No . . . wait. There's an old metal box stuck in a corner. Jammed in the mud. Toss down the shovel."

I did. In seconds I heard metal-on-metal sounds. "Limas? What's going on?"

Silence. "Hang on." He grunted and swore. "Ow! Damn it to hell."

"What happened?"

"Aw, scraped my knuckles is all. I've almost . . . got it. There, it's free. Get Cassidy over here, Gus. She'll want to see this."

I straightened and waved Cassidy close. "He's got a box of some sort, Cassidy. Take a look." I stood to cover Knorr and Greyson.

She knelt and peered over the edge. "Limas? What is it?"

"Don't know for sure, but it's pretty damn heavy."

I repeated what Limas had said for Cassidy's benefit and asked, "Can you open it?"

"Yeah, I think so. Need a minute or so . . ."

We heard another loud clanging noise, followed by a grating screech. "What was that?"

"Hinges rusted shut," Limas called.

Cassidy stared into the pit while I faced the other two. Limas fingered aside numerous old pipe wrenches and heavy iron bars from inside the box. "What's in there?" I asked.

"Just some old parts and tools for the windmill. Nuts."

"Look around. Has to be something else."

The flashlight played around the interior and stopped against one of the shored walls. "Toss down that crowbar."

I threw a quick look at Knorr and Greyson, grabbed the bar, and returned to the pit. "Here. Heads up." I dropped the heavy claw and heard it smack in the mud. "What is it?"

"Walls are shored with planks, but it looks like a panel was cut in one side." He set the light down and poked around on the walls. Soon Limas called out, "Hold it. Something is here." He pried some boards loose and shouted, "There's another box here . . . metal . . . heavy . . . rusted pretty bad. I'll slide it up the plank. See if you can reach it, Gus."

"Cassidy?" Tap, tap. "Watch those two." I handed the gun back to her and leaned over and grabbed an end of the container. Limas shoved at the other end. The metal box crept halfway up the plank, snagged on a spike, and wouldn't budge. "Damn thing weighs a hundred pounds, Limas," I grunted. Cassidy crouched and looked at me, her eyes wide, excited. Then she turned around to check on Knorr and Greyson. My pulse rose and thumped with each breath. We'd come so far and the cost so high . . . The box had a simple hasp and no lock.

I hesitated, then slid my upper body down the plank to help pull the box to the top. It was at that moment I heard Skunky's growl. But, Cassidy couldn't hear her warning. Too late. Cassidy shrieked. The noise from the .38 was dull and small.

I elbowed back up the plank in time to see a massive shape looming behind her. It was Prittie; his melon head tilted to one side at a crazy angle. His right foot dangled like a broken candle—splayed to one side, the ankle shattered and useless. He was an enraged bull, and it was impossible to tell if she'd hit him or not.

Cassidy tried to pull the trigger a second time but wasn't quick enough. Prittie howled—a frightening, guttural, "Arrggh!" He lunged for Cassidy, grabbed her coat, wrapped a beefy arm around her neck, and stuck a screwdriver against her throat.

I dug the Beretta out, aimed, but didn't fire. Cassidy was in the line of fire.

"Rop-ah-gann-ibee!" Prittie's tongue flopped uselessly from one side of his mouth. He was the Hunchback of Notre Dame—on a larger frame. Blood streamed into his eyes from a deep gash in his forehead. Seriously injured, possibly shot, he somehow managed to remain upright. Cassidy staggered under the hulk's weight and dropped her gun. Prittie lost his balance, and then Skunky darted forward and clamped down on his shin.

As if in slow motion, Cassidy ducked and grabbed the arm with the screwdriver. Prittie shook his leg to rid himself of the pesky little dog. Skunky held on as if she had a ewe by the nose.

Cassidy's knees bent as if flexing. She managed to get both hands on his wrist and found a pressure point. Slowly, she bent his hand back, which changed the angle of the screwdriver. She tensed for a final thrust and then erupted upward to drive the metal shaft into his right eye.

"Eeeyyyah!" Prittie waved his arms, clawed at the weapon. Cassidy scrambled away as Prittie fell to his knees, then pitched forward. The butt end of the screwdriver struck the ground, driving the shaft deep into his brainpan.

His feet and arms twitched. Then all movement ceased. Skunky let go and limped over to Cassidy.

Cassidy dropped to one knee, sobbing, and pulled the little dog into her arms.

I rushed over and lifted her chin. "Cassidy? How'd you manage . . ."

Her breathing leveled out. "Limas made me learn Judo as a teenager. It's all about leverage, Gus."

"Thank God for Limas."

"Gus? Gus? What the hell's going on?" Limas stuck his head out of the pit. When he saw Prittie on the ground, he crawled out, walked over to the body, then picked up the .38 Cassidy had fired.

"It's okay. Everything's okay now." Relief choked the words in my throat.

"I don't think so," Limas said.

Forty-Eight

SMEAD NODDED AT GREYSON and Knorr, beckoning them to rise from the snow. Limas stepped before me and pointed the gun at my chest. "Hand me your weapon, Gus. Easy. No one gets hurt if we all act smart."

"Limas? What are you doing?" Cassidy saw what was happening.

"It's about time, Smead!" Greyson stood, brushed off a layer of snow, walked over, and took the Beretta.

"What the hell were you waiting for?" Knorr asked as he stood and straightened his glasses. "Damn near froze my ass off." He reached into my cart, withdrew the .44, and waved it menacingly. "Now then, let's get back to business."

Cassidy was crying now. "Limas? Please tell me this is a mistake."

The old man turned so she could read his lips. "Sorry, Cassidy. I needed the money. Too many gambling debts." He nodded at Knorr and Greyson. "They bought my markers." He shrugged and turned away as if he couldn't look her in the eye.

"You didn't actually think we'd come this far without an ace in the hole, did you, Ivy?" Knorr exulted. "How'd you think we managed to keep pace? Smead was in on it from the beginning."

I felt stupid, small . . . sick with despair. If there were clues about Limas, I'd missed them all. Then I remembered the crumpled phone slip from Greyson's desk—L.S. And his frequent cell phone calls ostensibly gambling related. Dumb. Careless. Too late now. In a strange twist, the dice flopped again, and we crapped out.

"Enough," Greyson barked. "Get the box."

Skunky sensed the shift in energy. She growled and slipped off behind one of the four stanchions. "Easy, girl." I was surprisingly calm now as Greyson took over.

"Ivy. Go down and bring the box up," she commanded.

Shit. I stalled for a bit, then walked back and eased into the dark hole. My personal nightmare became reality. I was shivering by the time the box was back on the plank. "I need help with this." My head popped up to insure I'd been heard, but also to gain relief from the hole.

"Micah. Go," Greyson shouted.

Knorr muttered something unintelligible and leaned down to grab a handle of the box. He tugged while I pushed. Soon the box was resting on the planks. I lost sight of Knorr and was just about to climb out, when I heard, "No! You can't!" It was Limas.

"Oh, Yeah? Watch me," Knorr said. "End of the road, Ivy."

I ducked and pressed into a corner beneath Knorr. An explosion of noise followed. Mud and rocks sprayed around me from the .44s heavy load. My ears rang, but I was otherwise unharmed. I could barely hear Smead arguing with Knorr.

"You sonofabitch. You said there'd be no more killing," Limas shouted.

"I lied. Shut the hell up and get outta the way."

I heard a grunt, then feet scrambling for traction on the slippery planks. Limas must have tried to stop Knorr from firing a second time. I wasn't about to wait around. I grabbed the shovel, and peeked over the planks to the sound of more gunfire. I ducked, but the second shot was muffled, not in my direction. I heard a thump, as a body fell on the planks. I peered over the edge.

"Limas!" Cassidy shouted and cradled Limas's head in her arms.

Knorr stood and wiped his hands on his trousers. Greyson knelt next to the metal box. "Open it, Bailey."

She flipped open the latch and raised the lid. Her head flew back and she looked up. Her eyes narrowed, and she shouted, "What the hell is this?" She reached into the box.

In their excitement, they either forgot about me, or assumed I was dead because both hunched over the box. I had to do something.

"What do you mean?" Knorr demanded and peered inside. His chest heaved. He elbowed Greyson aside, reached in, and withdrew two small, blackened toy soldiers. He dumped the box over. A small pile of small cast replicas settled on the snowy timber. "This is your precious treasure?" Knorr exclaimed. "Toy soldiers?"

I only had one chance.

"We went to all this trouble for a bunch of toy soldiers?" Greyson continued, livid.

"Goddammit, there has to be more here someplace." Knorr held a soldier up against the dusky light, peered over his glasses, and studied it closely. He reached in his pocket, took out a knife, and flipped the blade open. He scratched against the dark surface of the small toy. "Wait a minute. Look." He held it up for her to see.

Now! I heaved myself out of the pit, rolled away with the shovel in one hand and slipped behind one of the carts. Cassidy watched me from fifteen feet away. She appeared traumatized. Her eyes weren't registering much of anything.

Knorr and Greyson focused on the toys. "I think it's gold, Bailey. Has to be! Feel how heavy these are."

"But there's only what . . . twelve? Where's the rest?" They both glanced at the pit. Greyson picked up a flat, cellophane-wrapped package that had been in the box. "Let's see your knife." She slit the waxed wrap and withdrew a sheet of yellowed paper. She stared at it and muttered, "It's a certificate of ownership, but there has to be more!" She stuffed the letter back in the wrap, dropped it in the container, and slammed the lid closed.

"Gotta be another box," Knorr offered.

"Then get your ass down there and look for it!" Bailey commanded.

Knorr considered her demand and countered with, "What if . . . uh . . . what if Ivy isn't dead? Maybe I should go get Boris."

"You have a gun, you chickenshit bastard. Go on!" Greyson shouted. She shoved him in the back. Knorr stumbled toward the opening.

Time to move. I rose up and ran toward Greyson. I slammed into her back and continued on toward Knorr. He had heard the scuffle and turned with the .44 in his hand. I swung the shovel and connected with the side of his head. The blow knocked his glasses back into the snow, and Knorr's feet left the ground. His body slammed into one of the stanchions. He collapsed as if run over by an truck. I stumbled, tripped over the toolbox and fell to the ground.

Before I could react, Greyson rose and kicked me in the head. White spots floated behind each eye. There was no pain—just a distant roar. My eyes were open, but I couldn't focus. Everything faded to a slow blur. I touched my ear, looked at my fingers, and saw blood. *Fascinating.* Numbed, I tried to work my jaw. It took forever to close my mouth. Stupidly, I looked up as the first wave of pain struck my brain. *Have to . . . get to Cassidy.* But I couldn't move.

Greyson picked up my Beretta. I watched a slow motion movie as she pointed the gun at my head, sneered, and squeezed the trigger. I struggled to see the bullet leave the muzzle. Here it comes . . . But, something moved just then, and the tape stopped. Cassidy. She lunged for the Beretta.

Both women fell into the deepening snow. They rolled and twisted and fought for possession. Their shrieks barely penetrated my torpid brain. I was helpless. I shook my head to clear the cobwebs, but that only made me nauseous.

Greyson had a choke hold on Cassidy as she kicked and fought for leverage. Cassidy's face reddened before turning purple. She flexed her back and with a desperate heave, threw Greyson aside, but it was a hopeless gesture. Greyson fumbled in the snow and picked up the Beretta. Both women were standing. Greyson pointed the gun at Cassidy. Her gloved finger pressed against the trigger.

I wanted to call out but couldn't. I tried to stand, but my legs were lifeless. Helpless, all I could do was watch. Something heavy whistled and spun past my head. It slammed against the pillowed fabric of Greyson's down parka with a *whumpf!*

An agonizing, painful, cry accompanied the airborne object. "Noooo!" Limas collapsed after a last, desperate attempt to protect Cassidy.

Greyson staggered, her mouth open in surprise. She backed into the golf cart. The black crowbar stuck in her chest grotesquely. Impaled, her green eyes stared in disbelief. She touched the bar gently as if it weren't really there and shook her head. Blood trickled from a corner of her mouth, then spread across her lips like some bizarre, morbid embellishment. Our eyes met briefly, then hers dulled and rolled up toward the darkened sky. She sagged to the ground in a sodden heap. A crimson circle spread out around the wicked iron in her chest.

Cassidy dropped next to Smead. "Why, Limas? I'd have given you money." Her tears mixed with sleety snow and streamed down each cheek.

Limas fought to speak. "Not enough, Cassidy. They promised . . . no one . . . would be hurt. Then it was too late."

"You should've told me. After all these years . . . we'd have figured something out."

"No . . ." He fought the pain. "When I tried to back out . . . said they'd kill you. I'm sorry. Didn't want this to happen." He touched her cheek briefly and smiled. Then his eyes fluttered, and his hand dropped away.

I stood on wobbly legs, went to Cassidy, and dropped down to my knees. I put my arm around her, and waited until she was ready to let him go. I lifted her up, and we embraced. When she could cry no more, we separated. Knorr sat dumbly shaking his head. Without his glasses, he was nearly blind. I picked up the shovel and whacked him a second time. He folded like soggy bread.

"Let's go, sweetheart."

She inhaled and nodded. "What about Knorr?"

"He can't go far." We brought Skunky over to the cart and put her on the floor. I gathered all the weapons, dumped them in the rear basket, picked up Limas's cell phone and handed it to Cassidy. "See if you get 911, or the sheriff's office. Tell 'em there's another bad guy in the barn." I gathered the toy soldiers along with the certificate and threw those in the basket as well. The wheels spun when I hit the gas pedal but finally gained traction. We slewed away from the windmill back toward the lodge.

We had to traverse back down the eighteenth fairway, but with the deepening snow, it soon proved impossible. It was pitch black. Snow fell at an alarming pace. I steered into the sandy areas adjacent to the fairway, but the snow was too deep here as well. Finally, the cart stalled and refused to move.

"Come on, Cassidy. We'll have to walk from here." I put the Beretta into my coat pocket and took her arm. "Skunky, come." The little dog hopped out and limped behind as we trudged down the fairway.

I don't know how long it took to reach the pole barn, but by the time we arrived, I was winded and dizzy. The lot was dark, silent. A yellow light flared from a small window near the door in the shed.

"Oh, my God!" Cassidy declared. "The guy in the shed."

"Yeah." Have to deal with this myself. "Luke Dalton and the others are still in there. Can't wait for the sheriff. Guy might spook and kill 'em all." I led her over to the Suburban and gave her the keys. "Wait ten minutes then drive away as fast as you can. Don't stop until you reach Rose." I put Skunky in the front seat and turned to leave.

"You don't have to do this, Gus. We can send the police back." She pleaded for me to reconsider.

"I've a score to settle with him. He shot Sam and Skunky." I withdrew the Beretta and finished with, "Remember, ten minutes. Go and don't look back."

She obeyed and climbed behind the wheel.

I waited until my breath settled, withdrew the Beretta, and crept close. *Make him think it's Knorr.* I pounded on the door and waited. The door opened a crack and began to swing inward. I slammed my shoulder against it and charged through. Lesard staggered and fell as his feet slipped on the greasy floor.

Lesard rose to one knee, raised his arm, and pointed a heavy pistol at my face. "Ivy!" His mouth twisted in fury.

I kicked out at his arm but missed and stumbled over his legs. An explosion sounded and the slug whizzed past my cheek. My ears rang as the shot echoed throughout the cavernous barn. As I hit the concrete, the Beretta slipped from my fingers and skidded away. Lesard spun around and aimed for a second shot.

My heart froze. I miscalculated, and now it was all going to end. *Cassidy. Leave now.* A low growl sounded from the open door. I turned in time to see a flash of brown as Sam clawed for traction and hurtled through the air. Ninety pounds of golden retriever landed on Lesard's head. His scream of terror mingled with Sam's throaty growl.

I rolled away, crab-crawled toward the Beretta, and wrapped my fingers around the butt. "Sam! Here!"

Sam had the meat of Lesard's right shoulder in his mouth and was shaking it like a dead rat. When he heard my voice, he let go and scrambled away. Lesard fumbled with his weapon. It slipped from his hand and land-ed with a metallic thud. His eyes bulged. He estimated his chances. He made a slight move for the pistol but hesitated when he saw the Beretta.

"Don't do it," I said. Sam stood off to the side, still growling.

Once again, the two of us faced off—but this time his weapon was just out of reach. "On second thought, go ahead. You won't get to it in time, but what the hell?"

I knew he'd try, and he did. And I was glad. With two hands on the pistol, I squeezed off a round as Lesard grabbed his gun.

The thirty-caliber slug struck him in the mouth. He fell back—hard. His head, slamming into the concrete, bounced once while both legs splayed outward. A puddle of blood and viscous brain matter spread over the oily concrete.

"Drop your weapon!" a voice commanded from the open doorway.

I laid my weapon down. "Sam. Down," I commanded. It was over.

Forty-Nine

I T TURNED OUT THAT Sam had six separate entry wounds in his rear end. We took both dogs to a wonderful vet named Mathew Secord from Rose. Sam had to be sedated to remove the heavy buckshot and to receive stitches. Skunky's wounds were not life threatening, so we decided to leave well enough alone. "Nothing more than what an old bird dog might accumulate," Dr. Secord said.

Ciphering things out, I decided that Sam must've returned to his hiding spot near the lodge that night, and he'd resurfaced on hearing the gunshot or possibly spotted me moments before.

Lesard's bullet had torn a hole in my ear; the medics patched me up and commented how lucky I'd been. That much I knew. I also know that Sam saved my life that night.

Micah Knorr was found huddled inside the Rosewater Lake pump house. The sheriff said he was hypothermic and delusional and kept muttering, "Cavity Lake my ass." The bodies of Greyson and Prittie were also recovered.

Luke Dalton and his men were freed, unharmed. Cassidy and I spent a few days with Luke and his wife, Annabel, while the dogs recovered. At which time Cassidy made arrangements to bury Limas in the local cemetery.

We found a total of twelve authenticasts along with the certificate of ownership from the pit beneath the windmill. We later determined that all twelve were cast from twenty-three carat gold. Each weighed from sixteen ounces to over two pounds The models depicted a variety of wartime figures, including: two small statues of both a German and Japanese soldier—rifles at the ready, two PZKW German Tiger tanks, an artillery piece of unknown replication, two A6M Japanese Zero fighter planes, a BF109 German

Messerschmidt, a pair of German submarines, and a Japanese aircraft carrier. Gold had reached a new high of over five hundred dollars an ounce, and collectively I thought the twelve might be worth over three hundred thousand dollars. I imagined their value to a collector might be substantially more.

After breakfast on the second day, Luke told us an interesting story about Preston's dream catcher. "Dad said that Preston drove into the ranch one day with Mary Beth in a big new Packard. Shortly after, two big trucks pulled into the yard, loaded with building material. Preston told Dad they were going to build a windmill. It was Memorial Day—Dad said he'd never forget it. When he asked the old man why they needed a windmill, he simply said, 'tradition.'"

"Why was that so odd?" I asked.

"The ranch already had a working well near the house and, along with the seep, they didn't need water."

"Then the windmill was just for show."

"Dad and Preston spent a month constructing that damned thing. Each of the four legs was imbedded in concrete. Mary Beth helped as much as she could," Luke said, "But the structural parts were extremely heavy. They used chain hoists and a homemade jib-crane to raise the tower. It was made entirely of some exotic metal encased in Spanish cedar. The blades and fins were standard gauge steel, of course."

"Why the exotic wood?"

"Kittridge imported it 'For its resistance to rot and insects.' Dad said Preston wanted it to stand for four hundred years. Probably will, too."

"Must've been quite a project."

"I imagine. Preston was an engineer. He knew what he was doing all right."

"How come you left it standing when you built the golf course?"

"Thought about taking it down—even tried a couple times, but Dad was still alive back then and put a stop to that."

"Was the golf course your idea or your dad's?"

"Mine. Thought it would be a good investment. Already sold off most of the property and had the money, so what the hell?" He threw up his hands and smiled.

"Any regrets?"

"Nope. I love the game. Play every chance I get. Besides, as you saw, we're still in the ranching business, so I keep plenty busy with that. Got the best superintendent I could find, though. Young fella name of Benjamin Vann. Hired him away from one of those fancy courses out in Palm Springs."

I asked Luke if he had ever opened up the pit beneath the windmill. "Nope," he said. "Never bothered to. No need."

Later that day, Luke drove us down the eighteenth fairway. Sam and Skunky trotted gingerly alongside. We pulled up next to the windmill. The snow was just about all gone and the sky was bright blue as I gazed up at the tower. The wind was up a bit so the opposite side of the fin showed. A faded hand-painted Circle MB stood out against the dull metal. "Look, Sweetheart." I tapped Cassidy and pointed. I could almost imagine old Preston up there while Mary Beth stood below directing his brush. I leaned against one of the uprights and picked idly at a wooden cross member while Luke gathered up the toolbox and spilled its contents.

"Old Preston sure built this thing to last," I said, and leaned over to see the backside of the weathered wood.

Luke accidentally kicked an iron bar across the plank deck, and it settled against my foot. I leaned down and picked it up. It looked like a spare piece from the structure. Its heft was substantial, even for iron. A portion of the blackened skin had been scraped away, and as I turned it over in my hands, the sun caught the exposed metal. A bright yellow glare flashed as the sun struck. The bright reflection momentarily blinded me. When my eyes cleared, I looked at it again. My heart suddenly landed in my throat, which'd gone dry as dirt. My mouth was full of sawdust.

Cassidy noticed my distress. "Gus? Are you all right?"

I cleared my throat and whispered, "Luke, hand me one of those wrenches."

His brows arched, but he reached into the box and withdrew an ancient pipe wrench. I banged it against the bar in my hand and swiped at the surface. "Cassidy. Luke. Look at this!" Both stepped close and stared at the slash of exposed yellow metal beneath.

Luke said, "That's not possible . . . is it?" He looked up at the windmill.

So did Cassidy. So did I. We each fingered one of the lower cross-members. We exchanged glances and nodded.

I took an eighteen-inch wrench in both hands and whacked it against the cross brace. *Bang! Bang! Bang!* came the resultant reverberations. The exotic wood began to splinter and break away. Both dogs stood with their ears pricked, poised for action.

Luke retrieved a machinist's hammer from the toolbox and soon we were both pounding away at the iron-hard Spanish cedar. It took five minutes before the outer skin fractured and fell away. The exposed iron was as black as coal. I whacked and scraped until a six-inch streak of pure yellow shone in the bright sunlight. Darkened by oxidation over many years, the black gold shimmered and gleamed.

My voice rasped . . . barely a whisper. "Cassidy! Luke! The windmill . . ."

"Yes, the entire thing," Cassidy replied. "It's made of pure gold!"

ON JUNE 17—sixty years to the day that Jack Kittridge was shot and killed by a sniper's bullet—I stood with Cassidy, Bryce, Allison, and Luke Dalton at the base of Preston's golden windmill. A demolition crew waited for a signal to begin deconstructing the wooden dream catcher. Security guards hired to protect the structure edged close for a peek.

As I stood with the others in the mid-day heat, I thought of Frankie and Manny and the old night watchman. *Was it all worth it?* I wondered.

Four golfers crested the last hill in front of the seventeenth green—Rosewater Seep. I watched as one of the four struck a nice wedge from a hundred yards. The ball arced high and settled like a dove ten feet from the pin. The wind blew in our direction, and I heard one of them say, "Nice shot there."

Yes, indeed, I thought. *Nice shot.*

His playing partner also hit a wedge from about the same distance, but his ball landed in a bunker. I could just see the top of the ball. *Oh, oh. A nasty buried lie. You're not going to like that shot, pal.*

My guardian hawks spun lazily overhead. I craned my neck to watch as they described indifferent circles against the deep blue sky. *Thanks, Nantan. Hope you are well*, I thought.

"Look, Gus," Cassidy called. "Aren't they beautiful?"

"Can you see those, Cashmere?" I asked incredulously.

"Why, yes. Of course."

"I'll be damned." I smiled and nodded to Luke.

He waved to the foreman and soon the large crane roared to life.

Epilogue

WE RECOVERED OVER two thousand pounds of twenty-three carat gold from Preston's windmill. It was sold to a dealer in Denver for a little more than twenty million dollars.

We offered Luke Dalton an equal share. He declined, citing Mary Beth's generosity with the ranch. We finally convinced him to accept two of the authenticasts—along with two million dollars. The balance was split between the Navajo Nation, Bryce and Allison, and Cassidy and me.

Cassidy gave her share to Gallaudet College and the National Foundation for the Hearing Impaired. The college planned to name a new wing after Mary Beth Bower.

Bryce and I decided we had more than enough with the authenticasts, so we each kept a million, and gave the rest to Nantan's people, Gallaudet, and a portion to the Animal Humane Society.

Sam never completely recovered from the shooting, and developed a severe limp. In my spare time, I managed to construct a windmill on the farm back in Minnesota . . . out of Spanish cedar, some reclaimed from Preston's windmill. Every time I looked at it, I thought of Nantan and the two hawks.

Cassidy and I kept the one remaining copy of her grandparent's book. The other copy—the one given to Knorr that night in the parking lot, was never recovered. I later heard that our jacketed copy was worth a great deal of money, but we refused all offers to sell.

Cassidy's dialysis treatments were suspended indefinitely. Other than periodic checkups, her doctor said she appeared to have had complete remission. He added that he had no sound medical explanation for her return to health. We all knew what had happened, of course.

We went back to the Nation in October. We had hoped to see Nantan, but we were too late. He had passed away in late August. We spent a few days on the ranch with Orenda and Sike, and on one glorious early autumn day, I took Cassidy with me to Spider Rock.

Sam recognized the place immediately, and soon we watched as he hobbled along, trailing some teasing critter into the scrub. Skunky trotted alongside, trusting that something fun was in the offing.

We sat on my flat rock and had lunch just as I'd once done alone. When we finished dining, Cassidy took my hand, and we lay back on the warm boulder.

Tap, tap. "Gus, why do you think grandfather only made twelve gold replicas?" Cassidy was sitting up to see me answer.

"I've been thinking on that . . . maybe he didn't."

"Didn't what?"

"Make only twelve." I watched her eyes widen.

"You mean?"

"Later, Cashmere." I pulled her down to nest in the fold of my arm. We stared at the sky. "Yup. Let's talk about that later, Cassidy."

"Look, Gus. They're back." She pointed above the monolith at the two redtails.

"I know." I closed my eyes and imagined that I could fly . . . that Cassidy could fly . . . that we could soar with the raptors.

The End.